Everything Here Belongs To You

Saborna Roychowdhury

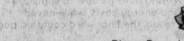

Black Rose Writing | Texas

The author grants the final approval for this literary material.

First printing

This is a work of fiction. Names, characters, businesses, places, events, and
incidents are either the products of the author's imagination or used in a
fictitious manner. Any resemblance to actual persons, living or dead, or
actual events is purely coincidental.

ISBN: 978-1-68433-959-4
PUBLISHED BY BLACK ROSE WRITING
www.blackrosewriting.com

Printed in the United States of America
Suggested Retail Price (SRP) $22.95

Everything Here Belongs to You is printed in Palatino Linotype

*As a planet-friendly publisher, Black Rose Writing does its best to eliminate
unnecessary waste to reduce paper usage and energy costs, while never
compromising the reading experience. As a result, the final word count vs. page
count may not meet common expectations.

Cover Image: Ritayan Mukherjee – award-winning Photographer, Kolkata, India

To my mother.

Acknowledments

There are several people I wish to thank.

A very special thanks to my husband, Partha Ganguly, for his support and encouragement and his comments on various drafts of the manuscript.

Many thanks to my wonderful agent, Julie Stevenson, for the interest she took and the guidance she provided at crucial junctures. My book would've been wandering around lost without her expertise and insight.

To my editor, Laura Chasen, who provided detailed and thoughtful 20-page editorial letter that elevated the book to a whole new level. Her countless comments made the book smarter, sharper, and more cohesive.

Cecilia Lewis for helping me fine-tune every scene with appropriate actions and emotions.

My fantastic readers throughout the many stages of this book: Lisa Falk Ellis, Kathleen Bucher, Laurie Claypool, Enos Russell, Alex Baker, Paige Bonnivier Hassall, Georgiana Steele Nelson, Mary Scheps, Joyce Yarrow and Mosarrap Khan. Thank you for being so patient, and for your helpful advice. Your feedback helped me grow as a writer.

Everything Here
Belongs To You

Everything Here
Belongs To You

Chapter 1

Mohini feared Parul was losing her mind. Sometimes she stood alone on the terrace, the evening wrapped around her frail form, the sadness of a day gone by mute and heavy in her eyes. Those days she talked very little, ate even less, and fell into prolonged silences. Sometimes Parul circled the potted plants on the terrace, but she mostly remained in her tiny room on the third floor.

Mohini knew that seeing Parul so detached and unresponsive unnerved much of the family. Mohini grew up with the sounds of Parul's tongue laboring to unload countless recollections on the family. Parul had talked about the shady banyan trees, the winding railway lines and shimmering ponds of her village. She told of the undulating rice fields, the red dirt roads and the one-eyed blacksmith who scared children by taking off his eye patch. Parul loved to tell stories of her earliest days. Whether they came from fragments of memory or concoctions of her imagination, it was hard to tell. In fact, Ma, Mohini's mother and Parul's employer, had often complained that Parul's chatter was driving her insane. Mohini understood Ma longed for a quiet moment, but Parul rarely left the house. She had nowhere to go. Instead, she stayed at home and helped Ma with chores, her tongue toiling in rhythmic accompaniment to her task. For every occasion Parul had a reminiscence; for every domestic discord, Parul offered a suggestion; for every concern, Parul showed compassion. Her anklets had danced on the cold marble floor, moss-covered staircases, and long winding hallways of the house. Her multicolored cotton saris occupied the clothesline between the east and west wing.

Her cheap glass bangles clattered as she ground spices rolling and thumping on the grinding stone in Ma's kitchen.

Ma often liked to tell Mohini stories about when Parul first came to the house. Ma had stared at the confused child half-hidden behind the door. She was only six years old then. Ma was not surprised by how young she was. Girls her age worked as maids in many neighborhood houses and businesses. From Ma's point of view, a little girl following the mistress around all day was a required part of a lady's equipment. Having her in the house, Ma said, would add to her social prestige.

The girl's father had told Ma the girl's name was Mumtaz.

"But she's Muslim," Ma had exclaimed. "I can't have a Muslim maid in my house."

Mumtaz's pigtails were infested with lice, her nose ran, and her stomach was bloated by years of malnutrition. Her bony arms displayed a few red and green glass bangles.

Mumtaz's father had spoken like a true salesman. "Don't worry, Ma. No one will know she's a Muslim. Change her name if you wish. Bring her up like a member of your family. I don't have a problem with that. She can light the stove, boil the rice, and get water for you from the tube-well."

"You don't mind if I give her a Hindu name?"

"We're small people, Ma. What is there to mind? First comes the empty stomach and then everything else."

Twirling the end of her sari on her finger, Ma had paced back and forth. "I'll be taking an enormous risk if I let her stay in this house." Taking a sharp breath, she had looked at Mumtaz's father. "This is not a simple decision for me. Ask her not to follow any of her Muslim rituals here. She'll have to forget her past."

Mumtaz's father waved his thin arms as if to wave away her concerns. "Ma, my daughter is like a piece of soft dough. She'll mold herself into any shape you want to give her. She's a very obedient child, selfless and good-natured like her mother was. She'll not let you down."

Ma had stared at the scared child for a long time and then said, "I'll name her Parul."

"Parul?"

"Yes, she reminds me of the Parul flower. Our garden is full of them."

"As you wish, Ma. My daughter is now your daughter." He slapped his hands together a few times, the way a man might if he just accomplished something big.

At first Ma gave Parul the simplest household chores: she folded clothes, fluffed the pillows and served tea and biscuits to the visitors. In the kitchen, she worked as Ma's helper: washed the rice grains, peeled the pea pods, removed shells from fresh shrimps, and measured out lentils with a cup. When Ma took her afternoon nap, Parul massaged her feet with warm mustard oil. In the evening, she picked flowers from the garden, made sandalwood paste and helped Ma with her *puja* preparation.

Mohini, who was couple years younger than Parul, was not asked to do any household chores. "Why do you always ask Parul*di* to do all this work and not me?" she protested. "Why can't I help her?"

"Don't bring such words to your lips, Mohini." Ma rolled her eyes. "You are from a respectable *bhadralok* family. This work is not for you."

When Mohini turned five, she was enrolled in a prestigious English medium convent. Parul was sent to the neighborhood Bengali medium, free school, for girls. "You focus on your work, Mohini," Ma would say. "You have to go to college. Parul'll study for a few days and then drop out."

After school, Parul got busy with her chores and Ma forbade Mohini to play with her, but it was no use—Mohini ran to Parul at every opportunity. She was happiest when she was with Parul. Parul braided her hair and put nail polish on her toes. She made tiny boats and fans out of folded paper and told her stories of *jinns* who lived in village wells. Their favorite game was dressing up like Bengali brides. They wrapped red saris around their small bodies and bent forward to help each other with the pleats and folds. They took out golden bangles out of cardboard boxes and slid them onto their tiny wrists. Standing in front of the dressing table, they piled their hair on top of their head and rolled it into buns. Then they exchanged plastic flower garlands with their male dolls and called them their husbands.

"My sister, Rehana, and I used to play this game," said Parul, one afternoon. "We were always together. We didn't need anyone else. People in our village were jealous of how happy we were when we were together."

"Why did you leave her, Parul*di*?" asked Mohini. "She must be so sad."

Parul gazed into the distance with her black eyes, and a sudden pained flush appeared on her face. Mohini's chest seized with guilt. She grasped her hand immediately, saying she was sorry. She didn't mean to ask a question that made her so miserable. Parul got up to go to the kitchen, and when Mohini followed her, she said she had to finish the work Ma gave her.

A few days later, Parul pulled Mohini aside and said, "Come sit close to me, and I'll tell you my story. I never wanted to leave my sisters. But we are such unlucky girls..." Her voice broke off.

Parul told Mohini that she had begged her father not to send her away. She had promised to be a good girl, be more obedient, and take better care of her sisters. But her father had made up his mind. After Parul's mother's death, things had become especially difficult for Parul's father. Alone, he took care of his three daughters and worked part time on other people's farms. But after three seasons of drought, most farmers didn't need his help to cut and gather the produce. He also had a considerable debt in the market, and the moneylenders had piled up at his doorstep. Getting rice grains for even one meal a day was becoming difficult. He had carefully thought things through and decided that it might be helpful to have a daughter in the city who could earn extra money. He could take the train to Kolkata once a month to collect her wages. He could pay for his food and rent with it.

"When my Abbu decides to do something, even God cannot sway him," Parul told Mohini.

Parul and her father walked several miles to the nearest station and boarded a crowded local train. When the train left the platform, she strained her neck and watched the emaciated forms of her sisters running alongside her window until they grew smaller and smaller, and she could see them no longer. She then rested her head against the window bars and fell asleep.

Parul was on the train for half the day. When the train reached Howrah, she was shocked at how crowded the station was. There were people pacing all around, shouting and screaming, and coolies ran back and forth with enormous trunks on their heads.

Her father slapped the back of her head and said, "This will be your new home, Mumtaz. You will make your old father very happy." As she made her way toward the exit, she had to squeeze through the sweating bodies and oily heads pasted against one another. She felt something tugging the end of her skirt. Looking down, she saw a leper on a skateboard asking her for money. Two dark eyes blazed in his crushed and bruised face. The arms he held out to her were like shriveled logs devoid of fingers. To six-year-old Parul, he looked like a monster from a fairy tale. She screamed and pushed past the crowd, chasing after her father.

For a moment, she lost sight of her father in the crowd. It was then she felt the sudden lightness of her shoulder bag. When she looked, the little bundle in which she had packed her clothes and little mementos of her mother and sister had disappeared from her bag. All she had left of them was the chain and locket around her neck that her mother had given her. She gripped it in between her fingers, just like a drowning man would clutch at a straw.

Mohini could not believe her friend's hardships. "Parul*di*—" Mohini could hear her own voice trembling. "Such terrible things have happened to you."

Parul leaned on her shoulder and released a deep sigh.

Mohini kissed her hands and her cheeks and brought her face close to Parul. "Look at me, Parul*di*. I am your sister now. I'm your Rehana."

Mohini grew up on the outskirts of the city. Most houses in her neighborhood had cement walls and red-tiled roofs, bordered by tall palm and oak trees. The roads were mostly narrow and pothole-covered, bordered by open drains. The primary means of transportation was the hand-pulled rickshaw that gyrated gaily on the narrow roads. In the afternoon, when the liquid shadow of the palm tree glimmered in the green pond, when smoke rose from the clay and charcoal ovens as the neighbors cooked their meals, Mohini loved to listen to the melodious tone of vendors selling utensils, vegetables, sweets, and ice cream outside her house. And after sunset, when she ran around the neighborhood holding Parul's hand, she heard crickets chirp and frogs sing and occasional night owl hoot in the dark unlit pockets of the road.

On the pavement outside her gates were tea stalls, flower stalls, laundry carts, and snow cone vendors. Further down the road, many makeshift shops made of bamboo, wood and canvas had sprung up like mushrooms in the night. Their rusty signboard had misspelled names like *Poonam's Beaty Parlor*, *Janta Breekstore* and *Mama's Cantin*. Mohini always giggled at the spellings as she pointed them out to Parul. Over the past decade-and-a-half, mango and banana groves in her neighborhood had been cleared to make way for multi-storied apartment buildings. Still, her family had to travel a great distance to enjoy multiplex theaters, large shopping malls, western style coffee shops and air-conditioned restaurants.

Mohini's home was at least a hundred years old. It had two wings. Some walls were covered with patches of flora with roots penetrating deep into the concrete. Mohini imagined them as coral reefs rising from the deep ocean floor. Had her family lived on the entire second floor, it would have been much more spacious, with a separate dining room, living room, and guest bedrooms. But living on the second floor of the west wing had become nearly impossible for them—it had long needed repair. Rainwater seeped through the cracks and crevices of these rooms, leaving behind damp patterns on the walls. The discolored windows hung from rusty hinges. The furniture had broken legs and torn upholstery. The floors creaked, the glass rattled, and dust and cement speckled down from the weary ceiling beams and lay scattered like snow on top of blue plastic sheets used to cover the furniture.

Downstairs on the first floor, a courtyard separated the west wing of Mohini's house from the east wing. In the center of this yard was a rusty tube-well, from which Parul pumped drinking water for the family. Mohini heard the clatter of her glass bangles every morning, accompanied by the screech of the old piston. Sometimes Mohini and Parul ran around the tube well, playing hopscotch and tag, screaming and giggling and racing past each other. On the days it rained, they stood in the courtyard, getting their clothes soaked through till Ma's face appeared on the second-floor balcony and she shouted, "Girls, how many times have I told you not to get wet like this? Do you want to miss school tomorrow? Come upstairs at once."

The two wings also connected on the second floor through a long moss-covered balcony. Over the years, although Mohini couldn't remember when it happened exactly, she had come to believe that she was eight and Parul ten when they figured out how to unlock the rusty door of the second-floor west wing and slip in unnoticed. Together they peered apprehensively around the dark crumbling hallways and cobweb-covered rooms, which looked sinister and infinitely mysterious to them. They walked down the musty, slippery verandas together, their hands sliding forward on the banister, imagining unknown figures lurking in the shadowy depths of the house, waiting to jump on them. Sometimes they crawled or squatted and edged along the wall to enter the drawing room of the west wing. This was the largest room of the house: the walls alternated between mirror panels and wood panels. In the corner of this neglected space, covered partly by termite- and rat-bitten curtains, stood a majestic black trophy—the grand piano.

"Listen," Mohini told Parul, as they crawled on the dusty floor around the piano. "Someone is playing a melody for us. Can you hear the notes?"

Immediately, Parul crawled away from her. "You're mad. You always imagine crazy things like this." And then she stopped and held her breath, cocked her head slightly to one side, and looked back at her as if to say she, too, could hear the beautiful melody from the keys of the piano buried under the dust and cobwebs.

Instantly, the dark room lightened up and all around them they saw figures, like porcelain dolls, walking around and sipping tea and stopping to say hello. There were women in dazzling saris and heavy gold jewelry, their long hair rolled into fashionable buns. The men wore dark suits and smoked tobacco pipes, their heels clicking on the shiny marble floor. The piano came alive, filling the room, rising above the chatter and drowning the guests in its sweet and simple melody.

Parul took Mohini's hand and pulled her under the long mahogany table to get away from the silhouetted figures, and they held each other tightly, shivering with their eyes closed, wishing the specters to go away. Eventually, they crawled out of their hiding place and stepped backwards, edging out of the room 'til their backs touched the rusty shell of the grandfather clock in the hallway. They stopped and listened to the faint tick-tock coming from its antique belly, as if life was still wrapped in those rickety metallic hinges and once magnificent black hands. Then Mohini squeezed Parul's hand and said, "Let's get out of here. Mad Shanti is watching us."

They rushed back to the east wing, slipping and sliding and rolling along the moss-covered balcony—breathless and excited.

• •

A few months after they had first set foot in the forbidden west wing, one evening, sitting by the grand piano, Parul turned around and demanded, "Why do you keep saying mad Shanti, mad Shanti! Who is this mad Shanti? Who is watching us?"

"He was my grandfather," Mohini said quietly. "He died in this piano room."

That was the first time Mohini told Parul the story of mad Shanti and the west wing, which she had heard from her parents. Over the years, she told Parul the same story repeatedly, changing it marginally each time, but she must have been a compelling storyteller because Parul listened with her mouth open.

In all his photos, Mohini's grandfather, Shanti Kumar Sen, looked like a tall, undernourished-looking man with disapproval etched permanently on his face. He lived a life of simplicity and moderation— he didn't eat meat, didn't touch cigarettes or alcohol, and had never set foot in a movie theater.

"It was because of his terrible ulcer, you know, poor Shanti, didn't even get to eat any spicy street food. Only rice and fish curry, two times a day, every day." Mohini told Parul.

He was also never seen wasting his time with young men who spent time at the street corner *addas* and played carrom and cards at the party clubhouse across the street. Everyone in the house carefully avoided making eye contact with him and spoke in low voices in his presence.

Every morning, Shanti fed the white pigeons who lined up on the parapet and sturdy wrought-iron railing of the curved balconies of the west wing. The pigeons were a symbol of wealth and prosperity, and Shanti thought of them as Ma Lakshmi, the goddess in disguise. He believed it was because of the white pigeons that their family business, "Sen Saris," was doing so well.

Wealthy ladies in dark sunglasses came in their Ambassador cars to look at the saris in his store. Their drivers respectfully opened the car door and then held an umbrella over their head as they walked up the stairs and into the showroom. Shanti greeted them at the door and guided them to the comfortable leather sofas. He waved to his employees, who appeared with glasses of chilled lime soda for the ladies. Shanti rolled out the saris—finely hand woven *jamdani* from Dhaka to the colorful *bandhni* from Rajasthan. He sprinted forward to fetch the ones they liked and refolded the giant pile they rejected. The ladies caressed the material with their painted fingers and fluttered their eyelashes. When they finally tried them on before the shop mirror, flattening the pleats and adjusting the *palla*, Shanti felt all his hard work had just been rewarded... the beautiful saris had met their genuine match.

Then one day a massive fire broke out at Sen Saris, and it gutted the entire shop. Smoke continued to billow till afternoon, and the flames slowly consumed the sari-filled shelves. The employees rushed out of the building and stood helplessly as the fire raged inside. Neighbors tried to throw buckets of water at the flame, but the fire roared like an ugly beast, determined to leave a trail of destruction in its path. Shanti's showroom and gorgeous sari collection were turned into charcoal and ashes. The loss was estimated to be over fifty lakh rupees.

Shanti could not recover from such a massive setback and re-open his store. No one was willing to loan him the money to start over. Around this time, he noticed that all the white pigeons have left the house. The parapets and railing were empty. The pigeons had flapped their wings and soared the skies and taken with them Shanti's good fortune. He knew then that his best days were over.

With no store left to open, no customers to serve, Shanti lost all motivation to work. As he started spending more time inside the house, it gradually became evident to everyone in the family that Shanti was undergoing a profound change. The man who was always punctual, maintained a busy schedule, ran his life like a clockwork, had suddenly loosened his grip over time and let it slip between his fingers. He spent most of his time in the piano room, reclined in his armchair. Next to him stood a hookah, or water pipe, with a long snakelike tube attached to it. Shanti put one end of the tube in his mouth and sucked in the smoke as the water bubbled noisily in a glass jar. Over time, his interest in family matters lessened and his attention confined itself within the four walls of the piano room. He stopped going for walks, attending social functions, and inviting relatives over to the house. His hair grew longer, and a dense prickly beard covered his face. Even his own children started to avoid him. To the people in the house, he seemed to sink deeper into the armchair every passing day—a shriveled, delicate, lost man enveloped in the smoke of his water pipe.

The house fell into a state of disrepair, but Shanti did not notice it. Instead, he sat contented next to the piano, remembering the golden days when fancy ladies came to his store to get their chiffon, georgette and chanderi saris. Shanti remembered their fair complexion, silky smooth skin, coquettish looks, and intoxicating laughter. The saris folded around them like lotus petals, and they left the store looking like brightly wrapped candy.

Sometimes through the open window came the whiff of their rich perfume, drowning him in its power. That's when he imagined those wealthy ladies from his store dancing around the room. Their dazzling saris rustled and their anklets rang. They spread out their arms and invited Shanti to dance with them. Shanti would get up to dance, waltzing around the room with jeweled beauties in his arms. He would twirl and posture with the dainty damsels, draw them closer and then spin them around. He would swing his hips and sway his torso and follow their rhythm stylishly and accurately. He would see their reflections slithering along the walled mirrors and hear their heels clicking in union on the marble floors.

Some days, Mohini's grandmother would see her husband moving around the piano room with his arms outstretched, looking dazed and happy. She would snap her fingers to bring him out of his trance.

Word of Shanti's strange fixations spread in the neighborhood. Rumors followed almost instantly—that the west wing was haunted, and Shanti danced with the ghosts. They started calling the west wing "Bhuter Bari"—the haunted house. Shanti too got a nickname. The local boys called him "mad Shanti."

It was on a moonless, Amavasya night, that the god of death came for Shanti. Next morning, Mohini's grandmother discovered him on the marble floor next to the piano. His eyes were open as if he was looking at someone, and his lips were twisted into a blissful smile. She threw herself on his body, banged her head against his chest and wailed, "Ogo, what have you done? How could you leave me like this? What will happen to us now?" She broke the red and white shell-bangles on her wrist and wiped the vermillion dust from her forehead.

Mohini's grandmother was only thirty-three years old then, with two young children and no source of income. In time, she had to sell off most of the family jewelry to pay for her son's school and daughter's wedding. The house went into a state of disrepair, and some of the most trusted servants were let go. The west wing became a crumbling silhouette of its former self.

"That's why we don't repair the west wing. No one should wake up mad Shanti," Mohini added at the end of her story each time.

She saw Parul shudder.

The east wing of Mohini's house was in better shape, though it received less sunlight, remained slightly damp, and was under a constant onslaught of mosquitoes. Mohini's father, Baba ran his weight-lifting camp on the first floor of the east wing. Baba was a powerfully built man who, of course, looked like a giant to Mohini. In his youth, Baba had a reputation for being "strong as an ox," and the local boys liked to call him "King Kong." He was a professional weight-lifter and trained students to take part in tournaments. When Mohini asked Ma how she met Baba, she always rolled her eyes. "What will you do by knowing all that?" asked Ma. "Little girls don't ask such questions."

But then, in the middle of a cutting and chopping vegetables in the kitchen, Ma began to wipe her eyes with the end of her sari. "Your Baba could have been internationally famous. He was a weight-lifting star... the Golden boy for the Moscow Olympics," she said. "He gave it all up for me." She looked at Mohini apologetically, as if to say, because of her, Mohini never got to see her father's glorious days.

When Mohini asked Baba about his stardom, he waved his hands and dismissed the memories. "There is nothing to tell. Those days are long gone. I'm now a middle-aged man." His silence frustrated Mohini. She had started to weight-lift with Baba in the gym downstairs and knowing what happened to him was important to her. After much insistence, he recounted a few stories from those years and an outline of their lives emerged.

Baba was the rising star of the Indian weight-lifting scene, winning multiple awards at the national and international level. In the National Championship at Vishakhapatnam in 1978, Baba won a silver medal. He was the Golden Boy, the chosen one for the prestigious Indian Olympic team to represent India in the 1980 Moscow Olympics.

Ma lived three houses down the street from Baba. She stood on her terrace every evening and watched Baba lift barbells in his driveway. She called him "elephant man" and told everyone in the family she wanted to marry him. Mohini didn't have a clear idea of how their romance progressed, but she knew that Ma's father was against their marriage. "What qualification does he have to marry my daughter?" he would say. "Does he hold any actual job?"

It was around this time that Baba had to travel to Delhi for a tournament. He was waiting in the wings when someone brought him a telegram from Ma.

Come home quickly. My father found a husband. Wedding in three days.

The competition officials announced Baba's name, and he entered the ring dazed. He bent down to pick up the barbell, his mind distraught over the recent news. Unable to concentrate on his technique, he lifted the barbell with a sudden jerk, and immediate pain shot up his arms and pierced his brain. He screamed in pain. An ambulance took him to the hospital where the doctor told him he had a lot of ligaments damage. Then the doctor gave him the most devastating news — "You may never go back to competitive weight-lifting again." Baba found it very difficult to talk about what happened after that, but he told her that Ma went against her entire family and visited him in the Delhi hospital.

After their wedding, Baba set up his gym in the dusty hallway of the east wing. He had a few manual treadmills, some barbells and a single bench press. Some neighborhood kids signed up with him. It was never clear to Mohini how the gym gained its good reputation and brought in so many students, but as far back as Mohini could remember, she had always seen it packed with sweaty boys pumping iron and steel. They came from all over India, and Baba put them through a rigorous training routine which started with a hundred push-ups at the crack of dawn.

Later, Baba told Mohini that he never wanted to look back and blame his fate. What had happened had happened. Baba believed in new beginnings and fresh starts, and when Mohini was born, he began a new chapter, the happiest chapter in his life with Mohini in it. The joy he felt when he held her in his arms undid the hurt and healed his wounds.

Mohini and her parents lived on the second floor of the east wing, above the gym. This wing had only two bedrooms. The larger one faced a few palm trees and the neighbor's cow barn. This room always smelled of cow dung and sodden leaves. Mohini covered her nose and closed the windows on hot days when the smell was especially intense. Her parents spent most of their time here, reclined on the large four-poster-bed by the window. Ma sat with her book of monthly expenses, chewing on her pencil and adding long columns of numbers. Baba reclined next to her with the daily newspaper covering most of his face. He was always tired after his morning gym sessions. Ma chatted with him constantly about the rising prices of fish and vegetables and household appliances that always needed repair. Baba inserted an occasional "Umm" or a "Hunh" in between Ma's rapid chatter till his eyes grew heavy and the newspaper fell flat on his face. Mohini smiled when this happened—the unabating stream of Ma's grumblings met with the desert like silence on Baba's side.

Mohini's aunt, Pishimoni, visited them frequently. They kept the single bed near the wall for her to spend the night. Next to the single bed was her parent's steel almirah and a wooden clotheshorse whose outlines were indistinct because of the layers of sari, blouse, pajama, and petticoat heaped on the bars rising like a mountain. A swarm of black ants lived in the wall cracks behind the clotheshorse.

Outside her parent's bedroom, there was a tiny balcony, barely big enough to hold two people. Sometimes Mohini and Parul bounced their balls against the walls of this balcony. A teacher and her niece lived in the house exactly opposite to them. Mohini detested them because they were the "gossipy people" who loved to spread rumors about their neighbors. When Mohini and Parul came out to the balcony, the pair observed them from behind the clothesline and then whispered and murmured and nudged each other. Other times, they pursed their mouth in self-satisfied smirks. Mohini wanted to throw her ball and break a flowerpot on their balcony, but Parul held her back. "Control your temper, Mohini. Don't you know what kind of people they are? You'll get yourself into heaps of trouble and those people will clap their hands and dance around." Parul was one who had a cooler head.

The smaller room served as Mohini's bedroom. It faced the main road and overlooked a gravelly driveway. The antique tri-fold dressing table had plastic trays filled with her clips, hair bands, hair ties, and *bindis*. Her bed had multi-colored cushions, and the windows had flowery cotton drapes. Near the window was Mohini's desk with her schoolbooks and weight-lifting books piled high on it. She used a set of dumbbells as paperweights.

Outside the window, a Gulmohor tree was always heavy with flowers. Little squirrels darted up the trunks and jumped from branch to branch. Every evening, Mohini did her homework in this room with Parul. She sat on her desk while Parul sat cross-legged on the floor with her exercise books and pencil. But instead of doing her homework, Parul stared at the Gulmohor tree with her big black eyes. Sometimes she walked over to the window to touch the enormous pink plumes and hold them gently to her nose.

One day, Mohini asked her, "Why do you like this tree so much, Parul*di*?"

For a moment Parul stood still, holding the flowers in her hand. Then she looked at Mohini and said dreamily, "We had a Gulmohor tree, just like this one, behind our house. I used to play under its leafy branches every day. My Ammi sat close by, rocking and feeding baby Rehana. I picked up the scattered pink flowers and put them in Ammi's hair. They sparkled as bright as stars. I could feel the flowers were alive—it was like holding a tiny heartbeat between my fingers." Parul held the flower to her nose and inhaled gently. "It was the same heartbeat that I felt everywhere I went in my village—it was in the sunrise and sunset, in the tall blades of grass, in the morning dewdrops. Everything I touched had life." A shadow like a stain spread over her features as she walked back to Mohini's desk and squatted on the floor. "I thought the Gulmohor tree with its giant branches will protect our family always. But look at what happened." Her voice cracked.

Parul ripped off the petals, crumpled them, and scattered the flowers onto the floor.

Mohini watched helplessly.

• • •

Once a month, Parul's father, Madhu*babu*, came to visit her. His real name was Ahmed *chacha*, but Ma had taught them to call him Madhu*babu*, a simple Hindu name. He was a middle-aged man with a

15

receding hairline and very dark complexion. White talcum powder coalesced in dull white beads at the base of his neck. He did not wear a skullcap and had a trimmed beard, so nothing in his dress and behavior betrayed his religion.

He bellowed Parul's name from the street below and then came up to the second-floor staircase to wait for her. Seeing him always made Parul nervous. Mohini knew it did. He came to take away most of Parul's monthly salary. But his demands on her never seem to end. Every month he came up with yet another compelling reason to ask for money: to treat his asthma, or to repair the leaky tin roof over their heads, or to buy a warm blanket for the coming winter nights. Mohini watched Parul meet each of his demands obediently, like an ox, which carries a heavy yolk on its shoulders and never questions its fate.

Mohini disliked the man so much that she tried to stay away from him. But then, one day when she was coming up the stairs, she found Parul in the middle of a heated argument with her father. "No, no, no," said Parul, tears running down her cheeks. "Abbu, I am telling you... it is not possible."

Madhu*babu* twisted her arm, and she yelped in pain. "Mumtaz," he said. "Only you can get me out of this mess. You're a clever girl. You can figure something out." He didn't let go of Parul's arm even when Mohini came up, and, not knowing what to do, Mohini stood there watching Madhu*babu* inflict more pain on Parul.

After he left, Parul faked a headache and stayed in her room. When she came to dinner that night, her eyes were red and swollen. Still, she didn't share her story with Ma and Mohini. The next evening, when Parul seemed particularly distracted, Mohini pushed aside her homework in frustration and demanded, "Parul*di*, what is it? What's wrong? Why was your Abbu bothering you? Tell me now or else I'll tell Ma your Abbu hurts you."

Parul's sigh carried the whole weight of her heart. "My Abbu went to play *teen patti* poker game at our village casino. He lost all his money... more than my month's salary. Now the debt collectors are after him." She took a deep breath and leaned against the wall. "He wants me to pay back his debt."

"How can that be?" cried out Mohini. "You're just a child."

"I don't know... I don't have the money—any money—and I can't make him understand that." Parul's tone trembled on the edge of anguish.

Mohini gripped Parul's elbow and turned her around. "Then why don't you ask Ma for the money?"

Parul shook her head. "Ma has already done so much for me. I can't ask for more."

Mohini released her and stepped back. Her head throbbed with rage. What a terrible man this Madhu*babu* was to put Parul under so much pressure. As if snatching her salary every month was not enough, now he wanted her to pay for all his bad habits.

The next morning, as Mohini sat combing her hair in front of her trifold dressing table, she puzzled over Parul's dilemma, and an idea came to her. Getting up, she rummaged through her cupboard and dug out a rusty tin can, hidden carefully under layers and layers of clothing. Inside the can were rolled bundles of ten and twenty-rupee notes tied neatly with red strings. Picking up the can, she ran to the courtyard, where Parul was pumping water from the tube-well. When Mohini called her name, Parul jumped, and then stepped back in surprise when Mohini shoved the tin can in her hand. She stared open-mouthed at the neatly tied crisp bundles inside. "Where did you get all this money from?" gasped Parul, covering her mouth with the flat of her palm.

"I robbed a bank," laughed Mohini. "Silly Parul*di*, don't you know I get money from my parents and relatives every birthday? Most of the time I can't think of anything to spend it on and I stick the notes in this can." Mohini rubbed Parul's hands. "No one knows this money exists. It doesn't have to be accounted for. It's yours now."

Parul neither spoke nor moved. Her eyes looked wet, but when she dabbed them with the end of her *dupatta*, there were no tears. Perhaps she had cried enough.

"Parul*di*," Mohini shook her arm urgently, "Why don't you say something?"

"I can't take your money, Mohini."

"Why not?"

Something shifted and stirred deep inside Parul's eyes. She sat on the mossy floor, hugging the tube well and shaking her head. "It's your pocket money... you need to spend it. If I take it... I won't be able to look at myself in the mirror."

Mohini felt a thousand needles prick her heart all at once. "Please don't say no," she said. Then she gathered Parul's hands in her fist and brought them close to her chest, "Don't you think Rehana would have done the same for you?"

Parul grew silent. Water dripped on her arm from the tube-well, but she didn't seem to notice it. She was pale, and for the first time, Mohini saw the dark circles underneath her eyes. Mohini sat down next to her and waited. After some time, Parul turned to her and wrapped her feeble, trembling body tightly around her. Holding her then, Mohini felt as though Parul had pulled out her soul and placed it in her hand.

That night from her bedroom window, Mohini looked at the Gulmohor tree shimmering in the moon light. Walking to the tree, she held the branches and made a wish. "Please god, take the village away from Parul. Set her free."

Chapter 2

Baba, Mohini thought, perhaps secretly wanted a boy who he could train to be weight-lifter. So when she was born, he mistook her for a son, and treated her in every respect like a little boy. He encouraged Ma to dress her up like a boy, to buy her sports outfits, and to keep her hair cut short. He started her training early on, teaching her to perform gymnastics, play soccer and practice swimming in the Ganga River. It terrified Ma that the strong currents would snatch her feeble body out of Baba's grasp. But Baba was oblivious to Ma's fear and pushed her to swim farther and faster.

Mohini joined Baba's other students in the weight-lifting class, and from the day she walked into the gym and picked up the barbells, she fell right into magic. Baba planned out a daily routine for her that increased the weights and the difficulty level gradually. He taught her to squat, deadlift, bench, and do overhead pressing. He initiated her into glute bridging by putting a barbell on her hips and asking her to lift her hips as high as possible, driving the barbell up and off the ground. He increased the weights by five pounds each month until Mohini could glute bridge almost twice her body weight.

"Careful Mohini, you'll break your back," warned Parul when she came to sweep the gym floor and watched her practice.

"If Baba says I can do it... I can do it, Paruldi. I am not scared," Mohini said.

Mohini was not afraid of any serious injury—she had too much faith in Baba for that—and the truth was that she liked being pushed, scolded and praised by him.

Parul bent down to lift Mohini's barbell, and even though she clenched her teeth, closed her eyes tightly shut and tried hard, she couldn't budge the bar even an inch.

"This is impossible," cried Parul. "How can you do this every day?"

Mohini laughed at her. "Silly Parul*di*. You need training for this. I'm just lucky to have Baba."

Parul flopped down on the floor and looked at her wistfully. "Wish my Abbu was like this... like your Baba... took a bit of interest in my life. But the man won't spend a single paisa on me."

There was such regret in Parul's voice that Mohini felt her shoulders tense up. "What did he do this time, Parul*di*? Be honest. You can't hide anything from me."

"*Arre* na, silly girl, you're always worried about me," Parul laughed. "It's nothing serious. For some time now, I have been begging him to bring me a kite from our village. Our village is famous for making the lightest and fastest kites. So yesterday he finally brought me a kite. I was so happy that I danced all around him. I told myself I was wrong about him all this time... he is not miserly at all. I really wanted to trust him... you know." Parul got up and moved towards the gym mirror and sighed at her reflection. "But my Abbu fooled me again. The kite was torn on the edges. He had patched it up with colored paper. My own Abbu couldn't get me a new kite. He picked up one from the roadside and did a few repairs on it."

Mohini felt her cheeks grow warm. "Really, Parul*di*, if you need a kite, just ask me. I'll get you one. But don't let your father lower you like this. He doesn't care for you and never will."

Then Mohini felt bad. She wanted to take back her cruel words. But they were already out, and she could see the cloud they left on Parul's features.

• • •

In her third year, Baba introduced Mohini to the "snatch technique" with the barbell, often used in weightlifting competitions. He showed her how to heave the bar overhead and then drop under the bar to catch and stabilize it. Mohini was in awe of Baba's herculean strength; his lifts were dynamic and explosive, yet supremely graceful. His knowledge excited her; she was privileged to be in the same room with Baba and see the beautiful lifts in such intimate proximity.

During her first lesson, Baba said, "The snatch is a finesse lift. If done right, the lift should feel like water making its way through cracks. It should never feel like ice cracking stones. Once I train you, even heavy weights will feel light." Mohini was quick to imitate Baba, wanting to bring forth this exquisite blending of ease and command in her own performance.

She practiced with his older students, who had already taken part in tournaments and brought back trophies. She saw them pant and sweat, squirm and curse through long workouts in the hot gym. Day and night, they obsessed over attempts and numbers. Mohini felt a strange camaraderie with Baba's students. Practicing with them, she was lifted out of ordinariness and transported into a world of possibilities.

Weightlifting soon became an obsession. She woke up early to help Baba with the general housekeeping and upkeep of the gym. Then she worked out for an hour till her whole body was covered in sweat. Often, she lost track of time and Ma had to come rushing down to get her ready for school.

•   •   •

Even in school, she let her mind wander and thought about how to tweak her technique. She played with the doorknobs and round tap handles, imagining them to be the knurling of her barbell. In her free time, she helped in the library, carrying heavy boxes of books up and down the stairs. After school, she rushed home to change into her gym clothes and practice with Baba's students.

By age eleven, Mohini had started to notice how some girls in her class looked at her with slight disdain. Her muscles seem to make her less attractive, less feminine in their eyes. Mohini had always been told she was a pretty girl, with long curly hair and lotus-like eyes. She tried to dress tastefully, with matching hair clips and *bindi*, and keep up with current fashion trends. She had a large group of friends she got along well with. But there was no doubt about it; after her weight-lifting journey, girls in her class no longer gravitated towards her—her biceps and thick set of thighs seemed to make them nervous. Mohini saw how they looked at her and rolled their eyes whenever they thought she was not looking. She knew she was an unusual specimen to them—a girl who was stronger than most boys in her class and who could knock out their teeth in one punch if she wanted to. Though she pretended not to notice their changing attitude, their hostility plagued Mohini, and she felt more and more lonely in school.

Then one day, Baba asked her to share her squat rack with a boy who had just joined the gym. His name was Rajkumar. Unlike the other students, Rajkumar did not have proper gym clothes. He belonged to the untouchable Chamar caste of tanners and leather workers. Baba told Mohini, his father skinned the carcasses of animals and tanned the hides, which were turned into shoes and bags for rich ladies. Rajkumar wore *lungis* and banyans with dime sized holes when he worked out in the gym.

Mohini wrinkled her nose when she saw him. The smell of the coconut oil in his hair mixed with his pungent body odor suffocated her. She dug out her handkerchief and tied it around her mouth and nose. Rajkumar studied her for a moment and whistled softly. Then he dropped and did a few push-ups looking at her sideways, and when Mohini turned around to look at him, he winked at her. She ignored him and moved to the barbell section of the room, but the boy followed her there too, humming an old Bollywood tune, *Mere Sapno Ki Rani Kab Aayegi Tu* (Oh my dream girl, when will you come to me).

This time Mohini cringed. The Chamar boy's boldness surprised her. It was, after all, her father's gym, and no boy in their right mind would dare to flirt with her. Yet this boy was whistling and winking at her. *Where did this idiot come from?*

They both started squatting at 135 pounds. It was a heavy strength day for Mohini and she set her target to 185 pounds for a double. As she warmed up to 150s, 160s, she noticed Rajkumar was trying to keep up with her and squatting way outside his comfort zone. At 165 pounds, she saw his face turn red and his eyes almost bulge out.

"Careful," said Mohini. "You want to break your bones or what?"

"I can do this," he said, panting. Then he howled and collapsed on the floor.

Baba and his students rushed to their side of the gym.

"What happened to you?" Baba asked Rajkumar.

Rajkumar extended his sore left arm and sobbed like a child. "I am dying here, Sir."

"He was competing with me, Baba," said Mohini. "I told him not to, but he didn't listen."

"You tried to lift like my daughter? How can you be so dense? I have been training her for years. You just started here."

"I can lift more than a girl." Rajkumar looked stubborn.

A disapproving frown appeared on Baba's face. "Nonsense," he said. "There are no boys and girls here. We are all weightlifters, that's all."

Baba reached out for a bottle of Himalaya herbal balm. "Come here, let me see what I can do."

He uncapped the bottle and spread the dark droplets on Rajkumar's shoulder and neck. Then Baba massaged the balm into his skin. "No weightlifting for three days. You will give these muscles some rest."

Mohini noticed how hairy his arms and shoulders were. *Like a bear*, she thought.

"No more carelessness," said Baba. "You will only lift what I tell you."

Rajkumar croaked something incoherent and nodded.

•   •   •

A few months went by and Mohini didn't speak to Rajkumar. Then one day, she came into the gym and found Rajkumar taking a nap on her yoga mat. Everyone in the gym knew not to touch Mohini's mat. It was bright orange and kept separate from rest of the mats. A tiny transistor radio pressed to his ear was playing *ghazals*. Mohini cranked up the radio to full volume, and Rajkumar jumped up from sleep like something hit him.

He sat, opening and closing his mouth like a goldfish. "Are you crazy? I could have lost my hearing."

"Don't touch my stuff. My mat, my towels, my water bottle are just mine. No one else can use them."

"Why don't you write your name on everything, then? After all, it is your father's gym. Everything here belongs to you."

"Think what you like. I don't care. I am telling you once and for all."

"*Array* go! Who are you to tell me?" He made a face at her. "A few more days and you will be gone from here. Then all this will belong to me."

Mohini was taken aback. "What do you mean, I will be gone? I live here. This is my house."

"Gone from this gym. Fussss..." Rajkumar made a hand gesture to show a bird flying away. "They will make you vanish. Just like magic."

"What nonsense are you talking about?"

"Your own family. They won't let you become a weightlifter."

"Why the hell not?"

"Because girls don't become weightlifters. They marry and have children. You're wasting your time here."

Mohini stared at Rajkumar wordlessly. His words pierced her chest like a poisoned arrow. Mohini didn't need Rajkumar to tell her it was impossible. She knew it well enough herself. It already horrified her relatives to see her practice with boys every day in the gym. Her changing physical appearance had shocked them even more. Ever since she had started weightlifting, the extended family that enforced a slow and strong acceptance on its members had tried to convince Ma to pull her out of the gym. "She will scare away all prospective grooms. You want her to stay single all her life?" Pishimoni told Ma, day in and day out.

Sometimes the aunts stood near the gym door and shouted at Mohini. "This is not America and Russia. Here, girls live a certain way. Look at all your cousins; they don't have boy-like hobbies... they are just normal girls." Those were the times Mohini wanted to point out to them that none of her cousins were talented, but she knew a stern lecture would follow if she dared to open her mouth. Instead, she had an argument in her head with her aunts as she walked around the gym, pumping iron and flexing her muscles—*I'm not like my cousins, I don't enjoy getting facials and manicures all day. I don't even like to go shopping or read Harlequin romance. My dreams are different. I want to be recognizable when I grow up, wear medals and hold a trophy over my head. I want to make Baba proud of me.*

When aunts came to the gym door, Baba always intervened and protected Mohini like a shield. "I have big dreams for her," he told them. "One day I will send her to the Commonwealth games." It was Baba who stood between Mohini and the rest of the family and defended her right to weightlift.

Looking at Rajkumar now, Mohini felt a tear sting her eye, but she quickly blinked it away and composed her face to assure Rajkumar that his words had no effect on her. Tossing her braid back firmly, she threw him a contemptuous look and marched towards the gym door. But as soon as she opened it, she found Parul standing outside, with a bamboo duster and dustpan in her hand. Mohini opened her mouth to say something, but her voice was so choked with emotion that no words came out.

"Mohini." Parul's hand pressed down on her shoulder. "Why are you crying? Did someone hurt you?"

"Crying?" Finding her voice, Mohini tried to make it airy and casual. "Really, Parul*di*, you imagine things. I just have something in my eye... that's all."

Parul shook her head. "You're lying. Something has happened for sure." She caught hold of Mohini's elbow. "Tell me who upset you?"

Still, Mohini kept quiet. She deliberately stood near the door, blocking Parul's view.

Parul grew impatient. "If you don't tell me, I'll find it out on my own." She pushed past Mohini and entered the gym, and almost immediately, Mohini heard her loud swearing. "Is that son of a pig, *shuyorer baccha*, lazing on *your* mat?"

Mohini tugged Parul's hand. "He is a new student. Doesn't know the rules. Please, Parul*di*, say nothing. Baba will get upset."

Ignoring her plea, Parul marched up to Rajkumar with the dustpan in her hand. Rajkumar sat up in a great hurry and, pointing to the dustpan, said, "Hey, do your work later. Why are you disturbing my afternoon nap?"

Parul shook her head. "Important work can't wait."

She bent forward and blew hard on the dustpan to scatter the dust all around Rajkumar. The dust swirled around him and settled on his hair, whiskers, and eyelashes. Mohini watched, fascinated, as he sneezed and coughed and rolled on the floor from side to side.

Finally, Parul gritted her teeth and squatted next to Rajkumar. "Open your ears and listen to me, you ass," she said. "If you use anything that belongs to Mohini again, I'll beat you with my duster so hard that you'll forget your own father's name. Do you understand me?"

• • •

After school, Mohini usually took the school bus home. That day, she missed the bus and took a shortcut through the slums across the railway line. It was afternoon, and the shops had their shutters down so that the people inside could take a midday nap. The narrow alley was deserted except for an occasional street dog or crows eating out of the trash cans. She had reached the corner where the alley turned toward the main road when she heard someone shout, "*Dekh, dekh...* look who is here. Is this a boy or a girl?"

"Could be something in between," suggested another male voice. A string of laughter followed.

Mohini turned around to look at them. They were three boys in faded T-shirts and checked *lungis*; all in their early teens. The boy in the middle was taller with dyed hair, red *paan* stained teeth and dark sunglasses that rested on the tip of his nose. The boys now surrounded and circled her slowly, looking her up and down, their eyes drilling holes through her school blouse.

"What do you want?" she asked nervously, trying to push past them.

"Come on," said the tall boy, touching her arm. "What's the rush? Tell us what you are. We've got to know."

Mohini gritted her teeth and brushed away his hand. "Leave me alone or I'll scream."

The boy looked at her, nonplussed. "You don't understand," he said. "We can't let you go till you tell us what gender you really are."

Mohini allowed herself to take a long breath. "Look, I... don't want any trouble. You know very well I am a girl. Why ask me a silly question like that?" She licked her dry lips.

The boy with a thin face and wispy mustache shook his head. "Liar."

"What?"

"I said you're lying."

"What kind of joke is this? I am telling you I am a girl."

"Prove it then."

"Ask anyone," said Mohini desperately. "I live across the railway line. Ask any of the neighbors. They know me."

"*Tsh tsh*, why do you want to bother your neighbors for such a minor matter? They are all busy folks. This matter can be sorted out quickly... just between us... right here, right now." He whistled softly.

Anger had replaced Mohini's fear. "What nonsense are you babbling? What do you want me to do? Show you my birth certificate?"

"Fortunately for you, we are in a good mood today. We don't want you to take so much trouble for us. Keep things simple. Just pull down your skirt."

"What?"

"Let's check what is under that skirt. Then you can go home."

Mohini folded her arms and inhaled sharply. Humiliation and anger reddened her face, and her fingers clenched into a fist. She made a low hissing sound with her tongue. "Do not touch me. I am warning you."

For a moment, everything went still. No one moved. Dogs stopped barking and crows stopped cawing. The usual breeze had stopped, and not one of the tall trees stirred. Not even a leaf moved. Mohini also stopped breathing—the air in her lungs felt like a block of ice.

The boy with sunglasses now stepped forward and brought his face very close to Mohini. His eyes gleamed with vicious intent. "What if I touch you, *haramzadi*? What will you do? Call your father?"

All her fears disappeared. Revulsion rose from the hot tarry road and made its way through her veins. "I don't need my father. My training is enough to take down cowards like you."

Almost immediately, the thin boy with the wispy mustache lunged forward and reached for her skirt. He tugged on the elastic band and released it sharply, causing it to snap against her waist. Anger exploded inside Mohini, almost blinding her. She grabbed the boy's collar, dragged him a couple of paces, and then struck his face. The boy yelped in pain. She placed the flat of her palm against his chest and propelled him backward. He fell on his back, hitting the pavement. The other two boys charged forward, swinging their fists to hit Mohini's face. She blocked them with her elbow and punched so hard that the boys staggered back for a good four feet before banging into a parked delivery truck. Mohini pointed a finger at them and screamed, "I warned you not to touch me. Next time listen to me." She felt exhausted. She shut her eyes and let her head drop till her chin touched her chest. Sweat drenched her school blouse, and she could barely breathe.

A crowd gathered around them. They were too stunned to say anything at first. Then an indistinct murmur broke out as they tried to help the boys get back on their feet. "A girl beat up three boys? How is this possible? What is the world coming to?" Their disapproving eyes bore into Mohini, making her cringe in shame. She ran home as fast as she could.

At home, Mohini didn't tell anyone about the slum incident, not even Parul. *I have to remain calm and do everything normally;* she told herself. *No one must know about my showdown with the slum boys, especially not Ma.*

A week went by and no one in the house mentioned the slum incident. Mohini started to relax—*her secret was safe.* She went back to her daily routine and didn't think too much about the slum boys.

It was six-thirty in the morning and Mohini was getting a little anxious. She was in Baba's gym downstairs, spraying the mats and wiping the upholstery with light bleach. She had already spent an hour: she had inspected the weight stacks for proper alignment and smoothness; tightened all the loose nuts and bolts; and gathered all the dirty towels in a big laundry basket. From the window, she glimpsed Baba's students swinging their clubs and doing push-ups below the tin awning.

The gym was uncomfortably hot, as it was between rains, and Mohini had to toss back her thick braid several times to wipe the sweat off her neck. There, in the gym, fresh plaster and paint were applied to places where chunks had fallen off. To her, these patches stood out like half-healed wounds. Baba's students had covered some patches with pictures of famous weightlifters cut out from magazines and calendars. The large glossy photo of in the center was that of Mr. Universe winner and Olympic weightlifter, Arnold Schwarzenegger. He loomed large over the gym with his sculpted physique. The students pressed their palms together and said a quick prayer before his life-size photo prior to starting their everyday exercise routine.

Looking at Arnold now, she noticed the layer of dust that had coated his picture. The early morning sunlight caught the cobwebs hanging down from the photo like strands of black silk. Mohini would have to leave for school in an hour if she was to be on time for her sixth-grade final exam. Still, she wanted to climb up on the three-legged wobbly stool and clean up the cobwebs before she left. She glanced at her watch to estimate the time it would take her to do this. Normally she would have pointed out the cobwebs to Parul, and Parul would have gone after the webs with her broom like an eagle swooping down on its prey. Cleaning the gym was, after all, Parul's job, not Mohini's. But Parul had a fever for a few days, and Mohini knew this cleaning couldn't wait. She clicked her tongue in annoyance and pulled out the stool from the tiny storeroom. The stool screeched and scraped the floor as she dragged it forward.

The door flew open, and she turned around to see Rajkumar, standing outside in his *lungi*, his skin glistening from the mustard oil massage he received every morning. Mohini did not hide her dislike for him. Turning back, she busied herself with the task at hand.

He walked past, looking at her sideways, and stopped before the gym mirror. Whistling softly, he rendered a flourish to his coconut-oil-soaked hair by running a small comb through it. Satisfied with his greasy pompadour, he wiped the oil and tucked away his comb in the banyan pocket.

Ignoring him, Mohini continued with her dusting. Rajkumar circled the room a few times and cleared his throat as if he had an important announcement to make. Still, Mohini pretended he was invisible, leaning forward to reach behind the weight racks. Finally, he approached her and tapped on the wooden shelves, forcing her to listen to him. "Someone saw you in the slum across the railway line last week."

"What?" Mohini stopped dusting.

"You were seen happily beating up boys—Bachchan style, you know our famous film star." Rajkumar grinned.

The stool wobbled under Mohini and she almost fell off it. Her head was spinning. "What nonsense are you blabbering?" She fought to keep her voice under control. "Have you gone completely insane?"

"I can see you are having some memory issues." He looked at her with pity. "Told you all this weight-lifting is not good for a girl's health."

Mohini climbed down from the stool and tried to walk past him, but he blocked her way. "What's the rush? Hear me out."

"I have no interest in anything you have to say."

"But your mother does. Something tells me she will have a lot of interest in what I have to say."

Mohini felt all the air leave her lungs. She grabbed Rajkumar's banyan and shook him. "How do you know it was me? It could have been anyone."

"Nah." He waved his hand to as if to wipe away other possibilities. "There is only one female, Mohammad Ali, in this neighborhood, who can beat up boys like that. I'm sure it was you. The description my slum friends gave me matches you... same to same." He grinned.

Anger and frustration bubbled up inside Mohini. "You won't tell anyone... specially not Ma."

All friendliness seemed to evaporate from Rajkumar's face. His eyes hardened like steel balls. "Try to stop me," he said.

She lunged forward and pounced on his oily arm. "I am warning you..."

She didn't finish when Rajkumar said, "*Array* go! Who are you threatening? This Rajkumar doesn't take threats from a girl." He paused and looked straight back at her. "I'll do what I please."

He slipped away from her fingers and ran out of the gym. Mohini watched him helplessly.

• • •

The next morning, when she opened her eyes, Mohini was lying in her own bed with the sun warming one side of her face. A voice was shouting in her ear, and at first, she couldn't tell what it was saying, or why it was so loud. Then the outlines of Parul's face slowly took form in front of her and she sat up.

"Get out of bed," she was saying, shaking Mohini's shoulder. "Your aunts are here and they are talking to Ma."

"Talking to Ma?" Mohini frowned. "About what?"

"I think it is about you."

This time Mohini listened carefully, and she too heard the voices in Ma's room. A slight shiver went down her spine. Brushing Parul's hand from her shoulder, she sprinted to Ma's door to see what the commotion was about. Parul followed closely behind, her anklets ringing rhythmically on the cold mosaic floor.

Inside the room, half-a-dozen aunts in multicolored saris and clattering bangles had surrounded Ma. They seemed to be in a volatile state of excitement. They all spoke simultaneously, over each other, their haughty opinions filling up the room and spilling out of the doorway. They fumed over her weightlifting: What was to become of this girl? Today she is beating up slum boys; who knows who she will beat up tomorrow? Is she going to grow up and become a full *goonda* mafia type? At this rate, she may even end up in jail for beating people up left and right.

Mohini's heart sank. Just as she had feared, her aunts had come to know about the slum incident, and that was causing them to flare up. *Rajkumar had carried out his threat.* Her scalp prickled, and her palms turned slightly damp.

Ma interrupted the aunts and pleaded with them to slow down. She was having trouble understanding them. Then Pishimoni took over as the spokesperson. "It is your affection for your daughter that is making you blind. She is getting completely out of hand and you cannot even see it. If you don't tighten the leash now, there will be terrible consequences later."

"What's all this, Mohini? Did you beat up some boys?" Parul poked her back and whispered close to her ear. "Why didn't you tell me?" Turning around, Mohini could see the lines of fear and anxiety etched on Parul's face.

Mohini forced herself to step into the room in full view of the aunts. The aunts wagged their fingers in unison, making ominous suggestions about her future. Finally, Pishimoni suggested they leave the room. "If you all keep on shouting, we can reach no solution to this problem. I think we should leave the mother and daughter to talk to each other. It is they who need to decide, after all."

The aunts got up reluctantly. They gathered their purses and followed Pishimoni out of the room, glaring at Mohini on their way out. Parul moved behind the curtain to hide from the angry aunts.

Mohini moved closer to Ma and opened her mouth to speak, but, looking at Ma, she changed her mind. Ma's eyes were red and swollen, as if she had been crying. Mohini poured Ma a glass of water, but she pushed away the glass and looked fiercely at her daughter. "Why didn't you tell me about what happened last week? Did you really beat up three slum boys?" Clearly everything the aunts had said had an acute effect on Ma, for she was trembling.

"Yes," said Mohini quietly. "But they attacked me first. They tried to..."

"You thought you could create such a racket on the streets and the word wouldn't reach me? I wouldn't find out?"

"No, Ma. I was about to tell you. I didn't have time to..."

Tears streamed down Ma's face. "I blame myself for what happened. I let this weightlifting foolishness go on for too long. I never tried to stop your Baba."

"No, no, you're getting this all wrong." Mohini gripped Ma's hand tightly. "The boys were terrible. They tried to—"

"Quiet," said Ma. "I don't want to hear one more word. I have listened to you and your Baba for years. You always got your way. I said nothing. But look at where it got us."

Mohini shuffled her feet. The conversation was going the wrong way, and she had to distract Ma. She made quick eye contact with Parul, who had come out from behind the curtain and kneeled next to Ma. *Save me. She* pleaded mutely.

Parul assessed the situation quickly and broke in. "Ma," she said, tugging on her hand. "I think you left the kitchen window open. The crows will take away all our fish. And fish these days have become so expensive that..."

Ma gave Parul's hand a stinging slap. "Stop trying to save Mohini by telling lies. I closed the window with my own hands." Ma turned to Mohini again. "After what happened in the slum, even Lord Shiva cannot protect you from me."

Mohini grabbed Ma's hand. "Please Ma, don't say that. It was a mistake to take that shortcut last week. I should have known that the slum boys would torment me." The words *don't take away my weightlifting* formed on her lips, but she could not utter them. The thought evoked so much emotion that she blinked back tears and looked away.

Ma took out her hanky and blew her nose loudly. "I have decided you're not going to the gym again. From now on, you will do things that girls do: play with dolls, sew and learn to cook."

Mohini grew still. She moved closer to the table fan. She was sweating.

"Don't look at me with big, big eyes. I should have done this long back. It was your father who made me weak."

Mohini opened her mouth to argue, but Ma waved her away. "Go, go now, you two. I need to sleep. I have first-class headache coming."

Outside in the hallway, Mohini slammed her fist into the wall. Then she spun around to face Parul. "Why did he do this to me?" she shouted.

Parul put her arms around her and pulled her close. Mohini hit her chest with her fist and asked Parul again and again: "Why, Parul*di*, why? Why did he do this to me? Why did he ruin my life?"—and each time she heard Parul ask her in a confused voice: "Who did this? Who ruined your life?"

Finally, Mohini screamed Rajkumar's name before breaking into a series of hiccups.

• • •

The next day, Mohini went to the gym to clear out all her belongings. Everything in the gym was as it had been. There was a layer of sweat on the old leather and dirty towels in the bin. Baba's students carried on with their lifting and pumping like it was an ordinary day. No one noticed her when she walked in except Rajkumar, who was using the leg press and waved happily at her.

Suddenly, Parul appeared next to her out of nowhere. She pressed a finger to her lips and smiled conspiratorially at Mohini.

Mohini was about to ask why she looked happy, but she stopped mid-sentence, when Parul took out a piece of chewing gum from her mouth and stuck it to the headrest of the machine Rajkumar was about to use. Rajkumar moved to the machine, and even before Mohini could comprehend Parul's actions, she saw him lean back and rest his head on the gum. Mohini felt her heart ready to explode. She had to insert all her fingers into her mouth to suppress a squeal of delight. Turning around, she saw Parul smiling at her.

At first, Rajkumar looked puzzled, frowning and tugging to move his neck forward. Then, running his fingers through his hair, he gave a surprised cry—bits and pieces of the white gum stretched and reattached to his hair like an elastic band. "Who did this to me?" he cried loudly as all heads turned toward him. Then, beating his chest and howling, he hopped and jumped all around the gym, asking for help as the chewing gum got more and more entangled deep into his hair. In the end, unable to get it out, the gym boys had to yank off entire tufts of hair, leaving bald spots on Rajkumar's scalp.

Mohini walked to Parul and squeezed her hand and whispered, "I may have lost my weight-lifting, but I still have you," she said. "You'll be my friend forever. No one can ever come between us."

There was a strange tingling—like a foreboding—deep inside her stomach as she spoke. Ma's words rang in her ears: "Just when you think things are perfect, life throws curveballs and googlies at you."

Chapter 3

Parul stood on the balcony with Ma overlooking the courtyard. Looking down, she saw the printing press widow standing in the courtyard, talking to some of her customers. The widow, who was Baba's distant relative, owned the printing press on the first floor of the west wing.

A crispy white sari covered most of her head and part of her face. She didn't wear any make-up, though her lips were always red from the *paan* leaves she chewed day and night.

Seeing the smiling widow downstairs, a dark cloud descended on Ma's face. She leaned over the parapet to look at the widow with slight disdain. Tension sizzled between Ma and the widow even though they were on separate floors. "Do you see that some people have no shame?" Ma asked Parul. "They live in other people's houses and think of it as their own."

Parul suppressed a smile. This was almost a daily occurrence in her life. Ever since she had first set her foot in their house, she had heard a variety of remarks from Ma about the widow, infused with some hidden provocation.

At first, Ma told Parul little about how the widow came to rent the first-floor west wing. "These are family matters," she announced, making it clear that Parul was not included in whatever definition of family Ma had in mind.

But on this day, Ma was agitated and seemed unable to hold herself back. She pulled Parul inside and told her about the widow's wicked plan.

Years ago, when the widow's husband passed away suddenly, she came to Mohini's parents for help. In Ma's memories, she was small and thin with one runny-nosed boy in her lap and another one clinging to her knee.

"*Dada*, we have nowhere to go. He left us with nothing. He left me with two children, but no way to feed them. If you don't do something, we will have to beg on the streets," she said.

Ma felt grave sorrow for a woman who had just lost her husband, and she could see how upset Baba was. After all, the widow was a cousin. A distant one, perhaps, but still a family member. How could they let her suffer alone? Together they consoled the widow and promised to stand by her till she got back on her feet. They offered her a generous sum of money and a temporary place to live.

"But do you know what she did?" A wry grimace twisted Ma's face.

"What, Ma?" asked Parul.

"She turned down our offer. She didn't accept a single paisa from us."

"The greedy widow didn't take your money?" asked Parul in amazement.

"Why would she? She had much bigger plans."

Ma looked out the window as if she could see everything play out again in her mind's eye. She continued with her story, speaking in a hushed tone.

The widow bent down to touch Baba's feet. "*Dada*, you are an angel-like man." Tears ran down her cheeks like an open tap. "All I ask is two rooms. I want to start my printing press. It was my husband's dream. Alas, he couldn't see it."

In her words, there was despondency, her sentiments were saccharine, and there was great strength in her persuasion. All their hesitation disappeared and Mohini's parents rented out the rooms to her. Together, they helped her set up the printing press on the first floor of the west wing.

Ma could not go on. She pressed her fingers to her temples and massaged them one by one.

Parul touched Ma's arm. "Calm down, Ma. What could you have done? You were just worried about her. Who can see the future?"

"We were so young and naïve in most practical matters—no match for that shrewd woman." Ma groaned. "From the day she came, the noise didn't stop. *Kachang kachang kachang* went the press... all morning, all afternoon. Not one moment of peace."

"Why didn't you throw her out, Ma?"

"Did we not try? Your *Babu* left no stone unturned."

Baba wanted to expand his gym and bring in new students. He wanted to create a new fitness centre with all modern equipment in that part of the west wing. So he requested the widow take the business elsewhere. But the widow refused to move. The rent was cheap, and business was good in the Garia area. Why would the widow care about Baba's students?

That's when the quarrels started between Ma and the widow. They never missed an opportunity to stab each other with their poisonous words. Over time, the quarrels only got worse. Finally, things came to such a head that Baba went to Kolkata High Court and brought a case against the widow.

"Just a few more days and the court will decide for us," Ma finished. Then she wagged a finger under Parul's nose, giving her a stern warning. "Never step inside that printing press. I'm warning you, Parul, you disobey me, and I'll send you back to your village."

"Am I crazy that I'll go there, Ma? I have no interest in that evil woman and her printing press."

That afternoon, when Parul came down to the courtyard to collect the dried clothes from the clothesline, she bumped into the printing press widow. "*Ei* girl, are you blind or what? Can't you see and walk?"

Parul kept quiet. The widow scowled at her, gathered her files and entered her office.

From the courtyard, Parul could see the outlines of her white sari near her office window as she talked on the phone with her customers. Beyond the main entrance of the printing press, in the dark hallway, there were more rooms, but Parul had seen none of them. In the seven years she had lived in their house, not once had she dared to enter the widow's printing-press. Nor had she talked to any of the employees. She had seen some of them in the back alley, smoking *bidi* and drinking tea on top of the water tank. There was a giant man whose belly stuck out from under his T-shirt like a small sized whale. Everyone called him the machine man. And then there was the thin man with thick glasses who always read a newspaper. He was known as the compositor. Next to the machine man, the compositor looked like a dried-up sugarcane stick. A small boy, hardly eight years old, followed them around like a shadow.

Parul had never dared to smile or start a conversation with any of them. When they walked by, coming in and out of the press rooms, she deliberately kept her head low to avoid eye contact.

Now, looking at the white outline of the widow standing near the window, Parul felt nothing but strong revulsion for the wicked woman. *She is nothing but trouble,* thought Parul. *I hope Ma wins her court case.*

• • •

That Saturday, Mohini's English medium, stylish friends came over to their house. They all spoke fluent English, wore expensive dresses and came in chauffeur-driven cars. Some of them wore light makeup, even though they were all in the sixth grade. Parul admired their golden skin, perfectly plucked eyebrows, and stylishly cut hair. She sniffed their fragrant shampoo and body lotion as they burst into Mohini's room.

Parul waited for Mohini to introduce her to her friends. She, too, was eager to play with them. She stood behind the door curtain and tried to make eye contact with Mohini, but Mohini didn't look at her even once.

The girls climbed up Mohini's bed and sat in one big circle. They shared photos of their favorite film-stars and cricket players, winked and giggled coyly and poked each other in a friendly manner. Mohini laughed loudly at their jokes and nodded frantically at everything they said. Parul was surprised by how eager Mohini was to please her school friends. In their presence, her whole behavior altered, as if she shed off her old self and entered a new one.

The girls brought out dolls with golden hair from their bags and tried out matching outfits on them. Excitement bubbled inside Parul. She, too, wanted to hold the gorgeous dolls and play family with them. This time, she looked pleadingly at Mohini and whispered her name. Mohini turned around for one moment but pretended not to notice her.

Parul could no longer hold herself back. She came out from behind the curtain and stepped inside the room. All heads turned to her at once and she felt like a deer caught in the beam of a car's headlight. She could well imagine how she appeared to them—a somewhat pathetic specimen in her faded and stained cotton dress, two oily braids and cheap rubber slippers. Contempt and pity crept across their faces as they studied her meticulously from head to toe. Someone said something about her in English and the other girls laughed.

"Is she your friend?" a girl asked Mohini. She had a superior smile.

"This is Parul*di*," Mohini replied quickly. "She is our maid. Let her know if you need anything and she will get it for you."

Parul turned around and rushed back to the kitchen. She closed the door to support herself against it.

"What's the matter?" Ma rushed to her in concern. "Are you ill?"

Parul knew she looked pale to Ma. She closed her eyes and tried to bring her heaving chest under control.

"Do you have a fever?" asked Ma again. She put a hand on her forehead.

"Nothing happened. I'm okay." Parul walked to the outside sink and splashed water on her face. Mohini's words had entered her heart like a splinter, leaving it bruised. She turned on the tap all the way to drown out the pain. *That's all I am to her?* Parul thought. *A maid who takes orders all day? She is ashamed to call me her friend before those rich girls?*

Parul spent the rest of the morning flattening out the *rotis* with her rolling pin and cooking them on the hot griddle. Then she cleaned the kitchen, washed the pots and pans, and took a plate of food to Baba in the gym. For lunch, Ma gave her two *rotis*, cooked lentils and hot pickles. Parul sat on the kitchen floor to eat, but much as she tried, she couldn't push the morsels down her throat.

After some time, she walked over to Ma. "I want a new dress. I want one with velvet and lace—just the kind Mohini has. I also want leather slippers, not the rubber ones you buy me from the street hawkers."

Ma seemed to sizzle like raw onions in a pan. "Now, you're crossing your limit. Don't forget you're a maid in this house. Ask around the neighborhood and show me one maid who wears a velvet and lace dress and leather slippers. I can guarantee that you won't find a single house where people are crazy enough to spoil their maids with expensive things like that."

"But Mohini gets all new clothes..."

"Don't compare yourself to Mohini. You were not born with a silver spoon in your mouth."

• • •

That night, Parul went to sleep in her narrow storeroom on the third floor of the east wing. Her room overlooked the large empty terrace, the potted *tulsi* plants and chili plants. Part of her room was filled with potatoes, onions and cooking oil. On the other side was Parul's bed, neatly made every morning, the mouth of her earthenware water pot covered with a steel cup.

Parul took off her dress and hung it on the clothesline. She untied her hair and ran a comb through it. Images and thoughts boiled her mind as she sat down on her bed. She thought of Mohini and her friends—their giggles, their smirks, and their snobbery. How they stared at her faded dress, her cheap glass bangles and her greasy braids. How they made her feel small, like an insect—insignificant and inadequate in their world. And Mohini, her dear Mohini, how casually and thoughtlessly she had switched teams. Overnight, those snobbish girls were her best friends and Parul an embarrassment. *If she loves me, then why does she hurt me?* thought Parul. *Is this the way to treat your sister?*

Getting up, Parul poured water in a steel cup from her earthenware water pot. She had to release the grip of emotion that restricted the breathing in her throat. She walked out to the dark terrace and stood under the starry night. Looking down, she saw a glimpse of the city: the yellow streetlights and red-tiled roofs running lengthwise from the park below and disappearing into the distant mango and bananas groves.

A tide of loneliness swept over her. She closed her eyes and leaned back against the terrace water tank. When she was with her own family, she couldn't imagine such loneliness. Ammi and Rehana didn't leave her alone even for a minute. She was the center of their universe, the brightest star in their sky. The thought of her family transported her seamlessly to that moment in her childhood when she had felt completely at peace with his surroundings, where there was no friction, no discord, no impediments.

The red *Gulmohar* trees blazed like fire behind the tin and clay house where her family lived. Marigold and hibiscus bordered the curved path leading to the house. The sweet fragrance filled the room when her mother opened the windows in the morning and cupped her palms together in the form of a prayer. Parul helped her mother pick the flowers and string them into a garland. That's when Rehana tugged her away, and they raided the landlord's java apple trees. They always snatched a few juicy fruits from the lower branches before the security guard chased them down the unpaved roads, swinging his long bamboo stick. They ran across the paddy fields and over the canals, all the way to the railway line. There they sat in the banyan's shade, sucking the nectar out of each fruit and aiming the seeds at the passing trains.

Those were such magical days, thought Parul, when Ammi was alive. Ammi knew how to make her worries disappear. She always made things all right.

Parul bit her lips and suppressed a tear. How much she wished she could talk to Ammi now, tell her how invisible and inconsequential she felt in Mohini's house. How much she tried to belong in Mohini's world, and how unsuitable and poorly matched she was.

Parul was so tired that she woke up at dawn and went back to sleep. When she finally woke again, the room was well lit, with the sun streaming in through the windows. Ma was knocking on her door, asking her to come downstairs. She dressed quickly and rushed to the kitchen to boil the milk before it turned sour. All morning she folded clothes, chopped vegetables and peeled potatoes. Despair chewed and mauled her inside and her concentration wavered several times.

What kind of justice is this? She thought, stealing a quick look at Ma working with her in the kitchen. *Mohini can have fifteen beautiful dresses and I can't own just one?*

Every morning when Parul walked to the *bazaar*, she saw the dresses at shop windows—hundreds of them–with intricate embroidery, glitters and laces. Unable to resist her craving, she entered the shops to touch the dresses and feel the smoothness of the material between her fingers. *Issh,* she thought, *if I could own just one of them.*

Sometimes she thought she could save a little from her salary and afford one or two of the slightly cheaper ones. But after her father's visit, there was rarely any money left. Whatever she set aside each month was taken away by her father on one pretext or another. Her father could not see or think beyond money. Nothing else ever interested him.

Parul picked up her bucket and went down to the courtyard to get drinking water. She slammed the bucket under the tube well to fill it up. The roar of the printing press made her jump back in surprise. The floor underneath her feet shook, and the gym windows rattled. The water in her bucket splashed on the sides. The roar startled the crows and sparrows, and they flapped their wings and soared into the sky.

It was early evening, and the widow had left for the day. Parul noticed that her office was completely dark, and a heavy lock hung from the door. She tiptoed to the main entrance of the printing press and peered into the gloomy hallway. She saw the sets of rubber slippers and umbrellas at the door belonging to the employees, but none of them seemed to be anywhere in sight.

Looking at dark interior of the press, Parul had the overwhelming urge to break just one of Ma's rules and explore the interior of the press. *Why shouldn't I?* she told herself. *Did she give me that dress? Does she listen to me? Does she care for me?*

Crossing the threshold, she took a few tentative steps to enter the hallway. As her eyes adjusted to the darkness, she saw a narrow room in front of her with the door slightly ajar. Parul pushed it open, caught an odd smell, and came to a sudden halt. It smelled like vinegar at first, but when she sniffed again, she was sure it was machine oil. The place looked like a storeroom of sorts—ladders, stools, hammers, and nylon ropes lay scattered all around. Frosty bottles of what looked like left over acid, thick tarry ink and paint cans sat around in half open cardboard boxes. She crept forward another yard, and her shoulders brushed against a solid object with sharp edges. Looking up, she saw the box-like shelves spread all over the wall like a honeycomb rising all the way to the ceiling. Inside the boxes were small metallic alphabets: both English and Bengali ones. Parul grabbed a few and put them inside her frock pocket.

She took a few more steps into the darkness and had a moment of panic when she stumbled on the widow's black cat. She saw the flashing green eyes and heard a loud yelp, and the cat jumped out of the widow and bolted down the back alley. Parul bit the inside of her cheeks to hold back her scream. She re-traced her footsteps and returned to the hallway quickly.

Leaning back on the wall, she tried to get her heartbeat under control. Looking around, she realized she was halfway inside the widow's printing press. There were many reasons why she should not go any further: the employees could see her and complain to the widow, or the widow could come back and discover her. Either way, it won't be long before word got to Ma upstairs. *Ma would send you back to your* Abbu said an ominous voice inside her head. Parul shuddered.

Ahead, the yellow glow of a bulb spilled out of a doorway, lighting up a part of the hallway. The mechanical roar in her ears was even louder now. She was very close to the main machine room where the employees worked. This time, Parul didn't allow herself to hear the voice in her head and deliberately inched forward, her body brushing against the wall and her arm stretched out in front of her.

She advanced a few more yards, till her toes touched the outer periphery of yellow light coming from the machine room. She heard voices and footsteps inside the room between the rhythmic gong of the letter press. A shadow came close to the door, and she quickly stepped behind the door curtain. She shut her eyes and breathed deeply, struggling to steady herself.

The figures inside the room took shape. She pushed closer to the open door to get a wider view of the room. She saw the machine man first, standing close to the enormous grease and oil covered letterpress. A single bulb, suspended from a ceiling wire, lit up his face and part of his giant belly. The bulb undulated in the gentle wind that came from the window, giving the machine man's ordinary appearance an atypical fluidity.

She saw him pull a lever and peddle the machine with a glowing *bidi* in his hand and a slightly bored expression on his face. Parul watched, fascinated, as the giant wheel spun, and the pistons went back and forth, and the large round plate in the center of the metal structure moved forward to slap ink against crispy white paper.

Behind the machine man, Parul detected a slight movement. At first, she could not see clearly who it was: the letterpress blocked her view. Then, standing on her tiptoes and raising her head as high as she dared, she saw couple more heads near the back workbench: it was the thin compositor and the small boy. The compositor worked with small heaps of alphabets, the kind she had in her pocket, setting them in ink-filled trays. His glasses gleamed in the light of the orange table lamp behind him. The little boy sat close to him, biting his nails and picking his nose.

Every now and again, the boy got up and took the tray over to the machine man. The machine man inserted the tray in his letter press machine and pulled the lever. Sometimes the boy waited around and tugged on the machine man's *kurta*. The man ruffled his hair affectionately and gave him a small packet of biscuits. The boy smiled at him and rushed back to the compositor.

Suddenly, between the loud gongs on the press machine, Parul heard Ma's shrill voice calling her name from upstairs. *Ma was looking for her*. She heard women in neighboring houses blowing on their conch shells and knew it was time for Ma's evening prayer. Parul always lit the lamp and helped her with the *puja* preparations.

Her chest contracted. Sweat drenched her frock, and she could barely remain standing. Fear made her legs numb and unable to support the weight of her body.

In seven years, Parul had never disobeyed Ma. She had thrown tantrums, fought with Ma and sulked, but she had never challenged Ma's authority... not once. It was impossible to show such insolence. Deep inside, Parul felt gratitude for all that Ma had done for her. It was because of Ma that she had food on her plate and a roof over her head. It was because of Ma that her sisters went to school and had money to buy clothes and books. How could Parul forget that? This was her family—the only family she had ever known. She could never hurt Ma's feelings.

Picking up her skirt, she ran out of the printing press and across the dark courtyard all the way up the stairs to the second-floor balcony. Looking out at the subdued light just after sunset, she said a quick prayer: "*Heye* god Shiva, *Heye* Mother Parvati, forgive me this once. I don't know what came over me and I made a grave mistake. I promise you; I'll never ever go back to that printing press again. I'll never disobey Ma."

Chapter 4

Today was a special day, Parul's eighteenth birthday. Mohini came back from school with a chocolate cake with Parul's name written in colorful icing. She went looking for Parul and found her on the terrace, absorbed in a glossy woman's magazine. Mohini cleared her throat and shuffled her feet, but still Parul didn't look up from her reading. Mohini put down the box, snatched the magazine from Parul's hand and flipped through the pages. It was called *Bollywood Beauties* and featured women with long shiny hair, glowing skin, lipsticked mouths, and painted nails, facing the camera with contented expressions on their faces. The magazine advised women on how to take care of their hair, their skin and their body and how to entice unsuspecting men into wedlock.

Parul's fascination with such magazines was not new. For a couple of years now, Mohini had seen her borrow them from the neighborhood beauty parlor and pour over the beauty tips. Sometimes she consulted Ma on how to enhance her looks. Should she wear sleeveless blouses? Would rubbing turmeric on her face make her skin glow? Would washing her hair with homemade yogurt make it softer and thicker?

Her self-absorption and constant barrage of inquires annoyed Ma. Mohini knew it did. A maid should be contented with housework and not worry about beauty tips. When Ma served tea to Baba in the morning, she complained about Parul's fascination with physical beauty. "If she only showed half that interest in the housework, I wouldn't have to bellow after her day and night." Baba, absorbed in his morning newspaper, told her, "Mohini's mother, at her age, you too spent time adjusting your sari folds and applying *kajal* around your eyes. Had I not seen those charcoal eyes on the bus to College Street that day, I would still be a free man."

Mohini waved the magazine before Parul's face. "Why do you keep reading these nonsense magazines, Parul*di*?" she asked. "You want to impress your boyfriend?"

"Don't say such things. If my Abbu sees me with a boy, he will break my legs."

"Let me tell you straight. All this rubbing milk cream on your face and lemon in your hair will not help. You need to go out there and woo someone. Or else you will sit here 'til your hair turns gray."

"*Chi*, what are you saying?" Parul wrinkled her nose. "I'm not that type of girl who goes around with boyfriends so shamelessly. When my marriage happens, it will be arranged."

"What is wrong with having a boyfriend?" demanded Mohini. "If you have to marry someone and spend the rest of your life with him, it's important to see if you're compatible. I'm not going into any arranged marriage."

"You have become a *pakka* memsahib, Mohini... an English woman. But I'm still a simple village girl. I have to follow my Abbu's wishes." She looked at the floor and fingered her ears studs shyly. "My Abbu will bring me alliances," she said.

The inside of Mohini's mouth felt warm, as if she had chewed on some green chilis. "Parul*di*, will you ever stop? You've been saying this for over three years now. When has your Abbu brought you a single alliance tell me?"

Parul blushed. "No, no, I'm sure my Abbu is looking. It is hard to find a good boy these days. Also, the boy must be from our own village, our community."

"You mean a Muslim boy?"

"Shh, Mohini! Not so loudly. Didn't Ma tell you never to mention that word in this house?"

Mohini bit her tongue. She had shouted out the forbidden word before she could stop herself. Parul's religion had to be kept a secret within their immediate family—she knew even their closest relative would have nothing but contempt for a Muslim maid.

"My Abbu knows what is best for me, Mohini," said Parul. She looked off into the distance and then clapped her hands together. "Once he finds the boy, everything will move ahead quickly. The date will be fixed, and all arrangements made. Half the village will come to my wedding. After all, I'm the oldest... the first born... it has to be a huge affair."

Mohini gripped her shoulder tightly. She said nothing for a while and then released her grip slowly, bit by bit. "What is this madness, Parul*di*? What has happened to you? Why are you putting so much trust in your Abbu? Don't you think he'll hurt you again?"

"It's okay. You don't have to worry about me," she said in a slightly cold voice.

"Not worry!" Mohini could no longer hold back her irritation. "How can I not when you choose to be so blind?" Then she heard herself spit out, "Don't get your hopes high again. Your Abbu only cares for your salary. If you get married, your salary will go to your husband. So he's not interested in finding a man for you...."

Mohini stopped abruptly. She felt she had crossed a line, overstepped an invisible boundary. Usually, when she said things like this about Madhu*babu*, Parul agreed with her, blaming her own fate. But today something flashed and shifted in Parul's eyes like a warning.

Abruptly, Parul got up and moved toward her terrace room. "We'll talk later, Mohini. I have to take some rest before I go back to work." She left the cake box unopened.

Silently, heavily, Mohini got up and picked up the cake. She went to her room reluctantly. Staring out her window at the crimson Gulmohar tree, she saw Parul's face again, distant and defiant, and she thought of how much Parul wanted to live in her fantasy world of husband, children, and family. She had dropped out of school in eighth grade and since then she had dreamed of having her own family. It was the only real thing to her—her entire purpose of living. She couldn't think or imagine anything concrete beyond that world.

Madhu*babu* came every month to see her, but showed neither any interest nor inclination to arrange a marriage for her. He conducted business as usual, collected the paper notes from Parul's hand, licked his lips when counting them, and then left in a great hurry, saying he would miss the train home. And Parul, foolish Parul, still believed in her heart that her father would one day transform into a responsible man and do his fatherly duty toward her.

· · ·

When Parul came downstairs an hour later, she heard Ma's voice calling her but couldn't find her. Eventually, she walked toward the *puja* room and discovered Ma.

"Sit down, Parul. You have to do today's *puja* with me."

"Why Ma?"

"Today is your special day. You should ask for god's blessings."

Parul sat on the mat cross-legged next to Ma. Various Hindu gods and goddesses stood or lounged in a variety of poses before her. Lord Shiva, the destroyer of evil, sat in lotus pose, and Krishna stood cross-legged playing the flute. Saraswati played the veena accompanied by her mascot, the white swan; Lakshmi, goddess of wealth and prosperity, held a pot of gold coins in her hand. In the center, featured prominently, was a tall bronze statue of Durga sitting on a tiger and carrying many weapons in her ten arms.

Ma placed some cut fruits, half a coconut, and a box of Sandesh before each god and filled up their tiny brass cups with water. Parul helped her in the *puja* preparation by lighting the incense sticks and making sandalwood paste. Then, closing her eyes, she chanted the mantras with Ma, swaying back and forth, and occasionally blowing the conch shell and ringing a brass bell.

When they finished, Ma turned around and put a sandalwood paste dot on her forehead. "You know what I asked our gods today?"

"What Ma?"

"To find you a good husband."

Parul blushed and lowered her gaze even though her heart leaped with joy. Like all good girls, she too had to look shy when her future husband came up.

"You have become a young woman now," said Ma. "When Madhu*babu* first brought you here, you were a tiny girl, but look at you now. You're old enough to have children of your own. I'll ask him to look for a suitable boy for you."

"Really, Ma? You'd do that for me?" Parul could no longer pretend to be shy.

"Of course, *pagli meye*, my crazy girl. All girls have to go to their husband's home when they grow up."

Parul bent down and touched Ma's feet and felt Ma's affectionate pat on her head.

"Stay happy always," said Ma. Then she placed a slim bundle of rupee notes in Parul's hand. "Take the afternoon off," she said. "Go watch a Hindi movie, but come back before eight. Don't be late or else I'll worry."

Parul felt heady with excitement — rarely did she step out of the house and go to the movie theater all by herself. Looking at the notes in her hand, she knew she would have enough for movie tickets, peanuts and ice cream soda.

• • •

When Parul reached the outside gate, she saw the security guard in *a khaki* uniform was leaning back on his stool, talking to Ram the janitor. The security guard drank cheap beer at night and slept most of the time while he was on duty. He stopped no one from coming or going.

But now he waved his stick at her. "Where to at this time?" he asked her.

"I'm going to a movie."

"What movie?"

"Why do you ask?"

He stepped forward to block her with his stick. "Are you going alone or with someone?"

"None of your business," Parul snapped, pushing away his stick.

"*Arre,* you get mad unnecessarily. I am just thinking of your safety," he said. Then he brought his face close to her and whispered, "Why go to the theater alone? Why not with me?"

Parul wrinkled her nose and turned away. She could smell the alcohol on his breath. "Look at yourself in the mirror and you'll know why."

Ram the janitor chuckled loudly. He was amused.

"What are you laughing at?" Parul rebuked him. "Ma was looking for you. Everything needs to be cleaned—the commodes, basins and toilet."

"Yes, yes, I was going," said Ram. He picked up his prickly duster and broken pail.

Parul walked away, ringing her anklets and tossing her braid from side to side. Even though she didn't look back, she knew they were watching her.

• • •

It was a sweltering summer afternoon, the kind when the hot tar leaves blisters on bare feet. Parul patted the sweat on her neck with the end of her sari and stopped to buy some shaved ice from a street vendor. The movie theater was in a narrow lane, inside an ancient building— the fading walls covered in red *paan* stains, spit and graffiti. Parul was glad to step into its dark interior, where a cool breeze from humming ceiling fans washed over her like waves. The hall was not too crowded, and she found a comfortable reclining seat on the ground floor.

The lights went off as soon as her back touched the chair, and the silver screen sprang to life. Instantly, Parul was swept into the mysterious and magical world of the Bollywood movie. The heroine, glamorous in her chiffon sari, danced around trees, ran through paddy fields and rolled over flower beds pining for love. Her quest was answered by the tall hero on a powerful motorbike, wearing dark sunglasses. The hero picked her up on the back of his motorbike and raced down the country road. The wind ruffled his hair and a romantic song played in the background. Tiny pinpricks of excitement went down Parul's thigh. A sweet warmth spread through her body, turning her cheeks a darker shade of red. Inside her stomach, the deep churning made her shift in her seat. She imagined it was she—not the heroine—who sat on the back of the motorbike, with her arms wrapped around the hero's waist, singing songs of love.

• • •

It was past eight when Parul got back home. The security guard was dozing at the gate. He woke up and got groggily to his feet. "So how was it?"

"How was what?"

"The movie. Was it full of masala?"

"Why should I tell you?"

"I am only asking if you liked it."

"You don't have to worry about my liking," she quipped and haughtily tossed her head. "Just stay here and do your job." Then she marched down the gravelly driveway toward the house. The security guard followed her, trying to keep pace. "*Arre*, don't you have one minute to talk to me?"

Parul made a face. "I have a lot of work."

She stepped inside the gym corridor that led to the dark courtyard. The letterpress machine was now silent. Her footsteps echoed on the concrete, as did those of the security guard panting to catch up with her. She was about to turn and go upstairs to the second floor when her eyes fell on the widow's office.

The door was open, and the room was well lit. Standing near the door was a bearded man in white *kurta* pajama and a matching white cap. Parul was surprised: the chances of the man being a customer at this hour were close to nil. The printing press was submerged in darkness and the widow and her employees long gone.

The security guard caught up with her. He was breathless.

"Tell me something," Parul threw back at him over her shoulder. "Who is that man in the widow's office?"

He took a few moments to recover before he answered. "His name is Rahim," he said in a low voice. "He is Muslim. The widow hired him as the new printing press manager."

Parul was stunned: *the widow had hired a Muslim manager for her printing press.*

She stood undecided for a moment and then took a few steps towards the printing press to take a better look at the man. She stayed in the shadows and peeked from behind the door. From here, she could see the man clearly. He was tall and slim, with a thick glossy beard. He wore a white taqiyah cap with embroidery, and his hands, face, and clothes were impeccably clean. Black *soorma* darkened his lower eyelids. On his feet were a pair of beautifully handcrafted nagra shoes. He looked stylish and dignified in every way. Her heart fluttered a little, and she swallowed hard.

"Are you okay?" whispered the security guard from behind.

"Yes... ah... yes." Parul stammered. "It's just that my throat feels dry. I think I need some water."

"Should I get you some?"

"No need. I was just going upstairs."

•   •   •

That Sunday, her father came to visit Parul. She was sweeping the balcony with her thinning bamboo duster when she saw him walk up the gravelly driveway. She ran to the kitchen to get him a cup of tea and some biscuits.

Her father poured the tea on the saucer and blew into it loudly, and with a pleasurable click of his tongue, he took a sip. "*Ahh*. I have some good news to tell you, Mumtaz," he said. "I know you will be so happy."

Parul's heart leaped when her father spoke. Did her father find a suitable boy for her? Was God answering her prayers at last? "What is the good news, Abbu?" she asked eagerly.

"It's about your sister, Rehana. I am getting her married," he said.

"Getting Rehana married?" Parul repeated mechanically, as if the string of words sounded absurd to her ears. Then the thought grew and expanded in her head like tornado siren rising above all other sounds. Abbu *had not found an alliance for her. He had found one for Rehana.* Again and again, the words washed over her. It shook her body and twisted her face.

"Why, Abbu?" she asked, struggling to find her voice. "She is only fifteen."

Her father looked hurt. "*Eh* Allah! I thought you would be happy for your sister. Instead, you make a face. What has this city done to you?"

"Abbu," Parul said wearily, "You were the one who sent me to the city, remember? I didn't want to come then, did I? Rehana is still in school. You say she has a sharp head. Why don't you let her study some more?"

Her father paid no attention to her advice. "Enough of that school, Mumtaz," he said, waving his hand. "Too much reading and writing spoils a girl. Besides, if she reads too much, no boy in the village will marry her. I thought you would be happy to hear about your sister's wedding. She always talks about you. She said only this morning: 'Didi will buy me a beautiful wedding sari from Kolkata. For my wedding gift she will give me real gold earrings, not the ones covered with gold water.'"

Parul felt a cramp wrench through her whole body. How easily her Abbu had forgotten her and made plans for Rehana. Not once did he think she was the oldest of the sisters, that her time was running out and that she, too, was waiting for a groom. And now he was asking for her contribution... how could her Abbu be so heartless? She winced.

"I cannot afford real gold earrings, you know that. I can hardly afford to buy her the sari," she said in a low voice.

Her father frowned. "Money, money, and money. That's all you can think of these days. Did you think how beautiful your sister will look in a red sari and gold earrings? Is her happiness no longer important to you?"

"But, Abbu, you take most of my wages every month anyway...." Parul stopped. It was futile to argue. She couldn't refuse her father, no matter how much she might want to. She knew exactly what would follow. She would ask Ma for an advance from her salary and take out a loan from the local women's cooperative and ride a bus to Bara Bazar. There she would comb the market for a red sari with gold thread at a reasonable price. She would also give away her only set of gold rings. She would send her father away as a happy man, ready to make wedding preparations.

A fly buzzed around her father's tea. Parul didn't bother to shoo it away. She got up and paced the floor. Her head felt full to bursting. Sweat gathered on her eyebrows and trickled down the sides of her face.

While I mop the floor, wash other people's dishes, and iron their clothes all day, my sisters get to wear red saris and scold children.

The thought was like a deluge she could drown in. She held her breath against it as she walked up to her terrace room. Her Abbu's voice called to her, but she didn't bother to turn around.

Chapter 5

That night, after her father left, Parul had a dream. She saw her village again — the green pond and the shimmering shadow of the palm trees. It was so clear that she could see her reflection in the water. *Reflection that shattered in the hot pond.* Her sisters' faces appeared one by one — just above the surface of the water. Their lips move as they gasped for air. Parul reached out to touch them, but they were slippery like fish. They drifted farther and farther away from her. Their heads bobbed up and down in the teeming waves till the green water enveloped them. The dream shattered. The village faded away.

She tried to calm herself and go back to sleep, but felt as though she'd stepped through a doorway into a black and desolate place. She had never felt such dread in her life. The fragments of fear that had fused themselves at the base of her heart were impossible to dislodge. She gripped her mother's locket and held it to her heart. How long ago that had been, how many years had passed by already. Over twelve years since she had left the village and yet... the village was still alive inside her, as if it had made a permanent nest for itself somewhere deep in her ribcage. Nights like this brought back all the pointless memories from a time that was gone forever, a time she could never go back to, a time that sat heavy in her chest.

Sometimes a memory came, so real that she could smell it. The sprawling banyan tree stood in the middle of the huge open field, just behind the graveyard. Parul and Rehana sat on rope swings tied to the green, protective branches of the tree. The sunlight flashed like fire between the branches. Ammi stood behind them, pushing the swings.

Her nose ring glittered, and the bangles clattered. She chanted melodically:

Dol dol duluni/Ranga mathay chiruni
Bor aasbe ekhuni/ Niye jaabe takhoni.
Swing, my child swing, with a comb in your beautiful hair
Any moment now, your bridegroom will come and take you away with him.

Ammi's song throbbed and pulsated through Parul's veins, immersing her in its cheeriness. The rhythm gushed through her like a torrent of life. She closed her eyes, staying in that happy dreamworld in which everything was hyperreal: Ammi throwing back her head and laughing at the children, her eyes sparkling and her skin glowing; Rehana tugging Parul's dress sleeves, jumping off the swing and rolling on the green grass.

The sound of dogs barking in the streets brought Parul back to the present. The moon had come out, and part of her room was lit by its silvery rays. Anxiety chewed her insides. *This is like spending an eternity in hell,* she told herself. *Doing meaningless housework for a family that is not mine.* While her future would remain enclosed by the claustrophobic walls of Mohini's house, Rehana would take off like a colorful butterfly who had just found new wings. She would soar high above the trees and the clouds, leaving Parul behind.

Parul walked over to the open window to look at the night sky. *Can you hear me,* Ammi? she said to the dark night. *A bridegroom may never come to take me away.* Abbu *snatched away my portion of happiness and put it in Rehana's lap.*

• • •

In the next few days, Parul felt as though her life had come to a complete halt. The seconds stretched out, and the days dragged on. She found herself uneasy, unable to focus on housework, unable to overcome the pinpricks of anxiety at the bottom of her chest. All she could think of was stepping out of the gates and losing herself in the crowd of shoppers and pedestrians.

She walked aimlessly through the neighborhood streets, lost in thought. Sometimes she walked all the way to the railway tracks and sat on a nearby bench looking at the passing trains. The wind blew silent and unimpeded in this open space. It played with her hair and lifted the free end of her sari to cover her face. Parul tucked the sari in her waist impatiently and secured the loose strands with hairpins. Some days, the wind picked up and blew dead leaves, newspapers, and dust all around her. Left-over teacups and ice-cream cups swirled between the tracks like a whirlpool. Stray dogs and crows dug through the trash as if looking for treasure.

Every hour, a packed commuter train came down the track and thundered past her. Parul heard the piercing whistle and felt the earth shake and vibrate under her feet. The trains brought back memories of the first day she had come to Kolkata with her father. Since then, she had never gone back to the village to see her sisters. Abbu had never asked her to visit her sisters or brought them over to Kolkata to meet her. Every time she tried to bring up the subject, he asked her to wait a little longer. "Focus on your work for now. You're lucky to live here, in this big house, with these generous people. What do you not get here—milk, fish, soap and hair oil? Your sisters can't dream of such luxury. If you take time off unnecessarily, these people will find a replacement."

Across from the railway line was the Muslim slum where some of Parul's friends lived. Some days she walked on the narrow winding alleys inside the slum, peering inside the hovels as if she were looking for a new home. She watched women in simple head coverings cook meals on charcoal stoves and serve it to their families, who sat in circles laughing and sharing the food. She watched a mother massage her baby with mustard oil, getting him ready for a bath. In another hovel, two sisters played a tickling game and rolled off a mattress. And behind a gossamer-thin curtain, a husband put a flower in his wife's hair and pulled her into his embrace.

My life is cursed, Parul thought. *God has given me a life, but put a curse on it. He has given me a roof over my head and food on my plate, but he has taken away from me what was only mine—my family. Instead, he has given me a cement and brick house where I can live but never belong.*

It was mid-day when she got back home. The printing press was completely silent. The widow had gone home, and the employees were taking their usual mid-afternoon nap. Parul heard a rhythmic chanting from the printing press office and walked to the window to look. Inside, the new manager, Rahim, was on his knees, and his hands were flat against the mat. He was engrossed in his prayer.

His prayer was one of the prettiest sounds on earth. The repetitive hums of his chant were alluring, hypnotizing. Listening to him, all her fear and anxiety, her sisters' ghosts, cleared away. A heavy calm descended on her mind and body. For that moment, her emotions overrode logic.

She forgot her promise to Ma and stepped inside the printing press office. She spread her *dupatta* and kneeled beside him. The words formed on her lips...*help me, Lord, you who see everything and understand everything.*

Her words froze. Next to her, Rahim had stopped praying. She heard his sudden and sharp inhalation and then what sounded like swearing. Before she could open her eyes, his iron-like fingers dug into her shoulders.

"You shameless Hindu woman. Who asked you to come here? How dare you disturb my prayer? Get out at once."

"I am sorry... so sorry. I didn't want to disturb you. Your prayer is so beautiful... I couldn't stay away. I wanted to pray with you," cried Parul.

"This is not your prayer. Go to your own priest; go to your own temple."

"But Allah is my God. I am a Muslim by birth." The words flew out of her mouth before she could stop herself.

"I don't want to hear your brazen lies."

"It's true. My father's name is Ahmed, and we come from Murshidabad."

"Not another word!" His face was very close to her now, and she could see the fury in his eyes. "Go before I beat you into shame."

She turned away from him. Rahim picked up her *dupatta* and tossed it to her. It landed on her head like a fine piece of mesh, covering her face and shoulders. Parul adjusted her *dupatta* and stepped outside. Rahim slammed the door behind her. He swore again.

She leaned against the door, unable to move. Fear and shame burned inside her. The man was insane. What a mistake it was to enter his room. She cursed herself for her own stupidity.

She heard him recite the opening of the prayer again. He was starting over.

Bismillah-ir-Rahman-ir-Rahim.
In the name of Allah, the Gracious, the Merciful.
Praise and glory be to You, O Allah.
Blessed be Your Name, exalted be Your Majesty and Glory.
There is no God but You.
I seek Allah's shelter from Satan, the condemned.
In the Name of Allah, the Most Compassionate, the Most Merciful.
Praise be to Allah, Lord of the Universe,
The Most Compassionate, the Most Merciful!
Master of the Day for Judgment!
You alone do we worship and You alone do we call on for help.
Guide us along the Straight Path,
The path of those whom You have favored,
Not the path of those who earned Your anger, nor of those who went astray.
Amen.

The power and rhythm of the prayer was fascinating... mesmerizing. The verses spread like a balm through her battered body. She closed her eyes and slid down the door till her bottom touched the floor. Rahim's rejection did not bother her anymore. Even he was nothing compared to God and his glory. To God belonged all the heaven and earth. To God belonged her soul and her entire being. No one and nothing could take that away from her. This new consciousness made Parul shiver. She closed her eyes to stay in that rare moment of serenity.

It was difficult to shake herself out of the trance, but the fear of being discovered forced her to dislodge herself from his door. As she went upstairs, she thought of the impact Rahim's prayers had on her. All around her, the universe glittered as if she felt she had stumbled into the center of bounteousness.

I must pray to Him to give me strength to bear this lonely life, away from my family, away from my dear village, thought Parul. *I must ask Allah to help me on nights when darkness and hopelessness try to swallow me from all sides. It is only He who can show me the way to go on when I feel like giving up.*

Chapter 6

At two o'clock in the afternoon, when it was too hot to move, a heavy lethargy descended upon the house. Mohini's family finished their lunch of rice, *dal* and fish and fell asleep with their bellies full and contented. Movement slowed down in the stairs and corridors. The rooms grew silent. The only sound came from the clothes that hung from the clotheslines on the terrace, undulating with a gentle swoosh when the wind blew from the direction of the railway slum.

Parul came out to the terrace with a bucket full of washed clothes. She pulled dried clothes from the clothesline and put them away for ironing. Then she spread the wet ones, wringing out the water and smoothening out the creases. The smell of soap and bleach still lingered on the trousers, shirts, petticoats, and blouses. Red, green and orange cotton saris swayed like the Indian flag when detangled to dry. Parul flicked her wrist and shooed away the crows and sparrows that came to swing on the clothesline; they squawked and flapped their wings in protest, before flying off to nearby houses.

From the neighbourhood mosque came the melodious call for midday prayer. The golden dome and the ornate minarets blazed in the bright sunlight. Leaning over the banister, Parul saw the shaded courtyard fill with men in white *kurta*, *pajama* and laced caps. When the second call to prayer sounded, the men coalesced into a long, orderly line for worship.

Looking at them, Parul remembered a time when Ammi used to take her and Rehana to the Mazar for Friday Jumu'ah prayers. They walked through the mango grove and over the bridge to the other side. Ammi carried little Rehana while Parul hopped happily behind her, humming a tune. Sometimes Ammi turned around to smile at her and ruffle her hair. But close to the Mazar, the tone of Ammi's voice changed, as if she wanted to tell something of great importance. "When you're in God's house, keep your head covered at all times. Don't let your *dupatta* slip off. You're grownup enough to understand this now."

Inside the namaz room, on the endless chequered floors, the women knelt down in rows, their hands flat against the mat. They chanted and swayed, bowed and prostrated. High near the multihued stained-glass windows, hundreds of candles burned to light up the semi-dark room. The wavering shadows from the candles gave Ammi's features peculiar fluidity. The light outlined her figure and emanated from her like an otherworldly aura. To little Parul, Ammi looked like a saint—so pure and untouchable that nothing worldly could ever taint her.

As Parul clipped the wet clothes on the clothesline, she thought of her Ammi's strong relationship with Allah. Five times a day she talked to Him, told Him everything from her heart. It was because of her faith that Ammi could wither all strong winds and storms with indifference. Her devotion was the road to her great strength.

Ammi *couldn't imagine living without her faith, even for a day. If she were alive, she never would have allowed* Abbu *to bring me to the city and work in a Hindu home. She would have taken poison before seeing this day.*

A hint of pain stirred in the deep recesses of her heart. After Ammi's death, her Abbu had tossed, twisted and turned her life upside down. Everything was chosen for her, everything was decided. Overnight, she was shoved into a Hindu household and asked to learn the Hindu way of life. Since then, she could not affirm her Islamic identity to anyone—to do so would be a matter of shame in Mohini's house.

Whatever Abbu *has done is done. Now I must do what* Ammi *would have wanted me to do.* The thought came to her, as emancipating as the accomplishment of an impossible task. The clamour of voices inside subsided, and the pain lessened.

Her mind instantly veered back to the printing press manager, Rahim. His melodic chanting had held her spellbound, as if some part of her, deep inside, recognized those verses from a very long time ago. The words had comforted her, left her satisfied.

She knew she had to see Rahim again.

•   •   •

She found him at his desk, bent over dusty piles of paper with a magnifying glass. All around him, stacks of paper tied with thin pieces of red string were heaped against the walls and on the windowsill. The cupboards in this room stored all kinds of acids, plates, and inks used in printing. Parul leaned back against the door to watch him work. She liked the way he picked each piece of crisp paper between his long fingers and smoothed out the creases. He underlined some words and then set the paper aside. Her eyes fell on the prayer mat rolled up in the corner, and she shuffled her feet impatiently.

"I have something to show you," she said.

"You are here again?" He leaned back in the chair and crossed his arms over his chest. "Woman, your skin is as thick as a rhino's."

"You called me a liar. I want to prove to you that whatever else I may be, I don't lie about my religion."

Rahim pushed back his chair, which scraped threateningly on the red mosaic. Parul wondered if she should just turn and flee. It took a lot of courage to come back to his door. Now that courage was failing her.

"I will leave. Just give me one chance to prove myself." She leaned back, dug into a cloth bag, and handed him a copper locket. "Here, this is all I have left of my mother. Everything else was stolen in the train station when I first came to Kolkata. My mother gave this to me before she died. I was very young then. See the inscription on it... it says *Mumtaz*. I am a Muslim girl."

"I don't need to look at anything. Just get out of here."

"Please, I beg of you. Take one look at this, and I will go."

Rahim took the locket from her and held it under the light of the table lamp. He squinted his eyes and studied the tiny inscription.

"How do I know you didn't steal this locket?"

"What kind of suspicious man are you? If I am lying about what my dead mother gave me, may my tongue fall off."

Parul took a tentative step forward, closer to his desk. As much as she tried not to look at him, she couldn't help herself. Thick glossy beard covered most of his face like a dark monsoon cloud. A fine golden chain clung to the smooth brown column of his throat. Parul swallowed hard. God had made him beautiful in every way.

Rahim's eyes narrowed to crinkled slits. "Why do you keep coming back here? What do you want from me?"

"I am looking for my God. Can I pray with you here?"

"You foolish girl! You are insulting Allah, and you don't even know it."

"How can I insult Him when all I want to do is pray?"

"You cannot pray with a man who is not related to you. That is un-Islamic." Rahim thrust the locket back into her hand.

Parul was in no mood to give up. "Then I will wait," she cried. "I will pray after you are done. I want to learn Allah's prayer. Tell me how I can reach my Lord."

"Find a Maulvi and he will teach you all that..."

Parul took a determined step and slapped both hands on his desk.

"Why do you keep pushing me away? I want to know Allah and follow His path."

"But you went off Allah's path long ago." He pointed his finger at her. "You followed the infidel's religion. I can't save you from what you have already done." His voice had a sense of finality that made Parul shiver. Her knees grew weak, and her muscles strained to hold the weight of her body.

"Everything has been noted," said Rahim. He seemed to enjoy her discomfort. "All your wicked deeds are now in His books. When the day of judgment comes, you will have to answer to the Supreme Lord."

Parul tingled with shame as if a thousand needles pricked the bottom of her feet. "But what is my fault in this? I did what my father asked me to do. My only sin is that I am poor and I don't get to choose."

"No, your sin is that you sold your religion for money. Allah will not forgive you."

"Don't say that, for I may not be able to bear it. My life is already cursed. Sometimes I don't feel any hope... any hope at all. Wherever I turn, I see darkness. Even in my dreams I see the darkness chasing me." She clasped her palms together. "Show me the way to my God. I will ask for his forgiveness."

Parul's heart was racing, but Rahim's face remained masked by a scowl. She now fell to his feet. "Please, don't turn me away. No one else here can help me."

Rahim's gaze seemed to flicker across her face and sweep over her body.

"Allah's path is one of struggle. He wants great sacrifice, great humility."

A chilly breeze grazed Parul's neck and shoulder. She felt as strongly as if Ammi, standing behind her, was urging her to accept Rahim's challenge. All her hesitation disappeared. She brought her focus back to Rahim. "I am ready for all that. I will do whatever you say."

"If you procrastinate, there will be terrible consequences."

"I swear on my mother's name that I will never give you any reason to complain. I will not stray from His path."

Rahim was lost in thought as he played with a black globe paperweight. He gave it one last spin and made up his mind.

"Tomorrow afternoon..."

"Yes?" Parul could hardly hold back her excitement.

"Buy yourself a scarf and cover your head," he said at last. "Don't come to my room with your hair uncovered."

"Thank you," said Parul. When she put a hand on her chest, she could feel it pounding. Happiness seared through her body. It made her feel lightheaded.

"There is a lot I have to teach an ignorant girl like you. Muslims must have the proper Taharah—purification—before performing the prayers," said Rahim. "Remove all your filthy clothes and put on a washed sari. You will perform *wudu*—ablution—with me before you get started. Then I will teach how to read the *kalma* and the *namaz*."

"I will do as you say," said Parul.

Chapter 7

Parul couldn't sleep. She looked at the ceiling beams and Ma's pickle jars. The rain outside softly and hesitantly knocked on her window like an uninvited guest. She scratched her arms and tossed and turned. The room felt hot and stuffy. She got up and poured herself a cup of water from her clay pot. She massaged her temples in deep circular motions with the ends of her thumb and forefinger. Her mind churned out images and thoughts faster than she could process them.

She had climbed down the stairs and visited Rahim a few times in the past month. He had read passages from the Quran in Arabic and then explained them to her in Bengali. She had observed him spread out his mat and listened to him pray. He had bowed, prostrated, chanted and swayed. His deep voice had bounced in her head and settled in her heart and stayed like a lump in her throat. She had looked into his charcoal-blackened eyes, the delicate tilt of his nose, the raised veins on his neck and arms, and felt a tug in her heart.

Sometimes when praying together, Rahim had reached out and adjusted her headscarf. He had tucked away the unruly tufts that escaped from beneath it. Parul's neck had grown warm. She watched the coarse hairs on the brown skin of his arms curl up and bunch together in places. His closeness made her own skin tingle. Occasionally, his hands brushed against her face and arms. An electric current zapped through her body. Her nipples hardened and her palms grew moist.

In moments like this, she was mindful of the two angels who recorded her *hasanat*, her good deeds, *sayyiat*, her bad deeds. They noted her every action, her every thought for the Day of Judgement.

The first-time Rahim had mentioned Allah Ta'ala's angels, the idea of being watched constantly dragged Parul into a torrent of hypertrophied consciousness. For days, when slipping off her sari, unbuttoning her blouse and rolling down her petticoat in her terrace room, she had wondered if she was alone or if the angels were hovering over her. She obsessed over every thought that came to her mind and every bit of every task she was asked to complete. She was determined to please the angels watching over her. It was only in Rahim's presence that she felt completely out of control.

One afternoon she went downstairs and found Rahim packing sugar, oil, and rice into small baskets and covering them with heavy jute blankets. He was thoughtful. The rose oil on his shirt clung to the air in the room and tickled Parul's nose. The smell churned her inner yearnings.

"What are these baskets for?"

"Ramadan is next month," said Rahim, keeping his voice low. Though Rahim's office was separate from the printing press, and the roar of the machine drowned their voices, he always used caution when Parul came to visit him. "Living with these infidels, you have forgotten the holiest month for us Muslims?"

Heat crept up her neck and blazed through her cheeks. She smiled apologetically. "But what are the baskets for?"

"Foolish woman. They are for charity. Ramadan is a time for generosity and giving. It is a time when we think about those who have less than us, as well as thank Allah for everything he has given us."

"Yes, yes, I remember that," Parul blurted. "I remember the rich landlords in our village gave out pretty clothes and money to the poor during Ramadan. Abbu made us stand in lines to get these gifts."

"What you remember is called *zakat*. During Ramadan, fasting people give a certain amount of money or property to the poor Muslims. I hope you remember that Muslims have to keep a fast during the holy month of Ramadan?"

"Fasting, *wasting*, is not for me. I need my rice and *roti* every day. I don't know how people even think of keeping such long fasts. If I don't eat for two hours, I can feel rats running around in my belly." Parul rubbed her stomach fondly.

"*Mumtaz*! You are becoming more and more impertinent. This childlike behavior does not suit you. Fasting is what a good Muslim does. He keeps a fast 'til sunset for the entire month of Ramadan. This shows devotion to Allah. Looks like I am wasting my time training you. You were never meant to be one of us."

He walked away from her and went to the back alley to wash. Parul opened her mouth and sucked in the warm air he left on his trail. Pain pounded in her heart, and she closed her eyes. She cursed herself for being so hasty. Ma always said there should be a veil between what comes to the mind and what falls out of the mouth. The tongue should never be given so much liberty.

Rahim came back and scowled. He gestured at her to leave the room and took out his prayer mat. He bowed, hands on knees, head covered in his lace cap. Beads of water lay scattered on his chin and back of his neck. They hung like jewels, bright and untouchable. He got up again to fetch a towel and pat down the water on his neck and shoulders.

Fear gripped Parul, making her sway.

"Please, forgive me for what I said earlier," she cried. "My head is filled with confusion. I do not know right from wrong. That's why I am here. To learn all that is righteous, all that is proper. I came to you to know what God wants from me. I want to know how to live my life like a proper Muslim. I want to understand the things that matter... what is real and what is moral."

Still, he ignored her. She took a few steps back, deliberately ringing her anklets on the red mosaic floor, but got no reaction from him. She picked up the black globe paperweight and rolled it on his desk. The paperweight skidded forward, spun rapidly, and stopped on the very edge of the desk.

"*Allahu Akbar*," chanted Rahim, standing on his prayer mat with his hands raised to his ears. Then he crossed his arms over his chest. Parul felt utterly non-existent. It was as if he had completely cut her off from all his senses.

"I am ready to do penance for all my sins," she said.

This time, Rahim stopped. His shoulder muscles stiffened.

"I will prove to you I am a good Muslim. I will keep a fast and ask Allah forgiveness for the sin I have committed by staying in a Hindu home."

His shoulders relaxed, and he turned around. "You will keep a fast for the entire month of Ramadan?"

"Yes. Yes, I will keep a fast."

Rahim brought his face close to her. His breath warmed her neck. The powerful smell of his *attar* perfume clouded her thoughts.

"Do you mean it?" he asked. "Fast for the entire month? Don't play games with me, little girl. I will hold you to your promise."

Parul's head spun. A deep cloud of fear formed and expanded in her head and settled in her stomach. *If I don't eat before sundown every day for an entire month,* she thought, *Ma will ask me a thousand questions. What will I say then? How will I hide my fasting?*

"You coward," Rahim said, close to her ears. "You are having second thoughts. I knew you would back out."

Parul tingled with shame and fear. Her cheeks grew warm.

"Ma will find out," she said at last. "I cannot hide my fasting from her."

"Why do you care what the infidel thinks of you? Disobey her."

"No, no. It's impossible." Parul bit her tongue and shook her head vehemently. Her mind was flooded with so many conflicting emotions she found it hard to breathe. A single thought dominated in the end, and Parul took control of it. Whatever her list of grievances against Ma, she couldn't just openly defy her.

She made eye contact with Rahim again. "I owe Ma a lot. She saved my family from starvation. She let me stay in this house as her daughter. I get respect here."

This time Rahim grabbed her shoulder, almost crushing her bones. "Asking someone to mop the floor and wash the dishes is not respect, Mumtaz."

"It isn't like that..." croaked Parul.

"I'll tell you this for the last time. Listen to me, you foolish woman. Whatever else the Hindus do, they do not respect you. They may give two *rotis* in charity, but never with respect."

"Why do you hate Hindus so much? They have done nothing to us."

"No more foolish talk," said Rahim. "I cannot make an ignorant woman like you understand the history and politics of this country. After the partition, those of us left on this side of the border are nothing but second-class citizens. The Indian government here comes to us for votes and then leaves. They do nothing for us or our children. They don't give us proper schools, water supply, roads or hospitals. On top of that, they always think of us as criminals. Anything happens and you hear the police boots stomping through Muslim ghettos arresting the Muslim youth. Every poor Muslim family has a son or father behind bars."

Parul's head spun again. "Ma is not like that...." she muttered, half to herself.

Rahim brought his face so close to Parul that she could see his pupils. The hairs on the back of her neck rose. She lowered her eyes from his gaze and focused on his throat. Small freckles and moles lay scattered on the velvety smooth brown skin. The smell of his hair oil and tobacco terrified and excited her.

His fingers on her wrist were both menacing and unforgiving. "Get out," he said. "If you ever come back here, I will break your leg."

• • •

A week later, Madhu*babu* came to invite them to Rehana's wedding. Mohini took him to the kitchen, where Ma was stirring the fish curry. Ma switched off the stove and wiped her oily hands with the end of her sari. She took the simple wedding card from Madhu*babu*'s hand and studied the flowery design. Then she put it on top of the rice cannister.

Madhu*babu* spread his palms and looked pleadingly at Ma. "I know we are small people. We cannot afford a big wedding. But we would be honored if your feet would touch my *garib khana*, my poor man's house. You'll find nothing but hospitality in our village."

Ma rolled her eyes. "Madhu*babu*, how can you expect us to accept this invitation when you forgot all about your elder daughter? This should have been Parul's wedding card, not Rehana's."

Madhu*babu* waved his arms in the air to dismiss the suggestion. "Parul doesn't need a husband. You've given her such a good life here. She lives like a princess. What good will marriage do her? Can her husband afford so much luxury?"

"What foolish talk, Madhu*babu*!" Ma said with bristling impatience. "Parul talks about having her own family day and night. What kind of father are you, breaking your daughter's heart like this?"

The lines on Madhu*babu's* face hardened. Mohini could tell that he didn't take kindly to her rebuke. "Ma, I know what is good for my daughter and what is bad. If I marry off all my daughters, who will take care of me in my old age? We don't have money in the bank like people who live in big houses. Our sons and daughters are all we have."

Ma snorted. "Just what I thought. You've chosen to think only of yourself. Don't you think your daughter deserves to be happy?"

"I have made a big sacrifice for my daughter already. You brought up my daughter like a Hindu girl in this house. I could not give my daughter my religion. Do you know how much that pains my heart?"

A knot strangled Mohini's throat. Madhu*babu* had the audacity to blame Ma for changing Parul's religion. After everything Ma did for his family, this was the way he returned the favor? The man was a true tyrant.

"You can worry about your daughter, and I will worry about mine," said Madhu*babu*.

After he left, Ma tossed the wedding card in the trash can. "*Chhotolok*, small people," she retorted. "Not from our class. What else can you expect from such people."

•　•　•

The next day, Ma gave Parul some money to buy saris and other gifts for her sister's wedding. Mohini accompanied her to Gariahat market. Hundreds of small hawking stands—usually makeshift—clogged the pavement, selling multi-colored nighties, petticoats, glass bangles, bright handbags and cheap shoes. It was a week before Durga Puja, and the streets were jammed with shoppers and pedestrians. As soon as she stepped onto the pavement, Mohini felt she was being lifted and carried forward by a vast tide of people. Elbows dug into her back and heeled shoes stepped on her toes. She ignored the peddlers, who tried to draw her attention toward a pile of chequered towels or fragrant jasmine strings for her hair. Instead, she focused on Parul, deftly weaving through the crowd, her red *dupatta* disappearing fleetingly and coming into view.

They crossed the street where the stalls ended and gave way to more permanent structures. The shops here looked slightly upscale. Parul scrutinized the stock of Nandi Brothers. *Designer Sari at throw away price,* said the board outside. She found nothing suitable, and then moved on to Suleman Tailors. She examined a sari in the storefront display, a multi-coloured chiffon with rose print.

"All this waiting and you finally get to go to your village. Are you excited?" Mohini asked her.

"I don't know." Parul let go of the sari. "A short while ago, I was certain I wanted to go, but I'm not so sure anymore. So many years have gone by. Will my sisters remember me? Am I not a stranger to them now?"

"Such silly thoughts, Parul*di.*" Mohini gave a small laugh. "How can they forget you? You have done so much for them; don't they know that? You'll see, once you go there, just how grateful they are."

Parul fingered a pink sari with a golden border draped on a faceless porcelain mannequin. "My younger sister, Parveen, was only two years old when I left. She had barely started to walk and talk. Who knows what she looks now? All these years, I kept asking Abbu for a photo. But you know how he is... always ready with one thousand excuses."

As they entered the shop, the shopkeeper rushed toward Mohini. With a slight bow, both arms spread wide, he gestured for her to come inside the store. "You have come to the right place." His voice was pleasing. "All our saris are unique. Only one piece made all over India. You'll not find same to same in any other store."

Mohini pointed to Parul. "I'm not your customer. She is."

The shopkeeper looked at Parul and all his enthusiasm diminished. He knew someone like her couldn't afford his expensive brands. He frowned. "What would you like to see?"

"Some cotton and chiffon saris," Parul told the shopkeeper. "Nothing expensive."

Bringing out a wooden ladder, the shopkeeper reached for the stocks lined up on the top shelf. He rolled them out, one by one, pointing to the printed border and the decorated *pallu*. "Nothing but top quality in my store," he repeated after each display.

Parul studied the texture, quality and craftmanship of each piece of cloth. She held them under a table lamp to judge the color. Occasionally, she threw them on her shoulder and swivelled around to check her reflection in the mirror. At last, she decided on a few maroon and rose-pink saris, enhanced with resham work and patch border.

"Do you think Rehana will like them?" asked Mohini.

"I'm not sure." Parul fingered her mother's locket around her neck. There was a wet look in her eyes, and she blinked hard a few times. "Who knows what Rehana likes these days? She is not the little girl who used to follow me around everywhere and say 'Didi, Didi,' all day long. Now she is a young woman, full of her own likings and dislikings." She sat heavily on a wooden chair as if she was suddenly out of energy.

Mohini sighed deeply. Shopping for her sister's wedding was causing Parul pain. "Wrap these saris," she told the shopkeeper.

Parul opened her purse and counted out the money Ma had given her. She was short by a hundred rupees. "Can you give a discount?" she asked the shopkeeper.

The shopkeeper didn't smile. "Everything here is fixed price."

Mohini squeezed Parul's shoulder. "Don't worry. I'll take care of it."

When the shopkeeper was at a safe distance, wrapping the saris in brown paper and tying them up with strings, Parul said, "I feel shame in going back like this. What must the villagers think of me? I am the oldest, but Rehana will be the one in a bridal sari and makeup."

"You have such old-fashioned ideas. These days no one thinks like that."

"Things change in big cities, Mohini, but not in tiny villages. No one will say anything to my face, but they'll talk behind my back." A hint of pain flashed in the dark recesses of her eyes. "They will call me an old maid. I know they will."

Mohini sighed. The village had never released its hold on Parul. It was the source of her strength and vulnerability—the most authentic and inseparable part of her. For years the hope to go back to her village had reigned her heart. Finding acceptance and approval from her family was an undying fantasy in her mind.

Who knew it would happen like this? thought Mohini. *That she will go back with a broken heart.*

Chapter 8

A week later, Parul went to her sister Rehana's wedding. Parul had been led to believe that her father would meet her at the station or send someone from the village to walk her home. But here she was, alone on the platform, and so far, there was not a soul around in the tiny station. Picking up her shoulder bag and lifting her sari, she stepped into the muddy unpaved road that went past the rice fields and the banana grove all the way to her house. Her father had given her a hand-drawn map, but she still had to stop and ask for directions. Closer to her house, Parul was so happy to see the old coconut trees, java apple trees, swings and bridges that she would have gladly embraced and kissed each one of them.

At last, she stood before the house where her Abbu and her sisters lived. Abbu had told her he built them a new house on the same spot where their old one used to be. The tin and clay hut where Ammi lived was now gone, and in its place stood a one-story brick house with clay roof tiles. Parul leaned against the outside wall and closed her eyes. *Look* Ammi, she muttered, *it took me a long time, but I'm finally home.*

She pushed open the door gingerly, a gust of wind closing it shut behind her. The brown stone floor felt cool under her feet as her eyes adjusted to the dim light in the room. She spotted a clothes horse, some mats and stools scattered throughout the room. On the *charpai*—string bed—pushed up against the far wall sat a girl, who she guessed was Rehana, looking into a handheld mirror. She wore a pink sari, her forehead decorated with red-and-white sandalwood paint.

Rehana dropped the mirror and stood to face Parul. A small smile played around her lips.

Parul's first reaction was tenderness, seeing Rehana after all these years. A bubble rose in her throat; she wanted to say so much to her sister. She moved toward her; her steps light and filled with joy, her arms outstretched, her eyes filled with tears. But Rehana did not close the distance between them. Her eyes were focused on the gift boxes in Parul's shoulder bag.

"Didi, did you get those saris for me from Kolkata? Show them to me. I can't wait!"

Parul froze. Her body swayed forward slightly and then came to a complete halt. Her sister was pointing to the red-and-white cardboard boxes peeking from her bag. They still smelled of the dirty train compartment filled with cigarette smoke, and the boxes had been crushed in her lap as the crowd pressed on her knees and thighs.

Parul stood still, looking at the boxes. She had expected her sisters to come running to her, hug her, and even cry. For years, she had pictured this moment: she would come back to her village and her sisters would treat her like a celebrity. "You kept us alive all these years," they would say. "We will not forget all the things you did for us. Didi, you are our hero."

Parul looked at her sister in her gossamer pink sari and gold blouse. Rehana's eyes were focused not on Parul's face but on the cardboard boxes in her shoulder bag. Their youngest sister, Parveen, didn't come out of the kitchen to greet her. The hug she had waited for never came.

"Can I open the boxes, Didi? What else did you get for me?"

Her words were like poisoned arrows aimed at Parul's chest, each one hitting its mark and burning in her rib cage.

"Rehana," Parul said as she struggled to keep her voice calm, "look how much you have grown. Your beauty is almost unbearable. One cannot take their eyes off you."

Her sister opened the boxes and ran her hands over each sari. She rubbed the material between her fingers to judge the thickness and the thread count. Not once did she look at Parul or ask, "How have you been, Didi? Is life treating you well?"

My going away has meant nothing to her, thought Parul. *She has erased me from her memory so effortlessly, as if I was never here, as if I was never a part of this family. I am just a provider of money and luxury items for them now, a cow that gives milk, nothing more.*

She looked at her sister's glowing face again: the red-and-white sandalwood flowers on her pink cheeks, the glistening of the nose ring, and those enormous lotus-like eyes. She tried to recall the four-year-old child she had left behind in the railway station, her tattered clothes, yellowing hair, and unwashed face running after the train. "Didi, Didi, don't go. Don't leave us."

Parul sighed and walked to the open window to look at the lush countryside. The smell of the freshly harvested fields brought back Ammi's memories. The lotus pond, the sugar cane fields and the fishermen's boats soothed her eyes. It reminded her of a time when she was wonderfully happy. The kind of happiness she had never experienced in the city.

Moving away from the window, she entered the kitchen to find her sister Parveen bent over the stove. Parveen didn't make eye contact with her—she seemed painfully shy. Parul slumped on the floor next to her and studied her face—she looked a lot like Ammi. A lump formed in her throat. "Parveen, Ammi loved you with all her heart. I wish you had time to know her before she left for Allah's house." She touched Parveen's cheeks one at a time, dragging her fingers along their contours.

Rehana poked her head into the kitchen. "Can you make a bun for me, Didi? Parveen here is no help." She handed her the bun pins. Parul followed her back to the room and picked up a comb. She twisted Rehana's long hair into a tight bun and secured each strand in place with the pins. The pins poked Rehana's scalp, and she grumbled. Parul laughed. "You were such a drama queen even then. Ammi called you the family clown."

"Didi, you were gone a long time ago. How do you remember so much?" asked Rehana.

Parul sighed. *"Dhat pagli meye*—my crazy girl—Is it possible to forget such things? I still remember the songs we sang together, the pranks we played on each other and the times we quarrelled and made up."

Sitting next to Rehana after years of separation, everything became heightened for Parul. She was even more aware of her loss—the years of childhood that had been purposefully and deceitfully snatched from her. She pulled her sister close and cupped her chin. "Don't you remember our time together?"

Rehana clicked her tongue impatiently. "*Dhat* Didi, those are just silly childhood memories," she groaned. "Today is my wedding day. You should help me put *mehndi* on my hands, flowers in my hair and the red *alta* dye on my feet. Instead, you are bringing up stuff from a hundred years ago."

Merciless disillusionment smacked Parul like an unexpected blow. It shattered the only fantasy she had held on to for years. Standing there, Parul realized the village had grown and moved past her. It no longer waited for her return. The cool pond and the long, shadowy trees now belonged to someone else. She was now a stranger here, an uneasy guest in her own house.

That night the *bor jatri*, the groom's family, came to the wedding *pandal*. Parul welcomed them by showing them the holy earthen lamp and sprinkling husked rice and trefoil on their heads.

The room, no bigger than a large classroom, was decorated with rugs and carpets for the guests to sit. There were no tables or chairs. Rehana sat like a queen on a big *charpai* surrounded by half-a-dozen girlfriends, sparkling in her *Banarasi* sari and golden *maang tikli*. A red veil covered her head and part of her forehead. Parveen sat next to her, tucking tendrils of hair behind her ears and adjusting her veil. The young, handsome groom was seated on a separate *charpai* across the room. He wore a silk *kurta* with golden cufflinks and matching turban on his head. A *purdah*, a net-like curtain, separated the bride and groom.

"Rehana," her friends whispered, "your husband is so attractive. You're such a lucky girl."

Rehana kept her head low, looking at the floor, pretending to be shy. Then she too stole a quick look at the handsome groom and blushed deeply. Pain exploded in Parul's chest. She had taken time off from work, bought a train ticket she could hardly afford, walked three miles from the railway station just to attend her sister's wedding. Yet her sister had not invited her to sit on the *charpai* with her. Not once had her sister looked at her and said, "Didi, I cannot go through such an important day in my life without you by my side." Only her best friends and Parveen had this special honor.

The room was crammed with villagers. The men wore embroidered *kurtas* and caps, and the women wore multi-coloured glass bangles and flowers in their buns. Sweat trickled down Parul's forehead. She picked up the end of her sari and patted her nose. For a moment, her eyes contacted the young and handsome groom, and something stirred deep inside her. She tried to imagine what it would be like to be in her sister's place, to be married to this rugged and vigorous man, to be protected and comforted in the journey of life. What would it be like to cook dinner for him every day, to make his bed, to scold his children, and to get saris and jewelry from him every Eid? What would it be like to be identified by his last name, to walk a step behind him, to wear a ring with his name engraved on it?

Anticipation formed a knot in her stomach as she looked at the fair face of the groom beneath the white turban. And before she could stop herself, another sinful thought crept in: What would it be like to be in bed with him every night, to be held and smothered with kisses?

Evil, rotten thoughts! Allah is testing me, and I am failing. I can't keep my thoughts under control. Parul muttered the prayer of forgiveness that Rahim taught her.

"Our Lord! Condemn us not if we forget or miss the mark! Our Lord! Lay not on us such a burden as thou didst lay on those before us! Our Lord! Impose not on us that which we have not the strength to bear! Pardon us, absolve us and have mercy on us, Thou, our Protector, and give us victory over the disbelieving folk."

The Qazi, marriage registrar, was an ancient man who suffered from crippling arthritis. His gait was laboured, and he leaned on his grandson's shoulders for support. His beard was twisted into three or four turns like a rope. Both his hair and beard were treated with a special *henna* that glowed as bright as the sun. His grandson guided him to the groom's side.

The Qazi took off his glasses and scrutinized the groom's face. He made a clicking sound with his tongue, and even though he did not verbalize his feelings, it was understood that he did not approve of the groom. Abruptly, the laughter and chatter in the room stopped, and the groom shifted nervously on his *charpai*.

Qazi read some scriptures from the holy Quran.

... And among His signs is this, that He created for you mates from among yourselves, that you may dwell in peace and tranquility with them, and He has put love and mercy between your (hearts): Verily in that are signs for those who reflect...

Then he stretched his upper torso to bring his head closer to the groom.

"Do you take Rehana Sheikh to be your wife?" asked the Qazi, his bloodshot eyes glowing in the hollows of his withered face.

"Yes," said the groom, nervously scratching his head. His friends laughed.

"He is having second thoughts," someone yelled from the crowd. There were giggles from the women's side.

"Quiet," barked the Qazi, raising his bony finger to warn the crowd. "This is a wedding, not a two-*paisa* street theatre show." He slapped the *nikah nama*, the marriage contract, onto the groom's lap and tapped on the line that needed his signature. Along with his two witnesses, the Qazi walked over to Rehana's side and stood facing the net-like curtain. All heads looked toward Rehana and her friends. The Qazi touched his beard and cleared his throat. His glasses were thick as bottles, but his gaze seemed to focus on Rehana and her girlfriends, individually and all at once. Not one of them even thought of talking, though they pinched each other and bit their lower lips to stop their giggles.

The Qazi recited from the Quran again.

... Allah, it requires that a husband and wife should be as garments for each other. Just as garments are for protection, comfort, show and concealment for human beings, Allah expects husbands and wives to be for one another.

Rehana nodded slightly, and it was understood that she accepted the holy words spoken by the Qazi.

"Do you take this man, Akram Arif, to be your husband?" asked the Qazi, pointing to the nikah nama.

Rehana reddened. She looked at the floor and said nothing. Her friends tugged her veil and poked her back. Still, she remained silent. Parul felt slightly irritated. Rehana was unnecessarily wasting the Qazi's time.

At last, the Qazi lost his patience. "Answer me, young lady, right now," he roared, his flaming beard swinging threateningly. "I have four other wedding ceremonies to conduct today. Allah, the most gracious one, wants me to be present at each one of them."

"Yes," squeaked Rehana, terrified of the Qazi. "Yes, yes, yes." Her hands trembled, and she dropped the pen before signing the wedding contract. The Qazi glared at her till his grandson stepped in and separated them. Everyone in the village agreed the Qazi had an evil temper, but he always got his job done. He was most capable.

The groom was brought to Rehana's side, and the guests held a thin cloth over their heads and placed a plate of sweetmeat before them. The groom took a bite from one piece and then lifted it to Rehana's lips. Rehana pecked at the sweetmeat timidly, and the women cheered. Then Rehana fed the groom from her plate, not looking at him directly. This time, the groom's side cheered.

A mirror was placed before the groom, and he was asked, "What do you see?"

"I see my life," declared the groom.

When Rehana was asked what she saw, she covered her face with her *mehndi*-covered hands and said nothing. Rehana, thought Parul, was trying to impress her in-laws. Most in-laws in their village didn't like girls who were free-spirited like the city women—ones who didn't care what society thinks. A Bengali bride is expected to be *lajjaboti lata*, shy like the "Touch me not" creeper, which cannot stand on its own. Speaking during her own wedding is unbecoming to a Bengali bride.

The bride and groom exchanged flower garlands, and the groom lifted Rehana's veil to look at her for the first time. Drums started to beat, and a group of women stood up to sing. One by one, the village elders came to bless the newlyweds.

At last, Rehana looked at Parul. A smile flickered on the rosy corners of her lipsticked mouth. Parul's blood stiffened. She felt a tear sting her eye and looked away.

Walima, the feast that followed, took Parul by surprise. The tables were loaded with trays of *korma*, *kabab*, and *biryani*. Parul's entire body lit with anger. She must have paid for most of this extravaganza, and no one thanked her. She was not asked to help with any of the wedding rituals. Nor was she invited to sit with the bride. She stood in a corner like a guest and observer, invisible and insignificant to most people in the room.

Parul crushed Ammi's locket between her fingers. All her life she had worn second-hand clothes and eaten other people's leftovers to earn money, only to see that money squandered on a lavish wedding for her sister. Looking at her father now, hatred churned in her stomach.

Mohini's words rang in her head. *"The truth is, Paruldi, your father only cares about your salary. If you get married, your salary will go to your husband. So he is not interested in finding a man for you."*

Parul focused on the pain, which started like the burning sensation after eating green chilis and then surged into a fierce burn spreading in her veins.

Her father stood near the door, greeting the guests.

"Ahmed *Bhai*, what a wedding. You really dazzled us," the guests said as they passed him, and he glowed.

"Abbu, I need to tell you something..." Parul took hold of her father and pulled him outside, away from the guests.

"What is it, Mumtaz? Why do you look so pale? Are you ill?"

"I am okay," said Parul slowly. "I am going back to Kolkata."

"When?"

"Right now."

"Mumtaz, what's the matter with you? I don't understand. How can you go back now? It is your own sister's wedding. What will people think?"

"Why would I care what they think?" said Parul. "Does anyone here care what I think?"

"Allah, what's the matter with you? Why are you being so belligerent? Aren't you happy to see your sister getting married?"

His words made her blood boil. *Her* Abbu *was asking if she was happy?* She clenched her fist so hard that her nails dug into her palm.

Guests walking in and out of the room cast curious glances their way. Throwing all caution to the wind, Parul lashed out at her father. "Really, Abbu, do you feel no shame asking me this? Did you really think I could stand here and watch the guests eat *biryani* and *korma* in a wedding that is not mine, even though I am the oldest? Did you really think I could stand here and watch my sister flaunt her handsome husband at me and not feel anything? Do you think I am made of stone, Abbu?"

"Mumtaz! Is it jealousy that I hear? Are you jealous of your sister?" Her father threw her a look of disbelief. Then he gave her shoulder a pat. "This kind of behavior does not suit you. You always had a big heart. I tell our relatives that you are not just my daughter... but the son I never had."

"Stop it." Parul pushed his hand away. "Those words mean nothing to me anymore. Before I came here, I had hope. I thought deep inside, you cared for me... that eventually you would start thinking of *my* future. But Allah, in his infinite mercy, brought me here and opened my eyes. The fog has lifted, Abbu, and I see everything clearly."

"What is all this nonsense, Mumtaz? Have you completely lost your mind? To say such inauspicious things on your sister's wedding day. What will Rehana think if she overhears what you are saying?"

Parul's chest constricted. She had difficulty getting the words out. "I am leaving. I don't want to stay here a moment longer."

"You can't leave the wedding like this," he said, gripping her arm.

She gave her father a small, humorless smile. "Don't worry so much, dear Abbu. Your bank account is not closing. I will continue to work for Ma and send money home." She slipped sandals onto her feet and started walking toward the exit.

"Mumtaz, I am asking you to stop."

"You cannot stop me. You lost that right today."

Chapter 9

"What! Tonight?" Mohini cried on the phone, tugging on the coiled cord of the handset.

"What happened?" said Ma.

Mohini hung up the phone, turned, and grabbed Ma's hand. "It's Parul*di*," she said. "She is taking the night train back to Kolkata. She is coming home early."

Ma stared at her in shock. "But why? Why is she coming back on the night of her sister's wedding? Why couldn't she stay for a few more days?"

"I don't know, Ma." Mohini shrugged. "She hung up before I could ask her. I think she was calling from a payphone."

"*Off*, telling me so late...," said Ma. "Now who will make the extra *rotis* for her dinner? I've already finished cooking."

• • •

Later that night, Ma and Mohini sat on the balcony overlooking the gravelly driveway and poured themselves cups of hot tea. Mosquitoes buzzed all around them, and from time to time, they clapped their hands in the air to kill a few. Even though they'd been waiting for an hour for Parul to come home, there was no sign of her. The driveway and the front garden remained submerged in inky darkness. Leaning over the banister, Mohini saw the security guard slouch on a wooden bench. He was probably drunk and fast asleep.

A thousand questions flooded Mohini's mind: Why was Parul rushing back like this? Did her Abbu say something? Or perhaps the sisters? Did the villagers call her an old maid?

"How can she be this irresponsible?" Ma bit her fingernails. "Why didn't she take an earlier train? She knows very well how dangerous the city is at this time of the night." Getting up, Ma leaned over the banister and yelled at the security guard, "Don't just lie there, do something. At least walk to the bus stop and look for her." The guard neither stirred nor opened his eyes. "Why does your Baba pay him?" Ma grumbled to Mohini.

When at last they heard the creak of the gate and Parul's anklets on the stairs, Ma rushed to the second-floor landing and began scolding her. "Why did you come home so late? Do you have no sense at all? Making us worried like this?"

"My train was late." Parul's voice sounded distant and broken. "But you shouldn't have stayed up so late, Ma—it's bad for your blood pressure."

"Come to the kitchen." Ma grabbed Parul's elbow. "I need to talk to you."

When Parul stepped into the yellow light of the kitchen, Ma and Mohini stood silent and aghast at her disheveled appearance. Hair disarrayed, eyes narrow slits. Her sari had slipped off her shoulder, revealing dirty stains on her blouse. The emptiness in her eyes made Mohini's stomach somersault. *This is even worse than I feared,* thought Mohini. *It is as if a different person is standing before us.*

"Look at you! What have you done to yourself?" cried Ma. "You look like a *bhutni,* a ghost."

"It's nothing. When I was making my way out of the crowded platform, someone pushed me and I fell."

"Are you hurt?" asked Mohini. "I'll get you the Dettol bottle."

"No need." Parul shook her head. "Just some minor scrapes."

Ma stepped forward and patted Parul's shoulder. "Tell me first: why are you back so soon? Did they cancel the wedding?"

Parul shook her head. "The ceremony is done. Rehana is married now." Parul tried to appear stoic, but her eyes, as far as Mohini could see, became glassy.

"And you left right after your own sister's wedding?" Ma looked at her in amazement.

"Yes," Parul said softly. Then she shrugged. "It makes no difference to them... whether I stay or leave."

A plateful of food was waiting for Parul on the countertop, under a net cover. Ma removed the net cover and handed the plate to Parul. "I saved two pieces of fish for you. There are extra *rotis* in the casserole."

"Food? No. I am not hungry, Ma." She rolled her bony shoulders. She sounded tired.

"Are you saying you won't eat anything?" Ma cried. "Tell me what I should do with this extra food I cooked for you? Throw it away like it costs nothing?"

Parul broke in quickly, before her remonstrations could get fully under way. "I'll put it in the fridge, Ma," she said. "I'll have it for breakfast tomorrow." She yawned and stretched her arms. "Now let me sleep."

· · ·

Late that night, Parul lay in bed alone, her stomach hurting with anger over her father's betrayal. She thought of her own bleak future and Rehana's scintillating one. She thought of the extravagant wedding feast and her Abbu's beaming face. Then, on an impulse, she picked up a rusty blade from the windowsill.

Bending down, she pulled up her sari to reveal the brown fleshy part of her inner thigh. She was still for a few moments, fascinated by the unblemished skin, and then, with a sharp, deliberate jerk, she pulled the blade across her skin. Her heart drummed in her ears, and her eyes glazed over.

For a long time, she stared at the gaping space between her skin, now filled and overflowing with blood. The red, sticky liquid oozed out and soaked her white petticoat and left dull patches on her sari. Looking at the blood, Parul suddenly wanted to laugh. For the first time in days, her pain dulled.

In that haze of pain and pleasure, Parul thought of Rahim. She remembered the last time she visited him. His prayers had eased her anguish. She muttered his name and buried her tear-stained face into her pillow.

The shadow of the pain followed her the next morning. By afternoon, she was ready to give up. She half-walked to Rahim's door, leaning on the outside wall, and thought of excuses to see him again: She could tell him she had left her bracelet in his room, she needed to use his phone to make an urgent call; she was looking for the widow's cat. All the while, the more practical part of her brain, the part which concerned itself with matters of self-respect, reminded her of his frequent insults and displays of ill-temper.

She ignored the voices in her head and knocked on his door.

"Go away," said Rahim, cracking the door open and then reaching for the knob to pull it shut. But before he could completely close it, Parul inserted her foot through the crack. She then pushed past him and entered the room.

Looking at his deep scowl, Parul braced herself for more threat-laden diatribe, but something in her appearance made him stop and stare at her.

"What happened to you?" he asked.

"Why?"

"Have you seen yourself in a mirror? You look like a corpse."

"What does it matter how I look? Who is going to notice me?"

Rahim gripped her shoulder. "Mumtaz," he demanded, "what's the matter? Did someone hurt you?"

Parul blinked and looked away from him.

"How was your sister's wedding? Were they happy to see you?"

"Of course they were happy to see me." Parul gave half a smile. "I am the hen that lays golden eggs."

"You don't sound happy at all. Did something happen there?"

Parul tried to answer him but couldn't. Her shoulders heaved. She pressed on her chest and bit her lower lip. Rahim stretched his hand out and cupped her chin in his palm. She stared at him, wide-eyed and speechless.

"Tell me." He urged. "What did the village do to you?"

"Nothing happened." She stepped away from him. "I am very happy. Why would I not be? After all, it was my sister's wedding. Weddings are joyous occasions."

"Listen," said Rahim, in a flat, harsh voice. "You have to stop deceiving yourself. Your Abbu is neither a religious nor an honorable man. He is a coward and a thief. He will always take your money, and in return he will give you only tears."

"Don't I know that?" muttered Parul, walking to the window overlooking the alley. Then she spun around to face him. "Fortunately, he can't bother me now."

He threw her a puzzled look. "Why is that?"

Parul pulled up her sari to expose part of her leg. The scar was still fresh, framed in crusty dried blood. "I have found a way to take care of the pain. I just let it out from here," she said, pointing to the recently inflicted wound.

"*Yeh*, Allah," gasped Rahim. "Are you out of your mind? Why would you do a stupid thing like this?"

Parul pressed her palm over her chest. "I had to. It was getting very crowded here. I could not breathe."

"This is not Allah's path, Mumtaz," said Rahim. "I am sure some evil jinn possessed you last night. Let me heat some turmeric paste and put it on that wound of yours before it gets infected."

Parul stared back at him, wide-eyed. The concern in his voice warmed her heart. His gaze was solemn and serious. Parul was suddenly struck by the ridiculous desire to sink her face into the fabric of his *kurta* and weep her heart out.

Rahim stepped into the back alley and lit a kerosene stove. Parul followed him outside. He crushed the turmeric, and with a few drops of water, made a thick paste. He held the bowl over the fire with a pair of tongs.

It stung Parul's heart to see him like this—warming up turmeric paste for her, the roaring stove lighting his handsomely shaped face. *He is doing this for me;* she thought. *He cares about my wound. He is healing my hurt.*

The anger and restlessness ebbed away from Parul. It was replaced with an unknown emotion that made her blush. She raised her hand to feel her ear stud and fingered it delicately to look away from him. She touched the wound high on her leg and felt shame. *How can I let him apply it in such a private place?*

As if sensing her gaze on him, Rahim turned his head and looked at her. "What are you thinking?"

"I am thinking of my bad luck, *amar pora kopal.* My Ammi was a very loving mother. I still remember how she used to comb my hair every evening and make tiny dresses for my dolls. She called me a princess and picked me up every time I was sad. At night, she told me stories about *farishtas* and jinns."

Parul bent down and picked up the hot turmeric bowl with the end of her sari. "But Allah had to take Ammi first. He left me with a father who thinks of me as a commodity, not a person."

They came back to Rahim's office, and Parul sat behind the desk to apply the turmeric paste. Rahim looked away as she exposed the upper part of her leg.

"What about your parents?" asked Parul.

"What about them?" Rahim raised his eyebrows.

"Are they nice?" Then she laughed out loud. "Of course, they are nice. Why even ask? Not everyone comes to this earth with bad luck, like me. I am sure your Abbu is much better than mine."

"Yes, my Abbu and Ammi were both nice. But now they are dead."

"*Hai,* Allah! Why did they die so soon?"

"What will you do with all this nonsense information? I said they are dead. The story is finished. Now let's talk about something else."

"No, no, I want to hear your parents' story. Allah *kasam,* I will tell no one. My lips are sealed." Parul pulled down her sari to cover her legs and stood up.

"Let it go, Mumtaz." Rahim made an impatient gesture with his hand to throw off those memories. "Why bring up the past? What has happened has happened."

Parul smiled despite her pain. "It is your past that will let me understand your present. I want to get to know my teacher."

After much insistence from Parul, Rahim finally told her his story. Parul leaned against the desk and listened breathlessly.

•　　•　　•

Rahim's family were not Bengali-speaking Muslims like Parul's family. They used mostly Hindi and Urdu words, and the Bengalis liked to call them "Bihari Muslims." Originally, they came from Uttar Pradesh, but to Bengalis, anyone who uses Urdu words is a "Bihari."

They no longer spoke in pure Urdu, but maintained some Persian cultural traditions and retained words from the Urdu language. The Bengali Muslims in Kolkata thought they were culturally superior to the Bihari Muslims. The Bihari Muslims tolerated this arrogance with the kind of patience shown to an errant brother or cousin.

Rahim had a clear head in school. His teachers always praised him in the Madrasa. He could recite passages from the Quran in Arabic with his eyes closed. When he was in middle school, his Abbu and Ammi sent him to the neighborhood public school.

The community leaders scorned and ridiculed their decision. Most of their neighbors and friends believed that government and public schools only taught Hindu culture and discouraged students from learning Islamic traditions. But Abbu was determined to send Rahim to public school. "Our Madrasa has produced hundreds of graduates before my own eyes. But how many of them hold an office job like those educated *babus... can anyone tell me*? How many of them have their own desk, own nameplate?" Abbu told his friends when they gathered to play cards. "Everyone in this neighborhood works menial jobs and lives paycheck to paycheck. Then what good is this madrasa education doing us... *you tell me*?"

Rahim surprised everyone when he got a first division in his high-secondary exam and enrolled in Maulana Azad College. He knew his parents were very proud of his achievement, even though they never expressed it in words. He saw them looking at him with pride: *look at what our son has done*, their eyes seem to say, *he has come so far*. When he graduated from college, they were full of hope that he would find a high-paying, respectable job. Much to their surprise, a year went by, but Rahim could not land a job. Every time he showed up in Hindu offices, seeking a position, they turned him down. Eventually, the job went to the Hindu candidates who were much less qualified than he was.

"It is your beard and lace cap," his friends told him. "When you walk in looking like this, you lose the innings even before you hit the first ball."

After searching for a year, Rahim shaved off his beard and gave up his cap. His Ammi cried all night, and his Abbu could not bear to look at him. But still he could not get a job.

"Your name gives you away," said his friends. "What Hindu has a name like Rahim? You won't get hired unless you take a Hindu name."

Still, Rahim was hesitant. How could he give up the only thing his Abbu and Ammi gave him? If the name went,... what was left?

"It is the only way," his friends insisted. "In Hindu land, you have to pretend to be one of them. How does the name 'Shiv Ghosh' sound? It suits you."

Rahim didn't blame his friends for giving him this advice. They were being pragmatic and wanted what was best for him. After much deliberation, he listened to them. His parents tried to stop him, but he was adamant. "Allah will understand why I have to do this. Our family needs the money, and I am the oldest son."

He went to the interview clean-shaven, his hair neatly combed and his head bare of skullcap. Instead of his usual *lungi* and *kurta*, he wore a tricot shirt and pants he borrowed from a laundry for a day. The friendly neighborhood cobbler let him borrow a shiny pair of leather shoes, which belonged to a rich business owner that had come in for repair.

On the day of the interview, Rahim sat in the hot waiting room with its dust-furred ceiling fans and black velvet benches. He kept repeating the name "Shiv Ghosh" to himself. He rolled it off his tongue in a perfect Bengali accent.

This was the right thing to do, he told no one in particular. *This will end our poverty and help ease* Abbu *and* Ammi's *everyday suffering.* He penned down the Hindu name neatly on the application.

Finally, they called that name, and he went inside. Three men sat behind a large conference table. They adjusted their glasses and asked him his name. He opened his mouth to say "Shiv Ghosh," but "Rahim" spilled out. He was so surprised that he stopped breathing for a few moments. But much as he tried, he could not bring himself to say the

Hindu name. The interview didn't go well. He left, knowing he didn't get the job.

Around this time, Rahim's father, who worked in a cloth mill, lost his job. The mill was owned by the central government, and for years, it had made no profit. His father blamed prime minister Rajiv Gandhi, and his mother blamed her fate.

The family needed money desperately. Rahim's youngest brother, Salim, could not bear it anymore. He felt trapped and frustrated. Much as he tried, he could not see a future for himself and his family. One day, a police convoy passed through the neighborhood, escorting a big minister. On an impulse, Salim pelted stones and empty bottles at the police, chanting, "You dog, you bastard, may you die a thousand deaths."

What happened that night would remain etched in Rahim's consciousness forever. They had gathered for dinner in their tiny one-floor house. The darkness sat heavily outside the door. The daytime rush had died down, and the entire neighborhood was sucked into an unusual stillness. The dogs barked near the railway tracks, and a drunkard sang in the back alley.

Rahim's Ammi brought out yogurt for them to eat. It was warm and sweet. Rahim's Abbu rolled up his prayer mat and put away his book and his prayer beads. They sat cross-legged on the floor. Salim sat across from them, facing the front door. He was restless. He kept glancing at the front door, and his fingers trembled when he picked up his yogurt bowl.

Suddenly, loud knock slammed against the front door, followed by a crash. The door was kicked in. Police officers in uniform with pistols hanging from their leather hip-holsters burst into the room.

"Against the wall," the inspector said to Salim. "Don't move or we will shoot."

Salim said nothing. He simply raised his hands in surrender. The constable handcuffed him and threw him inside a police van.

The family ran after them, all the way to the police station. Abbu was barefoot, and Ammi had forgotten her headscarf. They rushed into the station, looking for the inspector. The station was crowded with Muslim faces and skullcaps. There were men locked in what looked like tiny-animal cages. The smell of urine was so strong, they had to cover their noses. Salim waved to them from one cell. He looked like a frightened animal, nervous and vulnerable.

The inspector gave them a friendly smile and asked them to take a seat. "Jail is just like a resort," he told them. "Free food and plenty of rest. Look how dried out your boy looks now. Let him spend a few days with us, and you will see how oily and rounded his cheeks get."

"But what has he done?" Abbu demanded. "My son has never been in trouble before."

"Your son robbed a bank," the inspector said carelessly, almost like an afterthought. "The description matches him perfectly."

"That can't be true," Rahim said. "I read the news. No bank was robbed in the past few months."

The inspector's demeanor changed instantly. His friendliness vanished, and his eyes hardened. "Shut up you *nere baccha*, you dirty Muslim kid. One more word and I will pull out your tongue."

But Rahim didn't back down. "Let go of my brother or else..."

"Or else what?" asked the inspector in a dangerously low tone.

"I will break all these tables and chairs," said Rahim.

The inspector grabbed the material of Rahim's *kurta* and gave his chair a furious kick. The chair turned over, and Rahim fell onto the floor. Then the inspector waved his hand, and the room came alive. Two constables in white uniforms and thick leather belts appeared from nowhere.

"This dirty Muslim kid can use some of our hospitality," said the inspector. "Put him in the same lockup where his brother is."

"No, *Sahib*, no," cried Rahim's mother. "He is young and does not know what he is saying. Forgive him, *Sahib*, forgive him." She fell at the inspector's feet. "I can't have both sons behind bars, sir. We are old people... have mercy on us."

The inspector kicked Rahim's knee and tramped his bare toes with his leather boots. "Next time you talk to me with disrespect, I will pull out your tongue."

The constables escorted them out of the police station.

•   •   •

After that, days went by, and Salim didn't come home. The police did not produce him in court. He didn't get any lawyers or a trial. One day, mad with worry, Abbu and Ammi went back to the police station. The constable stopped them at the entrance. He asked for Salim's description: his height, weight, and complexion. He noted everything in his notepad. Then he slumped into a chair and read the description again and again—a knot dividing his forehead into two equal halves. In the end, he scratched his head and gave them an apologetic smile. "There is no one in our custody who looks like this. No Salim was ever brought to this station. You must have made a mistake."

The parents protested. They said it was impossible for them to make a mistake. They had left Salim in the police station two weeks back on a Wednesday. He was in the small lockup behind the inspector's desk.

The constable went inside and brought back a thick file and showed them all the names recorded in the past three weeks. "This is the complete list of people who were brought to this police station in the past few years. See, here is the Wednesday you are talking about. Just check the date. But there is no record of your son's arrest. We don't have an arrest made under that name. We never did."

Rahim's parent could not believe their eyes. Salim's name and existence had evaporated from the file and that jail. Not a trace of him remained anywhere. They came home heartbroken. They spoke very little and ate even less. Later, a neighborhood boy who was released from the same lockup told them that Salim was moved to a secret prison, but no one knew where. Rahim's family gave up hope of ever finding him.

A few months later, on a Sunday, a bomb went off in a busy market on Chowringhee Road, killing over twenty people and injuring more. There was a lot of pressure from the media and the public to see some sort of "action" from the police. Then, one ill-fated evening, Ammi switched on the small, black-and-white TV in the living room to watch her cooking show. To her horror, Salim's face flashed briefly on the silver screen. He looked emaciated and lifeless, his face full of bruises and half-healed scars. The evening news reporter praised the police for gunning down a dangerous jihadi named Salim Ali, responsible for the Chowringhee Road bomb blast.

Hearing this much, the entire family broke down in tears. Their son had met a cruel and unbearable fate at the hands of the Hindu police officers. Later, Rahim was picked up by the police and asked to identify Salim's body.

A few days after this incident, a Muslim police officer came to see them. He was one of Salim's interrogators. He was sure Salim was innocent, and the inspector had used him as a scapegoat in the bombing case. "I was the only Muslim interrogator in that room that night. I saw what happened with my own eyes."

After the Chowringhee Road bombing, the police had brought Salim in for questioning. They wanted a false confession from him. They wanted him to go on record, saying he was responsible for the bombings. They grilled him for hours in the hot room under a single bulb. *Which terrorist group did he belong to? How long had he trained with them?* Question after question was asked until Salim was exhausted. Still, he repeated each time, "I have nothing to do with the bombing... Allah *kasam*. I was here in a cell, and you know that. You guys are deliberately trying to frame me."

Finally, the inspector lost his patience. He undid the belt that held up his pants. The leather crashed on Salim's delicate back, leaving tire marks on his skin. Salim threw up blood with his vomit. His shirt was drenched in sweat. "I was not involved," Salim repeated.

That was when the torture stopped. The inspector accepted who he was—someone who was not involved. He signaled his men to let go of Salim.

Salim was put in a police jeep and driven to a landfill. The Muslim interrogator was in the jeep, too. When they reached the open field, the inspector turned to Salim and said, "Go home." He removed the handcuffs and said, "We are setting you free."

Salim moved away, the unending blue sky above him and the green grass under his feet. He walked faster and faster away from the inspector. And then he ran. That's when the inspector shot him. Salim turned around once, surprised, as if to tell the inspector he was shot by mistake. The inspector shot him nine times. Salim went down slowly, as if he was kneeling to pray. He faced the Qiblah and cupped his hands to offer his last prayer.

"Salim was a very brave boy," the Muslim interrogator told the family. "The inspector could not break him. Had he confessed to the crime, he would have gone on trial and then been hanged. But when the inspector could not get a confession from him, he killed him in a supposed encounter and declare him responsible for the bombing."

Parul's hands were shaking when Rahim finished his story. Her eyes grew misty as they moved from the cobweb-covered, dusty shelves to Rahim's heavily bearded face. Rahim got up, tied his *lungi*, and lit up a *bidi*. He moved away from her and sat on his chair with his feet up on the bamboo stool.

"Understand, Parul," he said, his voice heavy with sadness, "we Muslims are desperate in this Hindu land. I am now determined to take revenge on all those who disrespect Islam. We are always guilty of everything that happens in this *mulk*. At least now we will go to jail for something we actually do."

Eh Allah, thought Parul. *How did Rahim bear all this? How can a family endure this deluge of misfortune and not drown under it? How can his Abbu and Ammi accept this cruel ending for their beloved younger son?*

As if reading her mind, Rahim said, "Abbu and Ammi grew silent after that. They hardly went out or ate more than a few morsels. My sisters were all married by then. But they came to visit us often and tried to nurse Abbu and Ammi back to good health. But it was as if my parents had lost the will to fight. They had let go. In a few years, they went to meet Salim."

Parul sniffled. Rahim's story had touched her deep inside. She could feel his pain, feel the weight on his soul. Rahim stood and covered the distance between them quickly before lifting her and wrapping his arms around her. Parul nestled close to him.

Rahim drew a rough finger along the contours of her face. He brushed his fingers over her cheekbones and traced the corner of her lips. He kissed her tears; his breath warmed her face.

Then he said under his breath, "It is not your tears that we need, Mumtaz. We need your strength, your power to struggle and to prevail against all those who have been unfair to us, against all those who want to destroy our way of life, against all those who disrespect our God and want to wipe out our religion from the face of this Earth.

It is only when you join my struggle that Salim will get the justice he deserves." He pushed a tendril of her hair behind her ears and brushed her lips with his fingers. "Will you do that for me, Mumtaz? Will you be strong?"

"Yes," said Parul, pressing her body against his. "I will do whatever you tell me. I will not look back."

Rahim cupped her chin and examined her face. "Allah has given you such a pure heart, Mumtaz. You see our scars... you feel our pain."

The press machine roared, and the floor trembled. Behind the walls, the employees had finished their afternoon nap and were getting back to work. The room grew dark, casting long shadows on the wall as if to match their somber mood.

Rahim groaned. "You know, after Salim's death, a part of me had grown numb. I was sure I could feel nothing again." He patted his chest and exhaled. "There was only space for anger here... nothing else.

"Then you walked in and my resolve failed. Your sweet innocent eyes brought down my barriers." Rahim crushed her against his chest and held her close. "My heart is no longer in control."

Chapter 10

Something had changed about Parul. Mohini knew it had. Some days, she disappeared from the house for a very long time. She had rarely stayed outside the house before except to catch an occasional Hindi movie at the local theater or run little errands for Ma. "Where would I go in the afternoons?" she would say. "The shopping malls and amusement parks are for people with money and big cars."

Now she left the house at least twice a week, right after the 4 p.m. teatime, returning in the early part of the evening. Her attitude was less friendly, her pace more hurried, her answers more succinct. She burned the vegetables, over-boiled the milk, forgot to add salt to their meal or added too much. Some days she left a thick coat of dust under the bed while sweeping and cut her finger while peeling potatoes. A few times Mohini entered the terrace room to find Parul on her knees, her hands flat on the floor, her head covered with the end of her sari and the sides of the fabric tucked behind her ears.

"What are you doing?" demanded Mohini. "What is all this?"

Parul immediately pulled down the head covering. "Nothing," said Parul. "The fan here is making my head cold. So I wanted to keep my head covered."

Mohini grew even more concerned when Parul avoided the puja room. Every evening, Ma asked Parul to light a lamp before goddess Lakshmi. Yet when Mohini passed by the puja -room, it remained dark and silent. The lamp stood in the corner, untouched and undisturbed.

But Parul seemed to be blissfully unaware of Mohini's concerns. She spent more and more time in front of Ma's dressing-table, applying *kajal* to her eyes, lipstick to her lips, and talcum powder to her face and neck. She wrapped a sparkling sari around her body, adjusting the length of her *pallu* and ironing out any creases with her fingers. She slid her glass bangles onto her slim wrists and she looked at herself in the mirror, critically. She then slipped out the front door, leaving behind a trail of sweet-smelling talcum powder.

• • •

One evening, as Mohini made her way home from her tutor's with Ma, she saw a group of four or five women in burqa stepping out of a Mazar. The burqa covered most of their bodies, leaving bare only the wrists and feet. Their faces were hidden in veils that hung from their headscarves. Mohini was about to walk away from them when she heard one woman laugh from behind her veil. Mohini jumped and looked at the women again. Mohini was certain she had heard this laughter before. But where? She turned and stared at them. She studied the women's wrists, and her gaze slowly swept downward and froze at one woman's feet.

"Ma, that woman..." She poked Ma's elbow and pointed. "Look at her bangles and anklets. Don't they look familiar?"

"I would recognize those bangles and anklets anywhere," muttered Ma. "I gave them to her with my own hands. She thinks she can fool me!"

Ma stepped forward and grabbed the woman's veil. The surrounding women shrieked loudly and tried to stop her. Ma pushed them away and lifted the veil to expose the woman's face.

Mohini was aghast. *Hiding behind the veil and the burqa was Parul.*

"So you're hanging out with these Muslim women," Ma screamed as a crowd gathered around them. "After everything I have done for you, this is the way you repay me? Overnight, you have become a devout Muslim? I am going to put an end to this sham of yours. Let me remind you that you live in a Hindu household, and you better learn to live like a Hindu."

She yanked the headscarf from Parul's head, and her hair came tumbling down.

"*Eh* Allah!" exclaimed the Muslim women around her.

Mohini watched as Parul lowered her head in shame and covered her face with both hands.

"Ma, that's enough." Mohini caught hold of Ma's elbow. "Let's go home."

Ma pushed away Mohini's hand and turned to Parul. "Come home with me right now. See what I do to you!"

Ma dragged Parul along with her. Mohini tucked the heavy load of books under her elbow and chased after them. Embarrassment lent a note of shrillness to her voice as she pleaded: "Don't do this, Ma. Everyone is watching."

Near their house, with a sudden burst of speed, Mohini ran around them and tried to block the doorway. "Do nothing hasty, Ma. Let Paruldi explain."

But Ma was not in a mood to listen to anyone. She forced her way past the door and marched off to Baba's gym. She came back with a pair of scissors and ordered Parul to take off the burqa. Parul whimpered something incoherent; she was very close to tears. Ma didn't wait. She snatched off the burqa and shredded the fine material into thousands of tiny pieces. "Let me see now," she said at last, looking at the pile of ribboned black cloth, "how you go back to the Mazar after this."

•   •   •

The next day, Parul woke up and washed her face and hands. She took out a black *dupatta* and covered her head. Then she went down on her knees, her hands flat against the mat. Morning prayers. She closed her eyes and thought of Allah's infinite power and greatness. She put away her worries and gathered all her unruly thoughts. She prostrated and recited the words but couldn't fully engage in them. A vein in her forehead throbbed. An image came, and then another. *Ma yanking off her headscarf and dragging her down the street. Ma shredding her burqa to pieces.* Parul could no longer hold still. She gritted her teeth and rolled her fist.

It was only in the last month that Parul had attended some prayers at the railway slum Mazar. Rahim had introduced her to the Maulvi

Abdullah there. The Maulvi, a kind old man, had accepted that she was Mumtaz, a Muslim woman. He had made her feel included, accepted and wanted at the Mazar. Parul had loved her secret escapades from the house, her anonymity behind the burqa. She had even made friends with the Muslim women who lived in the slum and attended the Mazar.

Ma will never let me go back there. The thought unleashed a fierce burn in her chest.

Parul tried to bring the focus back to her prayer. Then she heard Ma's voice from downstairs: "*Eije,* princess. How long will you sleep? Why should I keep a maid if I have to do all the housework?"

Parul did not take off her head cover. She went down the stairs and walked boldly into the kitchen

In the kitchen, Ma was busy cooking chicken. Bits of cumin, coriander, and garam masala sizzled in hot oil. The fragrance filled the entire room.

Parul stepped inside the kitchen, deliberately ringing her anklets. She cleared her throat with a gentle cough. Ma turned around slowly, looking at her in disbelief. When she saw the black head-covering, the hot stirring spoon fell from her hand, almost burning Parul's feet. Then Ma gripped Parul's shoulder and began screaming, her voice rising from a soft hiss into a high-pitched shriek. "You are challenging me. Yes, that's what you are doing. You are bent on defying me. I thought I cured you of this lunacy last night; I thought you would behave sensibly from now on. But no, looks like the bug inside your head is acting up again."

"Ma," said Parul quietly, "I want to keep my head covered at all times."

"How dare you say that? I will—"

"Ma, I didn't ask for your permission. It is a decision I have made. I will be happy if you can respect my religion."

This time, Ma burst like a pressure-cooker. "Listen to what you are saying! You decided? You are a maid here. I decide because I am the mistress of this house. Do you understand?"

The *garam masala* in the pot burned. Wisps of smoke and an acrid smell rose and tickled Parul's nose. Ma turned, lifted the pot with a pair of tongs, and tossed it into the sink. The oil popped and splashed. Parul stepped forward to help, but Ma grabbed her wrist and pushed her against the kitchen wall. Parul gasped, trying to wriggle out of Ma's iron grip.

"I will teach you a lesson, Parul. I'll teach you how to live in a respected family. I will not let you rub lime and ink on our face. You will stay up in that terrace room of yours and not come out for any reason. Any reason at all, you hear me?"

Ma dragged Parul up the stairs and back to her terrace room. She flung the door open and pushed Parul inside. "We will send your meals up here until you come to your senses." She slammed the door shut.

• • •

A few days went by, and Parul stayed in her room. One day, Mohini brought her lunch tray and sat with her. Parul liked when Mohini came to visit with her in her terrace room, though she felt slightly embarrassed by how shabby and crowded the room was, and she could never find a proper chair for Mohini to sit. Mohini was always lively, full of energy, and eager to talk about herself. Words gushed out of her as if a cap had blown off a soda bottle.

Parul tried to follow all of Mohini's fast chatter about her college, her involvement in student politics and the non-profit she volunteered for after school. Mohini was a student of English and history at Presidency College. She wrote for her college newspaper and submitted poems and articles to various political magazines. "Once I get a job, I am going to be paid for writing these articles, you know," she said. "Right now, I am just building my reputation."

Mohini presented a world that differed vastly from what Parul had known and experienced. Parul tried to take in what Mohini was saying, but most of it went over her head. Still, she managed to look sufficiently interested, inserting a nod and a "yes" in the right places. She had gathered from her fast chatter Mohini wanted to work for a newspaper after she graduated. She wanted to report from remote places in the world amid famine, earthquake and war. She wanted to be a tough journalist who asked pointed questions, stormed into buildings, disrupted meetings and exposed corrupt leaders.

Mohini's ambition baffled Parul. After all, Mohini was from a rich family. She could do whatever she wanted. Why did she want to go to these dangerous places and risk her life? *Rich people are strange,* thought Parul. *They get bored so easily. They are always looking for more thrills and more escapades.*

Parul's own dreams got lost in the quagmire of family responsibility. The thought of seeking new adventures never crossed her mind. The need to earn money and keep her father satisfied kept her on her toes. Every day, she washed a vast pile of dishes, measured out flour for *rotis*, soaked clothes in soapy water and dried them on the clothesline. She carried out this painstaking routine throughout the year. Survival was her only *mantra*, her own happiness always buried under the burden of duty. *No wonder Mohini stopped listening to me,* thought Parul enviously. *I must seem very dull compared to all those interesting things happening in her college.*

Mohini's voice broke through her thoughts.

"Parul*di*," she said. "What is going on with you? Why are you so defiant?"

Parul shook her head in disbelief. Here she was, held captive in her own terrace room, and Mohini was asking her why she was so defiant? Was she blind or only pretending to be?

Looking at Mohini in her room that day, Parul found herself becoming unaccustomedly outraged. Mohini cared so much about her college that she was neither curious nor sensitive about what was happening in her own house. Lately, Parul was getting the feeling that it was a chore for Mohini to make an appearance in her terrace room even once in a while. She was immersed in her college books or talking in English on the phone with her friends.

"You know you can talk to me. Tell me everything," said Mohini.

Parul busied herself folding a sari.

"Why are you being so fussy about a stupid scarf?"

Parul inhaled sharply. "It is not a scarf. It is my identity."

"The scarf is your identity?"

"You won't understand."

"Who is putting all this nonsense in your head?"

"No one."

"You got this idea from somewhere... Is it from a Bollywood movie you went to watch?"

"No." Parul wished she could get rid of Mohini. She closed her eyes and wished her away. When she opened them, Mohini was still there, glaring at her.

"Wait a minute, I know! It was in a magazine you read. So the stupid beauty magazines are talking about identity these days? I wonder why... Did they run out of soap and shampoo stories?" asked Mohini.

"I told you, Mohini, you won't understand. You know your roots—you can follow your faith. I have been denied mine. I have nothing to call my own."

"Since when did you worry about roots?" Mohini frowned.

"I have worried for a long time."

"You didn't tell me..."

"You have a lot of college work, Mohini. You are very busy these days." Parul dropped her folded sari into a steel trunk and snapped it shut, signaling the end of the discussion.

Mohini seemed undeterred. She cleared her throat and folded her arms on top of her chest. "You think wearing Muslim clothes and pretending to be Muslim will solve all your problems?"

"I am not pretending to be a Muslim. I am a Muslim," Parul said, spitting the words through her teeth. "It is a matter of honor for me to be a Muslim."

"Parul*di*, whatever you are doing is not good. You are testing Ma's patience. You know our relatives believe drinking water from a Muslim woman will take away their religion. What will they say when they come to know we have been harboring a Muslim in our house all this time?"

Parul did not answer.

Mohini sighed and clicked her tongue. "What will you do if Ma throws you out of the house? Where will you go? Back to your village? Do you think your father and sisters will welcome you back with open arms—that they will hug you when you tell them you are no longer a wage earner?"

"Leave me alone, Mohini. I don't want to talk to you. I don't want to talk to anyone in this house. Just let me be." Parul dragged her fingernails across the metallic cover of the trunk, making a low, rasping sound. To her satisfaction, Mohini cringed. Then she pouted, stomped her feet and moved away from Parul.

• • •

Mohini climbed down the stairs slowly. She was astonished to hear Parul talk in this vein. She saw the confusion in Parul's eyes, and she wanted Parul to tell her what was bothering her; she wanted Parul to tell her why she was taking such a big risk and putting her livelihood at jeopardy. Hadn't Parul always considered Mohini her closest confidante? Why wouldn't she open up to her? Why did Parul no longer trust her enough to share her dilemma?

As children, they were inseparable, pouring out their hearts to each other with a perfect lack of self-consciousness which only children are capable of. They talked about all their experiences with innocent delight and responded to each other with affection. But as they'd grown older, Mohini had felt that Parul had spaces that were private, barriers that couldn't be crossed, and occasional mood swings that couldn't be explained.

Still, Mohini had assumed she knew everything she needed to know about Parul's life. She had believed that Parul was incapable of defiance or deceit. So seeing her in a burqa outside the Mazar had ripped something vital from Mohini, leaving a gaping hole. She knew then that something had changed between them. Some innocence faded like the setting sun.

Unbidden, a memory came of their childhood days. They played house and school in the broken room of the west wing. Mohini had pulled out the rectangular pieces of blue plastic covers from the furniture and spread them on the floor. Then she sculpted her imaginary world on top of it with bits of cotton, cardboard boxes, burned candles and notebook papers.

While Parul gazed at the blue sheets, spread like a fictional ocean floor, Mohini took her hand and pulled her inside each rectangle. "This is the bedroom where Ma and Baba sleep," Mohini told Parul. "The room next to it is mine."

"What are those?" Parul asked, pointing to a pile of moth-eaten pillows.

"Those are chairs and tables. And see, this is the bed. Don't bump into them."

"Can I sit in a chair?" Parul giggled.

"No, silly," Mohini scolded her. "You are the maid. Sit on the floor."

Parul grew quiet; something in that role-play bothered her. But she never protested or quit playing. Instead, she obeyed each of Mohini's instructions as she moved around from room to room, walking through the open doors marked with green tape and staying away from the closed ones marked in red. Mohini stacked the old encyclopedias to make a staircase, and they climbed on top of it to reach the terrace. "See that park down there?" Mohini pointed out to her. "My friends are already there. I have to play with them."

"Can I come?" asked Parul, looking down.

"You have to stay back. It is dinnertime now, and Ma will want you in the kitchen."

Parul was silent for a such a long time that Mohini had begun to wonder if her tongue had frozen. Then, most unexpectedly, Parul had stepped forward and trampled the cardboard boxes and cotton wool that represented the kitchen. She had flattened out each piece with great satisfaction. Looking at Mohini, she had asked, "My work here is done. Now can I come with you?"

Chapter 11

"Bring me some poison." Parul burst into Rahim's room. "I want to kill myself."

Rahim got up from his chair quickly. He moved toward her and held her hand.

"I mean it," said Parul. "I want to end my life."

"No, you don't."

"Fine, if you don't give me poison, I will drink the bottle of phenyl in Ma's bathroom."

Rahim shook his head. "No, you can't do that."

Parul snatched her hand away from him and placed it firmly on her waist. "What do you mean I can't? It is my life. I can end it whenever I want to."

"A Muslim cannot commit suicide," said Rahim. "He who kills himself with a sword, or takes poison, or throws himself off a mountain will be tormented on the Day of Resurrection by that very thing."

"So what does Allah want me to do? I cannot live and I am not allowed to die." Parul grimaced, turning her head away, and a tremor ran through her whole body.

Rahim's voice softened to tenderness or pity. "Shh, no more useless talk." He touched her shoulder and turned her around to face him. "You are getting excited unnecessarily. This is not Allah's way."

"How can I remain calm when my insides want to burst out of my body? Am I just born to suffer?"

"I told you. A good Muslim woman always finds peace and comfort through prayers."

Parul leaned against the wall. Her shoulders heaved. She pressed on her chest and chewed the end of her braid. Then she took a breath, forcing herself to look up again at his face. "Ma, upstairs, won't let me pray to my own God. She found out about my visits to the Mazar. She locked me up in the terrace room for one entire week."

Rahim's dark eyes flashed with an insane glaze. "She locked you up?"

Parul nodded. "She won't let me practice Islam. If she takes away God from a poor girl like me, what else is left?" She bit her lips fiercely, and tears poured from her brimming eyes.

Rahim muttered what sounded like a curse. Stepping forward, he squeezed her hand, holding the fingers hard, as if he wanted to squeeze out her pain. "The infidel woman will pay for making you cry like this."

The air around them was choked with sadness. It filled the space between them like little droplets of condensation. It held them still in an unspoken bond. Rahim took out a handkerchief from his chest pocket to wipe her tears. The sun was behind him, and half of his face was stuck in the shadows. His beard was thick like the monsoon clouds, his eyes more beleaguered than ever.

His tenderness toward her struck Parul. *It is as if he can feel the weight on my soul;* she thought. *He wants to take away my pain.*

"Allah has great plans for you, Mumtaz," said Rahim. "When the time comes, you will make the people in this house weep blood with their tears. They will regret the day they were born."

The room grew quiet. The quietness rose somehow above the indistinct babel of the neighboring press rooms. Rahim put his arms around her and pulled her toward him. His breathing was uneven, his voice slightly husky. Parul smelled the strong *attar* on his shirt and the tobacco on his lips.

Fear and excitement surged in her stomach. Her body hummed with a new awareness. Rahim raised his arm, and his fingers brushed against her hair and her neck. Parul gave a low moan and stepped back, but Rahim stepped forward to fill in the space. His hand came down to her waist, and his fingers curved against the smallness of her back. She moaned again.

"I will make things right for you. You will get the dignity and respect you deserve."

Parul licked her dry lips. She felt a hunger that scared her and thrilled her. Excitement rose like little pins in her stomach, making her armpits sweat and moisture rush between her legs. Rahim kissed her on the lips and pulled her to the floor. He rubbed his palm against her nipple and squeezed her breasts. She moaned and cupped his silky beard. The fan above her creaked, and the water pump hummed. Rahim pulled down her petticoat and covered her body with his. He kissed her neck and then her belly. She groaned and pulled him toward her.

Afterward, Parul said nothing. Her eyes became watery. She lay in Rahim's arms, contented. The warmth of his body radiated into her, enveloping her with security and wellness. She wanted him to take her again, to clamp his legs around her like forceps and squeeze out all her fear and anxiety. Under him, she felt invincible, protected, and sheltered from the outside world. He took away her worry, undid her hurt. She wanted him to stay there and hold her forever.

• • •

The next morning, when the warm sun hit her face and neck, she reluctantly got up and went to the terrace tap. Her body was sore, and her head throbbed. She turned on the tap and let the ice-cold water drip between her fingers. She cupped the water in her palm and splashed it on her face and neck. Her mind overflowed with fearsome thoughts, like she was drowning in the river while Ma and Mohini swam farther and farther away from her. She closed the tap and sat heavily on the floor. Her back felt stiff, and her head hung forward.

The unthinkable had happened.

Parul bit the back of her palm, full of trepidation. Rahim had seen her naked. She was unmarried, and he had touched her. Together, they had committed a grave crime. If Ma came to know about their lovemaking, the punishment would be swift and severe. Ma would never forgive her for ruining the good name of their family.

She came back to the room and spread the wet towel on the clothesline. The small wall mirror caught her reflection, and she grimaced. Slapped onto her neck, half-covered by her sari, was an unmistakable hickey. The sight twisted her stomach, and she wanted to throw up.

I am a fallen woman now. I brought this upon myself. I didn't think of my honor or this family's honor.

Parul opened her mouth and sucked in her breath. *This has to stop.* She wouldn't allow herself to be blown away by temptation again. She would avoid Rahim from now on. She would go nowhere near his office.

She kneeled and cupped her hands. Closing her eyes, she asked God for forgiveness.

•　　•　　•

Later that day, Parul came down the stairs to bathe. The printing press door was open and the press widow was talking to Rahim. It was payday, and the widow had come early. Usually, she visited the press in the early evening to look at the accounts. The widow turned, and her gaze lingered briefly on Parul. *She knows*, thought Parul. *She knows I have sinned.*

The widow signed some bills, covered her head with the end of her sari, and left the room. Parul sighed with relief. Maybe she did not know about them. A vindictive woman like her would descend upon them like wasps to honey; she would bring a thousand accusations if she had the slightest inkling of what went on behind her back. *Allah had saved them from her wrath.*

Rahim came out of the office and smiled at her. Parul flushed and glanced away. Warm tingles scattered over her skin. She picked up her bucket and rushed to the bathroom. The sun was just emerging from behind the cloud cover. The widow's cat jumped from the low brick wall behind her bathroom and rubbed against her feet. Parul picked it up and scratched its belly. The cat purred loudly.

Parul's bathroom was on one side of the courtyard, adjacent to the gym. The bathroom was tiny, with only one door and a single boarded-up window. Years ago, this room was used to store coal for the ovens used in cooking. When Ma switched to kerosene oil, Baba emptied the coal and installed a toilet and a drain. Parul was moved to the new bathroom quickly. "In all houses, servants have separate bathrooms," Ma told her. "This will be yours from now on."

The door creaked as Parul pushed it open. She opened the tap and placed the bucket under it. Her heart raced. Her body's reaction to Rahim horrified. She cursed herself for being a weak-willed fool.

The bucket overflowed, and she quickly turned off the tap. She rubbed lifebuoy soap over her naked body and rinsed till the bucket was empty. Then she lathered up again and refilled the bucket. Bending down, she examined the corns and calluses on her toes and the hair on her armpits. Her mind ambled to Rahim, and she wondered if he had noticed her imperfections. She pushed away the thought as soon as it came.

Parul washed her clothes in the remaining water, wringing out every drop before stuffing them into a dry bucket like lifeless snakes. A hint of coal dust still lined the windowsill and left a grayish coat on the walls and ceilings of her tiny bathroom. The cobwebbed gloom of the semi-dark room sent shivers down her spine. She stepped out of the bathroom wearing only a sari, no blouse, specks of water gleaming on her bare shoulders and back.

Two crows were swinging on the courtyard clothesline behind the bathroom. She shooed them away, and they flew over to the neighbor's cow barn. She pulled out the freshly washed sari and spread it on the clothesline, straightening the creases. The sari arched like a rainbow, undulating slightly, touched by a gentle breeze. She spread out her petticoat, blouse, and bra and secured them with plastic clothespins.

Suddenly Rahim's bearded face appeared from behind the sari. His soorma-outlined eyes seemed to bore through her. "I went to the Masjid this morning. I brought you some perfume and incense. Come to my office when you are done here."

A warm sensation filled her chest and spread through her limbs. Her face flushed. It took all her willpower to turn down his invitation.

"I can't stop by today," she said. "Ma has guests coming, and I've to cook."

She unwrapped the wet towel from her hair and spread it on the clothesline. Pulling down her hair, she ran her fingers through the wet, clumpy strands. Rahim reached out and rolled a strand of her hair around his finger.

"Come to the office," he said urgently.

She looked up at Rahim and the naked intent in his eyes. Her head spun; her pulse drummed in her ears.

It was not right the first time, and now he is asking to see you again. The voice inside her head was loud and clear. Parul shuddered. It had to stop. She needed to stop this before it became a ball of fire and swallowed the entire house in its fiery flames.

She picked up her bucket and headed for the stairs. She tried not to look back at him, but failed miserably.

"This is not Allah's path," she told Rahim under her breath. "This is a sin."

"Yes, you are right. In principle, what we did is a sin. But Allah forgives. We have to pray hard and ask for his forgiveness. 'My servants who have acted extravagantly against themselves still do not despair of God's mercy. God forgives all offences; He is the Forgiving, the Merciful.'"

"But if I visit you again, I can never control myself. I may repeat the sin. So it is best that we stay away from each other."

"Mumtaz, I'll marry you, and take care of you," he said suddenly.

She grew still. Then she took a gulp of air and forced out a laugh. "You don't mean that."

"Allah *kasam*."

"But I am just a maid."

"You don't need to be a maid much longer. After I marry you, you will live like a queen."

Parul's stomach surged with excitement and dread. She walked with him to his office.

Rahim closed the door and came close to her. "You will never clean floors and wash dishes in a *babu's* house. You will have your own home and your own children." He left a trail of kisses from her throat to her jaw and then her lips. "I will ask your Abbu for your hand."

She pushed him back. "My Abbu will not agree to my marriage. He wants me to supply him with paper notes 'til the day I die."

"Then we will not ask for your Abbu's blessings. The railway slum Maulvi can marry us. We will send a letter to your Abbu after it is all over."

"Maulvi Abdullah?"

"Yes, Maulvi Abdullah. You know he is a good friend."

Rahim reached for her and pulled her into the circle of his arm. He whispered caresses in her ear, biting and tugging her earlobe, wanting a moan from her in response. Still, Parul resisted. Could she really trust him? She looked at Rahim now, and the fear paralyzed her body. *What if he changes his mind? He may like me now, but soon he will realize I may not be a suitable wife for him. What will happen to me then? Allah, I am not worthy of him. He will leave me after all this is over.*

Rahim cupped her chin. "Why are you still worried? Did I not tell you there is nothing sinful about our relationship now? We are going to be husband and wife."

"I want to believe you, but..."

"But what?"

"Good things don't happen to me. I have bad luck... *amar pora kopal.*"

"You are being silly again."

"My heart wants to believe you, but my brain is afraid."

"Are you doubting my integrity?"

Parul bit her tongue. "Not in a thousand years. You are my messiah, my *Pir*. How can I ever doubt you? But it will be too difficult...."

"What?"

"For us to be together. I am just a maid, and you are a college-educated man."

"Get those nonsense thoughts out of your mind. I have given you my word."

He bit the fleshy section of her ear, and her body lit up instantly. The need to trust him overcame her fear. She scratched behind his ears with her long nails, and he cursed in Urdu. Rahim buried his face in the shallow hollow of her throat. His throaty groan filled her up with delight. She felt wanted, felt desired, felt like a woman.

"We can't meet in the office like this," whispered Rahim between his caresses. "It is not safe."

"Where do you want to go?"

"I have been thinking," said Rahim, "that we should meet in the *bhuter bari*, the west wing. No one will find us there."

"That's impossible."

"Why? Are you scared of ghosts?" Rahim laughed.

"No... no," said Parul uncertainly. "But the place is a dump now."

"Exactly what we need."

"But it remains closed."

"You know where the key is, don't you?"

"Yes... but..."

"It's settled then. I don't think the ghosts can bother us. Even better, the ghosts will protect us from nosy intruders. It is a perfect place to meet once a week."

"But there are mice and roaches and cobwebs... who knows what else."

"Then take your duster and clean a corner for us. That's all we need." Rahim smiled.

Chapter 12

It was unbearably hot in the afternoons. The city was on fire. It was as if the sun had moved closer to earth and was beating down on them relentlessly. Ma lay on the large four-poster-bed; she was resting after lunch. The doors and windows of the room were closed; the fan whirred over her head, imitating gentle waves lapping against the shore.

Parul sat on Ma's feet, dabbing hot mustard oil on her foot cracks. From time to time, she glanced at the cuckoo clock on the wall and then at Ma's face. She was eager for Ma to fall asleep. Rahim had asked her to meet him in the west wing. This would be their first-time making love in the west wing. A needle of excitement went down her stomach. Parul took in a deep, hissing breath, a sound of lust and anticipation.

Ma changed sides. Parul leaned in closer, and this time she heard soft snoring. Relaxing her tense shoulders, she propped her back against the side of the bed. Lately, getting away from Ma and going to meet Rahim was proving to be difficult. Ever since she was caught outside the Mazar, Ma watched her like a hawk. Some days Ma went up to her terrace room and looked under the bed, shook out the pillow covers and rifled through the belongings stored away in the tin trunk. She did it with the thoroughness of an investigator who wanted to build a strong case against Parul.

Anything I say or do is automatically under suspicion these days. Parul clicked her tongue. *She trusts Ram, the janitor, and the drunken security guard more than me.*

She wiped her hands and screwed the metal cap on the neck of the oil bottle. Rahim was waiting for her, and she didn't want to waste any more time. Fortunately, she knew where Ma hid the west wing keys; she took them out and slipped them inside her blouse.

Getting up, she tiptoed down the stairs and made her way to the fire escape behind the printing press. The spiral staircase went all the way up to the second floor of the west wing. Rahim was nowhere around. Parul wasn't sure what to do next. She edged along, back flat against the wall, to the machine room and looked in through the window. The room was slightly dark inside; she couldn't see clearly at first. As her eyes adjusted to the dark, she saw the machine-man sprawled on the cool mosaic floor, his mouth open and his belly pointed upward like a small mountain peak. He was fast asleep. The compositor lay curled up next to him, snoring like a boiling teapot. The helper boy, who was now a teenager, slept with his hands and legs half hanging from the window ledge. The widow's black cat lay as a furry lump on his stomach.

Reassured to see them heavy in sleep, Parul decided to go up the fire escape and wait for Rahim. She grabbed the curved banister and stepped on the rusty rungs. The stairs popped and creaked, swaying just a little as she shifted her weight. She went up warily, stepping from foothold to foothold, counting herself lucky when she reached the second-floor landing.

The heavy door groaned open as she turned the key. The cobweb gloom of the unused rooms made her shiver. After a few minutes, Rahim came in through the same door, his face partly covered in a brown shawl.

Together they swept and scrubbed a space on the floor near the grand piano. They removed some of the blue plastic sheets and dusted the tables and chairs. Still, most of the room lay covered in dust and cobwebs. Silverfish crawled between the pages of the books that lined the shelves, and termite mud tubes that looked like dried-up river channels climbed up the wall, almost touching the ceiling.

It was only when her eyes grew accustomed to the darkness that Parul noticed the lantern on the bottom shelf. She went over and gave the lantern a good shake, raising a cloud of swirling dust. Rahim unscrewed the glass top and wiped it clean. "It is in good condition. I'll get some kerosene oil from my office." He tiptoed down the stairs and brought back a small canister and soaked the dry wick. The lantern lit up part of the room, casting long and creepy shadows on the wall.

Rahim picked it up and held it close to Parul's face. "*Mashallah,* you are so beautiful."

"*Dhat*," said Parul. "Who calls a maid beautiful? You must be joking."

"I mean it," he said seriously. "Allah took great care when he made you."

Rahim pulled her toward him, loosening the pins in her hair. It came cascading down like a black waterfall. "You know this is what I wanted to do the first time I saw you." He slid his arms over her shoulders and wrapped them around her neck. Rahim drew her more firmly against his body. His hands slid down to her waist and rested on the smallness of her back. "You are my Anarkali and I am your Salim."

He pulled her sari, and it peeled off like petals of a flower, fold by fold. She stood before him in her blouse and petticoat, red as a beetroot and trembling like a leaf. He kissed her lips and then her cleavage, and she moaned in response.

•　　•　　•

The next day, Parul woke up early and rubbed turmeric and sandalwood paste on her face. She clipped her toenails and applied nail polish on each finger. She pulled her hair up into a topknot and checked herself in her tiny hand-held mirror. Her reflection stared back at her, and it did not make her happy. She braided her hair instead and tie a ribbon at the end. She changed her sari twice, unable to decide which one to wear. Then she picked up her purse and left for the bazaar. Halfway there, she remembered her tote bag and had to rush back home to get it.

Walking along the busy road, past the children's school and the Laxmi temple, Parul found herself savoring every moment as if she was living it for the first time. She climbed up the steep road that led to the muddy pond, and sitting there on the grass, she watched the ripples form and spread on the water. She listened to the cuckoo singing on the branches of the fig tree and sound of the water lapping against the shore. Life was now bursting with meaning, and she was aware of all the sounds and sensations that surrounded her. She lay back on the grass and hummed a tune. She checked her reflection in the water and adjusted her *bindi*. Looking up, she marveled at the cottony clouds scattered over her head and felt the soft glow of the early morning sun on her cheeks.

Just then, two young boys on bikes pulled up near her. "Come here, sexy girl," said one of them. The other boy whistled. As if waking from a dream, Parul sat up and adjusted her sari. She threw one of her slippers at the boys, and they rode away, laughing. She dusted herself and gathered her purse and tote bag. She hurried to the bridge and climbed down the spiraling stairs to enter the bazaar.

In the market, the shops were open, and the streets were crowded, as usual, with people and rickshaws and cars. A line of young women carrying wicker baskets filled with live chickens, fruits and vegetables on their head squeezed past Parul. Porters and vendors unloaded hundreds of banana stalks from a parked truck into a bamboo cart. Parul had to jump over the sleeping street dogs and fresh piles of cow dung to reach the entrance of the covered market. A beggar sat on the broken pavement with an aluminum bowl. "Give me one *paisa*, sister. god will bless you." He had sunken cheeks and hollow collarbones. Parul dropped a twenty rupee note in his bowl. He looked at her in disbelief. "Did you win a lottery, sister?" he asked.

"Something like that." Parul smiled mysteriously.

The inside of the market was darker, with narrower passages. Fruits, vegetable, meat and fishes were piled up high and measured with iron balances. Parul picked up the bottom of her sari to step over the puddles and garbage piles to reach her favorite fish seller.

"*Wah* Bibi," said the fish seller. "You look radiant these days. What cream and powder do you use? Please get me some of that."

Parul laughed. Kneeling, she examined the fish, pressing on its belly and pulling back the gills to determine its freshness. The fish seller gave her a cheerful smile. "They are all fresh, sister. They were jumping in my bucket just this morning."

Parul didn't argue with him. She picked out a tilapia and a cod and asked him to weigh it. She told him to cut and scale the fish and fill up her bag.

On her way back, she bought a heavily embroidered handkerchief for Rahim. She was meeting him in the west wing again that week, and the thought of being with him left her breathless with excitement. Closer to home, she changed her mind about the handkerchief. It was too risky, she decided with a click of her tongue. It wouldn't be long before Ma discovered the man's handkerchief in her purse and created a big scene. Reluctantly, she dropped the expensive purchase in a blind beggar's bowl.

Parul quickened her pace. It was office hours, and the printing press was open. The thought of catching a glimpse of Rahim's lace cap in the office kindled a sense of well-being in her. It surprised her to think that sometimes your own family could behave like strangers, and strangers could become dearer than family. Or else how was it possible that she could pour out her heart to Rahim, while she made every effort to conceal her true feelings from people in that house? To Mohini's family, Parul was invisible, and her grief insignificant. Daily she mopped their floor, ironed their clothes, carried their bags and polished their shoes. And daily, bit by bit, she died before them, unseen and uncared-for.

But Rahim was different. In the few months she had known him, he had cared for her highs and lows, her good days and bad days, given her hope and made her feel valuable. He had called her his "Anarkali" and filled her body with guilty pleasure. Pleasure she had not known before. Pleasure that she had taken shamelessly and demanded even more. Pleasure that had connected her to a world previously unknown to her; in his arms, nothing else existed outside the space that contained both of them.

Over the next few weeks, Parul and Rahim continued to meet secretly in the west wing. No one saw them except the crows and sparrows that lined the parapet in the scorching afternoons. Their union often left Parul unsatisfied and restless, and she found herself always wanting to be with him, waiting for him to come to her and missing him the moment he rolled off her.

At night she reached out for him in her sleep, only to find the cold hard floor next to her mat, lifeless and unresponsive. Other times, she found herself resisting going down to the printing press during office hours just to catch a glimpse of Rahim at his writing desk. It was a forbidden and a dangerous thing to do, and the likelihood of getting discovered by Ma or the printing press employees was considerable. Yet she struggled to stay focused on her work in Ma's kitchen, knowing the source of her attraction was only a few feet away, across the courtyard in the press office.

Rahim was her first man, the only man before whom she had undressed, and even now Parul felt desperately shy when he looked at her bare body in the dim light of the lantern. He was patient with her, treating her body with infinite tenderness, as if he was worshipping Allah's beautiful creation. When he moved over her, rubbing and kissing her neck and breasts, hot tears filled her eyes and rolled down her cheeks. That she should be on the receiving end of so much love still amazed her. Even in her dreams, Parul never could imagine life filling her to the brim with so much joy. When she lost her mother, everyone felt sorry for her. *She has no hope for a future*, Parul overheard them whisper. *She is the daughter of a dead mother. Suffering is all she has left.*

Who would have predicted then that one day a stranger would come to her life and shower her with so much love and attention? *Allah has unusual ways*, thought Parul. *He makes us suffer, but when he gives, he gives with both hands.*

Parul did not remember her Ammi very well. Ammi died giving birth to their youngest sister, Parveen. Everyone told Ammi not to get pregnant again. After Rehana was born, she was thin like a stick—only skin and bones. *You won't be able to carry another child in that belly,* everyone said. *Listen to us or else you will be dead. Your own child will kill you. You already have two daughters; why do you need a third child?*

But Ammi would not listen to them. She told everyone Abbu wanted a boy, and it was her duty to give him one. *If I die,* she told them, *that would be Allah's wish. Our fates are written even before we are born.*

After Parveen was born, Ammi would not stop bleeding. The midwife took Ammi to the village hospital in a buffalo-pulled cart. Abbu ran behind the cart like a madman. Parul and Rehana stayed with the newborn and their aunt. Their aunt was nursing her own baby and so she gave Parveen her first breastfeeding.

Parul could not sleep that night. She prayed hard for Ammi to come back. Many times during that night, she felt Ammi's presence in the room—her light tap on her shoulder, her affectionate pinch on her nose. Once she opened her eyes and saw Ammi standing outside the window, her sari-clad form silvery against the dark sky. Parul got up and ran to the window to look out for her. But there was no one there. A black dog scurried across the courtyard. The coconut tree swayed in the wind behind the moonlit paddy fields.

Next morning, Parul found her aunt crying. "Your Ammi has become dear to Allah," she said. "She is never coming back home."

Parul looked at her in disbelief. Anger boiled inside her.

"You are lying to me. Allah will make your teeth rot and fall out," yelled Parul. Her aunt reached out to embrace her, but she bit her hand and ran.

"You are hiding my mother somewhere," she yelled out. "But don't worry, I will find her."

Parul ran barefoot down the street, searching. She looked everywhere—behind her house, in the rice fields and near the train lines. She checked the riverbanks and the empty boats tied to the ferry *ghat*, but it was as if Ammi had vanished; not a trace of her remained.

Abbu found her that night, sitting on a low tree branch, her dress soaked in tears. He carried her home in his arms and handed her over to her aunt. Her aunt wrapped a blanket around her and pointed to the sky. "Your mother is up there now. She is a star looking down at us."

"But why does she have to be a star?" sobbed Parul. "Why does she have to leave us?"

"Because your mother was exceptionally nice. She was like a *farishta*, an angel. Allah had to take her early."

Chapter 13

Every morning, at the crack of dawn, Baba's shrill whistle rang outside Mohini's door. The whistle interrupted her heavy sleep, and she stepped out of her dreams. She yawned and stretched her arms like a reluctant child. She stayed under the covers a little longer, listening to the sights and sounds outside her window. Koel and nightingales sang on her windowsill, followed by the sweet melody of the *Azan* from a nearby mosque. Metallic buckets clattered as the milkman came to make a delivery, and in the puja room a conch shell was blown three times.

As soon as the second whistle went off, Mohini dragged herself out of bed and rushed to the bathroom. Then she ran downstairs to fill up the water bottles and collect fresh towels for Baba's students. Though she had never gone back to weightlifting, she helped Baba with all the gym housekeeping duties before and after her college classes.

All around her in the adjoining rooms, Baba's students climbed out of bed, shuffled their feet and opened and closed doors. She heard them cleaning their teeth in the bathrooms—accompanied by loud grunting, coughing, and the sound of water being swooshed around in their mouths and then spit out with an elaborate "waaak thuuu." Then they formed a single file and marched to the children's park behind their house for their morning exercises. Mohini walked behind them with heavy bags of equipment flung on each shoulder. In the park, she kept a careful inventory of the equipment before passing them out to the students.

Over the years, Baba had become the joint secretary of the National Weightlifting Association and general secretary of the Bengal Weightlifting Association. He had incorporated yoga and meditation into his training routine. This fresh approach toward the sport had brought him national recognition and respect from well-known trainers. Baba wrote a couple of books on meditation and spirituality that hit the best-sellers' list. His reputation grew, and his fame attracted even more out-of-state students. Each room now accommodated four people with two sets of bunk beds. Baba converted the outdoor shed into a meditation chamber.

The group started the morning with the twelve poses of Surya Namaskar (Sun Salutation), facing the rising sun in horizontal rows. This was followed by squats and free-hand exercises. Baba walked around straightening the rows, as if he was straightening the shaft of an arrow. He tucked in the tummies and pushed on the backs. They ran a few laps around the park and rested in the shadow of the banyan tree. A few minutes later, they all got up to swing Indian clubs over their heads.

Rajkumar approached Mohini and tapped her shoulder. When she turned around, he showed her a silver medal. "I have real good news! I was runner up in the Eastern India Weightlifting Championship. I am now your Baba's favorite student... me... myself... one and only. Everyone at the prize ceremony took my photo... *takatak takatak*." Rajkumar pressed an imaginary camera shutter button with his right thumb. Mohini almost dropped the folded towels from her hand. Her head was spinning.

Seeing Rajkumar hold out the medal brought back memories of her own weightlifting days. Years ago, she had wanted the recognition of the Eastern India Championship; that medal was meant for her. She had worked for it day and night till her efforts were abruptly and unfairly stopped. Ma had clipped off her wings even before she knew how to fly.

Rajkumar flashed an arrogant smile at her. He patted his greasy pompadour and combed his sideburns. His victory threw a film over everything around her, reminding her of what she had lost.

"She is completely normal now. Behaves just like her other cousins," Ma bragged to all their relatives. "That weightlifting ghost is gone from her head." The relatives agreed with her. It was a victory for all of them—they had succeeded in taming Mohini's wayward spirit and made her bow to their decree. Mohini was now one of them, a close copy of her cousins.

Over the years, her aunts had worked energetically to rectify all her deficiencies. They had taught her to tie her hair in the newest styles, to shape her eyebrows into perfect arches and wrap saris around her with symmetrical folds and pleats. They had taken her shopping and introduced her to high-heeled shoes and matching purses. They had found the perfect shade of lipstick for her and introduced her into the world of perfumes and lotions.

Mohini had resented the kindness her aunts had showered on her. She felt like a puppet getting remodeled into a special species — "marriageable women" who will one day appeal to the other species of "marriageable men." Still, she had felt compelled to obey them, submissively, reluctantly going through the transformations till the aunts had accepted unanimously that she was almost as "feminine" as them.

"I don't recognize you these days." Baba, who had never stopped thinking of Mohini as a weightlifter, had a hard time accepting her changed appearance. "You were meant to be a star," he said. "But look at what they have done to you."

While Ma had never allowed Baba to look back, he could never figure out how to look forward to either. Like the hands of a broken clock, Baba remained helplessly locked in time. The gym had brought in a lot of talent over the years. Baba's students qualified for state, regional and national level competitions. Still, Baba found no enjoyment in their success. He stubbornly fixed his sight on Mohini, as if she signified, aside from everything else, an unfulfilled dream—and he wanted badly to live that dream.

Rajkumar grabbed Mohini's elbow. He sounded impatient. "Did you even hear a word I said? I'm the most gifted student in your Baba's gym now."

The bindings of her envy loosened, and Mohini suddenly felt pity for Rajkumar. He was obviously living in his own fantasy land. Years ago, he had removed Mohini from the gym. He had played a nasty, cold-hearted game to end Mohini's weightlifting ambitions. Despite that, in all these years, Rajkumar had failed in making a special place in Baba's heart. His moderate success in regional competitions was not enough to fulfil Baba's Olympic dream.

She threw a contemptuous look at him and walked away. She found Baba in a sand pit, demonstrating a muscle-building technique to his senior-most students. He picked up a heavy wooden beam and held it between his shoulders. Then, maintaining proper posture and body balance, he dragged the heavy load, attached to the beam, over the thick sand. His students clapped when he finished circling the whole pit. Mohini cheered too, but from the sudden pained flush on Baba's face, she knew that the exercise had left him exhausted.

Regret and pity filled her heart. Her powerfully built father, who had a reputation in his youth for being "strong as an ox," was now showing signs of slowing down. At forty-eight, Baba's hair had started to thin and turn gray, the lines between his eyebrows had deepened, and dark circles marked the contours of his eyes. Even his beard was flecked with gray and white. When Baba discussed techniques with his students in the camp, Mohini saw the slight hopelessness that surfaced in the depths of his brown eyes as his shoulders drooped slightly, and his voice lacked his earlier conviction.

"Your Baba was like the god Hanuman in his youth," Ma told Mohini. "He could lift mountains with ease." Ma recounted many stories about his colossal force, but the one Mohini liked the best took place in their neighborhood before they were married. One evening, when Ma had gotten off the tram, she saw a rickshaw that had fallen into a roadside ditch, half-buried in mud. The woman in the backseat was screaming in terror. The scrawny rickshaw-puller could not straighten the rickshaw, much less pull it out of the mud. The surrounding crowd watched helplessly.

In the end, it was decided that the local boys would ask Baba for help. Baba came soon after and climbed into the ditch until the mud reached his waist. Then, with one simple jerk, all his shoulder muscles contracting in union, his knees bending forward, he lifted the rickshaw, complete with the lady in the backseat and the scrawny rickshaw-puller hanging from the rails, out of the mud. He lowered the rickshaw gently on to the pavement and consoled the terrified lady. On her way back, Ma heard the local boys call Baba "King Kong."

Ma reminded Mohini, and perhaps herself, that the gym downstairs was the center of Baba's universe. He had always found peace in those old rooms. But for the first time, Baba could not control his temper in the gym; he got upset over small things and held on to the grudges for a very long time. Some days he even got into fights with his senior-most students and threatened to send them back home. It was as if his phenomenal talent, not having a suitable successor, had embarked on a mission of self-destruction.

Baba needed, more than anything else, a new student in his gym. Only a high-caliber student could revive his Olympic dream and give him peace of mind.

•   •   •

A couple of months went by, and the rainy season started in Kolkata. The winds pounded against that house, and the sheeting rain hammered down on the tiled roofs. The water slid down the slanted roofs and ran off like a series of small waterfalls. It collected into muddy puddles in the driveway and swirled down the open manhole. Parul had to wade through several waterlogged streets where the water came up to her knees to reach the bazaar. She came back completely drenched, looking like a scarecrow.

Meeting Rahim in the west wing was becoming increasingly difficult. The rain impeded their lovemaking. Water leaked from the big cracks in the ceiling and flooded the piano room. There were very few dry spots left on the floor. So Rahim and Parul sat cross-legged on the chairs and discussed religion and politics. The wind rattled the windows, and cement and sand trickled down from the ceiling beams.

"Are you reading the book of Hadiths that I gave you?" asked Rahim. "Islam is the only way to Allahu ta'ala. It is impossible for humanity to lead a happy life without having faith."

Parul looked at Rahim's face, buried in the inky shadows of the room. His beard had grown, and the *soorma* on the lower rim of his eyes was darker than usual. The lines around his eyes and mouth seemed to have hardened, and he looked older somehow.

"It is not enough to understand the Hadith itself. The interpretation is even more important. I want you to think critically when I teach you a Hadith—which ones are weak, which ones are contrived and which ones are accurate. Don't take this lightly, Mumtaz. Entire books have been written explaining just one Hadith. You should take your education seriously."

Parul listened in awe. *He is so calm and focused. His knowledge is deeper than the deepest sea. He is a true Muslim scholar. I am an imposter. I don't understand half the things he says. My head is full of nonsense thoughts about a wedding, children and money.*

Rahim got up and stood in front of the grand piano, gazing at it distractedly. His fingers glided across the piano's dusty black and white keys. He turned around abruptly, kicking the piano stool out of his way, and walked over to her. "Every Muslim must ultimately aim to be a jihadi." His tall form towered over her. "We have to protect our religion from the infidels."

The lantern light flickered, and Parul shivered inadvertently.

Parul asked him, "But who is an infidel? Is it just the Hindus?"

"Anyone who tries to destroy our way of life is an infidel. And there are many enemies of Islam. But America is our biggest enemy."

Rahim told her about her Muslim brothers and sisters worldwide. She learned how large the Muslim population was, how mistreated, and how targeted by non-Muslims. She learned how much Muslim youth resented being on the receiving end of American-supported and American-tolerated oppression.

"America has always shown one-sided support in favor of Israel while our Palestinian brothers and sisters continue to struggle and die," said Rahim, sounding different, as if he were reading something he'd written for his printing press.

Parul learned about the American support for tyrannical government in Egypt, Saudi Arabia, Jordan, Pakistan, and the Gulf states. She learned how the America-backed gutless dictators continue to severely beat, incarcerate and silence their own citizens.

"America has permanent military bases in our holy land and regularly uses their military to interfere in our Muslim affairs," said Rahim. "It is a global fight for us. Our struggle for self-preservation and self-respect."

Rahim was so knowledgeable. How much he read and how much he cared. *While everyone around me is thinking of the price of potatoes and fish and worrying about their own children and their own health, this man cares deeply for all Allah's sons and daughters and their struggle all over the world.*

As Parul listened to Rahim, guilt gnawed at the base of her heart. Why did she waste her time worrying about her own future? Why couldn't she have important thoughts in her mind like Rahim? How insignificant her problems were before suffering of this scale and magnitude.

"Mumtaz, our identity is like a lamp that flickers in the wind, and there is a strong wind all around. Guard your lamp from the infidels in this house, Mumtaz. Don't let them destroy your life."

Parul blinked as the meaning of his preaching made sense. She shook her head. "Ma is not like that, you know... like these infidels you just described. She does not want to harm me or destroy me."

"There you go again, you foolish girl. The question you have to ask yourself is: why won't your mistress let you practice your own religion? That is the key question. The world may be sending satellites to space, but the Hindus won't drink water from Muslim hands, in fear of losing their religion. To this day, Muslim women cannot find work in Hindu homes. Take any train in the Sealdah line and you will see Muslim women from impoverished families dressed up like Hindu women, complete with shell bangles and vermillion dust in their hair parting, coming to Kolkata to work as nurses and domestic help in Hindu homes. The moment the Hindu employer finds out the maid is Muslim, she gets fired. Why should we be subject to so much discrimination when we make up fifteen percent of the population? Why do we always have to fake an identity to find employment?"

"But Ma has no such prejudice... *Allah Kasam*. She will eat and drink from Muslim hands. She lets me wash her offering plate and light her prayer lamp in the evening. Her relatives are different. They won't come near a Muslim woman."

"Mumtaz, you don't see it, do you? Your mistress is perfectly happy to put up with all this prejudice around her as long as it does not affect her life. It is the people who appear to be unaffected and uncaring of our suffering—they are the ones committing a crime. By keeping silent and not raising her voice against a tradition of injustice carried out over centuries in this country, your Ma is as guilty as her relatives."

Listening to Rahim talk like this, something shifted inside Parul. The heaviness that sat on her chest gradually transformed into a ball of anger burning below her throat. It was as if she has finally stumbled upon the object of all her deprivation and frustration. Both Mohini and Ma had always tried to hide that fact that she was Muslim. It was a contagious disease like plague or kala-azar to them. It was worse than being an untouchable. *They think my identity will contaminate their flawless house? Their god is pure, their temples pristine, and my God is something to be ashamed of? Rahim is right. Ma has a strange way of treating people.*

• • •

That night, while dusting Ma's favorite porcelain dolls, Parul deliberately dropped and broke one of them.

"I didn't do it, Ma. It was the widow's black cat. As I was dusting, she deliberately came between my legs. I tripped, and the doll flew out of my hand."

Ma could hardly hold back her tears as she gathered the broken pieces.

"I had this doll for thirty years, Parul. I cannot replace it. How could you be so careless?"

"It was the cat, Ma, I am telling you. That cat is actually an evil witch in disguise."

"Stop that nonsense talk. I don't want to hear another word from you. Go do your own work."

"Yes, Ma. Whatever you say...." Parul shrugged.

Breaking Ma's precious doll, and making her cry, gave way to a feeling of satisfaction that took Parul by surprise. It started at the edges and expanded inward till it felt like a tidal wave sweeping through her whole body. It was difficult for her to suppress a smile even as she continued to apologize to Ma. She considered just how long she must have wanted to do something like this and never found the courage to do it. Now she felt a charge run through her entire body, electrifying her.

You cannot control everything I do. I am not an obedient dog that I will always wag my tail. From now on, I will say what religion I want to practice. You will not choose for me, Parul whispered to herself. Her shoulders relaxed, and she exhaled deeply, as if she had been holding back the stale air in her lungs for years. She felt lighter somehow. *It is the beginning of something new.*

Chapter 14

"Quick, Parul*di*, get Ma and Baba here," said Mohini, her face glued to the television screen. "They need to see this."

"What is happening, Mohini?" Parul pushed away her bucket of brown water and mop and ran to the television screen. "Why are you screaming like a madwoman?"

"Don't ask questions now. Just get Baba and Ma. This is too important."

Parul looked at the screen. All she could see was a very tall building and thick, black smoke spurting out from the upper floors. She looked at Mohini, confused. "All those floors are on fire? Are there people inside?"

"Of course, there are people inside," snapped Mohini. "The TV reporter said something like a plane crashed into this building. They heard a big boom and now this."

"Is this in Kolkata?"

"Silly, Parul*di*! Does this look like Kolkata to you? Have you seen a building of this size in Kolkata? This is Manhattan. Do you understand Manhattan? No? I guess not. Do you understand U.S..A.?"

Parul shook her head. Mohini pressed her fingers against her temples as if she could already feel a headache coming. "America. Now do you understand?"

Parul moved closer to the screen. It was then, as if by magic, another plane appeared on the screen, moving slowly toward the back of the smoking building. At first, she could only make out the TV reporters screaming in English in the background. Then Mohini jumped up and down on the bed. "Oh my god, what's happening?

That looks like a big military plane. Parul*di*, get Ma and Baba, please. This is horrible."

But Parul felt someone had glued her feet to the floor. She couldn't turn away from the television. She watched the plane again and again, like a child hooked to a video game. The screen filled once more with dark black smoke. The smoke was brittle; it fragmented and collapsed. Emergency vehicles lined up below the building. Parul felt sick. She crouched on the floor on her haunches and grabbed her knees to stop them from trembling. A figure appeared at a broken window very high up. He leaned over and came down like an arrow in free-fall. Two other figures jumped, holding hands, swimming in the air like tiny insects. Mohini put her hands over her ears and screamed. Baba and Ma came running into the room. They stood on either side of Mohini and tried to console her.

• • •

The next day, it was clear to everyone in the house that a big city in America had come under a Muslim terrorist attack. Relatives stopped by to talk to Baba and Ma. Parul served them sweet tea and puffed rice.

Uncles and aunts fell on Baba's newspaper hungrily, devouring the news. Mohini sat as if glued to them, listening carefully to their analysis.

"*Aree*, we all know that Islam is not a religion of peace," said Baba's second cousin, and the rest looked grave.

"With that, Quran, who can be surprised?" said his wife. "It openly calls for the beheading of nonbelievers."

"Cruelty is in their blood," said Pishimoni. "It started from the Babar time... the looting and killings. Didn't stop after that." She said it with such conviction that it created an absoluteness, a reality that need not be questioned.

"Who can forget what they did to us in Bangladesh in 1947?" said the man with gray hair, as if he was jumping to his favorite topic. "I was a small boy then—hardly six or seven years old. When the riots started in our village, they burned down the Hindu houses and seized all Hindu land. Our family ran out in the middle of the night and boarded a small freighter. The freighter was packed... thousands of people, all trying to cross over to India. How could a boat like that handle such a load? One by one people fell off into the water and drowned before our eyes."

More than a few around the room sucked their breath in shock.

Parul shifted her weight uneasily from one foot to the other. Their accusation made her feel uneasy. How could they think all Muslims were to blame for the actions of a few?

Parul fully expected Mohini to protest. She was always different from her relatives. Yet when she looked at Mohini, she didn't appear to be flustered by the prejudice that had pervaded the room. Instead, she nodded.

Around midday, the relatives got up to leave. "The Muslims will pay for it. No one messes with the mighty Americans," they said. "It is a matter of time."

To Parul, their tone suggested an eagerness for this retribution. A chill ran down her spine.

• • •

Later that afternoon, when the activity inside the house died down, Parul slipped downstairs to meet Rahim.

"They said the Muslims did this."

Rahim flipped through the red and green files piled up on his desk. He didn't look up. Parul grabbed his arm and gave it a good shake. "Say something. Why would Muslims cause so much suffering? My heart wants to shatter into a thousand pieces."

"It was bound to happen one day," said Rahim quietly.

"Is that all you have to say? Is your heart made of stone?"

He pushed back his chair and crossed his legs. He appeared to look off into the distance with glazed, heavy-lidded eyes. "Don't get me wrong, Mumtaz. I feel the pain of the victims in this attack, but I also wonder who is feeling the pain of 'the victims of American aggression'?"

She grabbed the back of his chair and attempted to spin him around. "Don't say it. I can't hear it today."

"Mumtaz, your sympathy is clouding your judgement." Rahim grew more animated as he spoke. "I have already told you the U.S. is soaked in blood. The world over, they take and destroy and look down on anyone not born and raised there, of their same color and religion. All while they lead lives of corruption and basest sin." Rahim creaked and popped his knuckles as if attempting to break them.

For once, Parul did not want to listen to him. She walked around the room like a zombie. "It was horrible," she whispered at last. "There were people hanging from the buildings. Some were jumping from windows. I saw them with my own eyes." With the end of her sari, Parul wiped away the sweat from her forehead and eyebrows.

Rahim stood up and moved closer to her. He removed his skullcap and held it tightly to his chest. "You have seen nothing yet. Now you will see what the Americans do to our Muslim brothers. There will be backlash for sure. Save a few tears for your own brothers, Mumtaz. This is just the beginning."

Chapter 15

On October 7, 2001, when Mohini was in her second year of college, the United States, supported by some NATO countries, including the United Kingdom and Australia, as well as other allies, began an invasion of Afghanistan under Operation Enduring Freedom. The invasion was launched to capture Osama bin Laden, who was accused of masterminding the September 11, 2001, attacks. In the summer of 2003, Baba got an invitation to teach at the Olympic Training Center (OTC) in Colorado Springs.

We train some of the planet's best weight-lifters. Not only is our facility one of the best in the country, it's one of the best in the world. We have read your book, Mindful Muscle, *on meditative healing and yoga practices in professional weight-lifting. We feel our athletes need to master some of these techniques to increase their strength, concentration and overall sense of well-being. We are extending an invitation to you to join our camp this summer. If you accept the invitation, we will make travel arrangements and discuss suitable compensation.*

The letter came in the gym mailbox, and Mohini was the first one to open it. She read and reread the letter a thousand times, unable to believe her eyes. Then she ran to the meditation room, where Baba was in Lotus Pose with his eyes closed. She pulled him up and did a joyous dance all around the room, holding his hands. With a huge smile on her face, she leaned up on tiptoe and kissed his cheek.

"What are you doing, Mohini? Have you lost your mind? You disrupted my meditation. What kind of childish behavior is this?" Baba scolded her. But when she showed Baba the letter, he, too, couldn't believe his eyes. They both rushed to the kitchen to give Ma the good news.

Ma cleaned her oily hands with the end of her sari and read the letter. "This is such an honor. I must tell everyone in the neighborhood that you are going to America. They will die of envy," she said.

•   •   •

The next day, Mohini was still in bed when she heard Ma and Parul talking outside her door.

"Parul, get two suitcases from the storeroom," said Ma.

"Why, Ma?" asked Parul.

"Your *babu* is going to America. Didn't I always tell you that your *babu* is a big man now? Not only people in India know him, but now he is getting invitations from foreign countries." Ma sounded breathless with excitement.

"Ma, ask him not to go. I don't trust those Americans," Parul said in a soft, apathetic voice.

"What nonsense, Parul! Have you totally lost your mind?" asked Ma with an astonished laugh. "We should be flattered that your *babu* got this position. Instead, you are jinxing his trip?"

"Sorry, Ma."

"You should be," said Ma. "Oh, go now and get those suitcases. I don't have all day."

•   •   •

Baba came back from America after two months with lots of gifts in his two suitcases. Mohini unzipped the suitcases, plunged her arms inside and squealed. "So many beautiful gifts. Which one is mine?"

"Ah, wait. Let your mother see. I have something for everyone."

Ma came close and squatted beside the boxes. She picked up the soaps and lotions and smelled them one by one. Then she pulled out the costume jewelry, shawls, and purses. "Excellent selection. It is what I wanted," she said.

Mohini pulled out a yellow jacket and tried it on before the mirror. It fit her perfectly. She turned around and hugged Baba.

Parul came into the room with her bamboo duster. She seemed to glance at the open suitcases but showed no interest in their content. Baba pulled out a woolen blanket and handed it to her. "Use it in the winter. The terrace room gets very cold."

Parul took the gift with no semblance of gratitude.

What's wrong with her? thought Mohini. *She has a poor attitude these days.*

Early in the morning, two days later, Mohini and her parents sat in the bedroom, where Baba had called a family meeting. Baba looked slightly anxious. He paced back and forth and avoided looking at Ma.

"What is it?" Ma snapped. "Just tell us. I am late for my morning *puja*."

Baba cleared his throat and began. "Understand, Mohini's Ma, the OTC Colorado camp, really appreciated my help. Their weight-lifters liked my cleansing yoga and healing meditation techniques. They were really sad to see me leave." Baba sighed and paused. "Anyway, that is a story for another time. Today, I need to tell you about this twenty-one-year-old boy, Michael, who I met at this camp. This boy, understand, Mohini's Ma, has been blessed by Goddess Saraswati herself. He is so bright and so gifted—he could easily represent the U.S. in the Olympics, even bring in a medal, but the poor boy is now struck with a terrible tragedy. He lost his father in the Afghanistan war. The memory of his father haunts him and he wants to give up his career in weight-lifting and withdraw from the camp."

"*Aha re,*" said Ma. "So young to face such a tragedy."

"Yes." Baba nodded. "I knew you would understand, Mohini's Ma. When the boy told me about his father... I knew what I had to do." Baba poured himself a glass of water and continued. "I made a decision. I knew in my heart if anyone could help this boy overcome this stress, it was me. I called his mother and discussed her son's future. I told her I could help her son get his motivation back."

Ma's mouth opened wide in disbelief. "But why would you say such a thing?" she asked. "The boy is a foreigner. He lives so far away."

"Yes, yes. You're absolutely right. How could I help him from thousands of miles away? So, I told his mother to send the boy to my camp... here in Kolkata."

"Send him here... in our house?" cried Ma.

"Yes, that's what I told her."

Curiosity bubbled in Mohini's stomach. "And the mother of this boy... Did she agree?" she asked him eagerly.

"No, no, not at all. It was very hard to convince her. She was mad at me for even asking. She had just lost her husband in a foreign country, and she would not let her son leave America. She hung up on me the first few times I called her."

"So you gave up?" Ma sounded hopeful.

Baba paused for a moment. One corner of his mouth twitched nervously.

"At first I did. What could I have done then? If the mother does not seek my services, I cannot offer them to her son. So I gave up trying. But right around the time I was getting ready to leave, Michael's mother, Nancy, came to see me in person. She was short and pale and clearly in a lot of pain. 'Take my son with you,' she pleaded. 'He now wants to join the military, just like his father. He wants to go to Afghanistan where his father was killed. I cannot bear it... I cannot let him join the military. He is not listening to me... my boy. Save him, Mr. Sen. Take him to India.'"

Mohini leaped up and grabbed Baba's arm. "And the boy? What did he say?"

"At first the boy would not listen. He kept talking about Afghanistan and how much he wants to go there, but I persuaded him in the end. I told him, if he does not like our camp, I will send him home right away." Baba sucked in his breath before pushing out the next few words. "The boy will come here in two weeks."

Silence. Baba had dropped a bombshell, and Mohini knew the explosion would inevitably follow. She stepped in front of Baba as if to shield him.

The first notes of a moan escaped Ma's lips. "An American boy! Are you out of your mind?" she whimpered. "You want to bring an American boy to this house? Do you think he can live with us, eat our food and be happy?"

"*Arre*, why are you getting so tense?" Baba kneeled on the floor beside Ma and took her hand. "There was a time when the British lived in our country. They loved our mangoes, our tea and our hospitality."

"You are comparing the British with this twenty-year-old American boy? You think he can adjust to our middle-class lifestyle?"

"Mohini's Ma, have some faith. This boy needs us. Give him a chance; it is a matter of his career."

Ma closed her eyes and massaged her temples as if she felt a headache coming. Mohini glanced at her nervously. The breeze from the open window touched Mohini's cheeks and played with her hair. In the distance, she could hear the words of a prayer song. The teacher and her niece had started their morning *puja* next door.

Ma got up and closed the window. Her black eyes glittered when she looked at Baba. "You want to be charitable, that is your problem. I will not take any extra trouble for this boy... that much I am telling you. If he can live here like a regular rice-and-fish-eating Bengali boy, then he is welcome, but if he throws tantrums, you have to put him on the plane back to his mother."

"Okay, Mohini's Ma. I accept your conditions." Baba's shoulders relaxed, and he smiled. "Now forget your anger and make me a cup of first-class tea."

• • •

On the day of Michael's arrival, Mohini was surprised to see Baba rent an air-conditioned car. He got it washed till the metallic frame sparkled. He hung a garland of marigold flowers in the rearview mirror and lit some incense sticks on the dashboard to add mild fragrance to the interior.

"Get into the back seat," he ordered Mohini. "We don't want to keep the American boy waiting at the airport." Baba sat next to the driver, twiddling with the radio knob. As the car groaned and jerked forward, notes of Western classical music filled the air.

It was the week before the Durga Puja festival, with clear skies and fluffy white clouds. A gentle breeze came in from the window, caressing Mohini's cheeks and ruffling her hair. Brightly colored marquees had been set in almost every alley—some were still under construction, and others had beautiful images of Goddess Durga already installed with colorful lighting and booming loudspeakers.

Baba halted at Flurys at Park Street to buy boxes of chocolate pastries for Michael. He asked Mohini to hold the boxes on her lap all the way to the airport. Mohini found it difficult to understand why he was fussing so much over a single student visiting from America. She had never seen Baba so excited. He suddenly had the energy and the enthusiasm of a child. When Mohini complained the pastries might ruin her dress, Baba glared at her and told her sharply that she ought to have known how worldwide they respect Indians for their hospitality, and their American visitor would expect no less from them.

Mohini sat in the backseat of the red Maruti car with the boxes pressed against her chest, scowling as she looked out the window. As the car raced down Kolkata Street, she fell into a resentful silence. It was true that she had wished for a talented student in Baba's gym. She had wanted Baba to get back his fervor, revive his old passion. Still, Baba was taking a bit more interest in the foreign boy than she would have liked him to. The thought of sharing her father with the American boy made her shudder. *Things are happening too fast*, she thought. *I am not ready.*

By the time they reached the airport, the passengers had cleared their immigration and customs formalities and trickled out the automatic doors. Relatives and friends smiled and hugged them as they walked out with their loaded trolleys.

"There he is," cried Baba, pointing to a golden-haired boy with a backpack and a rolling suitcase. Baba pushed past the crowd, waving frantically to attract his attention. "Here, here... Michael, this way... this way." Baba jumped up and down on the pavement, waving his handkerchief. Michael turned his head, squinted, and made his way toward them almost reluctantly.

Mohini was shocked by how handsome the American boy was. He was taller than most of Baba's Indian students, his hair a golden blaze of yellow and his eyes the color of seaweed. She stared at him with her mouth open. To be fair to Mohini, she was not the only one staring at him — a few other heads had also turned in his direction because of his startling, good looks.

"Welcome... welcome to India, young man. How was your flight?" Baba hurried toward him and rapped him affectionately on the back.

"It was alright." Michael shrugged. "Got little sleep though."

"Oh, don't worry about sleep. Mohini's Ma has made first class arrangements for you at the camp. You will sleep like a baby."

If Michael was confused about who "Mohini's Ma" was, he didn't show it. Nor did he glance at Mohini, standing behind Baba, with any interest or seek an introduction with her. The sun was blazing hot in the sky, and Mohini felt foolish standing on the pavement, balancing three boxes of melting pastries in her hands. She glared at Baba for making her look silly in front of the foreign boy. "Can we go now?" she asked.

"Oh Mohini," said Baba. "What are you waiting for? Give Michael the pastries. The boy is hungry after his long plane ride." He snatched the boxes from Mohini's hand and held them out to Michael.

"No, Mr. Sen. They served us breakfast right before we landed."

"So what? You are a young man. This is the time to eat. At your age, I could chew on iron and steel balls and digest them easily. Eat, eat... Don't be shy."

"Really not hungry." Michael gently pushed away the box Baba offered him.

This time, Mohini gritted her teeth to suppress an outburst. "Did you hear him, Baba? He doesn't want your pastries. Can we go home now?" She turned around and marched toward the car. Baba picked up Michael's suitcase and ushered him into the crowded parking lot.

Michael climbed into the back seat next to Mohini. He seemed preoccupied, almost unaware of her presence by his side. Sitting so close to him, she was aware of his masculine smell. Even after almost seventeen hours on the plane, the American smelled of citrus and an ocean breeze. Suddenly, Mohini had an irresistible urge to sniff him all over. She leaned toward him and then quickly recoiled as if hit with an electric shock. She was mortified at her own imbecilic behavior.

She stole a quick look at his face. Much to her relief, Michael had brought out his headphones to listen to his iPod, tapping his foot and drumming his finger. He remained oblivious to her presence.

Even as Mohini pretended to stare out the window, she puzzled over the American boy and his lack of friendliness. Why? Why had he not once smiled at her? Why had he not noticed her? Was she that ordinary looking that she didn't deserve a second glance from him? Mohini touched her hair and straightened her dress. Then she chided herself for her foolishness. Why would she care if the American boy looked at her or not? He was Baba's student, and that's all he was. She had nothing to do with him expect the usual housekeeping duties she did for all the students in the camp. Other than that, she could see no reason why she would have to think about him at all after this car ride.

The car rolled through their gates, and the driver brought it to a dramatic halt. Baba's students, neighbors, and some curious onlookers had all assembled on the gravelly driveway. They were all eager to see Baba's foreign student, who had come all the way from America.

Mohini climbed out first and held the door open for Michael. Michael climbed out, slowly, and leaned against the car, chewing gum and listening to his iPod.

Suddenly, all together, Baba's students surrounded him. "What's Arnold Schwarzenegger like? Have you met him?"

"... and Chad Vaughn? Are you his friend?"

"Stop bothering him," Baba scolded them. "He is tired."

*   *   *

Ma seemed to have put aside her fear of having a foreign student in the camp. Mohini found her outside the camp rooms holding a puja plate filled with flowers, sandalwood paste and rice grains. Baba shot her a quick wink, and smiling broadly, proceeded to introduce her to Michael.

"Meet Mohini's mother. She can understand English but can't follow your American accent very well. So you must speak to her slowly," said Baba.

Mohini turned to look at Michael then, for she wanted to see how he greeted Ma. He was confused at first, she could tell, because he put his hand forward, possibly to shake Ma's hand, and then, seeing the *puja* plate in her hand, pulled it back quickly. Almost as an afterthought, he leaned forward again and put an arm around her shoulder, giving Ma an awkward hug.

Ma's eyes grew wide with disbelief. Her mouth opened, and she gasped.

"Oh, I'm sorry," Michael stepped away quickly. His cheeks flushed. "I probably shouldn't have done that."

Mohini pretended to cough to disguise the bubble of laughter she couldn't suppress. Baba flapped his arm to keep her quiet.

"Not to worry," Baba told Michael. "Mohini's Ma has never traveled to the west. In fact, she has never left India. So she doesn't know how Americans greet each other."

Ma recovered quickly and smiled at Michael. "It is all right. You're like my son. I was surprised, that's all." She dipped her finger into the sandalwood paste and applied a *Tilak* on Michael's forehead. Sprinkling some rice grains and flowers on top of the Tilak, she said, "... here in India, this is how we welcome our guests. You are a part of this family now. If you need anything, all you have to do is ask."

Michael was given the best room in the camp—a medium-sized, airy room overlooking the side garden. There were velvety curtains on the window, a new Dunlopillo mattress, and a large air cooler near his bed. Mohini knew Baba had put enormous effort into acquiring these rarities for him. He would do whatever he could to make Michael feel at home.

Walking around the room, Mohini recognized the bronze vase on the bedside table filled with red and white flowers. Years back, Ma had received it as a wedding gift. The vase always stayed locked in her steel almirah and was brought out only for very special occasions. *Even Ma is trying is trying to impress the foreign boy*, thought Mohini unhappily.

As soon as he entered the room, Michael threw down his backpack, yawned and fell on the bed.

"The poor boy is tired. He needs to sleep," announced Ma.

Immediately, Baba shepherded everyone out of the room. Mohini followed Baba's other students as they marched out. Before closing the door, Baba pointed to the black telephone on the desk. "Don't forget to call you mother, Michael. She must be so worried about you. You can make international calls from that one."

"We will send lunch to your room. No need to come upstairs," said Ma.

Mohini clenched her teeth. Michael was clearly getting the royal treatment in their house. Her parents were so eager to please him. Having a foreign boy in the house was perhaps a form of entertainment for them, about which they would talk for days with their neighbors and friends, a welcome distraction in their quiet suburban life where nothing much happened.

●　●　●

Later that evening, Mohini went to Michael's room to give him a white bedcover, a clean towel, a bar of soap and a few hangers for his clothes. He was sitting on his bed, writing in a journal and playing with his iPod. In the dim light of the table lamp, she could see the muscles of his arms and chest defined in shadowy dips and shimmering planes.

Mohini closed the curtains, put the laundry hamper next to his wardrobe, and lit the mosquito repellent coil. She put down a plate of pastries and a bottle of Coca Cola on his desk. His eyes followed her around the room silently.

"There is bottled drinking water in the fridge. The tap water here is not good for you," said Mohini.

Michael said nothing. He went back to writing.

After closing Michael's door behind her, Mohini ran upstairs to look for Baba. She found him standing before the bathroom mirror, trimming his mustache. It was a delicate matter, slicing off exact amounts from either side of his nose.

Mohini didn't wait. She barged into the bathroom and announced loudly, "Baba, the American boy does not talk to me."

Baba's hand trembled, and he accidentally sliced off a heavier chunk from one side. He looked at her in dismay. "Now look at what you have done!"

"Did you hear what I said, Baba? That boy is so snobbish... I don't like him one bit."

Baba smiled. "Give him some time, Mohini. You know he has just lost his father. He is still recovering."

"I know all that. But a 'thank you' would be nice after I did so much work for him."

The smile disappeared from Baba's face. He put down his scissors and turned sharply to look at her. "Maybe I did not make myself clear," said Baba. "The boy is here to heal and get stronger. He is still in shock. You cannot expect him to behave normally right away. I don't want you to say anything that will upset him."

"I won't, Baba, don't worry. But between us, I think he has a very arrogant attitude. It is as if he is just barely putting up with us."

"Mohini." Baba raised his voice. "If I hear Michael complain about anything in this house, I will hold you responsible. You will give him the things he needs without bothering him. Is that clear?"

"Do I have a choice?" Mohini jutted her lower lip out in a pout and left the room.

• • •

The next morning, Baba asked Mohini to give Michael a tour of the house. Mohini tried to protest at once—she couldn't stand the idea of having to face the rude, unappreciative boy again. "Just do what you're told," Baba said, leveling a glare at her.

Reluctantly, Mohini went to look for Michael in his camp room. She knocked on his door, and he opened it slowly and leaned against it, rubbing his eyes with his fists. His t-shirt stretched tightly over his broad shoulders and across his chest, and the muscles on his naked arms rippled and writhed. Despite herself, Mohini felt the stirring of a reluctant awe.

She swallowed hard. "Did you sleep well?" she asked.

He shook his head. "Dogs," he said. "Too many in the back alley. They barked all night."

Then he stretched his hands and yawned. "I need to wash myself."

Mohini led him to the camp bathrooms, where Baba's students were brushing their teeth and taking their morning bath. As soon as they entered, the boys, curious about the newly arrived American, stopped to talk to Michael. They asked him a great many questions about his life in America. Michael was courteous, but faintly aloof. He seemed rapt in thought, and although he answered some of their questions, he showed little or no interest in getting to know them.

Mohini showed him the corner bathroom that Baba had relegated to him for his daily use. She pointed out the tin buckets and tin mugs. "We don't have hot water and bathtubs like your America. You will have to use a bucket and a mug to take your bath." Michael said nothing, but he stared gloomily at the wet floor and chipped walls. Then he stepped inside uncertainly and closed the door.

When Michael came out, he looked wide awake, smelling of fresh soap and aftershave.

Mohini led him around the house, pointing out the rooms upstairs, rooms downstairs, terrace and gardens. She explained to him why the rooms of the west wing were unexpectedly closed and remained so year-round. "We don't enter that part of the house," she told Michael. "It has become very unsafe."

When they came downstairs to the courtyard, Mohini pointed at the printing press. "That place belongs to the evil widow. She is nothing but trouble. Never cross this courtyard and go over to her side."

Michael made a sound that sounded like an affirmation, but when she looked at him, she wasn't at all sure that he had listened to her.

Finally, she took him to the children's park behind the house. She showed him the Indian clubs, the sandpit, and the climbing ropes that hung from tall poles. On the edge of the park was Baba's prized possession—an enormous wheel that rested on the brick wall. "This is the Persian wheel, which, in some parts of India, people use to draw water from wells. It takes a couple of bullocks or camels to make the wheel turn. But our students turn the shaft of this wheel to harden their muscles." She paused and looked at Michael. "We may not have all the modern equipment like your American gyms, but our ancient Indian techniques can do miracles."

This time Michael looked at her with mocking eyes, and his mouth twisted into a humorless smile. "Sometimes I feel someone put me in a time capsule and sent me back a hundred years," he muttered.

Anger bubbled inside Mohini. *Obviously, Baba's gym was too out-of-date for the fancy American.* Tossing her braid over her shoulder, she walked away from the insufferable boy.

Over the next few days, Mohini avoided direct interaction with Michael. Instead, she eavesdropped on his conversations and watched him from behind doors and windows. Michael seemed to have a great deal of trouble adjusting to the way of life in their house. He found the rooms too hot, the food spicy, the crows noisy, and the people nosy. Mohini took great pleasure in his discomfort.

Ma, however, toiled endlessly to make the foreign boy feel comfortable. Mohini saw her resisting the urge to spice up her curries with green chilies, something she had done all her life. She instructed Parul to buy boneless fishes from the market. She turned up the ceiling fan even on cooler days and added ice to Michael's water to keep him from sweating profusely during his meals. But all her efforts seemed to be lost on him. He ended up teary-eyed after each meal and sometimes found the food so exotic that he had to run to the bathroom to throw up.

Then, one evening, when Mohini was doing her homework and Baba was reading the newspaper, Ma burst into the room and snatched the newspaper from Baba's hands. "What am I supposed to do with this, Michael?" she demanded. "I can't even add a bit of ginger to the *daal*. It makes him cry. And he can't stand the smell of asafetida... says it smells like human sweat. Have you heard anything more bizarre?"

Baba raised his eyebrows with a very amused expression on his face. "Then give him something he will like. Something he had at home."

Ma stared at him, wide-eyed, speechless. She turned around to face Mohini. "Did you hear that, Mohini? Did you hear what your father just said?" she cried. "He now wants me to cook American food for Michael. He will bring anyone and everyone to this house and expect the wife to feed them."

Mohini pouted. "Baba only thinks of Michael these days. Everyone else is invisible."

Ma swiveled back to Baba and shook her finger at him. "Tell your Michael that we are ordinary middle-class Bengalis. We can't buy him fancy American cakes and pastries every day."

Baba got up and placed his hand on Ma's shoulder to calm her down. "Why are you making a mountain of a molehill?" he asked wearily. "Michael will adjust in a few days. Give him a little time, that's all. He is made of very tough mettle, this American boy of ours. All we have to do is rub a little, and he will sparkle."

Mohini's heart sank. It was futile to argue with Baba. He had already put Michael on the pedestal and was ready to overlook all his flaws.

Nothing could change Baba's mind.

Chapter 16

The day after Michael arrived in the house, Parul burst into Rahim's room. She was breathless.

"I don't have time to talk now. Can't you hear the *Azan* coming from the Mosque? I have to pray," Rahim said.

"But I need to tell you something. It is urgent." Parul's face was hot with excitement.

"It can wait. Prayer comes first."

Parul stepped forward and grabbed his sleeve. "You won't believe what I am about to tell you."

"I said it can wait."

Parul ignored his warning. She feared her stomach would burst open if she didn't get the information out. "Baba brought back an American boy with him. His father died in the Afghanistan war."

Rahim's body stilled for a moment. A strange look came over his face. "An American boy in this house?"

"Yes, I saw him with my own eyes. He moved into a training camp room. The room near the garden."

"So he is on the first floor with me?"

"Yes."

"Who told you about his father?"

"Mohini."

"How old is he?"

"Oh, that I don't know. It is hard to guess the age of white people. But he is young—maybe my age or a little older."

Rahim sighed and looked up at the sky.

"*Eh* Allah, look at your glory, your grace. This poor lost girl wanted your forgiveness. Instead, you showed her the path to paradise. Your clemency has no boundaries... knows no limit. You are an ocean of kindness."

"I don't understand," said Parul.

"You will now kill two birds with one stone."

"What bird, what stone? Why are you talking in riddles?"

"Shhh, be patient. I have something to show you."

Rahim reached into his drawer. "These are Urdu newspaper cuttings from the Iraq war. The Americans killed our Muslim brothers and sisters in Afghanistan and now they are slaughtering them in Iraq. They are killing Muslim babies and Muslim children. They drop bombs in the darkness. The hospitals are full of burned bodies. Some of the dead are so burned that their flesh has melted into their bones. Their faces are beyond recognition."

Parul picked up the photos and her hands trembled. The pages of the newspaper featured maimed and bloodied children whose bodies had been torn apart by bombs. Their limbs and heads laid scattered near their dismembered bodies. She dropped the newspaper and ran to the outside tap to throw up, holding on to her stomach, afraid that some of her organs would spill out with her vomit. She washed her face and wiped it with the end of her sari. *Eh Allah*, she thought, *what kind of animals are these people? What had these children done to deserve such a brutal end of life?*

Rahim stood behind her and touched her shoulder. "I told you, Mumtaz, there will be backlash. The Americans are bloodthirsty."

"How can they do this? To our people..." whispered Parul.

"They call all civilian deaths collateral damage. Only the Americans know what that means. Insha'Allah, we will stand together against these infidels."

Rahim now sat very close to Parul and turned her chin to face him. "Now listen to me carefully, Mumtaz. An American boy coming to this house has a very special meaning. An ordinary girl like you is called to take part in something bigger and holier, far more grand than your lowly maid work. You will bring harm to the American boy, and, in doing so, you will shame the infidel family. You will kill two birds with one stone. You will do all Muslim brothers and sisters proud, Parul. You are going to fulfill His wish."

Parul thought of the American boy, with his broad shoulders, muscular body, and blonder-than-blond hair. Everything about him was expensive—his T-shirts, his haircut, his branded sneakers. His teeth were evenly shaped, his cheeks and chin red and round, and he always smelled fresh. He slept on a Dunlopillo mattress at night in a room that was cooled artificially just for him. Parul picked up the newspaper again. The pictures of malnourished bodies with ashen skin, swollen heads, and terrified eyes leaped at her. Tears formed at the corner of her eyes. She went to Rahim's desk and touched the Quran. "I swear by the Quran that I'll take revenge." Before she closed the door, she turned and looked at Rahim. "You'll see what happens to the American boy now."

Chapter 17

The next day, Mohini was woken by heavy banging on her door. The feeble frame shook, and the rusty hinges threatened to give way. Mohini sat up, startled, and instinctively reached for the heavy paperweight on her desk. Baba and Ma rushed into her room, and they all exchanged fearful looks.

"Mohini, Mr. Sen, Mrs. Sen, can you let me in?" This time, Michael's voice accompanied the banging.

Baba opened the door as quickly as he could. "What's the matter, son? Did you see a ghost?"

"They're everywhere," Michael said, panting. "It's like an alien invasion. They've taken over my room."

"What are you talking about?" asked Mohini, shuffling forward behind Baba, who blocked her view.

"Roaches! It's like a fucking living carpet on the floor of my room."

Mohini rocked back on her heels. It was true that the house was old and occasionally roaches had found their way into the camp rooms, but it had never felt like an invasion. How could this happen?

Baba took Michael's arm and gently guided him to a chair. Ma poured him a glass of water.

Panting slightly, Michael explained how, while sleeping in his room downstairs, he had felt something crawling up his leg. He leaped out of the bed and reached for the light switch. The floor was swarming with tiny brown cockroaches moving in all directions, forming constellations and then dispersing. Some were crawling into the cupboard, and some were climbing up his bed.

"No," Ma whimpered, her hands flying to her mouth. "How is that possible?"

Mohini was about to run downstairs to look at Michael's room when Parul walked in, yawning and rubbing her eyes. "What happened?" she asked. "I heard loud noises."

Ma gripped her shoulder and pulled her close. "Tell me something, Parul. Do you clean the camp rooms these days?"

"Of course, Ma. I sweep and mop every bit of the camp floor."

"Then tell me, why did Michael find roaches in his room?"

"Roaches?" Parul looked at Ma in astonishment.

"A hundred roaches," said Ma. "Look at the boy... how frightened he is."

Mohini carefully looked away from Michael and covered her mouth. The thought of Michael, with his elephant-like body and rippling muscles, scared by a bunch of tiny roaches, was enough to make her burst into helpless laughter.

"I don't know where they came from," said Parul.

"Don't look so innocent," snapped Ma. "Because of your laziness, this house is so filthy. Where is your mind these days? What must the foreign boy think of us? That we can't even keep our house clean?"

"Ma, you are blaming me for nothing. This is a hundred-year-old rickety house. The cockroaches keep coming through all the cracks and crevices in the floor. How can I stop them? You tell me," said Parul.

"You always have a thousand excuses. Have you ever seen roaches in a clean house? Now go get some Baygon spray and hit them with it."

"We don't have any spray."

"Then run to the store and get it. Sweep up the dead ones and throw them in the janitor's cart outside."

Poor Paruldi, thought Mohini. *Even though she sweeps and scrubs the camp rooms at least twice a day, she still gets blamed for the roaches.*

Later, Baba, Ma, and Mohini all waited for their afternoon tea at the dining room table. Baba and Ma talked enthusiastically and banged their fists on the table to make their points. The salt and pepper shakers trembled, and the empty teacups jumped on the saucers. Mohini remained quiet, secretly enjoying Michael's distress. The widow's cat lay curled at her feet like a black furry ball. Its tail circled its body, and the tip touched its forehead.

"This is a disaster," said Baba between clenched teeth. "Never have I seen so many crawling creatures in one room. It is almost like someone brought them in a bag and let them loose on the floor."

"Only an enemy could do such a thing," said Ma.

"Looks like we have an enemy in our own house." Baba sighed. "It must be the printing-press widow."

Ma passed a plate of ginger cookies to Baba. "What would the widow gain by letting cockroaches in Michael's room?"

"Oh, I think she just wants to punish us for suing her. This is her revenge." Baba picked up a cookie and crushed it between his fingers. The crumbs spilled on his clothes. The widow's cat jumped onto his lap to lick the crumbs. Baba pushed it away and glared at Mohini. "I don't want that evil woman's cat to come upstairs, do you understand? Keep it away from me."

Mohini pouted and chewed the end of her braid. *What was there to get so upset about?* She thought. *Why would you ever punish a poor cat for its owner's misdeeds?*

Parul brought in a pot of Darjeeling tea and golden samosas from the kitchen. She added generous amount of milk and sugar to each cup before pouring out the tea with a strainer. As she passed out the cups, beads of sweat sparkled on her forehead and nose. She had just finished cleaning and spraying the camp rooms. It was pretty hard labor, and Parul was surely exhausted.

As soon as Parul left the room, Ma moved her chair closer to the table. She lowered her voice. "If you ask me, I still think it is Parul's laziness that is turning this house into a giant dust bin." She pointed to a single string of cobweb glistening in a ray of light. "Dirt and filth is all over the house."

"You blame Parul for everything these days." Baba wiped off the oil from the samosa before dipping it into sweet tamarind chutney. He spoke with his mouth half full. "*Are,* she has caused no problems in a while. She listens to everything you say. She does not step out of the house unless you give her permission. So why are you still mad at her?"

"I find it difficult to trust her. It is as if she is hiding something from me. I see it in her eyes, but when I ask her, she denies any wrongdoing."

Baba turned to Mohini. "Do you agree with your mother?"

"Impossible," Mohini interjected eagerly. "Parul*di* is such a gentle person, and she loves our family. She would do nothing to hurt our guest."

Mohini's answer made Baba smile. "See what I'm saying, Mohini's Ma?" He thumped his fist on the table. "You're obsessed with Parul. Let go a little."

"Yes, yes, I'm the one who is crazy. Your Parul is so innocent. She can do nothing wrong." Ma scowled at him. "You two, father and daughter, always team up against me."

Baba reached across the table and touched Ma's hand. "What Parul does in her own time is not our business."

"*Dhat.* Why would you care about all these things? You spend all your time pumping iron with your students." She blew hard out of her nose, as if attempting to exhale her anger. "But remember, Mohini's father, we live in a society, not in a jungle. If the word gets out that we have sheltered a Muslim woman all these years... our relatives will shun us."

"Nothing like that will happen. Parul is a teenager now. She is just testing our patience. But she will come around." Baba took a long sip from his cup. "Whatever you say, no one can make tea like Parul. She has magic in her hands."

"Your affection has made you blind. Keep encouraging her, and you will see what trouble she brings to this house."

"Okay, okay, let it go now. All married men know: if you want peace in the house, always agree with the Mrs.," laughed Baba. He checked his reflection on a steel plate and touched the mole on his left cheek. He tapped the plate thoughtfully. "Let's focus on the future now. We can't let the poor American boy stay in the rooms downstairs. I have seen the way they live in America. They are not used to filth at all."

Mohini rolled her eyes. Baba was making such a big deal out of this roach incident. If the insects had bothered any other student in the gym, Baba probably wouldn't be half this concerned. But Michael was Baba's protégé, and he couldn't let him experience any hardship, however minor.

"So what are you suggesting?" asked Ma.

"I think we have to bring Michael upstairs. We have to give him one of our rooms."

"But that is impossible. All the rooms in the west wing are beyond repair now. We have only two good rooms here. Michael won't be comfortable in our bedroom."

"Then Mohini will have to move to our bedroom and let Michael use her room," said Baba. "There is no other way."

Mohini jumped up from her chair, nearly tripping on her long black skirt. "What are you saying, Baba? I can't give up my room."

"Shush," said Baba. "No silly talk. I have brought you up to show as much generosity as possible to a guest. You will accept my decision." Baba squeezed his jaws shut to show that the decision was already made, and nothing could make him change his mind.

• • •

Michael moved into her room as Mohini watched from behind the door curtain. She didn't feel generous at all. In fact, she felt great resentment as she watched him pack his belongings into her mahogany cupboard and lay his shaving items on her dressing table. His shirts appeared on the parallel bar of the clothes horse, and his books about famous weight-lifters lined her desk and bookshelf.

Envy and helplessness swelled like expanding dough inside her heart. How could her parents be so inconsiderate? How could they hand over her precious room to that arrogant, sulking foreign boy who did not have an ounce of appreciation for all he was receiving? While she curled up to fit into the small single bed in her parents' room, Michael's giant form rolled on every inch of her four-poster bed as if he were marking his territory like the king of the jungle.

"That boy has completely taken over my room," Mohini told Parul. "Does he care to know where I sleep and how I am getting by without my room?"

"That's how Americans are, Mohini. They like to occupy other people's rooms, houses and land. Then they stay there forever."

Mohini gave Parul a puzzled look. "I don't understand. You don't read newspapers, and your useless magazines don't contain any actual news. So who is telling you all this?"

"There is nothing to understand, Mohini. Just stay away from the American boy. He is no good."

For one brief instant, Mohini wondered if Parul had a new friend in her life. Then she dismissed the thought. All of Parul's friends were uneducated people who lived in the slum across the railway line. To them, America, Russia and Europe were all the same: just far-away countries where white *sahibs* lived. It was impossible for Parul to have a well-educated friend. Why would a person from a gentleman's family waste his time on a maid?

• • •

In the gym, Mohini saw Baba spend countless hours with Michael, teaching him yoga and meditation. Baba told Michael repeatedly how talented he was and that it was his duty to his parents and his country to nurture this talent carefully. "It is a sin to waste a gift, Michael. Discipline, you must have discipline. The mornings you will spend in meditation and the afternoons in the training room. The year is short and will go by quickly. So no breaks between now and the end of the year." Baba pointed to his beautifully sculpted body and continued, "Your body is like a temple. Listen to the God who lives in there; let him speak to you. You will win only if your body is happy."

Baba's advice fell on deaf ears. Mohini was sure of that. Michael continued to be distant and aloof. Apart from the training sessions, he mostly stayed in his room. He did not talk to the other boys in the camp, and even with Baba, he was very reticent, answering only what he was asked. In his room, he listened to the songs he had downloaded back home on his iPod as he paced the floor. Sometimes Mohini saw him sit at her desk, searching through piles of *The Telegraph* for the latest news on the Iraq conflict. When he found yet another story of a roadside bombing and a casket of an American soldier sent home, he sat and stared at the white wall, his fingers rolled into a fist.

· · · ·

Mohini tossed and turned in her single bed late at night. No matter which way she turned, her legs and arms seem to hang from the edge of the narrow bed. The neighborhood's stray dogs had started up with a chorus of howls. Occasionally, she heard the moaning of a cow that had gone into labor in the barn next door. The noise didn't disturb her parents, who snored in their king-size four-poster bed across from her.

Mohini covered her ears with her pillow and counted to one hundred in her mind. Still, sleep evaded her. The cuckoo clock ticked away stoically on the white wall, unsympathetic to her struggles. Sitting up, she punched her pillow a few times and wiped the sweat from her eyebrows. She tried to sleep again. This time she counted backward from one hundred. The clock became a blur and the white walls melted away. Her eyelids felt heavy, and everything else floated away.

Something must have woken her. A thin crack of light shone under the bedroom door. Someone had switched on the terrace stairwell light. She climbed out of her bed and felt her way around the room till she reached the door. Standing on her toes, she undid the tower bolt and pushed open the wooden panes. Light flooded her eyes, making her squint. She stuck her head around the bend in the stairwell and heard the click of the terrace door being pushed open. Leaning against the wall, she listened carefully. There was another sound—this time it was footsteps on the terrace floor. *Someone was walking on the terrace at this late hour of night.* For a moment Mohini hesitated, wondering if she should wake up her parents. What if a thief was trying to break in? She dismissed the thought as soon as it came. Thieves didn't switch on lights and go on a midnight stroll.

It was obviously Parul, who had stepped out of her room to get some fresh air on the terrace. Perhaps if Mohini listened carefully, she would hear the rhythmic ringing of Parul's anklets. She went up a few more stairs and held her breath to listen. Instead of the soft tinkling of anklets, heavy footsteps that could only belong to a man sounded on the terrace.

Mohini felt an indescribable urge to investigate. Tiptoeing up the stairs, she peered into the darkness, which shimmered like an ocean of gloom on the terrace. The clouds had almost completely covered the moon, and the buildings all around them were submerged in inky darkness. She caught a whiff of marigold and jasmine from the flowerpots. As her eyes adjusted to the dark, she located a big, bulky form on the parapet behind the water tank. *It was Michael.*

She couldn't think of what Michael might be doing there at this time of the night. She marched toward him and demanded, "Can you kindly explain why you are sitting on this parapet in the middle of the night?"

Michael was startled to see her there. "Oh, hold on a minute. Why are you shouting at me?"

"Because you scared me. I thought a thief was about to break in. I was getting ready to wake my parents."

"Brilliant detective work. Now you discovered me." Michael threw her a contemptuous glance. "Why don't you leave me alone and go back to bed?"

"It was hard enough falling asleep for the first time. I don't think I can do it again."

"Why? You have insomnia or something?"

"Ah, you didn't even notice?" she said, her voice rising. "I have been thrown out of my own room. My bed no longer belongs to me. Someone rolls on my king-size bed like he is taking a stroll in a park while I lie huddled in a corner of my parents' bedroom, in a single bed, dreaming of the privacy and space I once had. And you ask me if I have insomnia?"

Michael was taken aback. "Hey, looks like I pressed the wrong button. I didn't know you missed your room so much."

Mohini gritted her teeth. She remembered what Parul had said about Americans and lashed out. "I can completely understand how you missed that. You Americans always feel everyone should accommodate you—that you deserve the best always."

"Your father was the one to tell me to move in, so I did. Your beef is with him, not America," he said coldly.

Pain seared through Mohini. Ah, the humiliation and misery of being told that your own father has let you down. Before the American came to their house, Mohini was the best student Baba had ever known. In his mind, she was the only weightlifting star. But now Baba was ready to hand over that sacred place to Michael. Who knew that the foreign boy would unravel her world so quickly?

It was with difficulty that Mohini composed her face and looked back at the American. "We were being polite and offering you the best. Showing hospitality to our guest is part of our culture. But you think people should just bend over backward to please you. Did you care to find out what happened to the person you displaced?"

Michael climbed down from the parapet and walked toward her. "Look, I'm sorry your dad kicked you out of your room. That's not my fault. It's yours and his. How am I supposed to know what you mean if you don't say what you mean? If I'm not supposed to take the room, then don't offer it to me."

Mohini was not in the mood to back off. "Oh, you would have known if you had a heart. Too bad, in that giant body of yours, you could not find room for such a vital organ."

Michael took an angry breath. He seemed to struggle to control his rage.

"Thanks for sharing. I'm outta here."

"By all means. Enjoy your soft mattress while I sit behind this water tank all night."

Michael swore under his breath and went downstairs.

Chapter 18

On the day of the Lakshmi *Poornima*, Parul woke up in a bad mood. Ma had asked her to make *Alpana* designs on the stairs to welcome Goddess Lakshmi to the house. "Do it with all your devotion," Ma told her. "When Ma Lakshmi comes to our house, she will step on these rice-flour designs." Parul had nodded reluctantly. Since becoming educated in Islam, she had begun to avoid even minimal observance of Hindu rituals. But she knew she couldn't wriggle out of her *Alpana* obligations without raising Ma's suspicion.

Picking up her bowl of rice flour and water, she ran all the way to the first-floor. Ram, the janitor, had scrubbed away the bird droppings and cat hairs from the floor. The marble still felt cold and slippery under her feet. Bending down, she carved out Lakshmi's footmark on each step with deft, confident strokes, dipping her fingers into the rice flour bowl. The green and red glass bangles on her wrists tinkled gently with each circular motion of her hand. Her soft bun swung loosely at the nape, and occasionally she arched her back to relieve her aching muscles.

She had almost finished when heavy footsteps coming up the stairs made her cringe. Before she could discern who it was, two big black boots stepped over the beautifully carved footmarks, leaving muddy imprints on each of them. The American Sahib hurried past her in his muddy shoes. He had probably finished his exercise in the park and was just getting back.

Parul watched him in horror, unable to move at first, and then lunged forward to grab his elbow, anger boiling inside her. "Oh, Sahib, what have you done?" she said. "How could you ruin my *Alpana* designs?"

The American stared back at her in surprise. He opened his palms and spread his fingers in a gesture that meant he didn't know what she was talking about. "No Bengali." He shrugged his shoulder.

Parul refused to give up easily. The American had ruined all her hard work, and she would have to start over. "Are you blind?" She pointed to his eyes and mimicked the movements of a blind man. "Don't you have *Alpana* in your country?"

The American must have picked up on her angry tone, for he too raised his voice and hurled some angry English words at her. A muscle flexed in his arrogantly chiseled jaw, and a deep frown appeared between his eyebrows. His mossy-green eyes were devoid of any remorse.

She gritted her teeth and wiped her face. *Looks like he has already forgotten the cockroaches that I put in his room. The time has come to teach the American boy another lesson,* she thought.

She tightened her sari and picked up her bowl of rice-flour. Before turning away, she brought her face close to the American and whispered in Bengali, "Be careful, *Sahib*. Your bad times are about to start."

· · ·

Baba was getting frustrated by Michael's lax and laid-back attitude toward his yoga and meditation training. Mohini knew he was. Michael often showed up late for his classes. He wore shorts and T-shirts to the meditation room instead of the traditional *kurta pajama*. His cap was backward, and he chewed gum during his meditation routine. Sometimes when Mohini passed by the meditation room, she watched him from behind the curtains. He had his eyes closed, but occasionally he tapped his finger or feet. Sometimes, when he thought Baba was deep in his meditation, he opened his eyes and took a quick look around the room. *He is doing everything mechanically; his heart is not in it,* thought Mohini. *His body is here, but his soul is missing.*

One day, when she entered the meditation chamber to light some fresh candles, she found Baba and Michael in the middle of a heated argument. "Michael, you are not a robot," said Baba. "I made you of flesh and bones. Yoga and meditation are for people who want to live life happily, not walk around like corpses."

"I told you, Mr. Sen, I'm a tough case. The shrink back home gave up on me, but you insisted that the Eastern medicine has a special power. You can try east, west, north, south, everything on me, but I can't be fixed." Michael wiped his face with his towel. "I'm only here because I promised my mother I'd try for a few months. Do your best, but I'm out of here as soon as my time is up."

"In other words, you want to quit. You think this is too hard for you."

"I think this is just not working for me." Michael gave a casual shrug. "Besides, that's not the point. I have somewhere else I need to be. Something else I need to do."

Mohini watched as Baba's expression changed. He pulled on the back of his neck, as if he wanted to remove his head. Mohini wondered if Baba was on the verge of one of the periodic seizures of outrage that sometimes gripped him. Quickly, she handed him a glass of water. "Ignore the boy, Baba. You shouldn't get so excited—remember what the doctor said about your blood pressure?"

"I'm alright, Mohini." Baba pushed away the glass. "Don't worry about me."

Baba brought his focus to Michael again. "How easily you give up!" He leaned closer to him. "You think everything in life is easy to achieve? You think things will be served to you on a silver platter and all you have to do is accept them? The moment you experience your first loss, your first difficulty, you want to turn around and run? With this attitude, Michael, how will you succeed in anything in life, let alone in the Olympics? If you always want to play it safe, if you are always running from adversity, you will keep on running for the rest of your life."

The air in the room became colder somehow. Mohini felt it. Michael's eyes lit up, and he sucked air into his lungs. The words seem to have affected Michael in a raw and broken place somewhere inside.

"Mr. Sen, you live a peaceful life in the suburbs of Calcutta, where the biggest excitement is when the cat steals a piece of fish from the kitchen or your milkman dilutes the milk with water. You've told me that your family has never seen wars or deployments. But my family has. The truth is... running from difficulty was never an option for us. We're in the middle of it, whether or not we liked it." Michael's shoulders heaved.

Leaning against the wall, Mohini closed her eyes. It surprised her to hear Michael reveal something so personal about himself. Somehow, his melancholy unsettled her.

This time, Baba softened his voice. "It is true my life is lacking in that kind of experience, son. A civilian can never go near the pain felt by military families. But what baffles me is that you now want to join the military yourself and go to Afghanistan. Don't you think your mother has had enough grief?"

Michael fell into a long silence. Mohini wondered if he would answer Baba. Somewhere behind the walls, the widow's cat was crying. The ominous sound made her shiver. The burned-out candles lay around them in exhausted heaps, plunging the room into semi-darkness. Mohini bent down and lit fresh candles around the room. The slim lines of gray smoke curled upwards, almost touching the ceiling.

When Michael spoke, his voice was barely audible. "My father left a job unfinished, and I want to finish it. Or else the stuff he did for his country won't make sense."

"And the Olympics? That means nothing to you?"

"I want to do something bigger than the Olympics. They're just games."

Mohini sighed. Michael was clearly caught up in the past. Time had stopped for him at the point of separation from his father, and no successive experiences could leave an imprint on his mind. Baba's wisdom, however well-intended, was up against stubborn opposition.

Baba sighed and put his hand on Michael's shoulder. "People go through terrible experiences, but they also bounce back. Life, as you know, is not always fair. But you have to teach yourself how to deal with an unfair world. It is a skill that can be learned. Going to Afghanistan will not bring your father back."

Michael made a low hissing sound, like water boiling in a kettle. He crossed his arms across his chest and looked at Baba and then beyond him. "It may not bring him back, but it will take me near him. I've got to do this."

Baba clicked his tongue and shook his head. "It is no use arguing with you. You are a record with a broken needle. Only god can change your mind at this point."

⋅ ⋅ ⋅

The next morning, when Mohini came down the stairs, she found Baba waiting for her. "Tell Michael and your Ma to get ready," he said. "We're going to Kalighat temple."

"Why, Baba?"

"I'm going to start a new meditation routine for Michael. We will ask Ma Kali to give him motivation and patience."

Mohini wanted to point out that even Ma Kali couldn't help Michael. But she knew she wouldn't say it, no matter how much she might want to. Baba shifted his feet impatiently, and Mohini went to look for Michael.

When she came to the second-floor landing, Michael's voice floated out of her bedroom: he was talking rapidly on the phone, possibly to someone in America. Mohini was about to turn her doorknob when she heard the words, "Few more days and I'm out of this crazy house."

She flung the door open and found him sitting on her chair with his cell phone, his legs propped up on her desk. She deliberately slammed the door behind her and tried not to look too pleased when Michael jumped up in surprise.

"Hey, what do you want?" he asked.

"Baba wants you to get ready. We are visiting Ma Kali to offer our prayers."

"Who is Kali?"

"She is our goddess."

"Whatever." Michael shrugged. "I'll be there in a minute."

•　　•　　•

When they got close to the Kalighat temple, Michael and Mohini got out of the car. Baba and Ma stayed inside to help the driver park.

Though Mohini didn't want to go to the trouble of speaking to Michael, Baba had warned her to be extra nice to him that morning. So she pointed out to him various handicraft stores on the way—artisans sewing wicker baskets, carving out wooden cots and sharpening the strings of musical instruments. Idol makers worked hard to give shape to various clay statues of gods and goddesses. They polished the statues carefully and applied terra-cotta or red bronze paint on the faces and arms. Roadside peddlers sold everything from incense sticks to hair clips and rubber slippers on blue, waterproof plastic sheets.

As soon as Michael entered the main courtyard of the temple, he was accosted by beggars. The ragged little boys and girls with runny noses and yellowing hair tugged on Michael's shirt and asked for money. He was at a loss about what to do. At first, he dug into his pocket and handed them a chunk of change. As if by magic, ten more children appeared and started pulling on his shirt.

"Don't give them any more money." Mohini pulled him away from the children. "Walk fast and ignore them."

"Shouldn't they be in school?" asked Michael.

"Oh, you know so little about the world," Mohini laughed.

•　　•　　•

Below the giant banyan tree, two monkeys dressed in little red costumes and sunglasses sat next to a monkey *wallah*. A tiny lock secured the metallic collars around their necks, and the monkey *wallah* held on to the long leashes. He played his drum to gather a crowd.

"Oh, *Sahib*," he called out to Michael in English. "Why see only Hollywood? Bollywood very beautiful... *ekdom* top class *chokris*, pretty like foreign girls." He poked his monkeys with a wooden stick, speaking to them in soft Bengali. "Go, my Sridevi, go, my Zeenat, enchant our guest with your charisma." The monkeys held their skirts, swayed their hips and danced to *"naach meri bulbul... paisa milega."*

Pushing past the throngs of worshippers, Mohini and Michael turned left and walked across the courtyards, past the altar, and over the platform. In the alcove next to the temple, a young girl rolled on the floor, her body writhing like a snake. Her eyes looked blank, devoid of eyeballs. The girl's lips moved wordlessly as her head rocked from side to side.

"She is in the midst of a trance state," explained a priest in broken English. "Ma Kali has entered her body."

"Bullshit," said Michael, pointing to the girl. "This has nothing to do with your Kali. The girl is having an epileptic seizure. I've seen one of those before."

"Don't say all this... not here. These people have their own religious beliefs," Mohini whispered.

"But clearly they're wrong and I'll prove—"

Mohini pulled him away from the crowd and walked toward the flower carts. Bargaining heavily with the vendor, she picked out the flowers and the incense for their *puja*. Michael showed no interest in her purchase. Mohini rolled her eyes and tugged on his shirt. "Anyone looking at you would think you don't want to be here. It is as if we brought you here against your will."

He shrugged. "Don't know why your dad dragged me here."

"He is only trying to help you..."

"How can a place like this *help me*?"

"People come to visit this temple from all over the world. They say this Kali is powerful. Her blessing can wipe away our sufferings." They sat on a wooden bench, and a little boy poured them tea in tiny clay cups. "Baba didn't bring you to an ordinary temple. This place is very special."

Michael looked away, showing no interest in her story. Yet she felt compelled to go on.

"Sati, an incarnation of Kali, was the wife of Shiva and the daughter of Daksha Prajaapati, a descendant of god Brahma. Sati went against her father's wishes and married Lord Shiva. Seething with rage, the Daksha made a plan to insult his son-in-law, Shiva. He performed a *yagna*, sacrificial fire, where he invited all the gods, including Vishnu and Brahma, but left out Shiva. 'I'll show that Shiva is a nobody. He's not even worthy of being invited to my *yagna*.'

"Sati heard about this big *yagna* and wanted to attend. Her husband was deep in meditation when she went to ask for his permission. But Shiva urged her not to go. 'Remember, he didn't invite us,' he told Sati. 'You won't be respected there, and you will only find insult.' But Sati attended this *yagna* against her husband's wishes. On the day of the *yagna*, before all attending gods and goddesses, the Daksha ridiculed her and called her husband a dirty, roaming ascetic who hangs out with ghosts, ghouls and goblins.

"Sati, unable to bear this humiliation, jumped into the sacrificial fire and immolated herself. When the news reached Shiva, he started the dance of destruction. He cut off Daksha's head and replaced it with that of a goat. Crazed with grief, he picked up the charred body of Sati and danced the dance of destruction all over the Universe. The gods were desperate to stop Shiva's dance, which was causing tremendous suffering and devastation on Earth.

"There were floods, hurricanes, and earthquakes everywhere. Disease and famine wiped out half of the human population. The gods knew that as long as Shiva had Sati's charred body in his arms, his grief would not subside, and he would not be able to forget or forgive his insult. So Lord Vishnu, a powerful god, released his spinning disk, *chakram*, and chopped up Sati's body into pieces. These pieces fell in various spots all over India, which were later considered holy spots. Hindu pilgrims hope to visit these spots at least once in their lifetime. Sati's toe fell here, in this Kalighat temple."

Mohini turned to Michael, wanting to see his reaction. His eyes crinkled, and a smile played at the corners of his mouth. "So the woman, Sati, got bored with all the meditation stuff and crashed her dad's party? Hey, I completely get that. All this meditation gets tiresome after a while."

"Don't make fun of our beliefs." Mohini glared at him. "I don't know why I had to tell you that story. I should have known you wouldn't care for it. *Dhat*, I feel so foolish now." She started walking toward the temple. She had expected Michael to follow her, but when she turned around, he was still sitting on the bench, playing with his clay cup.

"Aren't you coming?"

"I'm not going in there to see someone's giant toe."

"Wait until I tell Baba what you just said."

"And that should scare me?" he scoffed. "What's he going to do? Spin a *chakram* and chop me up?"

"How can you talk about my father like this? He is your guru. Here in India, guru and god have equal status. Eklavya cut off his finger because his guru asked for it, and that destroyed his dream of becoming the best archer in the kingdom."

"That was a brutal thing to do for sure. Don't expect me to be even half that obliging to your dad. Look, your country is full of spirituality and mysticism. You seem to get advice from mythologies and folklores, and I'm happy for you. But this isn't working for me. I keep telling your dad that, but he just doesn't get it."

Mohini was surprised by the ferocity of her own reactions to Michael's careless comments. She took his nonchalance as a rejection of her world and her reality. To him, they were merely foreigners, an exotic species who sometimes amused him and sometimes irritated him with their quaint stories. She wondered why Baba had wasted his time on Michael. All he did was discount and trivialize their traditions and beliefs. He could never value Baba's sentiments, could never appreciate his effort. Mohini turned her back on him and paced forward. A tear stung the corner of her eye.

She walked down the steps behind the temple and came to the bank of the Adi Ganga river. There was a time when visitors used to dip in the holy water to get rid of their sins. The water had been so clear one could see the rounded pebbles and silvery fishes on the riverbed. Years of neglect and careless government policy changed that, and the river had thinned and clogged. The city dumped raw sewage directly into the water and stacked mountains of trash on the banks. The river turned dark and opaque; the stench unbearable.

Mohini took out a handkerchief and covered her nose. Her head throbbed from the effort of understanding Michael. She couldn't tell what load of feelings, what haunting memories had led up to this impertinence. He was truly weighed down by the ghosts of his past, which made it impossible for him to enjoy his new surroundings, appreciate their hospitality, and accept the friendship they extended toward him. He was determined to mock and reject everything they offered.

Taking out flowers and *bel* leaves from her bag, she threw them into the river as an offering. "Ma Kali, no one goes away from your door empty-handed. So, please, accept this small offering and fulfill my one wish. Send the American boy home as soon as possible. He does not belong here."

Climbing up the stairs, she walked past the Shiv Mandir and the Radha Krishna temple until she reached the Natmondir. Someone called her name from behind her. She looked over the devotees and located Baba on the other side of the courtyard. He was waving his black umbrella at her. "Hey, Mohini, we are here. Come here," he shouted. Ma waited in the shade of the sari store.

Carts and vendors crammed the square, and people weaved in and out. Tourists gathered around a half-naked *Sadhu*, a holy man, who lounged on a bed of nails. His assistant collected money from all spectators. A young man climbed off his bike and approached a schoolgirl. He handed her a rose, and she blushed. Her girlfriends poked her from behind and chuckled. A woman in a white sari with a red border poured milk and honey on the black cylindrical *Shiva Linga* stone. A cat lapped up the milk that washed off the *Linga* and flowed into the street.

"Where is Michael?" asked Baba as soon as Mohini crossed the courtyard.

"Over there." She pointed to the bench near the tea stall.

"Why did you leave him there?"

"Baba, he is not a child. He makes his own decisions." Mohini pouted.

"I will never understand this generation." Baba sighed and went to find him.

Mohini kneeled before the goddess, and the priest placed some flowers and *bel* leaves in her hand. A little later, Michael entered the temple and sat on the floor beside Mohini. She lifted her head a few degrees to better see his eyes, where she expected to see scorn and apathy, but to her amazement, they sparkled with interest.

"Holy cow," he exclaimed, leaning forward to take a better look at the goddess. "This is insane. I've seen nothing like this before." He pointed to the naked statue of Ma Kali—three huge eyes, a long protruding tongue made of gold, and four hands. Two of those hands held a sword and a severed head.

Mohini pinched his arm. "Don't be so loud," she whispered. "People are looking at you. Who knows what they are thinking?"

Michael didn't heed her warning. Instead, he got out a small camera and, getting in front of the crowd, he started taking pictures of Ma Kali.

Finally, Baba caught up with him. "Put the camera back, Michael," he said. "You're here to pray, not to click photos. Sit here and pray to our goddess. Ask her to help you sort things out. Our Kali is world famous. Your wishes will come true."

The head priest, who was Baba's friend, came forward to bless Michael. He put a large *Kumkum* dot on his forehead and tied holy threads on his wrist.

On their way back, Baba showed him the Victoria memorial and the Howrah bridge. "See how beautiful our Kolkata is. There is a lot to see here and a lot to do. Give the city a chance, Michael. It can do wonders for you."

Michael looked unconvinced.

Chapter 19

"Mohini, I am going to your Pishimoni's house. Do you want to come with me?" Ma asked.

Mohini raised her head from her pillow and opened one eye. She stared back at Ma in surprise.

"So early?"

"Yes, I don't want the sun to come out. You know how bad my migraine gets."

"I want to sleep some more." She pulled the blanket over her head.

"Fine, sleep all you want. But remember, your exams are only three months from now. College exams are nothing to joke about."

"I know, Ma," she groaned. "I will study."

"One more thing," said Ma. "Ask Parul to give you and Michael some lunch. Your Baba went to the interstate tournament. He won't join you for lunch."

"Baba left?"

"Yes, he took the car. I'll have to take an auto rickshaw."

Mohini sat up, her eyes wide. "Baba left, and now you are going? You're leaving me with that jerk?"

"Who are you talking about?"

"Ma, that Michael. I don't like him one bit."

"Mohini, your father has asked you many times not to be so rude to him. He is a guest in our house. Besides, you are not alone with him. Parul is in the kitchen, and I told her to keep an eye on you."

Mohini grabbed the pillow and squeezed it against her chest. "You know, American boy doesn't do things for himself. He'll expect me to put rice and *daal* on his plate. Now, why would I do anything for him? It is not like he is always oozing with gratitude."

"I don't have time for this now. If you don't want to attend to him, then just ask Parul to take a plate to his room."

"You tell her. I am not getting up."

• • •

It was two o'clock in the afternoon. Mohini lay in the large square bed in her parents' room; she was resting after lunch. She had stayed in bed with her books all day, only getting up to eat and take a bath. The door and windows of the room were closed; the gentle humming from the overhead fan made her eyelids grow heavy. She could never catch a good night's sleep in her single bed. So she enjoyed her afternoon naps in her parents' large bed when they were not around. A satisfied smile played on her lips. She gathered the pillows around herself and buried her head as the soft cotton molded around her.

She was getting ready to sleep when a strange sound from outside made her sit up. It sounded like a roar... or a cry. Then it was gone. The room was silent for a minute. Then the sound came again, less loud and distinct, but none the less unmistakable. It sounded like someone was swearing. She pushed away her pillow, rose from the bed, and tiptoed toward the door. Someone was cursing, followed by some angry kicking and banging. She followed the direction of the sound and found herself in front of Michael's room. The door was closed but not locked. She pushed it open.

Michael was in the chair with his back to the door. Everything in his room had been turned topsy-turvy. His mattress, pillow, and blanket were on the floor. His books and papers were scattered everywhere. On the wall, written with spray paint, were the English words, "GO BACK TO YOUR COUNTRY."

Fear gripped Mohini's heart, making it hard to breathe. "What happened here?"

Michael jumped up and turned around in one movement, his chair almost toppling. His cheeks trembled as he pointed to the writing on the wall. "Someone broke into my room." Then his gaze narrowed and flickered over her face. "Do you know who did this?"

"I have no idea." She swallowed hard, dismayed by the accusation in his voice. The air in the room crackled with the building tension.

"Stop acting all innocent and tell me who the fuck did all this!"

"I really don't know. I was in my room the whole morning."

"Are you fucking kidding me?"

"I am being honest with you." She tried her best to calm him down. "I am as shocked and confused as you are."

His lips tightened. "GO BACK TO YOUR COUNTRY? Are you serious? Is this Taliban land? Did I end up in the wrong country?"

"This sort of thing has never happened before. No one in this house would do such a thing. This is an outsider's job."

"This is fucking demented," he said, choking out the words. "First, they put roaches in my room and now this..." The veins on his neck bulged out.

"I am sorry..." she started to say and then stopped. She found him staring at the cupboard shelves. Then he sprang forward, rifling through the contents of the shelves. "My photo album... my photo album! The bastard destroyed my photos." His head and shoulders slumped forward, and he began to pant. He pointed to the torn and crumpled pictures that lay on the open cupboard shelves. Beads of sweat formed on his forehead. The light coming from the skylight made them sparkle.

"These are my dad's photographs... photos of him before he left for Afghanistan. My only copies." He cried out. "I can't believe someone dared to touch my dad's photos."

Mohini stood on her tiptoes and collected the shredded photos left scattered on the shelf. Tears threatened to choke her throat as she swept the pieces into her lap. In the drawer of her dressing table, she found a plastic bag and shoved the pieces into it.

"Look, I don't know who did this. No one in this house would do such a thing! All I can say is I'm deeply ashamed that such a thing has happened to you here... in my house." She stopped to catch her breath. "I'll get these photos fixed for you. Our neighborhood studio can piece these together and reconstruct and restore the original image. They're very good."

Michael did not listen. Instead, he got up and paced the floor like a wounded tiger. "What makes you think it's an outsider job?" he asked. "Maybe the maid did it. What's her name... Pa.. rr... ul or something. She is a real piece of work. Always gives me nasty looks."

Mohini suddenly remembered Parul's words. *That's how Americans are, Mohini. They like to occupy other people's rooms, houses and land. Then they stay there forever.* Was Michael justified in suspecting Parul? She dismissed the thought as soon as it came. Parul was incapable of such a vile act—Mohini was certain.

She grabbed Michael's arm. "Listen to me. It wasn't our maid. She is like our family. We have known her all our life."

Michael shook off her hand and twisted his face. It was as if a tornado were at work inside him. "Family, my ass," he said tersely. "I'll drag her sorry butt to the police station."

He pushed past her and moved toward the open door.

Almost instinctively, she paced forward and beat him to the door, pulling the panes shut. She turned the lock from the inside with a decisive click. "You will do no such thing. Try to be reasonable. What is her motive? Why would she try to harm you?"

Somehow, she felt the need to explain further. "These women are very different from the ones back home, Michael. They have very little education, and they know little about the world outside of Kolkata. They are just poor women who come to the city to find work. They're used to very hard work—cooking, washing, and cleaning. Outside that—they know nothing about history, politics, current affairs. They are simple people—such malicious acts are beyond them. Besides, Parul does not know any English. The graffiti on the wall is not her doing."

The words just sprang out of her, almost as a last line of defense between Parul and her humiliation. Mohini's head hurt from the effort, and her throat felt dry. "I can understand how you feel, believe me. But it is not our maid. If you drag her to the police station, she will never get over the shame. She will never trust us again."

Michael placed both his hands on his hips and glared at her. But she positioned herself solidly between him and the door. "We never go to the police. It is a bigger problem than solution."

"Move away. Do as I tell you. We'll know soon enough if Parul is all that innocent. Let the police interrogate her. The truth will come out."

Mohini remained immobile.

"You will not move, will you?" he asked.

"No."

"Don't behave like a fool."

"You left me no option."

"Okay, then." He reached out, grabbed her arm, and pinned her against the wall. Despite his anger, he was surprisingly gentle, as if he were disciplining a disobedient child. Holding her with one hand, he unlocked the door with a quick snap and pushed the panes open. He gave her a triumphant look that said *Try to stop me now.*

Almost on an impulse, Mohini freed her arm, bent forward, and bit his left ear. Michael howled in pain. She wriggled out of his clutches, pulled one pane shut and tried to squeeze out through the other. But he grabbed the neck of her dress and pulled her backward. A ripping sound froze her in her tracks. The slice of fabric covering her shoulders and chest tore open, and her entire blouse slid down to her waist, leaving her breasts exposed to the warm air outside the room. She screamed loudly.

Michael did not move. It was as if he had turned into a statue. His rage had disappeared, and in its place, all that remained was amazement. His gaze remained fixed on her breasts as if he did not expect her to have them and for them to appear in his view so suddenly.

"You asshole," she screamed again, placing a hard slap on his surprised face. "I'll never forgive you for this."

Then, covering her breasts with her palm, she flew across the hallway and through the door. She ran into the bedroom and slammed the door shut. She sat on the bed... *distraught.*

• • •

For a long time, Mohini sat in a kind of reverie. Multiple emotions threatened to tear her apart. Her first thought was that something

179

irreversible had happened to her—that she had somehow been made impure, and that stain would now mark her forever. To be half-naked before a complete stranger was unthinkable. The pressure in her chest was intense, as if her rib cage wanted to burst open and let the tears flow out like an uncontrolled river. There was only one thing left to do, she told herself: run away from the house and never see that American boy again. She wrapped a blanket tightly against her chest, covering every bit of her exposed skin. She wished that the earth would crack open and just swallow her with her pain and humiliation. She thought of running to the kitchen and telling Parul what had happened. Then, partly out of embarrassment and partly because Parul would probably say, "I told you to stay away from that American boy," she decided to bury her shame in her heart and not confide in anyone.

• • •

That afternoon, when Ma and Baba came home, she told them about the vandalism in Michael's room. Their faces flushed red with anger. Leaning on the balcony railing, Baba ordered the security guard to come upstairs.

"Who came to the house after we left?" Baba demanded, peering irritably at the guard's face.

The guard frowned and lifted his cap to scratch his head. "No one, *Babu*. I didn't see anyone."

"*Baadmash kothakar*! This is why we pay you?" Baba reprimanded the security guard. "Anyone and everyone can go up the stairs right under your nose. Are you sleeping all day or just going blind?"

Baba even talked to the press widow. "Didi, we hope you will remember we are family... despite our differences. Whatever your grievances, take them out on me. But don't harm the American boy. He is just a kid and a guest in our country."

The press widow could hardly disguise her glee. "Family, *hunh*? Did you remember we are family when you brought the court case against me? Now you are in trouble, and suddenly I am family? This is god's punishment for tormenting a helpless widow. Now go suffer... what do I care?"

And in the kitchen, Ma admonished Parul.

"I left you in charge. How is it possible that you did not see or hear anything?"

"I was in the kitchen the whole time," replied Parul. "So many people come and go, Ma. The security guard stops no one. The postman, the milkman, the newspaper *wallah,* and the vegetable sellers... they all come upstairs. It's easy for anyone to wander in."

"Stop the nonsense. You can't do one thing right these days."

"You blame me for everything," Parul whimpered.

"Let me tell you this straight, Parul. I don't like to beat around the bush. Strange things are happening to the American boy, things that have never happened in this house before. We don't know whose inauspicious shadow has fallen on this house. But if I ever find out you have anything to do with this, you will be out of this house at that very moment, do you hear me? You can't expect any forgiveness from us."

"What are you saying, Ma?" Parul covered her mouth with her hand. "I have nothing to do with that American boy."

From the sudden pained flush on Parul's face, Mohini knew Ma's accusation had deeply affected her. Mohini wanted to say something in Parul's defense, but she knew that the moment she opened her mouth, Ma's icy tone would turn into fury.

"All I do is clean the boy's room, wash his clothes and serve him food. That's all. Not an inch more and not an inch less. Why would I care if he stays or goes? A poor girl like me has a thousand problems of her own. Why waste my time on the American? Besides, do I know any English? How could I write those words on the wall... you tell me?"

•   •   •

And so it went, back and forth, accusations and blame flying around the house, all of them unwilling participants in the dark, sordid drama. Ma and Baba were worried about Michael and his safety. In the bed next to her, they discussed in hushed tones why someone would want to harm a sweet kid like Michael. *This,* Baba declared with great conviction, *is not an ordinary robbery.* The boy's wallet, passport, and other valuables were untouched. So the motivation was to intimidate him.

But why would anyone want to do that? The question hung in the air, slowly settling in Mohini's heart as a sense of foreboding and filling her with endless dread.

Michael's rage ebbed with some afterthought. He didn't mention getting the police involved in this incident. Instead, it was decided that Michael's room would be always locked, and only he would have a copy of the key. Once a day, he would let Parul clean his room in his presence. Baba fired the old security guard and hired a new one. Vendors and peddlers could no longer come inside the house.

Over the next few days, Mohini avoided Michael. "I can't study here," she told Ma. "This house is too noisy, and Baba always asks me to help in the camp. I don't have time so close to my exam." She packed her clothes and books and went to Pishimoni's house in Narendrapur.

When she came back a week later, she saw Michael standing on the small balcony outside his room. Her heart leaped. He looked back at her, and her face burned. She lowered her head and slipped into the house.

That evening, Mohini went up to Parul's terrace room. The door was closed but not locked. A thin slice of light escaped from under the door, illuminating part of the stairway landing. She pushed the door open and stared in amazement. Parul was on her prayer mat, her hands cupped together and her eyes closed. Her head was covered in a black scarf.

"Gosh, Parul*di*, you are at it again. When will you stop?" Mohini stared at her, her head reeling.

Parul's eyes flew open. "Mohini, are you here alone?"

"Who else would be with me?"

"You got me worried. I thought you brought Ma with you." Parul leaped up to roll away her mat. She yanked off her scarf and stuffed it away in her tin trunk.

"Maybe I should have," said Mohini. "She should see with her own eyes just how disobedient you are."

Parul put an affectionate finger under Mohini's chin and smiled. "Now, why would you do such a thing?" Her voice was sweet as a nightingale's. "You are like a sister to me. You tell me everything from your heart... Have I ever gone to Ma and given away any of your secrets? I am honored that you trust me so much, and I will never break that trust. I know you will do the same for me."

"Parul*di*, these words will not melt me." Mohini tapped a finger on her shoulder, looking directly into her eye. "I think you have gone too far this time — you are doing the only thing Ma told you not to do: practice your religion. Don't you know what our relatives and neighbors would say if they found out we have sheltered a Muslim woman all these years? What answer would Ma give them... *hna*? And please don't start with your 'identity' story with me. Don't think I will be impressed that you know big words like that."

"I wasn't trying to impress you. I was only telling the truth," Parul muttered, half to herself.

Mohini gritted her teeth. Parul was getting more and more stubborn. She turned to look at the door behind her, debating whether she should go downstairs and tell Ma what she had just witnessed.

Reading her mind, Parul rushed to the door and pulled it shut. She twisted the tower bolt and locked it. "Please... won't you listen to me?" she pleaded. When Mohini didn't answer, she snatched Mohini's hand and rubbed it between her fingers.

"Look, Mohini, no harm done. All I am doing is offering some prayers to my God in my room. No one will know...no one needs to know." Parul sat and pulled Mohini down next to her. "Now forget everything you have seen and tell me about Pishimoni's house. You left so suddenly, and the house was so empty without you."

Mollified, Mohini was eager to divulge information instead of worrying about Parul's changed behavior. She leaned back against the wall and began. "At first, I didn't want to tell you any of this. I was so ashamed. Such a thing has never happened before. It is unthinkable..."

"What's all this about?" Parul moved close to her. "Why are you blushing like this?"

Mohini lowered her voice. She told Parul what had happened in Michael's room—how he had tried to push her away from the door, and she had bitten him, and then he had ripped off her blouse, exposing her breasts.

Parul looked thunderstruck.

"The boy is totally crazy. He wanted to go to the police. I was only trying to stop him." She started to cry. "I feel so much shame, Paruldi. I wish I could become invisible."

Parul took her hand and squeezed it. "None of this is your fault, Mohini. You have done nothing. Don't cry like this."

"I don't want to see his face again. I don't want him to see me... ever. I want him gone from this house," she sobbed.

Parul's hand stilled on Mohini's fingers for a second. She looked outside the window, as if she could see the future, and said quietly, "God has strange ways, Mohini. Your wish may come true, and it may happen sooner than you think."

Mohini left Parul's room and went down the dark, steep stairs, holding onto the banister to avoid missing her footing. The bulb that lit up the stairs had died, and Baba had forgotten to replace it. She pondered on what Parul had said about her wish coming true. Did Parul know something she didn't? Or did she make the prediction about Michael leaving the house just to comfort her?

Mohini came to the landing and turned to head down the second flight of stairs. A hand touched her shoulder, and she jumped. But before she could scream, someone covered her mouth. "Mohini, it's Michael. Don't scream."

He released her, and she turned around to see his gigantic form in the dim light. He smelled faintly of cologne and his breath was warm on her cheek.

"Don't be afraid! I just want to give you this note," he said. He shoved a white envelope into her palm and ran down the stairs. She stood there for a long time, staring at the envelope, unable to move, unable to react. Then she slowly unfolded the note and read it.

Dear Mohini,

I can see that you are very upset with me. I'm sorry for the other day—it was just an accident. I know you won't believe me. You think I planned it. I can just see you saying, 'Of course he'd behave like this. He's an American, after all.' I know you have a very low opinion of me. You hold a very long list of qualities that I seem to lack... respect for elders, obedience, humbleness, modesty, gratitude, and devotion for the Guru... and so many more. Well, now you have one more thing to add to your list: my lack of honor. Obviously, you don't think of me as a gentleman, and I'm sure you think I take great pleasure in undressing and embarrassing the girls I meet. But I was raised in a military family and I've always been taught to act righteously and to respect and protect all women.

Anyway, I can't change what happened. I have some good news for you. It looks like your wish is coming true. You won't have to put up with me for much longer. I've spoken to my travel agent and arranged for a ticket to return home by the end of the month. I wanted to go sooner, but they didn't have any seats.

I know your father will not want me to leave because he has so many plans for me, but I don't think I can worry about his feelings right now. Right now, I don't even care about my own feelings very much. I'm not like that. I'm not the kind of person your father wants me to be, and I can't change myself.

I said much more than I wanted to say. The important thing is that you will get your room back. Once again, for whatever it is worth, here is my apology. Forgive me if you can.

Michael

Mohini read and reread the letter as if she had entered a trance. Her first sense was that she had misjudged the American. She had never given him an opportunity to reveal his true nature to her. Instead, she had always criticized and rejected him based on some assumptions she had about American boys—assumptions she had gathered from reading books, listening to the news, and watching Hollywood movies.

Not once did she think this boy might be different, that he might have the courage to take responsibility for what he had done and apologize for his mistake. If anything, she thought she should have apologized to him. From the day he had come to their house, she had behaved badly with him... greeting him with sentences tinged with sarcasm. Not once had she made any effort to make him feel welcome. *Now he was leaving.*

Mohini read the letter again. Yes, Michael was making travel arrangements. He would leave by the end of the month. His departure should have made her happy, yet she felt no pleasure at the thought of seeing him go. *What was happening to her?* She leaned against the wall. Tears gathered in her eyes again.

Chapter 20

Two days later was the festival of Holi. The excitement in the house was palpable in the air. Large buckets of colored water and several plastic syringes were lined up in the courtyard. Some buckets were filled with water balloons. Little mounds of green, orange, red, and pink powder blew gently in the wind, forming a mist before Mohini's eyes.

Baba had invited his weight-lifter friends and their students. Some of them went to college with Mohini, though it was hard to recognize them with color smeared all over their faces. They chased each other around with long syringes filled with colored water. A few boys with water-filled balloons chased after a girl. All around her, laughter rose and fell and turned into shrieks of joy.

A girl ran toward Mohini, chased by a weight-lifter from Baba's camp. "Stop him," she said, half laughing, half frightened. "He is going to drench me."

The boy poured a bucket of colored water on her and rubbed red powder on her neck and shoulders and brushed his hand against the edges of her breasts. The girl pushed him back and ran, half screaming, half giggling. Mohini was amazed by the boy's audacity and the amount of tolerance a day like this could bring. This kind of behavior was unthinkable on other days.

Michael stood below the awning watching them, unsmiling and unenthusiastic. Instead of joining the celebrations, he looked irritated by the incessant stream of laughter. He was wearing clothes the like of which were never worn on the day of Holi: dry-cleaned, well-ironed dress shirt and pants. *Anyone looking at him would know he had never played Holi in his life*, thought Mohini.

A group of students wearing old T-shirts and shorts came forward, pulled his hand and tried to drag him to the courtyard. There were even a few girls in the group, and they all giggled loudly.

"Here, let's ruin your fair face and golden hair," chuckled one of the girls. "We want you to look like a monkey, like the rest of us."

Michael pushed them back and stepped away. "I might have enjoyed playing paintball with my friends when I was ten, but I am a grown-up now. I don't like childish stuff."

He turned away from the crowd and walked toward the back of the house. Mohini caught up with him and blocked his path. "Wait, Michael."

Despite his grim mood, he did not push past her.

"About the note..."

It was a while before he spoke, and even then, he averted his eyes. "I'm sorry," he said at last. "I don't know what came over me that day."

Mohini felt a faint flush of color rising in her face. She couldn't look into his eyes. "It was just an accident, you know. I know you did not mean to do it... it is one of those things that happens before you can stop it, and no amount of regret can change that." Despite herself, she laughed nervously. "We all have regrets, you know... we all wish we had done things differently. But that does not mean we have to run away from an unpleasant situation."

"Go on," he said, narrowing his eyes. "What are your regrets?"

"Well, for one, I wish I had attempted to be nice to you. It can't be easy living so far away from home, in a country so new to you... after everything you have gone through. I should have made an effort to—"

"You are apologizing to me?" A small smile flickered at the corner of his lips. "This is an interesting twist in the story. Allow me to quote you after that very unfortunate wardrobe accident—if I remember correctly, you said, *'you asshole, I will never forgive you for this.'*"

Mohini's cheeks burned with embarrassment. It was with difficulty that she got back the will to stretch the conversation.

"Look, Michael, I was in shock then. I know what happened that day should not have happened. But that does not mean you just give up on your dreams, hop on a plane and go back home." Mohini stared back at him. She couldn't think of anything more to say. Her throat felt dry. "It was just an accident. Can't we move past it?" she asked.

"What are you suggesting?"

"We forget all the bad feelings and start over again."

He hesitated slightly and then shook his head.

"It's too late for that. I'll be leaving here at end of the month."

He turned around and headed toward the printing press. Mohini ran after him.

"Wait... I am not done. I need to talk some more."

"Don't come after me. Enjoy your silly festival."

Michael pushed her aside, barely pausing in his stride. He entered the printing press and disappeared into the dimly lit passage. Mohini stared after him, wide-eyed, speechless. That part of the house was strictly off limits. *Michael should have known that*, she thought. It was Mohini herself who told him about the wicked widow. Yet he disregarded her advice.

Picking up her skirt, Mohini chased after him, waving her hand and shouting: "Stop! You can't go there."

• • •

That day the press machine was silent, and big locks hung from the pressroom doors. Behind the office, a group of press employees and servants sat on the water tank, soaked in color and unrecognizable. Some of them played the *dhol*, a longish drum, and some got up to dance. They all had glasses of a syrupy liquid in their hands.

"*Saheb*," said the compositor to Michael in broken English, "sit with us and have a glass of thandai... *ekdom* first class... You won't get this in your country, this much I am telling you. It is our India special, and it will take you up there straight..." He pointed to the sky.

The drink was making the servants stumble as they got up to dance. *I can already see where the drinks can take them*, Mohini thought grimly.

"No, Michael." She grabbed his elbow. "Don't even think about it. This drink is spiked. You know the camp rule — 'stay away from all addictive substances.'"

"*Saheb*, fear not," said the machine man. "This is one hundred percent natural drink. No chemicals, none, and very good for your health... nutritious. Big man like you should drink nutritious drinks."

This time Michael turned to her and said, "If I want a drink, then I want a drink. Just stay out of it."

"Let *Saheb* have a drink, Mohini," said a female voice from behind her, making her jump.

It was Parul. She smiled at Mohini and held out a glass to Michael. Her nose ring sparkled in the bright sunlight. She looked clean and untouched in a yellow sari—not a drop of color had grazed her face and neck.

"What is this, Parul*di*? You are not playing Holi today?"

"It is not my festival, Mohini."

"Not your festival?" she asked. "Since when?"

"Let it go, Mohini. I decided not to play this year. As simple as that. Now stop your interrogation and let *Saheb* have some fun."

Michael grabbed the glass from Parul's hand and sat down on the edge of the water tank. He took a big sip of the sweet drink and closed his eyes. He took a few more sips and wiped his lips with the back of his hand.

"Have some more, *Saheb*," said Parul, filling up his glass. "Holi special."

"You are making a big mistake," Mohini warned Michael.

"I just turned twenty-one. I'm allowed to drink alcohol legally, so please, let me make my own decisions."

He drank a few more glasses and got up to dance. The rest of the gang cheered. "*Bahut achha, Saheb*," they said. "You are a superb dancer." They smeared color on his face and clothes. He did not protest.

Mohini turned around and went back to the courtyard. She could stay and quarrel with him, but that would only wear her out. He was adamant, and no amount of persuasion was going to work on him.

The color on her body felt hot and prickly. She needed to wash it off and wash it off quickly. Who cared what happened to Michael? If he wanted to break the number one rule of camp, then that was his problem. If he wanted to get in trouble with Baba, then that was his problem. Her earlier dislike for him crept back in; her hands shook with rage. *What right did he have to talk to me like that? What right?* She had tried to be nice to him that morning... she had almost apologized to him when, clearly; he was the one who was wrong that day—first yelling at her and then ripping off her blouse. Who behaved like that? Only a madman would do such a thing.

She ran up the stairs, past her bedroom, and into the bathroom. She splashed water on her face and neck and watched the red and green colors dripping into the sink and swirling down the drain. She poured a bucketful of water over her head, tasting the ice-cold water with her tongue. This time, her body seemed to cool down.

She opened the bathroom door and went back to the bedroom. She glanced at the cuckoo clock on the wall. Two o'clock! Baba would soon leave the Holi celebrations and come upstairs for his bath. Her heart skipped a beat. *She had to find Michael and get him back in his room.*

She went back to the water tank to find Michael, but a servant told her, "The *Saheb* just left. I don't know where he went."

Mohini walked around the house looking for him, but there was no sign of Michael. At last, she discovered him in the tiny room below the staircase where the security guard slept. His shirt and shorts were soaked in color, and his face was smeared with pink powder. He was fast asleep on an old dusty mattress.

She called his name. "Wake up, wake up. You can't sleep here. You need to go upstairs."

Michael's eyes fluttered a little and a tiny slit appeared. "Go away," he said. "Let me sleep."

"So you won't listen to me?" she asked. "Okay then, I am going to pour a bucket of water on you."

Her threat seemed to permeate his consciousness, and Michael opened his eyes. His glance swept over her face and moved to the empty bucket in her hand.

"No water." She smiled.

He sat with a sudden jerk and swung his legs down. He peered closely at her face. "You are here to save me," he whispered.

"What?"

"You're an angel. You're here to take me to heaven."

"What nonsense are you blabbering, Michael? I am Mohini..." She hesitated. "Your friend."

He rubbed his eyes and looked past her at the wall. He seemed to notice his surroundings for the first time. Then he fell back on the mattress as if the ordinariness of his environment disappointed him and he fully expected to be in a more exciting location. The powder from his clothes rose like dust, swirling around him and making him cough. Clumps of color slid down his hair and fell heavily on the bed.

He looked at her again. "Did you put paint on me?"

Mohini laid a calming hand on his shoulder. "Someone must have. They spiked the drinks you had with marijuana."

"Marijuana?"

"Yes. They grind the marijuana leaves and mix it with the *thandai*. This happens mostly during Holi."

Michael got to his knees and pulled himself up, holding the window ledge. "Marijuana," he said. He repeated the word to himself several times. He rolled it off his tongue and then sucked it back in and trapped it in his mouth by smacking his lips together.

"C'mon, you need to go upstairs to your room. If Baba sees you here in this condition, he will blame me."

Michael shook his legs one by one and gave her a confused look. "I don't think my legs work anymore. They're no good."

Mohini touched his arm gently. "Your legs are fine. Everything is fine. You just need to try."

He looked down at her hand. He took it between his fingers and rubbed it.

"What are you doing?"

"You look so clean. No paint on you."

"I am clean because I took a bath. See, I could not get everything off. There is still some color left here and there." She turned her head to show him a pink patch on her left cheek.

Michael leaned forward as if to examine the patch, and then, without warning, he rubbed his lips against her skin.

"Stop that!" Mohini shrieked and jumped back immediately. "What do you think you're doing?"

Her legs felt weak, and she placed her hand on the wall for support. She knew she was blushing. She touched her face—the place where his lips had touched her. It was still hot.

"I was just taking that color off." He rubbed his eyes, and shielding them from the light, he peered at her. "Can I be clean like you?" he asked. "Can I take a bath with you?"

"You're not in your senses. Let me take you upstairs before Baba finds out you are not in your room."

"But I don't want to go upstairs. I want to be here... with you."

"No, you don't."

"I do," he said. "I really do."

"Come with me. You're too drunk. Nothing will make sense to you. We'll talk tomorrow morning after you have a good night's sleep."

Mohini wrapped her fingers around his wrist and tugged on it. Michael lifted his leg to step forward, but lost his balance. His upper body swayed slightly, and he grabbed Mohini's shoulder to steady himself. In the next instant, he fell back on the mattress, pulling Mohini down with him. She fell on top of him, her head landing on his chest. She stayed there for a moment, hypnotized by the rhythm of his thudding heart in her ears. Then she raised her head to look at him. He was staring at her, wide-eyed, surprised by what he had done. But when she tried to scramble off of him, he pulled her back. "Don't go." He ran a finger through her wet hair. "You feel so good."

Mohini was trembling now. She was trembling because she was angry, she decided. Hard to believe he was acting like this with her. All this time he was in their house, he didn't so much as glance at her. He pretended she was invisible. And now that he'd had a few drinks, he had decided he wanted to be with her. Not only that... he was leaving in a few days. He had already made up his mind. Did he ask her before he made that big decision? No wonder she was angry.

Anyone would be if they were subjected to this kind of constant unpredictable behavior.

Mohini took in a deep breath, trying to calm her own racing heart. She would remind him of all the things he did when he came to his senses. He would feel like an idiot then. Just looking at his face would give her great satisfaction.

She was aware of his arm resting on the small of her back. She lifted her eyes to his face. Michael had closed his eyes again and was going off into a doze. His mouth hung slightly open, and he looked peaceful, so peaceful that she almost didn't want to wake him. She wanted to keep staring at his beautiful mouth and thick eyebrows, now stained with Holi colors at the edges.

Looking at her wristwatch, she scolded herself for her own foolishness. She had to get him to his room, and it was getting late. "C'mon, we have to go upstairs. This room belongs to our security guard. He will be back here any moment."

To her relief, Michael opened his eyes and sat up. "Fine, I'll go with you." Then he looked around the room. "Where is the elevator?" he asked.

Mohini let out an exasperated groan. "We don't have an elevator!"

"No elevator?" he said, looking annoyed. "That's against regulations."

"Why don't we take the stairs?" suggested Mohini as gently as possible.

Still, Michael hesitated. "Will you come with me?" he asked.

"Yes, of course. But please, don't make any noise going up the stairs," she said. "I don't want Baba to see you in this condition."

Michael covered his lips conspiratorially. "Not a word...my lips are sealed."

They tiptoed up the stairs and came to the second-floor landing. Michael's room came into view. Her heartbeat faster—just another flight of stairs and Michael would be back in his room safely. No one needed to know about the *thandai* drink. They climbed a few more steps.

Just then, Michael lost his balance, stumbled, and rolled down the stairs. His body thudded heavily on the landing.

"Ouch," he said, flashing an idiotic grin. "No worries...no worries...I'm okay."

"Did you get hurt?"

"I didn't fart."

Despite everything, Mohini laughed.

"Who is that? What is going on there?" Baba's voice came from his bedroom.

Her heart skipped a beat. She tried to keep her voice calm. "Nothing happened, Baba. Michael fell. But he is all right."

"Michael fell down?" Baba and Ma came rushing out of their room. "Are you all right, son?"

Baba flew down the stairs to pick him up.

"Mr. Sen, I feel great. No problem. None."

"You don't look well. Are you sick?"

"I feel great. Just g-r-e-a-t. This is the best I ever felt."

"Why do you still have color on you? Why didn't you take a bath? All these wet clothes will give you pneumonia!"

"There are no bathrooms in this house. You don't even have an elevator," complained Michael.

Baba narrowed his eyes. "Have you been drinking? Is that why you can't get up?"

"Get up? Of course I can *get up*," laughed Michael. He pulled himself up and stood proudly before Baba. "See... piece of cake." Then he bent forward and said, "I can do better than that... I can even do a headstand—watch me now. I'll be perfect."

"No, Michael, don't do it—" Mohini rushed forward to stop him. But before she could get to him, he pushed his legs up in the air, bringing his hands down. His legs swam in the air for a second and then came crashing down on the hard, cold stairs.

Baba's eyes grew wide with surprise that changed quickly to anger. He wrinkled his nose in disdain. "Michael, did someone give you *thandai* today?"

"Baba, listen." Mohini stepped between them quickly. "It's not his fault. Somebody..."

"Later, Mohini. You, I will deal with later. I want to hear what Michael has to say first."

Michael pulled himself up on his feet somehow, slipping and falling several times. He brought his face close to Baba's and looked him straight in the eye. "Sorry about that headstand. That one is always a killer. But I can do a full-body flip. I picked it up from the cheerleaders in my school. Watch me."

Baba grabbed Michael's shoulder and shook him. "I never thought I would see you in this condition. This is the most disrespectful thing you have done."

"Mr. Sen, can you please keep your voice down? You are hurting my ears."

"You didn't pay attention to any of my teachings. If you did, we would not see this day. You have now destroyed the sanctity and purity of your body. Your body is now contaminated, and the meditation techniques will not work."

"Stop," cried Michael. "You are always shouting or lecturing— lecturing or shouting... right here in my ear. Sometimes your voice gets stuck in my head...it goes blah blah blah all day. 'Michael, don't do this' and 'Michael, don't do that.'"

Baba's face turned purple with rage. "*Thandai* has marijuana in it. It is dope, Michael. Any kind of dope in your system will disqualify you from any weight-lifting contest, let alone the Olympics. You, of all people, should know this."

Michael paused and frowned.

"Olympics?" asked Michael. He rubbed his chin thoughtfully and repeated the word several times. "That reminds me of something I have to do right now."

"What?" Baba released his clasp on Michael's shoulder and stepped back.

"I have to pee." He laughed.

Before anyone could stop him, Michael turned to the wall, unzipped his pants, and peed on the cool cement wall. Ma gave a loud shriek, covering her face with the end of her sari. That moment, standing before her parents and dying of shame, Mohini prayed for an invisible hand to appear and turn her into a tiny insect that could fly away to outer space and never return to the human world.

Chapter 21

A shrill ring alerted Mohini the next morning. She had difficulty locating the source. She ran down the hallway and stopped outside Michael's door. It was his cell phone that was disturbing the peace of their morning. But what was he doing? Why hadn't he picked up the phone? Irritated, she pushed back the curtains and entered his room.

She found him fast asleep, his arms and legs half hanging from the bed. The color on his body had rubbed against the bed sheets and pillows. His lips were covered in a whitish drool that had dried to form a crust around his mouth.

The phone did not stop ringing. Unable to bear the sound, Mohini picked it up. "Hello?"

"Who am I speaking to? Where is Michael?" The woman on the phone had an American accent.

Mohini's heart skipped a beat. "Are you Michael's mother?"

"Yes. Can I speak to my son, please?"

"Sure... err... I will get him for you."

"Thanks."

Mohini moved closer to his bed and called his name. He ignored her and sank deeper into his pillow. "Wake up. It's your mother on the phone." Mohini raised her voice. When she didn't get a reaction from him, she deliberately aimed her right elbow and stabbed his rib cage.

This time, he groaned in pain and opened his eyes. "Go away," he gasped. "I don't want to talk to anyone. I'm having some problems."

Reluctantly, Mohini picked up his phone again. "Michael is still sleeping. Can he call you back later?"

"No, I need to speak to him *now*." Her voice was sharp and assertive. "I received a phone call from Mr. Sen this morning. He told me what Michael has done. So it is very important that I speak to him."

Fear snaked through Mohini. "Baba... I mean, my father called you in Massachusetts?"

There was a brief pause. "Are you Mr. Sen's daughter?"

"Yes."

"What is your name?"

"Mohini."

"I need a favor from you, Mohini. Please put this phone on speaker. I want Michael to hear what I have to say."

Michael sat up and rubbed his eyes. His mother's voice crackled through the speaker. "Michael, are you there?"

"Yes, Mom." He sounded slightly breathless. "Why so early...?"

"It's not early, Michael. You're not in your right mind. You should know that it is ten in the morning where you are."

"That's impossible... I always wake up at..." He didn't finish his sentence. His eyes flew to the wall clock, and he stilled.

"Michael." His mother's voice cracked as she said his name. "Is there something you need to tell me?"

He squinted and rubbed his eyes, trying to focus on what his mother was saying. An image flashed before Mohini's eyes—Michael unzipping his pants and peeing on the freshly painted cement wall. A look of horror spreading over Baba's face, followed by a piercing scream from Ma. Then other images gushed over from the previous day in excruciating detail. Looking at Michael, she could tell he, too, was reliving the moments from last evening.

"Son, are you there?" His mother's voice was soft. Mohini almost thought she was crying. "Mr. Sen said you urinated on his wall. What do you have to say for yourself?"

"He told you that?" Michael gasped.

"Yes, baby. He told me that. He wants you to leave immediately."

Michael's jaw fell slack and his mouth opened in shock.

Mohini's heart beat faster. *Baba wanted Michael to go home.*

"But you need to stay. You should stay. You promised me you would try."

Michael clenched his fists in frustration. Climbing out of bed, he grabbed his oversized sneakers and tossed them at the wall one by one. A shoe flew in Mohini's direction and she jumped out of the way. She covered her mouth to suppress a shriek.

"What're you doing, Michael? Are you listening to me...?" His mother sounded anxious.

"Yes, Mom," he said, so quietly that Mohini could barely hear him.

"Did you hear what I said?"

"Yes." His voice was louder this time.

"So what are you going to do about it?"

Michael seemed to strain his chest muscles, trying to force out the words. "It's his house... If he wants me to go, I've to go."

"You did a stupid thing, son. Mr. Sen gave you an opportunity, and you blew it."

"But I still can't believe he actually wants me to go."

"Does it matter? You didn't want to go to India in the first place."

Michael turned slightly to look at Mohini. His eyes flickered with an unknown emotion and he looked away quickly. "Do we always mean what we say and say what we mean?"

"Wait, a minute. Are you changing your mind? You don't want to leave his house?"

"I don't know, Mom. It's less... complicated here, somehow. So far away from things... all that stuff you know." Michael opened his mouth to suck in air. "But it's too late. Mr. Sen doesn't want me."

Mohini's shoulders heaved. Her heart went out to Michael. How much she wanted to wipe out the *thandai* incident and make everything right for him.

"It's most definitely not too late. You must make this right," his mother chided him.

"What do you want me to do?"

"Apologize! Act like the son of a captain."

Michael remained silent.

"Maybe then he'll let you remain there," his mother said. "Then you'll be safe, at least, for a little while longer."

"I don't know how..."

"Find a way, baby. Make it right."

"Mom, just so you know... it was a mistake," panted Michael. "I didn't... know that *thandai* stuff is so powerful."

"Why are you speaking like this, Michael? Are you having trouble breathing?"

"Yes... Mom."

"Is your asthma coming back?"

"I d-don't... know." His face grew red, and his veins stood out from the effort of breathing.

Mohini's heart beat faster.

"Michael, how could this happen? You didn't have this for years..."

"I..." His voice got caught in his throat, and he did not finish his sentence. His breath turned into a wheeze as if he were having trouble getting oxygen into his lungs. He leaned forward with his hands braced on his knees. His efforts became more frenzied as he hankered for a bit of fresh air. He stumbled forward, almost tripping over some scattered clothes.

A shiver ran down Mohini's spine. Her legs felt heavy, as if they were chained to the floor.

"Mohini!" His mother's voice cracked like a whip, bringing her out of trance. "Get your father on the phone... *now!*"

• • •

Soon, Baba, Ma, Parul, and some boys from the camp surrounded Michael. They supported him and helped him sit in a chair. Mohini looked sometimes at Michael, sometimes at Baba's face. Like everyone else, Baba looked distressed to see Michael in such anguish, fighting to bring his spasms under control.

"Your mother tells me you had this before?" asked Baba.

"Yes," Michael panted. "Only as a child. Mom took me to the emergency room. Then it went away."

"Call the doctor," Baba instructed Ma.

Ma looked up the number in the stained, fading address book and picked up the receiver with trembling hands.

"Doctor *babu*," Ma pleaded, "Please, come as quickly as you can. The American boy is having an asthma attack... No, we did not know he has asthma, he didn't mention it to us... He looks terrible... Please, come quickly."

•   •   •

The doctor came over shortly. He propped Michael on the pillow and examined him carefully. "It is curious what caused this attack after so many years. What was the trigger? Did something unusual happen in the last twenty-four hours?"

At the word "trigger," Baba glanced down at Mohini's face. Stepping forward, she hesitantly described the events of the previous day, starting from how the servants gave Michael *thandai* and how later she discovered him in the room below the stairs, fast asleep. She paused momentarily when she spotted Parul half-hidden behind Baba's students. An image came of Parul in a yellow sari offering a glass of *thandai* to Michael. Mohini picked up a finger to point at her, but she caught herself in time. *This has to wait*, she decided. *We must think of Michael's treatment first.*

When Mohini finished reporting Michael's inebriated behavior on the stairs, Baba shook his head with regret. "Michael must have fallen asleep in his wet clothes and colored powder from the festival. None of us were in the right mental state. So we did not check on him."

Ma stood silently behind Michael's chair, her hand on his shoulder. Tears formed in her eyes and rolled down her cheek.

The doctor clicked his tongue. "He may be allergic to all this colored powder, and it stayed on his body too long. I will inject some epinephrine subcutaneously. That will calm the spasms for now. But bring him to my chamber after he gets better. I will write him a prescription for an inhaler." He filled the syringe with medication and gently tapped on it. "Monitor him," he said. "If the spasms don't go down, we may have to give him oxygen. Call me and I will send an ambulance and take him to my hospital."

After the doctor left, Baba slumped on a chair next to Michael and took his hand. "I owe you an apology. It is because of my negligence that you are in this state today. I brought you here to a new country, new surroundings, and then I failed to protect you. I gave my word to your mother... I promised to look after you. But I could not do my duty, son."

Michael's fingers wrapped around his wrist. He opened his lips to say something, but another spasm hit him.

"You should not talk in this condition." Ma inserted a pillow behind Michael's back. "Mohini's father, leave the boy alone."

But Baba was visibly distressed. The words gushed out like water from a fire hydrant.

"Mistakes happen at your age. But instead of trying to counsel you, showing you the right path, I deserted you. I left you with your struggles, when you needed me most..."

"Mohini," Ma shouted. "Take your Baba out of this room. He is getting the poor boy excited. Look at how much he is suffering."

Her threat worked, and Baba reigned in his emotion. "You are right, Mohini's mother. I am being selfish again. I will not say another word."

Chapter 22

Rahim lay on his back with his arms behind his head. Parul's legs remained locked in his; her head rested on his hairy, sweat-soaked chest. The desire in her body drained away slowly, replaced with self-loathing. She moved away from him and turned on her side. Rahim reached for her and dragged her back into the circle of his arms. He whispered caresses in her ear, biting and tugging her earlobe and wanting her to moan in response. Parul freed herself from his embrace and sat up, her bare back turned toward him.

"You seem worried, Mumtaz," said Rahim.

She looked back at his dark eyes, which were filled with desire. He ran his finger down her bare back, and she shuddered.

"I am not worried."

"Okay, I can see something is bothering you." Rahim pulled her down and rubbed her nipple with the end of his thumb. "You think I will not give you a *tawfa* for Eid? I have already bought a pair of earrings for you."

Parul bit her lower lip and looked down at her hands. "I don't need a gift for Eid."

"Why are you throwing a fit? Did your *Abba* ask you for more money?"

She did not answer, and for several minutes she chewed on her lower lip. Then she turned to say something, but the words choked in her throat. Her fingers curled into a fist and dug into the mat. She shook her head.

"Are you worried about us meeting like this?" asked Rahim at last.

"Shouldn't I be?"

"Did Ma say something? Has Mohini seen you come to the west wing?"

"No, no one has said anything or seen anything. But they could have."

Parul pulled up her petticoat and stood. Her fingers trembled as she tried to clip the hooks of her bra. Rahim pulled himself up and stood behind her. He squeezed her shoulders and rubbed her neck. "You worry unnecessarily. Your mistress's family sleeps soundly in the afternoon. No one is keeping an eye on you."

"No one keeps an eye on me, but God is. Didn't you teach me that God knows everything? He knows what's going on in the stars and what's going on deep in the sea where no man can go. He knows me from the top of my head to the tip of my toe." Parul's eyes filled with tears. "The guilt won't let me sleep at night."

He put his finger under her chin and lifted her head so she was looking up into his eyes. "There is nothing to feel guilty about. It is because of Allah's wish that I am with you now. He is in control of your destiny and mine. God is sovereign. Nothing occurs without His divine permission."

"If this is Allah's wish, then why am I getting His punishment?" asked Parul.

"What punishment?" Rahim raised his eyebrows.

"These days I feel very tired, like my hands and legs are chained to the floor. I don't feel like working. I want to lie down all the time."

"*Byash*? Such a small thing and you are worried about it?" Rahim patted her cheeks and moved away. He ran his fingers through his beard. Taking out his beard comb, he tamed the tangles.

Parul grew impatient. "There is more," she cried out.

"More?"

"Yes. I vomited on the terrace all over Ma's chili plants. I never vomit. I don't get stomach upsets."

"So? Just one vomit and you got terrified? Is this the kind of courage you want to show God? Is this how you will pass all his tests, overcome the thousand obstacles he puts in your path?"

"But what if I am with child...?" The words sprang from her lips before she could stop them.

Rahim gave a disgusted grunt and tied his *lungi* around his waist. He inserted the beard comb back in his vest pocket.

Parul apologized with a smile and added quickly, "Silly thoughts, right? I know I worry too much. It's just that I have never felt like this before... I don't feel like myself at all. It is as if an evil jinni has taken over my body."

Rahim did not answer. He moved to the cobweb-covered bookshelf and studied the moth-eaten collection of *Encyclopedia Britannica*. He picked up a book, blew away the dust, and scanned the pages. He snapped the book shut and walked back to her.

"Get all these nonsense thoughts out of your mind and focus on your task. The cockroaches and ransacking the American's room were both good plans. The spray paint on the wall in English was a nice touch. That really irritated him." He turned to look at his own reflection on the mirrored wall. He stroked his hair and adjusted his cap. "Of course, I had to sneak upstairs and write those words for you. Can't expect an ignorant girl like you to know any English.

"But remember, I can't do everything for you." He placed his hand firmly on her shoulder. "I am only your mentor, your guide. I can show you the way to God and paradise. But you have to execute your own plans."

"I am trying," mumbled Parul. "For instance, on the day of Holi..."

"Yes, I know. You gave the American some *thandai*, and he acted like a fool. The drink did more than we expected." Parul listened to him with trepidation and then, unexpectedly, an appreciative smile flickered briefly in the corners of Rahim's mouth. "That is the kind of good work we expect from you."

His approval warmed Parul's heart. She moved closer to him, looking into his dark eyes. For a few moments, a tide of longing swept over her body. Her mouth went dry, her pulse pounded so loudly she feared he could hear it.

Rahim drew a single finger down her cheek, making her quiver. "But everything you did till now is kid's stuff. I want to see some grown-up action."

Parul nodded and adjusted her headscarf to cover every bit of her hair. Then she dropped to her knees, extended her hands to grab Rahim's palms, and touched her lips to his knuckles. She drew his hands to her forehead and held them there.

Chapter 23

As Michael recovered from his asthma attacks, it became gradually clear that a change was coming over him. Michael's apathetic, resentful presence was slowly receding, and a more cheerful persona was taking its place. Mohini noticed he smiled more, showed up on time for his meditation classes, and acted friendly with Baba's students. Impossible as this might have seemed, Michael, who liked to sit on the sidelines and be a sullen observer, was finally showing willingness to play along.

One day, when Mohini had finished her chores and was about to leave the gym, Michael left his exercise mat and walked over to Baba. He kneeled before Baba and touched his feet.

Mohini's eyes widened. *This is new*, she thought. *Why is he showing so much respect?*

Baba pulled him up quickly. "What are you doing, son? You are an American. Your customs are different."

"Mr. Sen, I know I acted like a real douchebag," he said. "I hope you can forgive me."

"Why bring up all that?" Baba waved his hands in the air. "Gone... gone. All in the past."

Michael shook his head. "I was wrong. Very wrong. I hurt your feelings."

Baba patted his shoulder and smiled affectionately. "You are here, aren't you? Ma Kali has brought you back."

Michael picked up two barbells and stroked them wistfully. The sweat on his forehead glittered like jewels. He stretched both his arms and held out the barbells to Baba. "Don't know if I deserve a second chance. But if I get one, I'll do things right this time."

Baba didn't wait. He stepped forward and pulled Michael into his embrace.

Relief washed over Mohini like a wave. They were starting over.

．　　．　　．

When Baba made his students, do their morning exercises in the side garden, Mohini stood with her cup of tea on the balcony and watched. During push-ups, Michael's body extended forward like a sleek panther, almost devoid of any bones, and then arched as the muscles stacked on top of each other and quivered down his back. When Michael swung the Indian clubs, Mohini became wonder-struck. Watching Michael was like watching Baba in his younger days—there was the same ease, beauty, and mastery in all his movements.

Rajkumar, who, Mohini decided, looked even more ridiculous in his *lungi* and torn sleeveless vest next to the fair American boy, deliberately bumped into him and stepped on his feet while exercising. Rajkumar had been in unhappy spirits ever since Michael had walked into Baba's camp. He was furious with Baba for keeping the American close to himself and constantly praising his superior "western" technique. Rajkumar blamed Baba for showering almost all his attention on the white boy when, clearly, he, Rajkumar, was equally talented and deserving of such affection.

Seeing Rajkumar fuming and frustrated brought a satisfied smile to Mohini's lips. She tilted her head slightly and flicked her hair from one side to the other. Her eyes contacted Michael as he swung his Indian club, and he winked back at her. *Shameless*, thought Mohini, blushing deeply. She pretended to look away from him and then glanced back quickly, hoping he was still staring at her.

A figure came out of the shadows and blocked her view of Michael: it was Parul, and she had a disdainful expression on her face. "Mohini, you are behaving like a fool."

"What?"

"Around that foreign boy. You say silly things, laugh more than necessary, and stand too close to him."

"Why would you say something like that? It is not true." Mohini gritted her teeth. Parul was always spying on her. Clearly, she had nothing better to do.

"Don't believe me, then," said Parul. "But those foreign boys are not to be trusted. If he knows you are soft for him, he may try some hanky-panky stuff with you."

"Michael is not like that," said Mohini vehemently. *The drunken kiss on the day of Holi does not count,* she told herself. She would never doubt Michael again, no matter how much Parul tried to convince her otherwise.

"Overnight he became a good boy? A few days back, he ripped your blouse, and you came crying to me. Looks like you have forgotten all that. Anyway, why would you listen to me? After all, you are an educated girl, capable of making your own decisions. Why would you listen to a poor, half-educated maid like me?"

Parul's words were like shards sticking in Mohini's ribs. "Stop it, Paruldi. I know what I am doing," she shouted. "This is not your village, where women cover their heads with a sari and don't make eye contact with men. You don't understand our world at all. And if you don't, you shouldn't act as if you do."

•   •   •

One Saturday, Ma labored for hours in the kitchen, preparing fish and eggplant curry with just the right amount of cumin, coriander and cayenne powder. Mohini thought the food was finger-licking good. She gulped it down quickly, but Michael, sitting across from her, pushed the food around on his plate instead of eating.

Ma fell into hysterics. "Michael, I give up," she wailed. "I really don't know what to feed you."

"I'm sorry, Mrs. Sen. It's good food. I just can't eat it today."

"Don't think even for a moment that I am a fool. I know exactly what is going on here. You don't like our middle-class Bengali food."

Ma wiped sweat from her brow with the free end of her sari. "My hours in front of the hot stove mean nothing to you."

"You're getting this all wrong. My lack of appetite has nothing to do with your food, and I mean it! I just wanted something different today. I have had this craving all day..."

"Craving? Craving for what? Why didn't you tell me you have a craving?"

Mohini shifted uncomfortably in her chair. She knew how much Michael cringed at Ma's interrogations. *He would rather be anywhere else but here,* she thought.

"It's no big deal," Michael laughed awkwardly. "Forget I said that."

"No, no, tell me," Ma pressed on, unwilling to let him off. "After all, you are our guest."

"You won't get more upset?" asked Michael cautiously.

"Oh, Michael, I can't possibly be more upset than this. For the last three months, I have cut down on spices and green chili so much that I can't recognize my own cooking. Sometimes I think I am chewing on sawdust. My food has no taste... none! And still I can't make you eat it."

Michael put his fingers to his temples as though he had a headache.

It was unbearable. *I have to get him out of here,* thought Mohini.

"Michael..." She cocked her head to one side. "I just heard Baba yell your name from downstairs. You're late for your class." She winked back at Michael.

Ma glared at Mohini. "Get your ears checked. How can you hear your Baba's voice when he is not even home?"

"Not home?" Mohini swallowed hard.

"Your father left for his court date. The Kolkata High Court will hear our case against that evil widow."

"Sorry, Ma," stammered Mohini. "I... err... didn't know."

"All right," Michael said, in resignation. "The truth is, I'm craving a hamburger today, with fries and Coke. When I left home, my buddies told me that the first thing an American miss in a foreign country is a McDonald's, and he looks for hamburgers wherever he goes. They sure were right."

"A hamburger? You are craving a hamburger? The one that is made from cow meat?" Ma pinched her nose with her fingers and looked at Michael with disgust. "*Chi chi*. I cannot let such dirty food enter my house."

"And I wouldn't dream of asking you to do that," said Michael quickly, before the whining could get fully underway. "This is exactly why I didn't want to tell you. Don't worry, the craving will pass."

Ma dabbed her eyes and blew her nose.

"Ma." Mohini touched her shoulder gently. "McDonald's does not sell any beef or pork in India."

"Are you sure?"

"I am certain. They only have chicken and *paneer* items."

Ma's shoulders relaxed. She sighed and looked at Michael. "Go, go," she said. "I will not stop you."

"What?"

"I said go to your favorite McDonald's. Eat whatever you want."

Michael just stared at Ma as if he couldn't believe his ears. "Are you sure, Mrs. Sen? You really mean it?"

"Does it look like I am joking? Just eat your American food for one day and be happy. But tomorrow you have to chew on our *roti* and curry. No complaining then... I am telling you right now." She waved him off.

. . .

That evening, Ma told Mohini to take Michael to the big McDonald's on Park Street. When they reached the entrance, the doorman opened the heavy glass door for them. Inside, throngs of boys and girls, most of them their age, sat around sipping Coke and eating French fries from large brown trays. The aroma of fried chicken and stale ketchup hit Mohini's nostrils, making her feel slightly ill.

Michael placed an order for three McSpicy Paneer, two McChicken, three large fries, two ice-cream sundaes, and a two-liter Coke. Half a dozen high school girls standing behind him in the queue started giggling as the food piled up on his tray like a small mountain. But when Michael turned around and glanced at them, they were awed by his muscular good looks. They pinched each other and fluttered their eyelashes at him. Michael returned the effort almost carelessly with his most disarming smile, and the girls gasped. When he took off his thin jacket, the girls let out a small chorus of admiration at the sinuous, powerful muscles on his arms. "Are you a wrestler or something?" one squealed.

"Can we touch your muscles?" said her friend with a giggle.

Michael did not seem to mind the attention. Leaning toward them, he said, "Sure, why not?"

Beautifully painted, long fingernails grazed the rock-hard bumps of his arm and shoulders as the girls crowded around him, complimenting and approving.

Mohini rolled her eyes. *Why is he encouraging the silly schoolgirls to behave like this?*

"You shouldn't have done that," she said as they moved away from the group. "You ought to know that; this is not your America. You cannot behave like this here."

He shrugged. "They don't seem to have a problem with it." He checked out the girls, and this time, much to Mohini's annoyance, some of them winked back at him. She gritted her teeth, suppressing her irritation, but she could not think of anything more to say. They made their way past the red stools, toward the corner tables, and pulled back the chairs to sit. Michael occupied the chair across from her. A teasing smile played on his lips.

"It's true that I come from a different country and may not understand everything that goes on here. But back home, if a girl behaved like you are doing now, people might say she's jealous."

"Jealous? Now why would I be jealous? You were making a fool of yourself, and I thought, as your host, I should acquaint you with some of our norms."

"What kind of norms?"

"Like I told you—we don't wink, wave or talk to girls we don't know. And we certainly don't ask strange girls to touch us... That sort of thing is unthinkable here. You can do what you like in America, but here this action is called 'eve-teasing.' Only roadside loafers, thugs and good-for-nothing fellows indulge in such offensive behavior."

Michael seemed to ponder this for a minute. He scratched his head and asked, "What about holding hands?"

"What?"

"If I were to hold your hand, what would I be? A loafer, thug, or a good-for-nothing- fellow?" he asked. Then he took her hand and locked them in between his fingers with gentle and deliberate pressure. Awareness rushed through her body, and she looked back at him, flushed and self-conscious. He grinned, fully enjoying her discomfort.

"What does your book of norms tell you to do now? Call the cops?" He traced lines on her palms with his thumb.

"Why would I do that?"

"If smiling and winking at girls is considered such a big offense in your country, then surely holding hands deserves jail time, wouldn't you agree?" His fingers trailed up to her wrist, and he pulled her hand closer.

Mohini stared at him, wide-eyed and speechless. Her cheeks turned pink, and she looked away. He picked up her hand and placed a tiny kiss on the back. "And this... I'm sure this deserves nothing less than a life sentence."

"You are impossible, you know." She found it difficult to catch her breath.

Her phone rang somewhere in her purse. She pushed him away, freeing her hand from his grasp, and answered it.

"Hello," she said, pressing the "Talk" button. Ma was on the other end of the line, wanting to know if they had reached McDonald's safely. Without waiting for a reply, she bestowed upon Mohini her usual litany: how unsafe Park Street was at night, and how many robberies had taken place in recent times, especially targeting women her age, and though Ma felt having a muscular man like Michael with Mohini would work to her advantage, she also felt bad for putting their American guest in harm's way, asking him to defend her from strangers who may be armed, and if something were to happen to him, what face would Ma show to Michael's mother?

After hearing this much, Mohini hung up the phone and shoved it back into her purse. But before she could pull the zipper, the small bubble envelope she had placed in it earlier caught her eye. She pulled it out carefully and laid it on the table.

"I have something to show you," she told Michael.

"What is it?"

"The photography studio could put together all the pieces and restore your father's photos."

"Are you serious?" said Michael in astonishment.

"You were very upset that day when the pictures were destroyed. This is the least I could have done."

Michael took out a photo from the envelope and laid it on the table. In the picture, he stood with his father on the banks of a beautiful mountain stream. They both wore wet clothes that clung to their bodies, their uncombed hair soaking wet, and beads of water glistened on their foreheads and noses.

"Were you both swimming.... in that stream?" Mohini asked, studying the picture carefully.

"No."

"How did you get so wet then?"

There was an awkward moment of silence as he played with the salt dispenser on their table, twisting and twirling it with his fingers. "Long story." He smiled thinly.

"In other words, you don't want to share." She nodded and tried to hide her disappointment.

They focused on the food now, dipping the oily fries in ketchup and eating them one by one. Michael ate his hamburgers heartily, stopping only to wipe his face with the thin paper napkins. Mohini's own chicken burger had a rubbery patty with a bland bread coating. The smell of onions and mustard made her feel slightly ill. She put down her half-eaten burger and focused more closely on the photo laid out on the table.

"He looks like you," she said after a while.

"Who?" Michael tasted his ice-cream sundae and smacked his lips.

"Your father."

His smile was almost a grimace. "I've heard that before."

He grew even quieter, looking down at his tray and focusing solely on his food. Mohini shifted in her chair. She longed to talk to him and tell him how much she sympathized with him about his father, but she didn't know how to do it without upsetting him. She was still unsure of how Michael would react if she asked him very personal questions. His behavior toward her was so unpredictable. One moment he was drawn to her, and the next he rejected her.

Mohini tried to think of something casual and airy to say. "Massachusetts is so beautiful. Just love these mountains," she said, pointing to the photo. Talking about nature felt safe somehow. "The stream looks like melted emeralds." Michael drummed his fingers on the table and got up to pace the floor. A knot formed somewhere in her stomach. By showing him the photos, she had stepped over an invisible boundary, disturbed a part of his world completely unknown to her.

At last, he sat down and took a long sip from his drink.

"This isn't Massachusetts," he said at length. He paused and drummed his fingers again. Then he continued as if he were talking to himself. "The photo was taken before my father's deployment to Afghanistan. We'd taken a trip to the White Mountains in New Hampshire. While the family was setting up the camp, I wandered off on my own to see the nearby river. I went knee-deep into the water to look at the rocks underneath. Then I lowered myself into the raging water. I liked the rush of it, the force and power of the torrents forming and dispersing under me as it tried to pull me downstream. I held on to some big rocks. It was exciting... the danger of the swirling water, the mystery.

"Suddenly, my father appeared and pulled me out of the current with both hands. His face was white, and he was shaken — 'Never do that again,' he said. 'I thought I lost you.'"

"At that moment in the silent forest, I could hear the gentle gurgle of the stream and my father's heartbeat. 'Remember this, son... Remember this always. I can go to wars and face enemy fire and stare at death only an arm's length away because I have you. In my darkest hours and most difficult moments, I think of you, my son, and life surges through me again... The will to live comes back. I come back from a thousand deaths for you. I am because you are. So don't do foolish things like this and scare the living daylight out of me.'"

Michael paused and looked at her. "After that, my father left for Afghanistan. I still remember him waving goodbye as he went past the glass doors through the security gates to join the rest of his unit. I received occasional phone calls and letters from him, always asking me about my preparation for the Olympics. 'You, Michael, you have the power to make our country very proud. This old man of yours dreams of the day when you'll bring a medal home.'"

He got up to put away his tray. Mohini stared back at him, speechless.

Chapter 24

Mohini sat in a chair on the balcony pretending to read, but instead she watched Michael use the balcony sink and mirror to shave his face. He ran a quick hand over his stubble and put foam on his brush. He swished the rich lather in a circular motion until it spread like tiny, foaming rapids all over his face. It looked like a beard that even Santa Claus would envy. He carefully dug into the foam with his razor, scooping it out and washing it down the sink.

"You're staring," said Michael.

"It's just that I have only seen blond, blue-eyed men in Hollywood posters. Sometimes I don't know if you are real."

Michael laughed. "You want to see if I'm real?" He moved toward her table and brought his head close to her. The gentle fragrance from the wet lather both comforted and disturbed her.

"Touch me," said Michael.

"What?"

"See if I'm real."

"I will not touch you!"

"Too bad. You won't know then."

Mohini looked into his mischievous eyes and clicked her tongue. She stood in front of him and placed both hands on her hips. "I have a better way of testing if you are made of flesh and blood."

"What?"

She reached out and pinched his nose. He shrieked with pain. *What the hell*? That hurts."

"You don't like my touch?" She pretended to be offended. "Is it not womanly?"

"You'll pay for this," Michael vowed.

In typical weight-lifter fashion, he scooped her off the floor like a dumbbell and held her over his head like a trophy.

"Put me down at once."

"Why should I?"

"Michael, this is not funny."

"The pinch didn't make me laugh, either."

"Okay, Baba, I am sorry. I will not pinch you again."

"Louder... I didn't hear you."

"I said, *I am sorry.*"

Michael lowered her to the floor. "Much better. I always enjoy hearing the 's' word from you."

"You are really disgusting. How do the American girls put up with you?"

"Why do American girls have to put up with me?"

"Surely you have many girlfriends back home?"

Michael laughed. "Look who's getting all curious today, asking me about my girlfriends. Does that mean you're falling for me?"

"I am not that demented. You would be the last person I would fall for." She made a face. "Besides, you've already been here for five months. Soon your training will end and you'll hop on the plane and go back to all your American girlfriends... Who knows how many there are?"

"Oh, I lost count long ago." Michael grinned. "Who can keep track of so many? My math is weak to begin with."

"You know what? Your personal life is of no interest to me. So, please, keep this precious calculation to yourself."

"You started it, Mohini. You brought up my girlfriends."

"Talking to you is a big waste of time. Leave me alone."

Michael chuckled and moved away from her, going back to shaving. The faint fragrance of his aftershave left her, and suddenly she felt forsaken and forlorn. She wanted his fragrance to stay with her, to linger in her conscious and unconscious world, to wrap itself around her and to remind her of him all the time. *What was happening to her?* She didn't expect to feel this way about Michael. Yet as he moved away from her with long, bold strides, all she could feel was anxiety and anguish, as if she was trapped in a tiny room with no doors and windows and the air around her was running out.

Michael came from a world unknown to her. She didn't know if she could ever travel the distance to meet him at his beginning. From what he had described, she had drawn many pictures of him in his raised ranch-style house in the suburbs of Boston. In her mind, she had wandered from room to room of this wooden house, where thick carpet muffled the sound of her footsteps and a steep wooden staircase led down to a warm, dark basement where washers and dryers hummed gently and a single incandescent bulb cast dark shadows on the walls and behind the water heaters. The kitchen was large and airy, with green wallpaper and dark cherry-brown cabinets.

The living room had a stone fireplace where the logs were piled for winter months. The glass door slid back to reveal a wooden deck with lounge chairs and an oversized barbeque grill. Mohini was intrigued by these pictures Michael painted for her, and yet there were big gaps in her understanding of his world. Having lived like a frog in the well, she could not imagine the aroma that rose from that barbeque grill on his deck or picture the flames that leaped from his fireplace and quickly transformed into thick black smoke.

Yet she listened to him, spellbound, when he talked about the snow in winter and changing color of leaves in the fall. Michael described the soft, cottony wonder that fell softly from the night sky and settled on the front porch, the backyard, the chimney, and the stairs. She couldn't help feeling a gentle shiver go down her spine. Michael pushed back the snow with his shovel, and it collected into a small pristine heap in his backyard, cold and untouchable. And in the fall, every inch of his green backyard was covered with yellowing leaves. The leaves rose and floated and swirled all around him as he chased them with a leaf blower.

Sometimes at night she had dreams in which she had landed in Boston with Michael, and together they drove to his house in the suburbs to meet his mother. Mohini stood outside, hesitating and panicking. The sidewalk looked like glass, and the lawn was neatly trimmed. The bushes were pruned to perfection, and every grass in his front yard sparkled like emeralds. She was afraid to touch the blades and destroy their flawlessness.

Michael's mother, Nancy, met her at the door; she was perfect, like all military wives. Her long hair was pulled back with a single clasp, her blouse neatly buttoned to her neck and her skirt starched and ironed, gathered around her in long pleats. She reached out to shake Mohini's hand, her expression remote and unfriendly. Mohini expected it to be unfriendly. Even in her dreams, she knew Nancy wouldn't be thrilled about Michael's involvement with a brown-skinned foreigner. Mohini was hardly the kind of girl Nancy would want as a future daughter-in-law for her tall, blond, athlete son. Nancy would see instantly the improbableness of their coupling—Mohini's short next to Michael's tall, her brown next to his white, her black hair in contrast with his blond.

Out of habit, Mohini took off her slippers at the door before entering the house. Nancy looked at her bare feet with icy disapproval, a thin line dividing her forehead into two exact halves. "We like to keep our feet covered in this country," she said.

Michael's sister was missing from Mohini's dreams. Michael had excluded her from their conversations, and Mohini couldn't picture her. But she dreamed of the table Michael's mother set for them. The polenta and risotto, the lasagna and meatballs, chicken casseroles and shrimp scampi all exhibited in heavy serving trays. She had never seen or tasted any of these dishes, but Michael had described each of them in so much detail that she could identify them with ease. They sat down to eat with silver knives and forks. The weight of the flatware felt strange in her hands, and she shifted awkwardly, trying to adjust the partially folded napkin in her lap. After Nancy had taken a baked chicken out of the oven, Mohini struggled clumsily with her knife and fork, trying to cut off a modest piece. To her horror, she cut her finger. The dream shattered.

· · ·

"I don't think your mother will like me," Mohini told Michael.

He stopped shaving and looked at her, astonished. "So you were sitting here all this time thinking of *my* mother? Why on earth would you worry about what my mother thinks of you?"

"Why would I think of your mother?" she lied. "I am just asking, that's all. Do you think she would like me?"

"That possibility arises only if you meet my mother. Are you planning to meet my mother?"

"You are so rude. Can't I visit you after you leave? No invitation for me, *huh*?"

"Didn't think that far." Michael shrugged. "For me it's usually *out of sight, out of mind*." He grinned broadly, and she picked up an apple and threw it in his direction. He caught it with ease and sunk his teeth into it.

"Why the sudden interest in my mother?" he asked after a while.

"I just thought she may not like me. It's just a passing thought. Nothing important." Mohini picked up a newspaper and unfolded its pages.

"What makes you think she may not like you?"

"Oh, I am sure she will not. I am... you know... a foreigner." She pretended to read the newspaper.

"That's the dumbest thing I've ever heard. So what if you're a foreigner?"

"You know what I mean."

"Mohini, your head is filled with sawdust." He poked his head over her newspaper. "My mom's a sweetheart."

"Did you ever bring a girl of a different race to meet your parents? Like a girlfriend? Were they okay with that?"

Michael scooped some shaving cream from his chin and dabbed it on her nose. "Look who wants to know everything about my past. Are you thinking of running away to America with me?"

Mohini pushed him back. "Shut up. I will go nowhere with you, even if the earth gets invaded by aliens and you are the last man left."

"So you prefer an alien over me?"

"Something like that."

"Don't trouble yourself with such thoughts. Notice I didn't actually ask you to come with me."

"You are the most annoying boy I have ever met. Baba made a big mistake by bringing you here." Mohini rushed to the sink to wash off the shaving cream. When she lifted her head, she could see him in the mirror. He stopped behind her and surveyed her with a mocking smile.

Mohini's cheeks burned. Pushing him aside, barely pausing to pick up her newspaper, she marched off, down the stairs, all the way to the children's park. Michael's footsteps followed her, but she didn't turn back to look. She sat on the park bench and covered her face with the newspaper. After some time, Michael flopped down on the children's swing next to her, but she pretended not to notice him.

"Are you mad at me?" he asked.

"Shouldn't I be?"

"Look, if you really wanted to know about my girlfriend, all you had to do was ask. Why were you beating around the bush?"

"Who said I want to know about your girlfriend?" She made a face.

"There you go again. Why are you women so complicated?" He got up and sat next to her on the bench. He took the newspaper out of her hands and turned her around. "I had a girlfriend once, back in high school, after which I decided never to go down that road again."

Curiosity bubbled up inside her stomach, demanding to get out. Yet she composed her face, restrained her voice, and asked calmly, "And why would you decide that?"

"Because she was a big mistake," he said with a laugh. "Her name was Liz, and she was superbly clingy. The moment she spotted me in school, she rushed toward me, wrapped her arms around me, and showed me off to her friends. She used me like a trophy won in a contest. I was forced to spend all my free periods and lunchtime with her."

"You didn't enjoy being with her?"

"It was okay at first." Michael shrugged. "Then things changed. She wanted to go out and party, and I wanted to be in the gym. She didn't take my dreams seriously. Some days, she showed up at the gym and interrupted my training. We fought then." Michael folded the newspaper noisily and put it away. "The fights got bigger over time. In the end... it just all got too much for me."

Michael leaned back, and looked away into the distant horizon, "Everything was totally fine after we broke up."

Mohini's heart sank. Michael had come out of a bad relationship. *He would be double cautious in the future.*

Chapter 25

Over the next few days, Parul continued to battle her feelings. No one else noticed her suffering. Life went on normally in the house. The rice got cooked, the rooms swept, the cat yelled at and the crows shooed away when they perched on the windowpane. The weather was getting warmer. Winter was ending. Baba sat with his newspaper on the balcony, enjoying the mild midday sun. On one side, a variety of pickles made from red chilies, lime and carrots were laid out to dry, spread on old newspapers. Ma made these every winter, stored them in bottles, and used them year-round. The widow's cat sat next to them now, guarding them carefully from crows and sparrows that swung from the TV antennas on the nearby houses.

Parul climbed down the stairs, where the shadows grew longer and weather-beaten concrete pillars supported the remnant of a once lofty veranda. The metallic beams were breeding grounds for sparrows and pigeons, their monotonous cooing drowned by the roar of the printing press. Parul walked to the park behind the house. She stood next to the playground, where children slipped down plastic slides at dizzying speeds. They lined up to make a train and circle all around her. "Coooo," said the engine boy. "Jhik-jhik-jhik" said the little human compartments while the guard waved goodbye. Parul's head reeled. Normally, she would laugh at their antics and join their train, circling the park and stopping at imaginary stations. But today was different. Today she was not in the mood for company. The laughter and chatter and bright sunlight made her feel light-headed. She flopped onto a bench next to the playground.

Rahim had asked her to go after the American boy again. This time, he wanted her to cause him serious harm. "There should be a big *dhamaka*... like an explosion. People should talk about it for days. The white boy should be gone from this house... no no... not just this house... he should leave our *mulk*, our land. He should tell his American brothers never to come here. This city is not safe for Western disbelievers like him. Rely upon Allah and do this in any manner, or way, however it may be."

Parul did not know how to do a big *dhamaka*. She was, after all, a poor maid from a small village. One thing she knew: by going after the American boy, she would cause Mohini great pain. She had seen the way Mohini looked at the boy; the boy had become all-important in her life, and though Mohini never discussed her feelings for him, Parul knew if the boy were disgraced, it would break Mohini's heart. How low Parul had fallen to betray the family that had given her shelter and saved her sisters from starvation. How unlucky she was that she was plagued with this choice.

This isn't right, Parul thought.

But what choice did she have? Could she stop seeing Rahim? Did she have the power to control her own desire for him? She liked being wanted by him, hunted down by him, and lusted after. She liked his promises of a wedding and children and a home of her own. Most of all, she liked the pleasure he gave her body—every inch of her flesh heated in his presence.

In recent weeks, she had grown more and more careless. In her desire to be with Rahim all the time, she had even ignored his advice. She had gone downstairs to the printing press during office hours and loitered in the alley behind the press room windows. The machine man glanced at her, forgetting to peddle his machine, and the compositor fumbled with the typefaces, spilling ink on his clothes. Even the teenager boy whistled at her from behind the window curtains. They all pretended to be busy and then exchanged swift, meaningful looks with her.

Awful thoughts... sinful deed. I am a fallen woman, a slut. I hope Mohini comes home early from college and catches me near the press room. I hope she finds out I am sleeping with Rahim. I want her to find out. I want her to know how I am betraying this family. She will probably think I am a little whore. But that's exactly what I deserve, to be called that name.

Parul sat on the bench. She took deep breaths and tried to fight her tears. Then another fear snaked through her body, making her feel unusually cold. Earlier that day, she had thrown up again on the potted chili-plants. What if it was already too late? What if she had already brought her own destruction by what she had so foolishly begun? What if she was already carrying his sin in her belly? She could never turn her back to him then. She would have to do as he said.

The seriousness of her situation beleaguered Parul. How badly she wanted to share this fear, this moment with Mohini. The only trouble was that she didn't know how to reach Mohini anymore; Mohini had become so different from who Parul was. Mohini had left Parul, her childhood friend, behind, left her to find her own pleasures. The American boy played the lead role in her story, and Parul only played an insignificant side character. When Parul had urged Mohini to stay away from Michael, Mohini had fought back like a jungle cat, making it clear that Parul had overstepped her bounds. Parul could only agree with everything Mohini did and said; she couldn't even mildly disapprove without drawing attention to her subservient status in their house.

Mohini's snobbery pained Parul. Mohini believed she belonged to a class of "superior people"—people who attended college, spoke fluent English, wore mini-skirts and considered themselves cultured. Parul was hopelessly unfit in Mohini's circle of friends. The invisible line that existed between them was now sharper than ever.

No, Parul couldn't share her secret with Mohini. She could no longer fully trust her.

She paced the park, clenching her fist until her nails dug into the soft flesh of her palm.

The sunlight pricked her neck as she walked back home. On the first floor, she passed by the printing press. Rahim stood near the office window, gazing at her patiently. *He was waiting for her to act.*

"Sometimes we have to make sacrifices for the greater good," was part of Rahim's teaching. "We may have to hurt the people who love us the most. It is a tough choice, but if you are a true *jihadi*, you will make the right choice."

The pigeons above her head beat their wings and flew toward the empty sky. Their sudden movement startled Parul. A cool breeze chilled her body. She wrapped her sari around her.

Chapter 26

By the time Mohini had organized her notes, stuffed them in her backpack, ironed out her *salwar* suit, and gobbled down two pieces of toast with milk, it was already ten in the morning. Sweet, melodious Tagore songs spilled out of Ma's radio, rising and ebbing like a tide and leaving behind a dull yearning in their wake. Ma sat in her rocking chair, her eyes closed, her fingers curled around a hot cup of tea. Ma saved these fifteen minutes of peace and calm for herself every morning before she went back to her cutting, chopping, boiling of milk, and keeping an exact account of expenses. They all knew, barring an earthquake, not to disturb her intimate moments with this radio. The song played in Mohini's head long after she left home, repeating itself like a broken record.

That day, like every day, she adjusted the strap of her backpack and stepped outside the door.

"*Eije meye*," said a voice next to her, making her jump. "Is your mother at home?"

Standing on the top of the stairs was the press widow, her head covered with the end of a white sari. She appeared excited, a little impatient, as if she did not want to wait for Mohini's answer, but wanted to push past her and come inside.

Instinctively, Mohini put up her hand to block the widow's way. "I'm afraid she is busy. Anything I can help you with?"

"*O, Ma!* Look at this little girl's audacity. She wants to talk to me. *Arre!* You were not even born when I came to this house. I have seen you crawl on the floor in your nappies and burp milk on your mother's shoulder." The press widow patted Mohini on the head and said,

"Now, don't waste my time. Go get your mother. I have some grown-up discussions with her."

"I can't disturb her now; she is in the middle of something. She will be very upset if I interrupt..."

"*Oh*, no problem." The widow pushed past her. "Let me do the disturbing, then. As it has been ever since I came to this house, your parents have done nothing but disturb me. Without notice, they cut off the water supply to the press bathroom. *Arre*, where will all those employees pee? On my head? Or should I ask them to use the city's sidewalks as their toilet? *You tell me, Mohini...*"

"Please do not create a racket here. The neighbors can hear you. Wait until Baba comes home. Then you can tell him everything. Now, please, go downstairs." Mohini pulled the widow's hand and dragged her to the staircase. But she freed herself from Mohini's grip and dashed back inside to do some more yelling.

"And your mother uses the back alley as her personal dump yard. Rotten and stinking fruits, vegetables, eggs, and sanitary napkins. Everything ends up right outside the press window. *Ma go ma chi chi*. The stench makes us want to throw up. Feels like we live next to the landfill... Flies and mosquitoes use the back alley as their breeding ground these days. Every year they lay more and more eggs, proliferating like the Ravan family."

The widow covered her nose with the end of her sari as if she could still smell the stench.

"I should be the one bringing lawsuits against such homeowners. We are legal, rent-paying tenants. Instead, your father goes to court. Has he no shame? Bringing a lawsuit against a helpless widow like me?"

Ma appeared at the door. The commotion must have disturbed her few precious moments of peace. Her face was firm and cold. "Are you here to talk about the lawsuit? We told you a thousand times we are not taking it back."

"Ah, here you are. The mistress of this palace. Won't you ask me to come inside for some hot tea? After all, I am your relative, and that, too, from your husband's side. Don't I deserve some hospitality?"

"Didi, I have a lot of work. If you need drama so badly, perhaps you should join a television soap opera cast."

"*Hna hna...* Don't show me work. I know what kind of work you do. As if cutting off our water and suffocating us with filth were not enough. Now you are sending your slutty maid to use the press for prostitution. I have to say your cunningness has surprised me. You will fall to the lowest of lows to get us out of your property."

Ma and Mohini exchanged glances and returned to the widow with confused looks.

"What are you talking about? I don't understand one word of what you are saying," said Ma.

"Oh, so you are going to deny everything? Is this where it is going? Well... well... then two can play this game. For weeks, your maid has been loitering around the doorway, the windows, and the back alley of my press, doing all sorts of shameless things. After her midday wash, she hangs her blouse, petticoat and underclothes to dry from the clothesline just outside the press room window. Sometimes she takes a bucket downstairs and bathes directly from the water tank."

Ma stepped back so fast that she almost stumbled. "You are lying. Parul would not go near that press. She has promised me."

"Don't think my head is stuffed with cow dung. I, too, went to school and graduated eighth grade." The widow sneered. "You have planned all this out in that wicked head of yours. You want me to go out of business. Yes, that is exactly why you are doing all this."

"Believe me, Didi, I do not know what you are talking about."

"Your maid's antics have caused quite a stir in the press room. All the employees do is look at her. The compositor man poured acid on himself, and the machine man almost got his fingers smashed between the plates. The printed material that comes out looks like junk—the alphabets are upside down, and I can't tell if it is Bengali or Chinese script I am reading."

"But, Didi, that's impossible. Parul would not behave so shamelessly. I didn't bring her up like this," Ma squeaked.

"Stop upsetting my mother with your lies!" shouted Mohini. "Parul*di* has no interest in your lousy press."

"*Arre,* ask the teacher and her niece next door. They have seen your maid's comings and goings. I don't come here in the afternoon... The afternoon dust aggravates my asthma. Or else I, too, would have caught her red-handed, behaving flagrantly before my press men. The teacher and her niece have told everyone in the neighborhood. All the neighbors are talking about her. They are calling my press a brothel."

Ma's face got more and more red. "If what you are saying is true, Parul will pay for this dearly. I have given her enough warnings. This time she will pay for her misdeeds."

Ma turned around and slammed the door in the widow's face.

After the widow left, Mohini forced Ma back into her chair and poured her a fresh cup of tea. She tried to calm her down, but Ma was inconsolable. Sneaking a quick look at her watch, Mohini realized she would have to leave right away if she was to be on time for her honors class. Reluctantly, she squeezed Ma's shoulders, kissed her cheeks, and rushed down the stairs.

A few minutes after Mohini left, Parul got back from the bazaar and found Ma sitting on the rocking chair with her eyes closed. Knowing nothing of the widow's visit, Parul sat down to discuss the market prices with Ma.

"Ma," she said, pouring the contents of her grocery bag on the floor, "the tomatoes have gone up to twenty rupees a kilo and the price of cauliflowers and flat beans almost gave me a heart attack. They are selling at thirty to thirty-five rupees a kilo! I told the vegetable seller, this is robbery in broad daylight. He said floods have destroyed most of the crops and this year is going to be like this." Parul moved closer to Ma to hand her the receipts and the change. When Ma didn't open her eyes, she patted her hand to get her attention.

A deep frown appeared on Ma's forehead and she sprang out of her chair. "You shameless girl! You think I don't know what you're up to, behaving like a whore in front of all those grown men."

"What are you talking about, Ma?" gasped Parul.

"Don't lie to me. The press widow was just here. She told us you go down to the printing press in the afternoons. How could you break our trust like this, Parul? How could you rub lime and ink on our face?"

"Ma, believe me." Parul dropped to her knees and touched Ma's feet. "The widow is lying. I did nothing. I stay up in my terrace room all afternoon."

"What about the teacher and her niece? Are they lying, too? The widow said they have seen this brazen behavior from their window."

Parul felt her pulse quicken. She fought to keep her voice steady. "Ma, you know that the teacher and her niece like to gossip. They are making up all these stories. They are trying to poison your mind."

"Parul, lie after lie after lie! This is what you have become?" She flopped back into her rocking chair as if the interaction had suddenly sapped her energy. "Where have I gone wrong? What did I not do for you? I gave you everything we could afford. Cream, soap, shampoo, towels... whenever you wanted something, did I say no? If we ate fish, we put one on your plate. When Mohini drank milk, we poured you a glass, too. Show me one house where the maid gets this kind of treatment. Still, you bring shame to this family. I don't know where we failed you, Parul, that we have to see this day." Ma covered her face and wept.

"Ma, please don't cry like this." Parul folded her hands in front of herself like she was praying and whimpered. "Please, give me one more chance. I will not fail you this time."

"Go away, Parul. Leave this house. I have no more forgiveness left in me. Don't show me your face ever again."

"Don't say that," said Parul. "Where would I go? This is the only home I have known."

"Anywhere you wish. My doors are closed to you. You have humiliated and disrespected this family enough. You have ruined the reputation of this house. We can't support you anymore. Go where your two feet carry you. Go where your two eyes tell you to go. Just don't come back here. Just let us live in this neighborhood with whatever is left of our respect."

A sensational pain exploded inside of Parul. The world spun around her. She grasped the side of Ma's chair to steady herself. Bits and pieces of her life in their house flashed through her mind in a kaleidoscope of images, sounds, and colors. She squeezed her eyes shut, trying to block the overwhelming flood of memories. Still they persisted, each one unleashing a fierce burn in her chest. A whimper that sounded like an animal noise of anguish escaped from her lips.

Chapter 27

Baba decided to include Ma in his senior class field trip to Bakkhali, a seaside hamlet four hours south of Kolkata. "Your Ma is very upset, as am I, over the way Parul has behaved behind our backs," he told Mohini. "A day on the beach would take her mind off things. She needs a change." Mohini agreed with him wholeheartedly.

Ma was reluctant to go, but Baba was determined to take her. Mohini heard them arguing behind the thin walls of her bedroom. "If you don't come, we will cancel the trip," Baba told her. "Do you want to disappoint my students? You know how much they are looking forward to this outing."

So Ma had no choice but to agree.

"I'll go, too," Mohini told Baba. "I don't have any major tests or assignments due this week. I can take a day off."

There were nine students in all, including Michael and Rajkumar. Baba rented a second car from the local garage. In the end, it was decided that Baba would take Michael, Ma, and Mohini in the family car and the rest of them would follow in the large rented van. They would start early, have breakfast on the way, and reach Bakkhali around lunchtime.

When Mohini came down to their driveway the next morning, Baba was in a grim mood. His driver had not shown up, and when Baba tried to start his car himself, the ignition didn't turn on. He sat behind the steering wheel with the windows rolled down, shouting instructions to his students, who leaned forward to push the car. The rented van and its owner waited patiently below the big banyan tree.

"Mohini," said Baba. "Where is Michael this morning? Didn't I tell him to come downstairs by six?"

Mohini told him Michael had left the house early that morning and she had not seen him since. Baba grew impatient and leaned on the horn, making her jump. The disappointed look on his face made her heart sink. He always looked forward to an excellent breakfast on the way to Bakkhali, and now his car would not start, and on top of that, Michael had gone missing.

Mohini thought of the small Dhaba on the highway where they would stop to buy hot *chole*, *bhature*, *aloo tikki* and *samosas*, accompanied by a strong milky tea. Baba knew the Dhaba owner personally—years ago, they were both in competitive weightlifting. Baba stayed on, but his friend, a Sikh man from Punjab, left weightlifting to start this Punjabi Dhaba. Baba always visited him with his students on every field trip, and they sat on wicker chairs or cot beds in the shade of large trees and ate the mouthwatering food while licking the oil and syrup from their fingers. It was only on trips like this that Baba let himself ease off his diet regimen and indulge a little. So it was not surprising that the delay was irritating him.

"Seriously, where is Michael?" snapped Baba. "Why doesn't the boy have any sense of time?"

Mohini leaped into his defense. "I'm sure he went out to get his morning exercise, Baba. He will be here any moment now." She scanned the horizon, hoping she was right.

Rajkumar, who had already finished his morning bath and freshly oiled his hair, saw this as a perfect opportunity to disparage Michael before Baba. "What else can you expect from him, sir? He doesn't think your time is valuable. Only an American boy would keep his Guru waiting."

"Michael is never late," Mohini said. "There must be a very good reason why he is not here."

"It's called laziness," quipped Rajkumar. Mohini suppressed an urge to shake him hard. She would have loved to wipe that smirk off his face.

A gate creaked, and footsteps crunched on the gravelly driveway. Michael walked up the path carrying some plastic bags. As soon as he came close to the car, Baba leaped out and scolded him: Why did he not inform him before leaving the house? Why did he go off on his own?

Michael didn't look offended by Baba's sudden outburst. Instead, his eyes gleamed and his lips curled into a smile. He leaned on the car, rubbing his hands as if he were eager to share some news.

"My mother called from Massachusetts," he said. "My dad is being given the Congressional Medal of Honor."

"What honor?" Baba looked confused.

"They give it to soldiers who risk their life during wartime to save another soldier."

"And your father is being given that honor?" Baba's eyes popped with astonishment.

"Yes." Michael drummed his fingers on the metallic body of the car. "My father was severely injured trying to save the life of another soldier during the Gulf War. He is getting the award because of that." He stopped to give them an eager, animated look. "There will be a formal ceremony in the White House. President Bush has invited us all. My mother will receive the medal on his behalf."

Baba shook his head in amazement. "This is very good news. Very good news indeed." He pulled Michael into a bear hug.

Little butterflies of excitement twirled deep in Mohini's stomach. Ever since that day at McDonald's, Michael had not spoken of his dad. Mohini had tried to bring up the topic again, but he had stopped her with a wave of his hand and grimace. It was clear that he wanted to battle his own inner ghosts and didn't want her help. But today he had mentioned his father with palpable pride. This rare bit of good news had changed his demeanor—*he was glowing*.

Michael dipped his hand inside the plastic bag and pulled out bright cardboard boxes. "I went out to get some *Sandesh* for you. Isn't that how Bengalis celebrate all good news, eating lots of sweetmeats?"

One by one, Baba's students congratulated Michael. They shook his hand, squeezed his shoulder, and ate *Sandesh* from his box. Rajkumar reached for sweetmeat but didn't bother to congratulate Michael. Mohini glared at him.

When Ma came and heard the news, she gave a little cry of pleasure and touched Michael's forehead to bless him. She brought out her *puja* plate and put a sandalwood paste dot on Michael's forehead.

Baba climbed back in the car and turned the key in the ignition one more time. The car came alive with a roar. The engine whimpered and shuddered as if waking from a deep slumber, and the car lurched forward.

"Follow me," Baba barked to the owner of the rented van. "We should leave before the day gets too hot."

One by one they all got in, and the two cars took off for Bakkhali. Michael climbed in beside Baba while Ma and Mohini sat in the back. Soon they were driving out of the city, racing down roads that ran between rice fields and green ponds. Old farmers labored with iron plow standing in knee-deep water. Herds of cattle ruminated in the cool shade of trees. Sari-clad women carried water pots on their heads, their hips swaying gently as they walked back from the pond. The lush coconut tree leaves undulated in the wind like waving flags.

As the old car rattled and jolted and swerved over the rice fields, Mohini stuck her head out the window, letting the wind blow through her hair. The greenery all around her was bathed in tranquil sunlight: bees buzzed over sunflowers and wind blew over the paddy stalks, creating rippling waves of yellow. Small birds sang on the tree branches, and a crane stood patiently on one leg by the water. The musty smell of the freshly plowed fields hit her nose and filled her with a strange sense of wistfulness. She hummed a familiar tune from her childhood. Michael looked at her in the rearview mirror and smiled. The soft sunlight glittered in his green eyes, and the wind blew his blond hair across his forehead. He looked boyish and vulnerable, and suddenly Mohini ached to reach out and push back the hair from his forehead. She leaned forward slightly, but, hearing Ma shift in her seat next to her, quickly restrained her gesture and composed her face. She picked up a magazine and pretended to read it.

Baba turned off the radio and, keeping one hand on the stiff steering wheel, turned slightly to Michael. "So who is coming to your father's award ceremony?"

"Oh, our entire family will be there. Twenty of our cousins from all across the country. Dozens of Dad's friends—many who served alongside him. Some of them will fly in from other countries. They all want to be there for Dad."

Baba patted Michael on the shoulder. "Your family deserves this honor. After all you have gone through."

"Yes, it's a good thing for Mom to be going to this ceremony. She always said people around us don't recognize the sacrifice we make as military families. We lay down our lives for others, but very few come to thank us," said Michael. "We are a nation of three hundred million Americans. Of these, less than one percent wear the uniform of our armed forces. But my dad always wanted to serve his country."

There was a catch in his voice that made Mohini put down her magazine and look at him in the rearview mirror. The news clearly moved Michael. His eyes were dark with emotion. For the first time in a long time, he was eager to share his past. That he was moved, moved her.

She leaned out of the window and looked at the silvery road disappearing under the rolling tyres of the car. Shading her eyes, she looked back at the miles of green countryside they had left behind and marveled at how much her feelings for Michael had evolved over these months and how much she had come to care for him. The wind blew her hair, and the sunlight warmed her face. A lump rose in her throat and tugged at her heart.

When had the stranger become so important in her life?

•   •   •

The Dhaba was a modest shack with a placard reading, "Pure Punjabi." Some truck drivers and locals sat on wicker chairs or cot beds in the shade of large trees, eating and drinking from steel plates and cups. A few tables inside the tin shade offered relief from the glare of the morning sun.

The Dhaba owner came out to embrace Baba. His long hair was rolled up on top of his head and covered with a turban. He clearly had been bent over a hot stove in the kitchen: perspiration dripped off the side of his face onto his grease-spotted banyan. "Namaste, namaste, *Pahalwanji*." His face glowed with pleasure. "Long time no see. Where to this time?"

"We are on our way to Bakkhali, *Sardarji*. And we have an American guest with us."

"You brought an American to my *garib khana*, poor man's restaurant?" The *Sardarji* glowed with pleasure. "I'm honored."

"He is not just any American, *Sardarji*. He is one of the most gifted athletes who will grace the Olympic stage one day. It is by God's immense grace that I have this boy with me here. He will do what I couldn't do in this lifetime."

"And you were the best we ever had," said *Sardarji*, nodding his head in regret. "We had so much hope for you."

"Let bygones be bygones." Baba waved his hand to dismiss the thought. "We are all old people now."

Ma and Mohini took off their sunglasses and went to sit under the tin shade, away from the sun. Michael and Baba followed them inside. The rest of Baba's students stayed outside to play cards and *antakshari*.

Inside, the Dhaba was just the way Mohini remembered it. The walls were decorated with wicker baskets and truck tires. The smell of roasting spices laced with onion and garlic wafted through the air, while griddles sizzled inside the kitchen, and the sound of bhangra music blasted from small, black speakers.

Baba pulled a chair next to Michael. "You are only used to air-conditioned restaurants with fancy furniture and modern bathrooms. But it is in this simple Dhaba that we get the most authentic and tasty *desi* food."

Michael glanced uncertainly at the flies buzzing over the steel plates and water cups. Baba laughed. "This is clean, hot food, son. No need to get concerned."

The *Sardarji* brought out a roasted whole chicken on a plate with several bowls of almonds and clarified butter on the side. "This is our *Pahalwani* special. A complimentary dish for our American guest. May you go to the Olympics and make us proud."

Michael blinked at the enormous chicken on his plate in an anxious, dismayed kind of way. He picked up the clarified butter and held it close to his nose. He seemed reluctant to taste it.

"Eat, son, eat. All American are sons of lions," said the *Sardarji*. "The ancient Indian body builders ate this food for breakfast."

Michael took a small bite of the chicken and his face turned bright red. "Water, water..." he begged hoarsely, clutching his throat. Then he grabbed the folded napkins from the table and wiped his eyes. Baba and *Sardarji* started to laugh, but Ma glared at them. She pulled the plate of chicken away from Michael and scraped the outer layer with a spoon to remove the spices. She asked Michael to take another bite. "The spices won't bother you now," she assured him.

After lunch, *Sardarji* invited Baba and the students to play cards with him. Michael and Mohini went for a walk behind the Dhaba, where there was a river. For a while, they walked silently on the beach, occasionally dropping small pebbles into the water. Michael, deep in thought, walked faster and moved ahead of Mohini. When Mohini caught up with him and tried to fall in step, he gave her an awkward, apologetic smile. "Sorry. I think I'm a little homesick today."

They sat on the edge of the water and watched it lap against the shore. Mohini turned her head slightly to look at him. Michael, still distracted, twirled the ring on his finger.

"Remembering your dad?" she asked.

"Yes," he said quietly. "Dad's award brought back memories of his Kuwait deployment in 1991. That was the year he got shot." Michael folded his legs and brought his knees closer to his chest. He wanted to say something more—something that was important to him—but some internal checkpoint held him back.

"How old were you then?" she asked gently.

"I was only eight, and my sister, Anna, was six. We lived on a base then... It was Fort Dix, New Jersey."

"You were that young! It must have been shocking to get such bad news."

"What made the situation shocking was that the way the news was delivered to us." A sardonic smile twisted his lips. "It was the worst possible way to find out that your dad was shot."

"What do you mean?"

A faraway look came into his eyes as he gazed at the opposite bank of the river. Michael cleared his throat before he spoke. "One day, when Anna and I got back from school, we heard water running in the bathroom upstairs. We ran up the stairs and found Mom sitting on the edge of the bathtub, eyes glazed, looking into the space before her. I reached over and turned off the water so it wouldn't overflow the tub. Mom finally noticed us and said, in this weird, calm way, 'Your father has been shot. He may not come home.' I didn't know what to say or do. I just rushed over to our neighbor's house to get help. The neighbors called the doctor. The doctor gave mom some pills and ordered her to stay in bed."

"Who took care of you then?" cried Mohini. "You were both so young."

"No one, really. I had to take care of Anna on my own. She was sure that Dad was not coming back. She would hide under her bed or go inside her closet and cry. I pulled her out and assured her that everything would be okay."

"And your mom? Did she get better?"

"Not for a while. She mostly stayed in her bedroom. Anna and I made our own peanut-butter-and-jelly sandwiches and got to school by ourselves. When we got home, we saw her sleeping under the covers or staring out the window." Michael leaned back on a rock and stretched his legs. "One night, I woke up, hearing her crying through the bedroom wall. I found her propped up on the bed, her face buried in her palms. 'Your father is going to lose his leg now,' she said. 'He'll be disabled for the rest of his life.'"

Mohini shivered. She thought of little Michael and his sister alone in a big house, while their mother lay in her bedroom and their father was thousands of miles away. Those must have been terrible days for the children — spent cowering in the background, listening, while their mother sobbed wildly and an uncertain future hung over their head. No one came to comfort them and answer the thousand questions that plagued their young minds as they tiptoed around the house, huddled together in closets and speaking only in whispers.

Michael picked up a pebble and splashed it into the water. "For a long time, I didn't know what really happened to my dad. There was no one who could explain things to us. I wished I was old enough to take charge of the family and fix everything... make things normal again," he said with a forced smile. "It was frustrating to be just eight."

"When did you see your father again?"

"After a few months, Mom told us that Dad was coming back to the states to be treated at Walter Reed near Washington. We all went down to see him. Dad smiled at us weakly from his hospital bed. He looked so much older—his hair and beard had turned gray. I still remember how swollen his left leg looked. The skin was so transparent that I could see where it was cut and stapled together. Anna ran up to him and buried her curly head in his chest. Mom poked his left leg many times to see if it was working. In the end, the nurse asked her to leave the room."

Mohini took out a handkerchief and blew her nose loudly. How unfair that such a heavy burden had been placed on Michael's young shoulders. It was as if the world had singled out Michael to reveal its evil ...so early in his life.

"Did he tell you how he got shot?"

A frown appeared on Michael's forehead, and he bit his lip and said, "I didn't ask him."

"Didn't ask him?" Mohini was astonished.

"What did you expect me to do? I was so young then; I couldn't bear to hear a story where my dad almost died." A grimace clouded his face.

Mohini said nothing. She turned around and put a hand on his arm—shifting closer to him—and they looked at each other for a long, long time.

Michael broke the silence. "Dad told me later how he got shot... when I was older."

Mohini moved quickly to put a finger on his lips. "Let it be," she said. "You don't need to go there. It'll only give you pain."

"But I want you to know," he said firmly. "I want you to understand who my Dad was."

Blood thumped dully in Mohini's ears. A door had cracked open, and she was allowed to glance in. Gratitude surged through her. It was with difficulty that she focused on his next words.

"Two months after Dad was deployed to Kuwait, he was traveling with the scout platoon he led. He had a senior scout sniper and two or three spotters with him. They came across a roadblock made of rubber tires and tree trunks. The scout sniper jumped off the vehicle to clear up the block. Out of nowhere, a rocket-propelled grenade appeared and exploded in front of the vehicle close to the roadblock. As the smoke cleared, Dad saw that the scout sniper was on the ground, squirming in pain.

"Dad made a quick calculation. He understood how risky it was to save him, but he couldn't just walk away and let his friend bleed out. So he asked the driver to move their vehicle alongside the injured man to shield him from more gunfire. He grabbed his emergency bag and rushed toward the injured man.

"Dad heard the injured guy groan next to him. He was covered in hot, sticky blood. Dad opened his emergency bag to take out the tourniquets. Just then, he heard his friends inside the vehicle yell out to him. He opened his mouth to say something, but his voice died in a roar of gunfire. He felt as if a chainsaw was ripping open his leg. The pain was so intense that he almost lost consciousness. The machine gunfire hit him—on his left leg. He blacked out."

Michael shook himself as if to get rid of the image. Mohini gave his hand a squeeze to drive away the pain, to absorb some for herself. The sky was darkening above them and the threat of rain was eminent. She saw the birds circle the trees and the water lap wildly against the shore.

"And the leg?" Her voice trembled.

"Dad did not lose his leg. At the end of the year, he was back in our home in New Jersey. He walked around the house on crutches at first, and after months of physical therapy, he slowly learned to walk without them. Over the next couple year's dad made an amazing recovery—the injured leg regained most of its function, and dad was called back to active duty."

The clamor of voices in her head subsided slowly, and a single thought reigned: Michael had revealed himself to her, finally and unexpectedly. She understood his dilemma, felt his burden. His experiences made him familiar; the words he shared bridged the visible, invisible chasm between them. It brought back memories of her own weight-lifting journey, which was interrupted so early, all her hopes and dreams dashed forever. Like Michael, she too stood defenseless before life, enduring its reckless blows.

It no longer mattered he was an American, a foreigner, whose culture and language had at times felt alien to her. His admission had given her a glimpse of his soft and vulnerable side and erased all incongruity.

Chapter 28

Parul left the house in a haze, numbly walking down the lane, past the children's park and the tea stall. A part of her felt relief that she had finally been reproached; she needed Ma to be severe and unsympathetic, to acknowledge her betrayal and hand out a suitable punishment. Ever since the day she had first slept with Rahim, she had been burning in hell. She had behaved like a madwoman.

My life is really cursed, Parul thought. *I have lost all control over myself. I lust after a man day and night like a hungry animal. I am sick. I have no womanly restraint left in me. I follow Rahim like a dog—drooling and wagging my tail. All this time I thought I was being untruthful to Ma and to Mohini—the truth is, I was being untruthful to myself. It was not the path of Islam I was after; it was not God I was seeking... All this time, like a shameless woman, I was desiring carnal pleasure that only a man can give me. This is the sort of person I am—and I deserve to be homeless now, walking the streets with a bundle of belongings. This is my penance—this is God's punishment for my misdeeds.*

She walked the steep, uphill road next to the hyacinth-covered stream and the tall bamboo bushes until she came to the Shiv temple under the banyan tree. As a child, she came here with Mohini and Ma for puja. She brought flower garlands, incense sticks, half a coconut, and a box of *Sandesh.* Ma always said, "If Lord Shiva is pleased with you, you will get a groom just like him." *In my quest for a groom, I became a slut.* Parul smiled sadly.

It was mid-afternoon, and the sun was hot in the sky. People were bathing and washing their clothes next to the roadside tap. Some people ate lunch from roadside stalls—they poured *daal* into little mounds of rice. A plate of onion and lemon sat on each table. Little boys sold tea in clay cups to the shopkeepers.

Parul pressed the bundle against her chest and turned around to retrace her footsteps. Her heart told her to go back to the house and ask Ma for her forgiveness. No one else could take her place in the house. No other maid knew how to fold Ma's clothes, shine her silver, scale the fish, and grind ginger and garlic just the way she liked it. No other maid could reach into the narrow corners behind the armoire and under the bed and dust the floor just the way Ma liked it.

Parul got as far as the children's park, and then her courage failed her. Her betrayal was still fresh in Ma's mind. The wound Parul had inflicted was too deep and too recent. Forgiveness would not come to her so easily. Only time could act as a balm and heal. Discouraged, Parul sank into the doorsteps of the court building. Her throat was dry, and she wiped the beads of perspiration on her forehead. Then she got up and walked to the nearest tube-well to get water.

A familiar tingling sensation touched the back of Parul's neck. She shivered inadvertently, aware of who was standing behind her. The hair on her arms stood up, and she slowly turned to face Rahim.

"What are you doing here?" he asked.

Parul's lips quivered, but no sound came out. Water from her lips dripped on her blouse, leaving a wet patch.

"Why are your eyes red? Were you crying?" Rahim's shadow loomed over her, blocking her escape.

"Answer me," Rahim pressed. "What is in that bundle?"

Big drops of water made their way down Parul's cheeks. Rahim squeezed her shoulder and then withdrew his arm quickly as if he had touched hot iron. Word spread quickly in the neighborhood, and for them to be seen in public, touching each other would get a lot of tongues wagging. "Meet me behind the courthouse," he whispered. "We can talk privately."

Ten minutes later, Rahim met Parul in the alley behind the courthouse. He pulled her behind a parked truck.

"What is it? What are the tears for?"

"Ma kicked me out of her house. I don't have a home now."

"She kicked you out? Why?"

"The press widow came to talk to her. She told Ma that I sometimes go downstairs to the printing press."

Rahim grabbed her wrist. He tightened his grip on her arm until she winced in pain. "How many times have I told you not to come downstairs, you foolish woman? When will you learn to behave like a proper Muslim woman? You are not only irreligious but also irreverent. I pray every day that Allah forgives you for your blasphemy."

"I am sorry," sobbed Parul. "I feel like an evil jinni has taken over my body. I cannot control myself anymore. You must take me to a *Pir* and ask him to cure me. My body is no longer under my control."

"Stop this foolish talk. I have heard enough from you already." Rahim snapped his fingers. He lowered his voice and asked urgently, "Does Ma know about us? About you and me?"

"I don't know," stammered Parul. "I don't think so. Ma only said that the press widow has seen me in the printing press. She said nothing about our meeting in the west wing."

"That's all?" Rahim exhaled deeply, as if he had been holding the air for a bit too long. "Are you sure?"

"Yes, I am certain. Ma said nothing about you."

"*Subhan Allah*," said Rahim. "It is God's will. God, the holiest and the exalted of all beings, protected us from the press widow. Our secret is still safe."

A bubble expanded deep inside Parul's chest. "You look so pleased. How can you be so pleased? Here I am, with no roof over my head, nowhere to go, no one to turn to. I am walking the streets with nothing but two saris and petticoats in my hand... *and all you can think of is our secret?*" She tugged on the material of his *kurta*. "Where will I sleep? What will I eat? Will I have to beg in the streets now?" Sadness crushed her chest as she searched his dark eyes, looking for answers.

"Calm down." Rahim removed the decorated *chador* from his shoulder and wrapped it around her to stop her from shivering. He massaged her arms inch by inch to rub away the tension. "Your problems will appear as mountains if you focus on them too closely. When you focus on your own problem, Allah looks small, but when you focus on Allah, your own problem looks small. The truth is your problem is like a grain of sand and may not even be visible to the naked eye, but Allah and his mission are like mountains—much more important than the problem you are crying over."

For once, his words of mission and greater purpose failed to sway Parul. Wrapped in her own misery, she could only think of her own bleak future, the immediate threat that hung over her head like a guillotine waiting to drop. *Where will I go? What will I do? Going back to Abbu and my sisters in Murshidabad is not an option. Abbu will break both my legs when he hears how and why I lost my job.* Parul closed her eyes, and the surrounding noise receded, and all she could hear was the loud thumping of her own heart.

"Did you listen to anything I said?" Rahim shook her shoulder. Parul opened her eyes slowly to look at Rahim.

"I am homeless," she wheezed. She sank onto the pavement and covered her face with the flat of her palm. "I have nowhere to go."

"You know what your problem is? You have no faith in God, no faith in me. My teachings have made no difference in you." He folded his arms on his chest. "You want me to leave you alone?"

Parul sprang up and gripped his arm. "No, no... don't go. I have endless faith in you. I take every word you say to heart. I do everything you tell me to do. You are my teacher."

Her candid admission temporarily soothed Rahim. He pressed his palm on her cheek.

"You need to stop acting foolishly now," he said. "Lie low for a few days. Ma is upset. She may remain upset for a week... maybe two weeks. But in the end, she will forgive you."

"What if she does not?"

"Do not question me." His forehead creased as he frowned. "I am wiser than you, and I understand the ways of this world. That is why I am your teacher. The infidel woman will not find a maid who can satisfy her needs. She is used to you and your ways. When the anger dies down, she will miss you. That is when you will make another appearance and assure her you have become a new person. You will beg her to give you one more chance, and she will give in."

"She will give in..." whispered Parul. "She will give in..." she repeated, rolling and relishing each word on her tongue. "*Eh Allah*, I hope that day comes soon, for I can't bear this separation for long."

"Calm down. This overload of feeling gets you into trouble. You are on Allah's mission. Too much attachment to that infidel woman and her daughter will not help you achieve your goal."

"Forgive me." Parul dried her eyes with the back of her hand. "It was my home for so long. It is the only home I have ever known."

"An infidel's home cannot be your true home. It was a shelter at best."

Rahim played with his beard and reached a decision. "The time has come for you to meet your own people."

"My own people?"

"Yes, your own people."

"You mean my Muslim brothers and sisters?" Parul rubbed her hands together. "Will they give me food and shelter? I can't pay much rent. I have very little money. Will they keep me as a maid?"

"Leave the thinking to your teacher. Whatever decision I make is for your own good. Now come with me, and I will take you to your new home."

Parul hesitated. She tightened the muscles of her stomach, and a wave of nausea hit her suddenly. A complete range of conflicting emotions swept through her body, making her feel cold and hot at the same time. Rahim was asking her to follow him. He was taking her to an unknown destination—to an unknown house.

What would happen if she followed Rahim with her little bundle of clothes? How much did she really know about this man, even though their bodies had been intertwined from head to toe and she had tasted every inch of his salty flesh? She still did not feel close to him—close enough to know what went on in that twisted and complicated head of his.

She was not sure if he truly loved her. She was reminded of his repeated promises of marriage, children and family, but he never followed these promises with a specific date and wedding plans.

Even now that she was homeless and helpless, and to a great extent he was to be blamed for it... she saw no compunction, no remorse in his eyes. All she could see was arrogance. She had risked everything for him—her honor, her life, and what had he risked for her?

There will be no marriage proposal, a voice whispered in her head. *You are homeless, penniless. This man does not want to reach out and ask for your hand. Can you really trust him?*

The pain rose in her chest. She didn't have a choice now. Either she followed Rahim and went where he wanted her to go, or she would have to live on the streets and get mauled and chewed by the street corner gangsters, thugs, and ruffians. She had lost her privilege of deciding. Her own irresponsible behavior had closed all doors for her. Now she was dependent on him, and her future was in his hands.

She covered her head with the end of her sari and looked at Rahim decisively. "I will go wherever you take me."

Rahim nodded in satisfaction.

Chapter 29

The Muslim neighborhood was near Park Circus. Parul and Rahim got off the bus and walked the mesh of narrow alleys, so narrow that even hand-pulled rickshaws had trouble navigating this territory.

"But where are we going?" asked Parul, panting and trying to keep up with Rahim.

"To Hasina's house. She is my older sister. Her husband passed away last year. She has two young daughters."

"You are taking me to your sister's house?" A feeling of relief washed over her.

"Where else can I take you? A Muslim woman can't live in a house with a male who is not related to her. I have to find you a Zenana quarter for women."

"One million thanks," said Parul.

She struggled to match Rahim's long strides through muddy unpaved streets and courtyards where chickens ran around, stopping to peck on scattered grains. They passed through narrow winding alleyways where sunlight struggled to find its way. They went past the barbershop, the locksmith, the carpet maker's, and the tailor's. Beggars and flower sellers in white crochet caps lined up outside the mosques, khanqahs and dargahs. The pavement vendors sold rose water and prayer beads.

Parul had never visited this neighborhood. It was nothing like the Garia Narendrapur area she knew so well, where there were Hindu temples at every corner and very few mosques and mazars. The Urdu writing instead of Bengali on the shop signboards surprised her. The shops sold everything from Islamic books to decorative book rests, attar and headscarves. The store windows displayed prayer rugs and gold-printed green chadors used to cover graves of the Sufi *Pirs*.

The women in these streets wore black niqabs that covered their faces and showed only their eyes. They cast stony, disapproving gazes in Parul's direction. A five-year-old girl walked by in a hijab. She turned around to stare at Parul. *She is so young*, thought Parul. *How can she run around and play with her friends in that attire?*

All around her, cycle rickshaws, autorickshaws and even school buses had their curtains drawn, the riders made invisible to the public eye. Parul, who had her head covered with the end of her sari, suddenly felt under-dressed. Many faces looked at her from behind the half-open windows of two-story buildings, horrified to see her bare arms and uncovered face. A shiver ran down her body. Even in the slum across the railway line, which was predominantly Muslim, women did not wear a niqab. Some wore a hijab, while others covered their heads with scarves or with the end of their saris.

Parul folded her arms over her chest and walked a little faster, trying to catch up with Rahim. At the next bend, they passed the halal meat shops where butchers sharpened their slaughter knives. Scrawny, half-starved chickens huddled together inside claustrophobic cages. Severed goat heads were on display on the outside tables. The live goats lined up next to the dead ones in a pool of blood. The dead eyes of the slaughtered goats stared back at Parul from the butchers' table and sweat trickled down her forehead.

She almost bumped into the carcasses of dead cows swinging from steel hooks and had to cover her nose with the end of her sari. She had become a practicing Muslim, but she still had trouble consuming beef. The first time Rahim had asked her to taste a beef roll from Nizam, she almost threw up. Much as she wanted to, she could not shrug off all her Hindu habits overnight.

At last, Rahim stopped in front of a small single-story house with a red-tiled roof and knocked on the old, discolored door. Seconds later, a woman flung open the door and almost stepped on Parul.

"*Eh*, Allah," cried the woman, pointing at Parul. "Who did you bring back with you?"

"Offo, Apa, calm down," said Rahim. "She is the maid in the house where I work. Her name is Mumtaz."

"So, why did you bring her here? I don't need a maid. I can't afford to feed my own children; how will I keep a maid?"

"Apa, you are becoming more and more like Ammi. You blurt out whatever comes to your mind. You don't give people time to explain."

"*Hna hna*, I am not reserved like you, measuring out my words carefully with a balance beam. I am a simple uneducated woman—I say what comes to my mind."

"Forget your anger, Apa. I take back what I said. Allah gave you a pure heart. You always go out of your way to help people. Mumtaz here needs your help."

"What kind of help?" asked the woman. Her eyes were small and hard like steel balls; a line of worry stretched thin across her forehead. When Rahim had called her "Apa," older sister; it had become clear to Parul that the woman was none other than Rahim's older sister, Hasina.

Her heart hammered in her chest. If ever her life was out of her hands, it was now. A woman who she just met would decide her fate. She licked her lips and looked away.

"Mumtaz became homeless," said Rahim. "She needs a place to hide her head, that's all. Just for a few days... at most a week. And then she will be gone."

"Homeless?" Hasina screwed up her face. She covered her nose with the end of her sari. "Why did you bring her here?" she snapped. "Does my home look like a roadside motel?"

"Apa, the girl is in distress. She can't spend the night on the street."

"There are thousands of pavement dwellers in this city. Are you going to bring them to my house one by one? Have I opened up a charity house for all destitute women?"

Parul grew hot with embarrassment. Her lungs swelled with charged air. "I don't want to stay here for free, Apa," she said. "I have a few rupees for rent. I can also help with housework. Cooking, cleaning, and taking care of your children. I do a good job. You can ask your brother here. My mistress is lost without me."

"So why don't you go back to your mistress? If she likes you so much, why are you homeless?"

"I can't go back. Not yet, anyway. She is very upset with me. She won't take me back."

"Upset with you? What have you done? Stolen her money and gold jewelry?"

Parul gasped and took a step backward. Rahim looked at his sister fiercely. "You just insulted my future wife, Apa. This is the girl I am going to marry. When she needed help, I thought of you first. Where else would I have taken her, if not to my own Apa? I took care of you when your husband passed away last year. I paid your rent and your grocery bills. So I thought you would do this much for me."

His words seemed to shame Hasina. Her voice lost its former piquancy, and her shoulder dropped in mild surrender. "Why didn't you tell me this is your future wife? Allah knows what nonsense I spoke to her," she said.

Parul looked rapidly from one to the other. She had not expected Rahim to introduce her as his prospective bride and his sister, Hasina, to accept her as one. She wanted to pinch herself to make sure she was not dreaming.

Hasina pulled Parul into her embrace and said, "I spoke harshly to you, sister. I don't know what came over me. If possible, forgive me."

"Forget it," said Rahim. "Clearly you don't want Mumtaz to stay with you. I don't want you to do anything against your own wishes. I am taking Mumtaz back to her mistress."

"*Eh,* Allah," said Hasina. "How much punishment will you give your Apa for one mistake? Can't you forgive this silly woman just this once? Mumtaz will stay with us for as long as she wants. I will even buy her a new mat and blanket."

"Are you sure, Apa?" asked Rahim. He folded his arms and stood with his legs wide apart. "I don't want you to do anything against your will."

"Please, don't make me feel more guilty. Come inside, sister. I will tell everyone you are my cousin. That will be a safe thing to do. You two are not married yet. Your staying here could fuel a lot of gossip."

"Okay," said Rahim. "I am going back to the printing press, and you will not see me anywhere near her. I will only come here to take her back."

"I think that will be the right thing to do," said Hasina. "Don't worry, Rahim, I will take good care of your young bride."

Parul relaxed. She let out a warm puff of air, as if someone had lifted a heavy burden off her shoulders. Rahim had given a name to their relationship before his sister. He had argued with her to provide a roof over her head. *I am safe now*, she thought, *at least for the next few days. Allah is most merciful, most gracious. He never forgets his helpless children.*

Before Rahim could leave, two little girls stepped out of the house. Their heads were covered in black scarves. "*Salaam, Mama.*"

Rahim patted their heads. To Parul, he said, "This is Nikhat, my older niece. And this is my little doll, Lubna. She is only five, but she behaves like a hundred-year-old lady."

"Who is she?" asked Lubna, shyly pointing at Parul.

"Your *khala*," said Hasina hastily. "My cousin. She is going to live with us for a few days. Now go inside and get the room ready for her."

•

Parul woke early next morning. The sun was slowly rising in the east, an opalescent ball peeping from behind the white marble-like clouds. The children were all asleep on the floor mats, their hair matted around their faces like angelic halos, their cheeks flattened against their pillows.

How innocent they look, Parul thought to herself. *Just like two flowers. So secure in their sleep... so trusting of this world.* She tiptoed away and entered the kitchen.

Hasina was already there, cutting and scaling the fish. She had laid out yogurt, tomatoes, and cumin powder in small bowls next to the kitchen blade. Rice boiled in a big pot on the coal-burning stove. The rice water oozed into the flames, making them crackle. Parul entered the kitchen, and the two of them exchanged smiles.

"Why didn't you wake me up, Apa? You need not do all this alone."

"*Arre*, it is my habit to wake up early. Ever since my children's Abbu left me, I toss and turn and wake up before dawn."

"It must be hard for you, bringing up the children all by yourself."

Hasina wiped the kitchen blade and put it away. "I have friends in this community who keep me going. Women in this neighborhood check on me every day. We are all sisters here."

"Thanks to Allah for giving you such a helpful community!"

"That they are. Here we pray in small groups, share our meals, and our children play together. You could say that my children grew up in these neighborhood houses. I hardly saw them during the day. They ate and slept in other people's homes. I cannot think of a life outside this community."

"It is hard for me to imagine such a life. I have lived in a house for thirteen years, and I cannot tell you for sure if I really belong there... if I am one of them." Parul smiled sadly. She rubbed turmeric and chili powder on the freshly scaled fish.

Hasina moved closer to her. "Sister, if you don't mind my asking... why do you work as a maid? Why don't you live with your own family?"

"We don't get to choose our own destiny," said Parul with a sigh. "We do what Allah wants. Ammi died when I was only five years old. Abbu could not support me and my two sisters. So he sent me to Kolkata to work at Ma's house and send my wages home."

Hasina cupped a hand over her mouth. "*Hai Allah*. Your family has seen such bad days?"

"Yes, it was very hard then." Parul shrugged slightly. "My sisters were very young, and there was no one to look after them. God was testing us." She drew the back of her hand across her forehead. The chili dust on her fingers stained her brows and burned her skin. She wiped her face quickly with the end of her sari.

Hasina took her hand, lacing her fingers between Parul's. "Allah gives you suffering to make you a better person. And he never gives you more than you can bear."

"Yes, Apa. You are right."

"Your suffering has made you a very special girl," Hasina whispered in her ears. "That's why my brother likes you."

Parul tried not to blush and busied herself around the kitchen. She peeled the garlic and collected it in a bowl. She washed the mortar and pestle to grind up the wedges.

Hasina took pickle slices from a jar and inserted them into her mouth. "I didn't think my brother would ever get married. He has always been so against marriage. He spends most of his time buried in Arabic books or praying at the mosque. He says marriage is for ordinary people. Allah expects more from him.

"All of us, of course, want him to get married. We sisters talk about it all the time. But who is going to bell the cat, you tell me? We don't have the courage to bring up the subject when Rahim is in the room."

Parul bit her lip and glanced away. She got up to wash her hands below the kitchen tap. Hasina handed her a pickle slice from the jar.

"So how did you do it?" asked Hasina.

"What?"

"Convince my brother to marry you. You made the impossible possible. Wait 'til I tell our other sisters what you have done. They will jump up and down with joy."

"Really, it is nothing like that. He is my *Pir* and I am his *Murid*. He shows me the path to salvation, and I have nothing but respect and unending devotion for him."

"Respect and devotion are good, Mumtaz. But now you are more than his disciple. You have ownership of his heart." Hasina smiled.

Parul shook her head. "Rahim is doing me a favor. I am nothing but a poor, uneducated maid. I never dreamed that an educated man like him would take me as his wife." Her eyes grew wet, and she looked away.

"Now look at what I have done!" Hasina placed her hand on Parul's shoulder. "You are my guest and I made you cry. What kind of host am I? My brother is right. I talk too much, and I don't think before I let the words out."

"I am okay," said Parul. "There is something in my eye."

She walked back to the tap and splashed water in her eyes.

• • •

Later that day, Parul filled two buckets from the outside tube-well and carried them to the covered area behind the house. She took a long bath, lathering up to take the fish stench from her skin. She changed into a fresh sari and combed her long hair.

"You have beautiful hair."

Parul turned to face the older child, Nikhat. Two dark eyes blazed between a maze of dark, curly hair. The younger child, Lubna, peeped from behind her sister's back.

Parul laughed, happy to see them.

"Are you going to be our new *Maami*, our uncle's wife?" asked Lubna.

"What makes you think that?"

"We heard everything our uncle said to Ammi yesterday," said Lubna. "We were standing behind that door listening. You will make a beautiful *Maami*. I will braid your princess-like hair every day."

"Stop it, Lubna." Nikhat pinched her. "Don't let Ammi hear you."

"I did nothing," wailed Lubna.

"It's all right, Nikhat," said Parul. "I don't mind."

She pulled Lubna into her arms and kissed her rounded cheeks. "It will make me very happy to be your *maami* someday, but things only happen when Allah wants them to happen. Nothing is in your hand or mine."

"But it is in our uncle's hand," contradicted Lubna. "He can make it happen."

Parul turned away so that the children couldn't see her eyes. How could she explain to the two innocent faces that even she didn't know what would happen? Rahim had seemed sincere when he had declared her as his "future bride" before Hasina, but how could she be sure? What if they were just utterances meant to placate his sister— perhaps a means to persuade her to take Parul in?

"Be quiet," cried Nikhat. She grabbed her sister and shook her. "You will get us all in trouble."

The commotion soon reached the kitchen, and Hasina's face appeared at the window. "What's going on here? Are you two fighting?"

"Nothing, Ammi. I was just getting Lubna ready for the morning prayer."

"Then why do I hear shouting? Come inside and change your clothes."

"Yes, Ammi."

The two girls rushed inside, pushing and poking each other.

Hasina smiled at Parul. "They are curious about you, but don't let them bother you too much. They can really tire you out with their unending questions."

"No, no, Apa. They don't bother me at all. I love small children."

"Yes, I can already see that." Hasina looked at her approvingly. "Now, get ready quickly. We are starting morning prayers."

"I will be there in five minutes." Parul stuck a *bindi* between her eyebrows and put away the mirror.

•••

A little later, Parul came back inside and stood by the door. The children were on their knees, their heads covered with scarves. Hasina rolled out a mat for Parul and she kneeled next to the children. Lubna shifted closer. Her arms and thighs touched hers. *The children are excited to have me in their house,* Parul thought. *I am already their new aunt... Rahim's young bride.* She closed her eyes and tried to focus on her prayer.

She opened her eyes to see Hasina watching her. Her gaze was friendly, even motherly. *She likes me,* thought Parul. *Like the children, she, too, is dreaming about the future. She wants me to come here as a bride. If only it were that simple.*

Over the next two days, Parul got used to the patterns and sounds that permeated the tiny house. The sense of Islam was everywhere. Three times a day, Hasina and her daughters covered their heads, stood facing the direction of Qiblah, and began their prayers by chanting, "Allahu Akbar." During the prayer, they bowed, sat, and prostrated in unison, their voices rising and falling and vibrating deeply between the four walls of the room. Parul prostrated with them and joined them in chanting, "*Subhaanallah wal-hamdu lillaah walaa ilaaha illallaahu wallaahu akbar.*"

Women from the neighborhood visited them one afternoon. They wore all-covering niqab on the streets. But inside the house, in the absence of men, they discarded the cover and conducted themselves with no restraints or inhibitions. They gathered in the kitchen and helped Hasina cut vegetables and make dough.

The kitchen shelves were lined with tin canisters holding supplies of rice, *daal*, sugar, and molasses. Glass bottles with plastic lids contained sticks of cinnamon, cumin, hot paprika, and turmeric. The women picked out pieces of cardamom and cinnamon and crushed them with the heavy mortar and pestle. Hasina brought out the meat, and the women soaked it in yogurt and the flavored spice. Some of them rolled out the dough and baked *rotis* over the charcoal stove.

The women ate from the same plate; they placed the plate on a mat in the center and sat in a circle around it. Parul joined their meal, dipping small pieces of thick roti into rich brown gravy. Their soft banter, easy camaraderie, and endless affection for each other warmed her. Their sinuous laughter rose like thick, heavy dough and filled the room with its sweet, long-lasting smell.

After lunch, the women brought out an old harmonium with broken keys. One of them played a *ghazal*, and the rest got up to dance. Parul joined them shyly, her torso swaying gently with the sweet tenderness of the melody. She felt an immediate kinship with the women in the room.

Parul thought of her empty terrace room in Ma's house, where she lay on the threadbare mat alone with her thoughts, burdened by her hopeless future, isolated in her struggles. She knew at that moment what being a Muslim meant. She knew what she had been searching for all along. For once in her life, Parul was fully at home.

Chapter 30

On Friday, Hasina's family went to the local Mazar. Parul joined them. They put on their best clothes; both Hasina and her daughters wore the full niqab that covered them from head to toe, leaving only two slits for their eyes. Parul slipped into a borrowed hijab that left her face uncovered.

The Mazar itself was a white marble building with smooth arches and Arabic blue tile mosaic forming most of the front entrance. The porch had an austere chessboard floor that led to the main flower-covered entrance. The men, dressed in white *kurta*, loose *lungi*, and white caps, exchanged greetings by embracing each other. A series of water tap outlined the boundary of the Mazar, and men and women stepped up to wash their hands and feet. Hasina signaled Parul to clean herself from a tap.

The interior of the building was so dark that the men and women turned into long black figures with spectral faces. Their prayer areas were separate. The women prayed sitting outside in the covered hallway while the men went inside the burial room.

The mothers signaled their children to be quiet and pulled them to their sides. A powerful scent of incense and perfume rose in the air, mingling with the sweat and the heat and creating a haze around them. Parul's senses now enhanced in the dark, mysterious interior, the splendor and divinity of her surroundings astounded her. A beautiful, melodious voice cut through all the chatter and signaled the time for *namaz*. The men bent down beside the body of the saint and closed their eyes to pray, and the women cupped their palms to join them.

Parul closed her eyes to pray but could not concentrate. Instead, she imagined going back to Ma's house and having a conversation with her. She played it out in her mind, reading both parts and delivering her lines with emotion. *I will never betray you again.* Ma looked skeptical. *We women may fall and fall badly, but we also know how to get up and move forward.* Ma laughed now, a sort of hollow, mocking laugh that did not disclose any genuine amusement. *Just one chance, Ma, and you will not regret it.* Parul kept repeating these lines in her mind until they became a prayer, and her eyes overflowed with tears. Hasina touched her shoulder, her expression sympathetic. Parul turned away from her and dried her eyes quickly.

The women and the children moved out to the courtyard and lit candles and incense sticks below a big banyan tree. Hasina handed her a ribbon and said, "Tie it on the tree, sister. All your wishes will come true. No one goes back empty-handed from this saint."

· · ·

Later, the children gathered under a shady tree for their Sunday afternoon Quran class. Hasina's daughters moved to the front row and kneeled before the Maulvi. The Maulvi looked aged. His body bent forward from his waist, and his hands trembled as he passed out incense and perfume. He gave Hasina a bottle filled with holy water. "Sprinkle the water on the pillows and bedcovers where the children sleep. This will keep blasphemous thoughts out of their mind."

The Maulvi then opened the Holy Book and started his preaching. The mothers, covered in niqabs, sat behind the children to follow the holy man's words.

Even though the Maulvi's gait was sluggish and his breath was shallow and labored, his voice during the sermon was clear and crisp and filled with conviction. Parul listened, mesmerized, as the old master read verses from the Quran and then explained them with ease to the children. Suddenly, he closed the book and leaned forward to look at his audience closely. Rage burned in the depths of his aged eyes.

"The poverty, plague, immortality and scandal we are slave to in this neighborhood can only be attributed to our having distanced ourselves from the Islam of the time of Our Prophet, Apostle of God, to adopting new and vile customs of the heathens. Good Muslim children who are true followers of Islam should never watch the images on the silver screen. By showing us those vile images of half-naked women, the heathens want our sons and daughters to get corrupted and move away from the path of Islam."

Lubna fidgeted and played with the tiny red bangles on her arm. "I am thirsty," she whispered to Parul. "Can you get me some water?"

"Okay, wait here. I will fill your bottle."

Parul gathered her *hijab* and moved towards the taps. She uncapped the small plastic bottle and bent forward to fill it. Just then, glancing at the crowd of men pouring out of the prayer room, Parul's heart leaped into her mouth. Rahim stood with a group of men, discussing something in earnest. He was dressed in immaculate *kurta* and *pajama* and a lacy skullcap.

She swallowed back the lump of hurt in her throat. He must have known she was here. Yet he had not stopped by to say *Salaam*. Why was he ignoring her?

She looked up to see Rahim break away from the crowd and move toward the back tables lined up against the boundary wall. He picked up a glass of chilled pink *shorbot* and poured it down his throat.

Parul hastened her steps and caught up with him instantly.

"Why didn't you tell me you were coming here?"

Rahim did not turn around. He lowered his voice and said, "I always come to this Mazar on a Sunday. Everyone here knows me. So I can't talk to you here."

"Why not? Why can't you talk to me? And why are you pretending you don't know me?" Parul put her hands on her hips, challenging him.

"Because that is the proper thing to do." He turned reluctantly to look at her. "We are not related. I am not your husband yet."

"But do you know how much I worry about what is going to happen to me? I have been away from Ma's house for almost a week. No one else can tell me what's going on there."

Rahim made an impatient gesture. "Learn to keep your thoughts under control. When you are in God's house, be humble, be calm."

"How can I remain calm when I feel so helpless?" she asked, incredulous.

His face contorted into a grimace. "Do you think Ma will take you back if you scream and cry like this?"

"Tell me what happened after I left Ma's house. I have to know."

"Nothing happened."

"Does Ma miss me? Did she find a maid to replace me? Does she want me back?"

Rahim slapped his hand on the table, making the *shorbot* glasses jump. "I am on the first-floor printing press. How would I know what Ma is thinking upstairs?"

Some heads turned in their direction to see where the commotion came from. Parul could feel the color rise in her cheeks. She put a hand on the wall to support herself. "But you must know something. Do you see a new maid going up and down the stairs?"

"Enough," snapped Rahim. "I don't want to hear another word. This is not the time or place to talk. When the time comes, you will know everything." He waved his hands, indicating he wanted her to move away.

Parul took a few steps back, her shoulders touching the boundary wall of the Mazar. She picked up a glass of *shorbot* and sipped from it to calm her nerves. She pleaded with him one last time. "Why don't you understand? I can't wait. Anxiety is gnawing at my bones. Bad thoughts buzz in my head like a thousand bees."

Rahim's scowl deepened. "Looks like you will not listen to me. You are both stubborn and disrespectful. I am leaving now. Don't come after me, or there will be consequences." He slammed the empty *shorbot* glass on to the tray and headed for the back of the Mazar.

The Maulvi waved at Rahim, and Rahim stopped to speak to him. The old man stooped forward to whisper something, and Rahim nodded. They walked toward the back of the building, where they slipped into one of the half-open dark rooms.

He just wanted to get rid of me, thought Parul. *As if my presence is shameful. He does not want to be associated with me. Did he care even for a*

*minute how worried I am about my future? Where will I go? What will I do
if Ma does not take me back? Here I am fighting for my survival, and all he
can think about is his reputation. I spit on such reputation.*

Parul picked up Lubna's bottle and headed back to the tap. She
rinsed the bottle before filling it with clear, cold water. She put down
the bottle and splashed some of the cold water on her face and neck.
She rubbed her temples to relieve the pressure and calm the voices
battling inside her head.

A queasy feeling hit her. She had felt nauseous every morning of
this week. It had lasted a few minutes like a passing wave, but this
time the feeling persisted, and she clutched her sides to let out a small
gasp.

She dropped the bottle and ran for the bathroom at the back of the
building. The bathroom was dark and slippery. Parul almost lost her
footing and clutched the cold tiles on the wall for support. A small
reservoir of water and several buckets hung from the sides. Parul
dipped a bucket into the water, but as she tried to pull it out, a fresh
episode of nausea and pain hit her. For a moment, the inside of the
room felt dark, and she sat on the floor, her head reeling from the
effort.

To her dismay, she vomited over her hijab, emptying her entire
stomach. Clumps of rice and tiny pieces of vegetables clung to the side
of her mouth and weighed down the material of the hijab, stretching
between her knees. The sour taste in her mouth mixed with the inner
terror. She sat on the cold, wet floor and wept.

She could deny it no more. Allah had served her the evidence on a
platter. She was with child, and no matter how many times she told
herself it was indigestion and gas, the life that had implanted itself in
her uterus would not disappear overnight. She would have to talk to
Rahim. She would have to tell him everything. *He will have to decide
what to do. He will have to take the next step. After all, he is as responsible as
I am. This is not all my doing.*

Parul took off the hijab and washed it with the reservoir water. She
wiped her face and rinsed her mouth. Stepping outside, she laid the
hijab to dry in the sun.

Parul looked for Rahim in the crowd, but couldn't spot him anywhere. She moved to the rooms in the back of the Mazar. He was nowhere to be found. Crossing the hallway, she took a few tentative steps to the stairwell to the basement. She opened the stairwell door to listen. Her ears picked up faint voices coming from the basement. She climbed down the stairs and waited outside a half-closed door. Then she peeped inside.

From here she could make out Rahim's figure. He was talking to some heavily bearded men. They all spoke in hushed, low tones, as if they were in the middle of an important discussion. Around her, the air felt heavy with anticipation of something ominous unfolding inside the room. The low rumblings made her feel unwelcome, and she shifted her feet nervously.

Parul turned to leave. She got as far as the staircase and changed her mind. She came back, put a firm hand on the door, and pushed until it was completely open. From here, the men surrounding Rahim were clearly visible. Taking a sharp breath, she stepped inside the room in full view of the men inside.

"I... err... need to talk," she addressed Rahim. "There is something very important I need to—"

She wanted to tell him about her pregnancy and ask him what her options were, but his angry, disapproving gaze stopped her in mid-sentence. Rahim sprang up from his seat, grabbed her hands, and pulled her outside the room, closing the door behind him. "Have you gone out of your mind?"

"What did I do?"

"This is the men's section of the Mazar. Who asked you to come here?"

"I didn't know," stammered Parul.

"Why did you take off your covering?" hissed Rahim next to her ear. "Did you forget this is a place of worship?"

"No. But you are not letting me explain..."

"You have nothing to explain. You ought to know girls don't behave like this here."

"What do you mean by *behave*? What have I done?"

"You can do whatever you like in the Hindu house," he said. "You can walk around like a shameless woman. But there are certain things you cannot do in this neighborhood. That's our religion, our culture. That's how we live here."

For a moment, she stared at him, speechless. "But I did nothing. I had to wash my hijab. It is still wet..."

"Enough excuses. Now go away."

"I didn't come here to discuss my hijab. I just have something very important to tell you."

"It can wait."

"No, it can't. I need to tell you right now."

"I am very busy."

"You talk about our wedding, our life together. But you are not willing to listen to me. You won't even *let me speak*."

"All right," said Rahim. He glanced back at the room with the bearded men. The door was slightly ajar. "I'm in a meeting all day today. I will stop by later."

"You can't spare five minutes to hear what I have to say?"

"I have thousands of things to do."

"Then add this to your list of a thousand things. *You are going to be a father*."

She put her hand on his arm. His muscles tensed against her fingers.

"Aren't you going to say something?" she asked.

For a fleeting moment, she thought she saw a glimmer of emotion in his eyes. What was it? Was it hope, joy, or just plain fury? He stood in front of her now, his legs slightly apart, the *soorma* in his eyes dark as midnight. His hair was damp, curling on the ends, reaching for his shoulders. *So much strength in those powerful shoulders. Allah has blessed him with such a beautiful body.* Rahim's kurta smelled of neem soap. It made her belly tickle with yearning. *He is still young. A lot of years left in his life to take care of a family.* For a moment, she imagined a baby in his arms, a tiny body nestled safely in the triangle of his elbow. The baby reached out and touched the thick beard that covered most of his chin, and Rahim looked down to smile at him.

His voice cracked like a whip in her ears, shattering the fleeting fantasy.

"Go home," he said.

"What?" Parul couldn't believe what she heard.

He pulled free from her hand and stepped back. "I said go home."

"That's all? Did you even hear what I just said?"

"We can talk later. I have things to do."

"Things to do? What can be more important than this?" It was as if she was stuck in a nightmare. "Look at me." She cupped his chin in her hands. "I'm telling you the truth. This is our baby. This time I'm sure... one hundred percent."

"This is not the time or place to discuss this." He pushed her away.

She bit the insides of her cheeks and tasted bitter blood in her mouth. This was worse than a nightmare. She tried to squeeze the pain out and look at him again.

"But we need to. Don't you see this is important? I need to know what will happen to me now. I am going to be an unwed mother!"

He glanced at the door again. His face hardened as if it was carved out of ice. "This is not a place for girlish drama. Disappear from my sight at once."

Parul was feeling lightheaded again. She shivered.

She moved back, away from him, slowly making her way up the stairs. Quran classes were over, and the crowd had moved to the other side of the courtyard. Women and children sat in long queues under the *shamiana* eating fruits, chickpeas, sweets, and *shorbot*. Hasina and her daughters were there, too. They waved at Parul, and she walked over to sit with them. An elderly woman with a friendly smile placed a paper plate before her.

Sunshine wrapped around her, warming her face and arms. All around her, children laughed and their mothers chatted. She shut her eyes and breathed deeply, struggling to steady herself. She took a small bite of the food but could not force it down her throat. In the crowd of unfamiliar faces, her eyes longed to glimpse Mohini. *What an absurd wish*, she thought. *Mohini can never come here.*

The worst thing was, she did not know if she would ever see Mohini again. If Ma didn't forgive her and take her back in, would that determine the end of her relationship with Mohini? As a tear trickled from her eye, she realized how much she'd been missing Mohini, how much she longed to tell her about her troubles.

But what can you tell her? The voice in her head was nagging and nasty. *Can you tell her you sneaked behind her back and went to see Rahim? Can you tell her you are an unmarried, expectant mother? Can you tell her that the baby may never get his father's name?*

The horrible thoughts hit her like a punch to the guts. She could imagine what trauma her revelation would bring Mohini. Accusation and hate would burn deep into her eyes. "This time you've gone too far," she would say. "After everything my parents did for you... you brought them such unbearable shame."

No, Parul shook her head vehemently. *I can never tell Mohini about this baby.*

She swivelled toward Hasina and clutched her wrist. "I want to go home."

"So soon?"

"Yes, right now."

"As you say, sister. Just wait till the girls finish their food."

Chapter 31

Five days went by, and there was no news from Parul. Ma claimed to be relieved not to have heard from her. "A girl like her can only bring shame and bad luck to a family," she told Mohini and Baba, her face hard and dangerous like an arrow. "I would not let her shadow enter this house." Her threatening words crushed Mohini. It was true that Parul had made a terrible mistake, but how could Ma stay mad at her for so long?

It was on the sixth day that the first chink appeared in the armor of Ma's indifference. Early in the morning, on her way to the terrace, Mohini found Ma in Parul's room. She sat beside Parul's open tin-trunk and gazed emptily at her belongings. Mohini decided not to disturb Ma. She tiptoed down the stairs.

That evening, when they all sat down for dinner, Ma pushed her plate away and turned toward Baba. "Where is Parul? Tell me... where is she?" she cried. "She hasn't come home for five days, and no one in this house is bothered."

"You sent her away, Mohini's Ma," said Baba softly. "You told the girl never to come back. She is just following your orders."

"Yes, yes, blame me. All fault is mine. I am the one who sent her away." She slammed her hands on the table. "But what about you, Mohini's father? Don't you have any responsibility? The girl has been away from home. What is she eating? Where is she sleeping? Do you worry about her or not?"

"Calm down, Ma." Mohini rubbed her fingers. "I'm sure she went back to her father's house in Murshidabad."

Ma shook her head. "That's what I thought at first. But I know Madhu*babu's* nature. He will not let her miss her work. The moment he hears what has happened, he will drag her back here."

"So you think she went somewhere else?" Baba narrowed his eyes.

"Yes. I am worried sick now. This is a very bad city, so full of crime... and a young girl like her alone..." Ma's voice choked. "She is, after all, my responsibility. What will I tell her father when he comes here? What face will I show him?"

Ma had gone very pale. Beads of sweat gathered above her eyebrows. Mohini leaned closer and fanned her with a newspaper. "Nothing will happen to Parul*di*." She tried to sound confident and wasn't sure how well she did. "She knows how to take care of herself. I am sure she is staying with one of her slum friends."

"Yes, I think so too." Baba nodded in agreement. "Tomorrow we will walk to the slum and ask around."

"And if you don't find her there?" Ma chewed her nails.

Baba wiped the sweet yogurt from his lips and gulped down a big glass of water. "Then we have to go down to the Police Station to file a missing person report."

"No, no." Ma gripped Baba's arm. "What will the police do in all this?"

"Try to find her, of course."

"No, let it be."

"Let it be?" Baba threw her a look of disbelief.

"We are respectable folks. It does not look good when the police get involved in our matters."

Baba gritted his teeth. "Did you hear that, Mohini?" He looked up at her. "I'll never understand your mother. Why me...? I am a mere mortal. Even the gods can't understand the female species."

"Ma, listen to Baba." Mohini nudged her gently. "Finding Parul*di* is more important to us than anything else right now."

"*Offo!* Your father gets upset over nothing." Ma clicked her tongue. "Did I say we shouldn't try to find her?"

"How will you find her if you don't get the police involved?" demanded Baba.

"All I am saying is... we should try to find Parul ourselves first."

"Yes, Mohini's Ma, that is a very sensible plan," mocked Baba. "I am sure I can easily spot her in this city of millions."

• • •

A week went by, and Parul did not come home. Mohini asked Michael for help to find Parul. At first, they did everything to find her without involving the police. They went to the slum across the railway line to show her photo and ask people if they had seen her. Most of the women who recognized her claimed not to have seen her lately. They even stopped by the mosque and talked to the Maulvi, looking for leads, but he had no information. On the seventh day, Baba went to the police station and filed a missing person First Information Report.

When Michael and Mohini came home, they climbed the stairs all the way to Parul's terrace room. Mohini paused briefly outside Parul's door. Inside the room, everything was as it always was—Parul's soap, crème, hair oil, water pot, and the clothesline sagging beneath the weight of her saris. Mohini walked out on the terrace and leaned on the banister just as Parul used to do every morning.

The multi-storied buildings of Highland Park glistened in the afternoon light. The vast expanse of the city sprawled before her eyes—the old, discolored buildings, the narrow alleys, the dusty roads, and the green parks. Gazing beyond the vast labyrinth of houses and the rising dust, Mohini was filled with a sense of loss.

Michael placed his hand on her shoulder. "You're taking this very hard."

"You don't understand what Parul*di* is to me. She is my sister."

"Make me understand," he urged gently.

Mohini told him about how they ran up and down the stairs playing hide-and-seek, stole pickles from Ma's kitchen, and played soccer in the rain. They would race each other in the park or skip forward on their jumping ropes, chanting their childhood songs.

Sometimes they climbed the guava trees bordering the pavement and dropped small, rounded guavas on the pedestrians, their tiny bodies shielded deep inside the foliage. Then they jumped down from the lower branches and ran back home, slipping, tumbling, and screaming, chased by the angry pedestrians. They would close the main door of their house and hear the men pounding on it from outside, swearing and bellowing words of revenge.

"Most of my memories would be incomplete without her," Mohini told Michael. "For she is the one who can confirm that they really happened."

Michael put his arm around her shoulder and pulled her into his embrace. She moved away immediately, conscious of people looking at them from the terrace of nearby houses. There was no privacy anywhere in their house. She imagined a place where they could hide away from the nosy neighbors. Ultimately, they squeezed into the space between the water reservoir and the concrete banister. Mohini put her head on Michael's shoulder.

Michael reached for her hand and placed it purposefully on his chest. His heart beat fast against her palm. He brought his face close to hers. Her mind was floating. There was a strange disconnect with reality; it was as if her body was no longer in her control. Her lips trembled, and her left leg vibrated up and down. He pulled her into his embrace and stroked her hair. His hand was awkward and hesitant at first, but then he bent down and kissed her lightly on her mouth. She looked back at him, startled. For a moment, she thought he was going to apologize. Instead, he kissed her again, and this time his kiss was passionate.

• • •

Their house was getting out of shape—a thin layer of dust coated the floors and stairs, and dirty clothes piled up in laundry baskets. One day, Mohini picked up Parul's bamboo duster and offered to sweep the floor, but Ma glared at her. "Don't forget you are the daughter of a *bhadralok*. This kind of task doesn't suit you."

This reasoning, Mohini knew from having heard it many times before, formed a fundamental pillar of Hindu belief, and it went like this: God made two kinds of people, the *bhadralok* and *chotolok*—literally respectable people and small people. The *bhadraloks*, who were generally the higher caste, were refined and cultured. They valued education, attended college and refrained from manual labor. *Chotoloks* came from low caste (and poor Muslims) and took part only in menial jobs. They were simply paying for the mistakes of their previous life.

Though this reasoning made Mohini uneasy, she couldn't let herself feel very much about it. After all, most middle-class Bengali families made this distinction. Why would she risk getting Ma upset by questioning it? Reluctantly, she put down the duster and asked Ma to look for Parul's replacement. "The house won't clean itself," she urged Ma. "Just for a few days, let's try someone new."

The next day, some women, young and old, came to interview for Parul's position. Ma briskly and fiercely ordered them around the house. The women scrubbed the floors, starched the saris and cooked fish in hot mustard sauce. They swept under the bed and behind the armoires and wrung every drop of water from Ma's sari. But their efforts were in vain. As soon as they left, Ma wrinkled her nose and said, "Useless, all of them. Nothing but cow dung inside their heads."

Mohini knew seeing the maids in their house reminded Ma all the more of Parul's absence. For years Parul and Ma had worked together, argued, sulked and reconciled in the propinquity of their tiny kitchen. They had laughed together, sung old Bengali songs and shared neighborhood gossip. As a child, Parul had followed Ma around the house like a shadow, snug and wound around her feet. As a young woman, she was Ma's only confidant, her closest friend. So it was perhaps inevitable that Ma could not find a replacement for Parul easily. The most efficient of maids, one who could make the floors sparkle and the steel plates shine, could not take that special and untouchable place in Ma's heart that Parul occupied.

One evening, when Ma seemed particularly anxious, Mohini grabbed her hand and took her up the stairs to Parul's room. "Let's search through all her belongings. Who knows? We may find a clue that may help us locate her."

Ma glanced at her in surprise and patted her shoulder. "Good idea. Why didn't I think of that?"

Sitting cross-legged on the floor, they rummaged through Parul's tin trunk, pulling out her saris, bras, dupattas, petticoats, and purses.

Mohini shook the clothes and emptied the purses, while Ma sieved through the contents. A photograph slipped from an inner pocket of a purse and landed on the floor with a gentle swoosh. Mohini picked it up and scrutinized the photo. A thin, almost skeleton-like girl in a big cotton frock stared back at her. *No more than six or seven years old*, Mohini guessed. Her hair was short and cropped unevenly. Various religious beads and strings covered her bony arms. The girl looked familiar, but Mohini couldn't quite remember where she had seen her. Then it dawned on her that the girl in the photo was none other than Parul. She snapped her fingers and looked at Ma with great excitement. "Is this how she looked as a child?"

"Yes," said Ma, bending down to look at the photograph. "This was around the time she came to our house. Your father took this photo with a Polaroid camera."

Mohini inspected the picture. There were very few photos of Parul in their house, and this photograph may be only one of her childhood. Her hands hung limp in her lap, her shoulders drooped, and her eyes were downcast. *The pain of estrangement from her beloved village is inscribed on her body*, thought Mohini.

Taking the photo from Mohini's hand, Ma sighed deeply. "She was such a naughty girl. Created big trouble on her very first day."

"What did she do?" asked Mohini.

Ma stared at the sunny terrace with a distant look in her eyes as though, years later, she could see little Parul standing there still.

"When she came to our house from her village, she was absolutely filthy. She hadn't bathed in days," Ma said. "Her arms and face were covered in a thin film of dirt, and her thick hair was knotted, sticking out like rhino horns all around her face.

"After her father left, I took it upon myself to clean that little girl. I took her to the bathroom and filled up buckets with soap and water. Parul stood in the middle of the bathroom, her hand on her waist, staring back at me defiantly. Taking off her drab, threadbare clothes, I tossed them into the trash pile for the janitor to collect. I turned her to face the wall and poured a bucket of soapy water on her head.

"She stood still for a moment, blinking as the soap foam reached her eyes, gulping air like a fish. Then she grabbed my arm and pleaded. 'I want my Abbu. Let me go home.' I pretended not to hear her. But she slammed the tin mug on the side of the metallic bucket and chanted, 'I want my Abbu, I want my Abbu.' That's when I lost my temper and scolded her. But I knew I had made a mistake the moment I did it; I should have known she would react badly."

"What did she do?" Mohini asked anxiously.

"She backed away from me and darted out of the bathroom. She ran through the house barefoot and naked, her body dripping with soap and water. I chased after her, urging her to come back, but she didn't turn around to look at me. Slipping and sliding, she went down the stairs all the way to the front entrance. She was about to open the front door when I reminded her, she was naked. That's when she stopped, lowered her head and tiptoed back to me. I stepped forward and covered her with my sari."

"Oh, poor Parul*di*." Mohini covered her mouth. "She must have been mortified."

Ma shook her head. "If she was, she wouldn't show it to us. She had a permanent armor of unfriendliness on her face from the moment she entered our house. That was her way of distancing herself from us."

Ma adjusted her sari and got up. She pulled out the last item from Parul's tin trunk. It was the blanket Baba had brought back from America. Locked in the box, untouched for months, the blanket had a musty odor to it. Mohini helped Ma carry it out to the terrace and spread it on the clothesline. Together, they smoothened out the creases and secured it with clothespins.

"What happened after that, Ma?" asked Mohini. "How did you convince her to stay?"

A deep frown appeared on Ma's forehead, and she shook her head. "Took a long time. She was a stubborn child." Ma shooed away the crows who came to sit on Parul's blanket.

"In the next few days, Parul pouted, scowled at us and refused to make eye contact. You were four years old then, eager to follow her around. But she didn't want to play with you... nor did she want any of your toys. When I served her rice and vegetables, she put a few small morsels in her mouth and pushed the plate away. 'I'm not hungry,' she said. It broke my heart, Mohini, to see a little girl like her resisting and fighting her hunger. I didn't know what to do."

"Then?"

Ma lowered her voice. "Then one day, she disappeared."

Mohini stared at Ma in surprise. "Disappeared?"

"Yes." Ma nodded. "She was gone from the house. I looked everywhere for her—the terrace, the gym, the west wing, even the widow's printing press. But it was as if the girl had vanished. When I couldn't find her inside the house, I sent your Baba to look for her in the neighborhood. He circled the house, wandering into the back alleys and the children's park. He asked the street vendors if Parul bought puffed rice or chickpea curry from them. No one had seen the child."

"Oh my God," gasped Mohini. "Where did she go?"

"There was a bus garage in our neighborhood. That evening, one of the bus drivers was starting his bus when he heard a sniffle from the back of his empty bus. He discovered Parul hiding under a seat. Of course, he didn't know who she was. When he pulled her out, she begged him to drive her to Murshidabad. The bus driver asked around and finally found out that she worked in our house. He brought the hungry and thirsty girl back to us."

"What was she thinking?" cried Mohini. "Someone could have kidnapped her, raped or killed..."

"Look at my bad luck, Mohini." Ma dried her eyes with the end of her sari. "Years later I am having the same bad thoughts about her."

Chapter 32

After coming back to Hasina's house from the Mazar, Parul packed her things and cleared her room. She folded up her saris, blouse, comb, and hairpins. She picked up her mirror from the windowsill and threw it into her small bag. She dusted the floor with a bamboo duster. She made up the bed and emptied the clay water pot. She gathered her used soap, hair oil, and towel and handed them back to Hasina.

"Stop, sister," said Hasina. "Don't leave us like this. This is wrong. At least wait until my brother comes to get you."

"Why should I wait for him when he himself told me to disappear from his sight? That's exactly what I am doing. Disappearing from his sight... *forever*. I am going back where I came from."

Parul pulled her half-dried petticoat from the clothesline and stuffed it into her bundle. She folded Hasina's scarf, hijab, and prayer mat, but Hasina refused to take them back.

"Now, why would my brother say such a thing?" asked Hasina. "In a few days, you two will get married... Insha'Allah. This is such a happy time for us. Our family is preparing for the wedding. And you are leaving this house? What has gotten into you?"

"Nothing. I am fine. Why don't you ask your brother what has gotten into him?"

"Look, Mumtaz, this makes little sense," pressed Hasina. "My brother does not lose his temper easily. You must have done something that got him upset."

"*I* did something to upset him?" snapped Parul. "From the day I met him, I've listened to everything he said... I obeyed him and worshipped him. But look where that got me. He asked me to

277

disappear. Disappear when I need him the most. Disappear when..." Parul could not finish.

Hasina went to her, took her hand and stroked it as gently as if it were a bird. "Now, now, sister, I am sure he did not mean that. Things that are said in anger must not be taken seriously."

"Of course you will support him, Apa." Parul's bottom lip quivered. "Why would you not? He is, after all, your brother. You cannot see anything bad in him."

"It is not like that. Try to understand. I am just worried about you. Decisions made hastily and angrily are almost always wrong. At times like this, we need to think of Allah and his glory. We need to flush all the crabby thoughts out of our minds and ask God to fill our bodies and minds with peace and calmness."

Parul's insides burned. Her throat was parched, and beads of sweat gathered around her temple. She felt dizzy. "I trusted your brother and he..." Clumps of darkness gathered around her, and the cramps came back. Clutching her sides, she slowly slid down the wall and squatted on the floor.

"Mumtaz!" Hasina's voice seemed to come from a great distance. "Are you sick?"

Parul did not answer.

• • •

Parul opened her eyes with difficulty. Hasina and her daughters were bending over her, studying her face. She was on her mat, covered lightly with a cotton blanket.

Lubna's face broke into a broad grin as she looked closely at Parul. "Ammi was worried about you," she said. "But I told her, *khala* is only sleeping. She will wake up soon."

"How are you feeling now?" asked Hasina.

Parul tried to lift herself up. She felt dizzy again.

"No, no," rebuked Hasina. "Don't get up. You are very weak."

"Did I faint?"

"Yes. You got us really worried."

278

"It's nothing." Parul tried to stretch her lips into a smile. "I ate little this morning...."

"That's what I thought, sister. As it is, you eat like a bird. On top of that, you are skipping meals. You have to be careful about your health..."

"Can I have some water?" asked Parul.

Suddenly, Parul's eyes located movement in the room's corner next to the clotheshorse, and her heart stopped. Rahim stepped out of the shadows and moved toward her slowly—with some difficulty, for the room was crowded with furniture, mats and pillows.

"Why is he here?" Parul turned to Hasina. "Please, ask him to leave."

"Calm down, sister. I called my brother here to talk to you. Whatever is going on between the two of you can be sorted out right now. I only ask that you speak to each other with a curtain in between. You are not married, and we have to follow some propriety."

The glow of the low-wattage bulb behind Rahim cast ominous shadows on his face, making him look even more mysterious and unapproachable.

Hasina got up and spread out a sari on a clothesline between them. "There," she said. "For now, this sari will have to do the curtain's job."

Parul glanced at Rahim, standing behind the translucent material of the sari. Like an image on the silver screen, he floated on the other side of the shimmering sari, coming into focus and then dissolving away. He was in a long *kurta* and a *lungi*, and instead of his usual white cap, he had a black turban.

Hasina and her daughters left the room. Parul was suddenly aware she was alone with Rahim. He pulled a bamboo sitting stool against the sari, purposefully sitting very close to her.

"How are you feeling?" he asked.

"Why do you care?" She turned her back to him.

"I looked for you at the Mazar. You had already left."

"You asked me to disappear from your sight. So I did."

"Turn around. Look at me."

Parul's muscles contracted all at once, making her body rigid and tight. She closed her fingers and made a fist. She squeezed her eyes shut, wishing him to go away.

"Don't be childish," urged Rahim. "We need to discuss this."

"What is left to say? You don't want me or the baby. You want to be a free man."

Rahim inserted his hand under the curtain and placed it on her belly. She flinched, but didn't push him away. His finger trembled, and he exhaled deeply. "Children are Allah's most beautiful creation," said Rahim. "The greatest joy a man can have."

His words were like a tiny gem of white light in an otherwise unending dark sky. She gripped his hand and pulled it to her chest. They looked at each other for a long time. His gaze was friendly, compassionate.

"This is your baby... your own flesh and blood," Parul whispered to him. "He needs your support, your protection."

Perhaps it was a mistake to utter those words, for a look of anguish came over his face. He pulled his hand from her grip. "What you're dreaming can't happen," he told her, a pained intensity lighting up his eyes. "I can never live up to your desire—to father this baby and bestow upon it a safe and secure world."

Parul's chest compressed, and the pain surged. When Rahim had touched her belly, she had felt hope. There was tenderness in his touch—Parul was sure of it—as he had pressed his fingers against her skin, feeling for the life growing inside her. But now the hardness in his eyes was back, and the lines on his face were even more rigid.

Parul pushed the sari curtain and moved closer to his bamboo stool. "Look into my eyes and tell me you don't care for this baby— the baby means nothing to you."

"Stop being stubborn, Mumtaz. I already gave you my answer."

"What's the real reason? Why won't you ever consider this?" Her chest heaved, and her lips trembled. "Don't you want happiness?"

"My happiness ended the day Salim died. Now only the dead live in my world. I have no room left for the living."

"Why are you saying crazy things like that?" cried Parul.

"Are you calling me crazy?" he snapped.

"No, but I think you're changing the subject."

Rahim got up and paced the room like a wounded tiger. "Get all the nonsense thoughts of children out of your mind," he said. "Don't forget you came to this earth to carry out Allah Ta'ala's mission."

This time, Parul glared at him. "Mission? So you came to talk to me about the mission? Does anything else matter to you?"

"Keep your voice down, woman," warned Rahim. "I don't want my sister to hear you."

"But she will have to know, won't she? After all, this is your baby. You cannot keep denying it."

Rahim's face darkened. His eyes gleamed as his chin settled into a line of contempt. "What if I deny it? Who will believe you then?"

Parul gasped. She couldn't believe what she was hearing. "*Yeh Allah*, what a mistake I have made in trusting this man. I gave him my body, my innocence, and all along he was planning to ruin my life. And I hung on to his every word, like a child lured by candy. Why didn't I jump into a well and die first? Why did I have to see this day of shame?"

"Stop the melodrama," snapped Rahim. "And keep your voice low. Becoming pregnant was not part of the plan. I expected you to complete the mission for which I was training you. Now you spoiled everything with your foolishness."

"You pretend as if all this is my fault."

"Maybe you wished for this baby. You asked Allah to give you one. You didn't put your heart on the mission. I sensed your lack of interest from the first day."

"What are you saying?" Parul sobbed. "That I would wish for this baby and bring disgrace to myself? That I would deliberately ask the entire world to point a finger at me, to say, 'there goes the shameless unmarried woman with a child?' Who would pray for such a fate? This is worse than death."

"Enough! I don't want to hear any more nonsense from you. What I am saying is very simple. I spent long hours training you. All my hard work is ruined."

"You forced me to sleep with you..." hissed Parul.

"I did not force you. You came on your own."

Parul opened her mouth and sucked in air. "You lured me and trapped me."

Rahim narrowed his eyes to slits. "You could not restrain your lust. You have no self-control. Didn't the neighbors see you lurking in the back alley, displaying yourself to the employees? No good Muslim woman behaves like that.".

"How can you be so cruel! Do you have any humanity left in you?"

Rahim kicked back the bamboo stool, and it rolled over the tiled floor. His voice was ice cold when he spoke. "Listen carefully to what I am saying. I can't let my hard work go to waste because of your careless behavior. You will now go back to the Hindu house and finish what you left undone."

"I can't go back there. They will know I am with child."

"No, they won't. You don't show. Even my sister could not guess by looking at you that you are with child." He gripped her shoulder and studied her belly. "You're okay for now. You can still fool the people in that house."

"You cannot force me to go back there."

"The choice is yours." Rahim gave a humorless smile. "Succeed in the mission and the child will have my name. Or else..."

"Or else?"

"People disappear in these winding narrow alleys all the time. Even the police are scared to come here."

Parul shivered. She clutched the blanket and wrapped it around her.

"Pack your bags," said Rahim. "Tomorrow you go back to the Hindu house."

Chapter 33

The next morning, Parul woke as the sunlight from the windows spread warmth on her hands and cheeks. After Rahim left, she had spoken to no one. She had even refused dinner and stayed wrapped in her blanket, drowning in her own misery.

Now she picked up her toothbrush and went to the back tap. Hasina was there, next to the charcoal stove, blowing and fanning the flames. She smiled at Parul but mentioned nothing about the previous day. A feeling of relief washed over Parul. Hasina must not have heard their argument. *She doesn't know I'm pregnant*, thought Parul. *My secret is safe.*

Later, Parul joined Hasina in the kitchen. She squatted on the floor to scale the fish with the kitchen blade. Hasina warmed some milk and poured it carefully into a frosty glass. She added sugar and a spoonful of turmeric powder and walked over to Parul. Her eyes were soft and moist as she crouched next to Parul and said, "Drink this, sister. Our Ammi always said there is magic in turmeric milk. All your frustrations disappear like this..." Hasina snapped her fingers.

Her kindness touched Parul. Her hands trembled as she accepted the glass from Hasina and took a long sip of the delicious milk. "Apa, please don't get upset when I tell you this. But you remind me so much of my own Ammi. She had big, beautiful eyes like yours, always filled with such kindness."

"Sister, if I remind you of your own Ammi, then why did you keep such a big secret from me?" Hasina said, making Parul squirm. "You could have shared your troubles with me."

"You know?" Parul avoided Hasina's eyes. "But how...?"

Hasina smiled. "The walls in this house are so thin, they hold back nothing."

"What did you hear?"

"Everything. I know you are with child," Hasina said matter-of-factly.

Parul's heart stopped. She dug her nails into her palms.

"It's all right, sister. I am not here to judge you. I leave all the judgement to Allah."

Parul fixed her gaze on the floor. When she spoke, she couldn't hide the disappointment in her voice. "I know you will want me to leave as soon as possible now that you know what kind of girl I am. My being here is not good for your reputation."

"Calm down, sister. We will worry about reputation later."

"No, Apa, you have done enough for me. You took me in when I needed a home. Allah knows how much gratitude I feel in my heart. I don't want to cause any more trouble for you or your family. I will leave this afternoon."

The room was hot. Parul stuck her nose between the bars of the open window and inhaled deep breaths of fresh air. Outside, a yellow cat jumped over the corrugated tin roofs and landed on the brick fence, its tail hoisted up. It sat on the neighbor's awning and licked its paws at a leisurely pace, as if to mock Parul's racing heart. For one insane moment, Parul wanted to hit the cat with a rolling pin. Resisting her impulse, she moved away from the window.

She walked over to the kitchen tap to rinse the leftover dinner plates. Beads of sweat gathered above her eyebrows. She massaged the side of her face, temples, and jaw. Only one thought repeated itself over and over again: Where would she go after she left Hasina's house?

"The house is empty without you. Won't you come back?" Mohini's face appeared on the back of a steel plate she had picked up to wash. Parul's hands trembled, and she dropped the plate. She opened the tap all the way. Water splashed off the sink and onto her sari and blouse. The face faded away. But when she looked up, it was in the mirror above the sink. It stared back at her with anguish-filled eyes. "Where are you, Parul*di*? We looked everywhere, but still we can't find you."

Parul squealed and backed away from the sink.

Hasina looked concerned. "What is it?" she asked.

"Nothing." Parul paused and tried to control her trembling voice. "It's just that I've never been away from my mistress's home for so long. I'm missing Mohini, my mistress's daughter." Parul dried herself with a kitchen towel. She turned to Hasina and forced a smile. "I want to leave before it gets dark. It's an unfamiliar neighborhood, and I may get lost."

Hasina stepped forward and gripped her shoulder. "Running away will not solve your problems. Sometimes you have to confront them head-on."

Parul did not reply.

"You are not listening, Mumtaz. Leaving this house could get you into even more trouble."

"Then what do you want me to do?" cried Parul. "I know no other way."

Hasina reached out and touched Parul's chin. Her touch was affectionate, even motherly. "You want to know what I really want? I want a wedding. A wedding right now, between you and my brother. That way we can stop all tongues from wagging when your belly shows."

Parul sighed. "Don't I wish that, sister? But your brother is a complicated man. Only Allah knows what goes on inside his head."

"Wash your hands," said Hasina. "I will make you some ginger tea, and we will talk. We can solve all problems over a cup of excellent tea."

•   •   •

A little later, Parul accepted the tea from Hasina and leaned back against the wall.

Hasina patted her on the shoulder. "Tell me how all this happened."

Still, Parul did not look at her.

"Talk to me." Hasina gave her a gentle nudge. "It will unburden your chest."

Parul started from the beginning, telling Hasina how she had met Rahim in the printing press. She told her about their meetings in the west wing, his religious teachings and his assurances of marriage and family. Much as she wanted to, she could not bring herself to talk about the American boy. So he remained absent from her story.

Hasina remained calm and listened to all she had to say, keeping her interjections to a minimum. At last, Parul finished her story and blew her nose loudly. "I behaved like an insane woman, shameless and totally out of control. I brought this upon myself, sister. I sullied my father's name and Mohini's family's name. All because of my foolishness. Mohini's family will never take me back. I have nowhere to go now. I don't know what to do with this child."

"Have patience, sister, have patience. If Allah gave you this child, he will also show you the way to take care of it."

"But your brother does not want the child..."

"You judge him too harshly, sister. My brother never breaks a promise. If he promised to marry you, then he will." Hasina squeezed her hand.

"The marriage now comes with conditions. He is asking me to go back to Ma's house."

"If you don't mind my asking you, sister, why is my brother pushing you to go back to that house? This is only part of your story that I find puzzling."

Parul hesitated again. Guilt and fear gripped her as she stared at the hot brown liquid inside her teacup. How could she share with Hasina all the terrible things she had done to the American boy? How could she tell her how she had betrayed her host family? How would she explain her forbidden lust for Rahim and his severe and relentless control over her?

If she told Hasina all her misdeeds, she would fall in her eyes. Hasina would never respect her again or look at her with open affection. And then another thought came to her mind, making her laugh despite the pain she felt inside. *How can Hasina possibly think any worse of me? I have already fallen in her eyes. I am unmarried and I am carrying Rahim's child. Nothing can be more sinful and dreadful than this. I am already a social outcast.*

She opened up and told Hasina about the American boy and her attempts to harm him, holding back nothing from her. "So you see, sister, I have betrayed Ma and Mohini, who is a sister to me. I have caused so much pain. Still, your brother wants me to go back there and do more damage. I am powerless against him."

Hasina was reflective. She played with her teacup, tapping the sides and rotating it between her fingers.

"I see," she said at last. Her lips trembled, and she placed a hand on her heart. "I had a feeling this day would come. My brother would do something foolish like this. He has seen too much injustice in his life. Ever since our younger brother Salim died, he has never been the same. It is as if he has a volcano inside him, ready to erupt." Hasina dried her eyes with the end of her sari. "And lately I see him spending too much time with the Maulvi *Saheb*. I don't know what they talk about, but that man is no good."

"The Maulvi *Saheb*?"

"Yes, the old man you met at the Mazar yesterday morning. He is the one. He is what they call a radical. And now it looks like he is becoming Rahim's mentor."

"What is a radical?" This was an unfamiliar word for Parul.

"Sister, I am not an educated woman. I don't understand everything about everything. But I don't like the things that man asks our community here to do. He wants us to live our life following the Sharia law," explained Hasina. She went on to say it was because of the Maulvi and a handful of very militant followers that the women in the neighborhood had to keep themselves covered from head to toe.

Most Muslim neighborhoods in Kolkata did not require women to wear so much veil. But the women in this pocket of Park Circus were forced to keep themselves covered whenever they stepped outside the house. Not only that, the Maulvi and his men discouraged little girls from attending government-run schools. They only permitted the girls to attend Madrasas in the neighborhood, which taught from religious literature. Lately, the Maulvi had even started to interfere with children's health. When the government health workers came to give oral polio vaccines, his followers chased them away. They said the health care workers were government spies.

"It may sound like I am saying big things from a small mouth... but my heart says all these things are wrong. Things have gone too far in this neighborhood. We are peaceful men and women here. We would not harm a fly if we could help it. But now a handful of militant Islamists throw their weight around and ask us to do many evil deeds."

Parul sat with her back against the wall and drew her knees together. Hasina's suffering pained her.

Hasina stopped and poured her some more ginger tea. "This neighborhood is changing so rapidly it frightens me. Sometimes I just want to pack my belongings and leave. People here are suffering, but no one has the power to oppose these radical men.

"I am telling you this, sister, but don't tell anyone. *Allah Kasam* to you. Last year, I witnessed a terrible celebration in the local clubhouse. That morning some Islamic militants had attacked the American center near Park Street, killing five policemen. All of us feared a backlash and stayed inside that day. The boys didn't go out in the alley to play cricket, and the shopkeepers closed their shops early and went home. In the afternoon, the police were here knocking on every door, interrogating and rounding up the suspects. We were really terrified.

"Later that night, when most of the neighborhood was deep in sleep, I had to go to the outside tube-well to get drinking water. As I passed by the clubhouse on my way to the tube-well, a sound, somewhat muffled, coming from inside the clubhouse made me stop. The doors and windows were tightly shut. So I peeked in from a hole where a brick had chipped off. What I saw left me speechless. The Maulvi *Saheb* and his mullah friends were inside with some local boys. They were celebrating something. They wore garlands and frequently embraced each other. They danced around the room, clapping rhythmically with music. They ate sweet meats out of cardboard boxes. Their celebration terrified me and I left before they discovered me.

"These dangerous men are now my brother's friends. We are all peace-loving folks here... we have nothing against others and how they love their god. But these men, they give us a bad name.

"The Maulvi controls my brother's mind. Heaven knows what that man wants from him."

"What are you saying, Apa?" Parul slapped her forehead. "That the Maulvi and his mullah friends are terrorists? They shot the police guards at the American Center?"

"I don't know that, sister. I don't know if they are actual terrorists or just their sympathizers. But I have seen foreign men come and go. They have secret meetings in the Mazar basement."

This new knowledge chilled Parul. It was as if Rahim had shed his old self for a new one, and she was no longer sure she knew him. Of course, Parul had known he wanted to take revenge on the enemies of Islam, but that he would sympathize with terrorists who killed innocent victims was unthinkable. She wiped sweat from her face with the free end of her sari. Unwittingly she had brought upon herself trouble, whose scale and magnitude was beyond her imagination.

"Don't do what my brother is asking you to do." Hasina's voice was urgent. "He is not in his senses. We believe in peace and brotherhood. Don't harm others in our name."

Parul didn't look at her. She focused on the pain ripping her apart inside.

"It may already be too late for me," she said after a while. "Sister, my child needs a father."

Chapter 34

On Saturday, Mohini took Ma and Michael to the big stadium in Eden Gardens to watch a cricket match. It was India versus Pakistan, and the crowd in the stadium was wild and impatient. Mohini had to explain all the rules of the game to Michael, who watched with great interest, sitting on the edge of his seat and asking Mohini many questions. They took the metro on the way back.

It was raining hard when they stepped out of the metro station. Ma and Mohini drew their saris and dupattas over their heads as they stood under the awning of an old building. Michael covered his head with the hood of his jacket and stuffed his iPod into its waterproof cover.

Sheets of rain rolled down the corrugated metal roofs and gushed out of rooftop scuppers. The rain soaked the billboards and posters, danced on the glass windowpanes and dripped off the power lines. It washed the pavements and swirled around the open drains. The homeless huddled at the entrances and doorways of stores and banks while the stray dogs crawled under parked cars and trucks. A gust of wind swept in and blew leaves and dust all around them.

A taxi swooshed past within inches of Michael, splashing dark brown water on his denims.

"Watch out." Mohini pulled him back. "The taxi drivers in Kolkata think they own the road. They can do whatever they please."

Michael bent down to roll up his pants. Ma stuck out her hand to test the rain. It had thinned to a light drizzle now. "Come on." She lifted her sari and stepped into the water-logged street. "Let's get a rickshaw." She waved her hand, and two hand-pulled rickshaws waded through the water and pulled up in front of them.

"Get up quickly," Ma instructed Michael and Mohini. "All the streets are now waterlogged. We can't walk in this dirty water."

Michael inspected the rickshaw and the old rickety rickshaw-puller and shook his head. "I'm not getting up on that thing."

Mohini gave Michael a sharp prod in the ribs. "What's your problem with a rickshaw? These poor men are just trying to make a living. Help them."

"People don't ride on people. This is immoral."

"That's an American notion," snapped Mohini.

"No, it's a universal notion."

"Oh, you are so idealistic. These people cannot afford your ideals. They have a family to feed."

"The man who sells his kidneys does it to feed his family. Should I then purchase kidneys from him?" asked Michael.

"It's not the same—" began Mohini, but Ma interrupted her.

"Stop arguing, you two, and get up on that rickshaw," said Ma. "I have to go home and make tea for Mohini's father."

The rain was once again changing, from a sporadic drizzle to a steady shower. Drops of rain bounced off Michael's nose and rolled down his cheeks. The rickshaw pullers rang their handbells to show their growing impatience. Still, Michael showed no interest in climbing up. It was as if his feet were nailed to the ground, and nothing less than an earthquake could make him move.

Mohini looked at him, irritated. "Didn't you hear my mother? She is late."

He was thoughtful for a moment, and then he made up his mind. "I'll pull," he told Ma.

"What?"

"Why don't you and the rickshaw puller sit on the back, and I will do the pulling," said Michael.

Ma and Mohini looked at each other, astounded. *Michael wanted to pull the rickshaw.* Such a thing was unthinkable in Kolkata.

Ma walked over to him and gripped his wrist. "You'll do no such thing. Pulling a rickshaw is beneath you. You come from a *bhadralok* family."

"What is a *bhadralok*?" asked Michael.

"I can't explain all that to you. Just know this much: people from good families don't pull the rickshaw."

"But what's the big deal? I am just—"

"This is our culture, Michael." Ma clenched her mouth shut, signaling the end of the argument.

Michael folded his arms on his chest and took a long breath. "Very well, you two can come on the rickshaw, but I'm walking." He stepped into the water and splashed through it, taking long strides.

"Do you even know the way back home?" Ma cried.

"You keep going. I'll follow you," Michael replied without turning back.

Ma and Mohini climbed into the rickshaw and went past Michael, who didn't glance at them. The rickshaw-puller rang his bell and ran through the narrow side streets, away from the main road, and turned the corner near their house. Suddenly, Ma let out a surprised cry. She pointed to a woman in an orange sari sitting outside their house. "Is that Parul?" she gasped.

Looking at her figure, Mohini's heart stopped.

They paid the rickshaw-puller and hastened toward the woman. She was lost in thought and did not notice them approaching her. It was only when they were a few feet from her that she seemed to wake from her daydreaming and turned her head in their direction. Her nose ring glittered below her long, dark eyelashes.

"Parul," Ma squeaked, unable to rein in her delight. "You came back?"

"Yes, Ma."

"Are you okay? Everything all right?"

"Yes, Ma."

Michael caught up with them. He was slightly breathless after trudging through the garbage-filled Kolkata water. Annoyance was writ large on his face. He pulled out his shoe and squeezed out the dark water. Seeing Parul standing close to Mohini, his frustration seemed to dissipate quickly. *Are you happy now?* His eyes questioned Mohini.

"Where were you all this time?" Ma asked Parul.

"In a temple."

"Temple?"

"I went to the Mayapur ISKON temple. They took good care of me."

"Parul, tell me the truth. I will not tolerate any more lies."

"I swear on Ma Kali's name. The head-priest there felt sorry for me and let me sleep on the temple premises. He said... all I had to do was... sweep the temple floor for him. For that he let me eat the *prasad* twice a day."

Ma looked unconvinced. Her lips tightened, and the fleeting friendliness disappeared. It was clear to Mohini that the events of the past few months had destroyed Parul's credibility, and Ma was careful not to trust her so easily.

"So why are you back here?" Ma asked her sternly.

Parul stepped forward and clasped her hands in a gesture of a *Namaste*. "Ma, please, take me back. I have nowhere to go. Forgive me for all I have done. I will never bring shame to this house again."

"Not possible," said Ma.

"I will not disappoint you. Trust me just once," she pleaded.

"It is too late for forgiveness, Parul. I have found a replacement for you. I have a new maid—someone who respects this house and adheres to the rules. That is enough for me. You can go back to where you came from."

Fear flickered in Parul's eyes, and Mohini felt sorry for her. The truth was that they had hired no one new. Ram the janitor cleaned the floors, and the security guard ran all of Ma's errands. But Ma was determined to make the reunion painful for Parul.

"Don't say that, Ma." Parul fell on Ma's feet. "You are like a mother to me. I have nowhere else to go. Please, don't turn me away."

"Enough. I said no. You can't live in this house anymore. You will go back to your father. I will send him a message."

"Then I don't have a choice, Ma," cried Parul. "I have to end this cursed life of mine. If you don't want me... I can't go on living."

Abruptly and deliberately, Parul stepped off the pavement and ran toward the rapidly moving traffic. A speeding truck came to a screeching halt, missing her by inches. The driver honked loudly and rolled down his window to drown Parul in a string of profanities.

Michael rushed forward and pulled her away from the oncoming traffic. "Are you out of your freaking mind?" he roared. "Who the fuck does this sort of thing?"

"*Saheb*, you stay out of it," snapped Parul in Bengali. "I want to kill myself, and don't poke your nose in my matter."

Ma and Mohini exchanged smiles. They were used to Parul's attention-grabbing antics, but Michael, being a foreigner, was so easily fooled. *He will learn*, Ma's eyes seemed to say.

Parul rushed back to Ma and fell on her feet again. "Take me back, Ma. I will follow all the house rules. You can trust me. You can trust me one hundred percent."

Still Ma did not respond. "Please," wept Parul. "You are the only mother I have ever known. Mohini here is my sister. Can't you forgive me just once?"

For a moment, Ma seemed to hesitate. Then she exhaled deeply and made up her mind. "Go upstairs to your room and remain there until I order you to come downstairs."

"Are you taking me back?" Parul's eyes lit up with hope.

"I am not making any promises," snapped Ma. "I am just letting you stay in my house 'til I talk to your father and sort out things. He is the one who brought you to this house years ago. I have done my duty and raised you. For good or for bad, I don't know. But this much I know: it is time for me to relinquish this responsibility and hand you back to your father. That would be the proper thing to do."

"Ma, please, don't say that...."

"Not another word. Go upstairs."

And that's how Parul got a temporary entry into their house. For a few days, things seemed to fall back into their cozy, familiar routine. The multicolored cotton saris came back to the clothesline, and Parul's anklets danced rhythmically on the stairs.

The house was spotlessly clean again, the laundry folded, and the food had the familiar aroma. And at night, Mohini tiptoed up the stairs to stand outside Parul's door, her feet pressed on the thin strip of yellow light that spilled from underneath it and illuminated part of the stairs. There was great comfort in that warm glow of light, comfort that came from the knowledge that Parul was back in her life—her sister, her best friend.

Chapter 35

Mohini sat on the windowsill of her parents' room, staring at the impenetrable text of her heavy college textbook, her mind weighed down in anguish and far removed from the printed words. From her window, she could see the sun disappearing beyond the horizon and the birds circling the tall palm trees. The book slipped from her fingers, and her mind drifted to Michael.

Love was not the joyful phenomenon described by poets and writers, she thought. If anything, it was agony and longing, night and day, with no end in sight. The possibility of falling in love with Michael came with far more fear and trepidation than actual happiness. Ever since their kiss behind the water reservoir, she was even more aware of him—responding to his glances, his sudden movements and the modulations and quiet undertones of his deep voice. She listened for his footsteps on the stairs, looked for his shorts and T-shirts on the clothesline, and smelled his aftershave when he left the bathroom in the morning. And when she was alone in bed at night and the life outside her window died down, she worried about their future together. Did he care for her as deeply as she cared for him? Would his feelings lessen in intensity once he went back home? Would he wait for her? Come back to get her?

Every evening, Mohini rushed up to the terrace to meet Michael. He pulled her behind the water reservoir, drew her close, and cupped her chin to kiss her. There they sat, hand in hand, talking attentively, wrapped in each other's stories—mystified by the omissions and exclusions they had made in their narratives when they first described their lives to each other. There had been so many barriers then, so much distrust between them. Mohini had not liked Michael's sudden intrusion into her space, and he had looked upon her as the annoying Indian girl. But now they shared their past with a sense of urgency, knowing they were running out of time and sharing this with each other was of great importance.

One such evening, as the sun disappeared behind the tall buildings of Highland Park and the sound of conch shells echoed through the neighborhood, Michael finally allowed himself to talk about his father's deployment to Afghanistan. He admitted his father hadn't really wanted to go on this deployment. He had a premonition of what was to come and didn't want to leave the children, but being in the army, he had felt trapped. He had to follow orders. "What I'm about to tell you... I have told no one else before," Michael told Mohini. "It was a private conversation between my dad and me. Even my mother doesn't know about this...

"The night before my dad left, I was hanging out in my room. There was a knock, and I looked up. I saw my dad in his pajamas outside the door. He had a haircut and a shave, but he looked dead tired. I knew he was coming to say goodbye to me, and I couldn't believe we were doing this again. He was going to leave the next day, and there wasn't a damn thing I could do to stop him.

"Dad went over to my bookshelf and flipped through some of my books. He shuffled around, staring at my weightlifting trophies and medals, and he couldn't look me in the eye. After a long time, he cleared his throat and said, 'They say it is a quick and easy type of war. We'll be in and out in no time. As soon as our boots touch the ground, we'll get to Osama. Then all we have got to do is get the Taliban out.'"

"And you?" asked Mohini. "You believed him?"

Michael seemed to wince. "Every cell in my body wanted to believe him."

A lump formed in Mohini's throat. She pulled his hand in to her lap and held it there.

Michael sucked in a gasp of air before continuing. "After that, Dad did something I couldn't believe. He leaned forward and brought his face close to me, like he was going to tell me a secret. His voice was a whisper, and I listened carefully. 'Son, I'm tired and wish I didn't have to go.'

"I couldn't believe he said that. When it came to wars and his deployments, Dad never discussed his feelings. Like most military men, he remained silent—sometimes too silent. So I was worried... you know... Why was Dad telling me this?"

"Then?" she asked, gently.

"Dad placed his hand on my shoulder. 'In the beginning, going to war has its own thrill. It gives you a sense of accomplishment, just enduring it and coming out alive. What I was doing out there seemed so much grander and so much more important than anything I could have done back here.'

'But years of living in the shadow of death can teach you a few things about life. Each time I came back home, and I held you and your sister in my arms, I said to myself, thank God I am alive and I can still do this. Each time I dropped you off at school and helped you with your homework at night, I said to myself, thank God I can still do this. War made me realize that the most boring, ordinary moments of our life leave behind the most powerful memories.'"

Mohini's throat constricted, and she swallowed hard. "What a beautiful thing to say." She pulled out a handkerchief from her pocket and blew her nose.

Daylight was rapidly fading, plunging them into darkness. The birds circled the sky and settled on branches of tall trees. The cool breeze brought the smell of jasmine and marigold—divine, comforting and temple-like. Dust rose from the terrace floor and swirled around them like golden sparkles.

Michael folded his legs and brought them closer to his chest. His fingers drummed nervously on the back of the water reservoir. "It was hard for me to see Dad so conflicted. Through the long deployments, the death of his close friends, and the injury that almost took his leg, my dad had never lost his will to serve his country. He always had amazing energy, amazing vitality and a sense of purpose. But that night, he seemed troubled. 'You know, son—there is nothing heroic about watching someone's head get blown away or torso starting to melt. You don't unveil any secret about human life... You don't imbibe a deeper reality from experiencing such scenes. My eyes have seen too much blood of friends—these hands have lifted too many body bags of comrades. I just don't know if I'm up for all this again.'"

A tear rolled down Mohini's cheek. She took a deep breath and forced herself to look at Michael. "Did you try to stop him?"

"Stop him?"

"From going to Afghanistan."

Michael smiled ruefully. "It doesn't work like that, Mohini. His orders had come. He'd passed his physical inspection. He had to go."

Michael placed a hand on his chest and looked at Mohini as though he had just realized how powerless he was before the greater forces that controlled his life. Beads of sweat tickled the sides of his face. He got up and leaned over the parapet. Mohini touched his arm, and when he turned to face her, she rose on her tiptoes to wipe away his sweat with her *dupatta*.

Michael turned away so that she couldn't see his eyes. "When my dad died, I was touring the Olympic training center in Colorado. Anna was out visiting friends. My mom was alone when the men in uniform showed up at her door. When she heard the news, she fainted." Michael kicked the flowerpot next to him. "I wasn't even there for her."

•　　•　　•

It was dusk when Michael finished his story. "My father was my best friend from childhood. He was my bud. But he was gone just like that... *just like that*... not even a goodbye. I don't know why... but I am still mad at him."

They went downstairs and straight to Michael's room. Mohini's heartbeat fast. After hearing Michael's story, she just wanted to put her arms around him and make him forget all his suffering. But something told her to stay away from him as he paced the floor like a wounded cheetah. Telling her the story had taken enormous effort, and Michael was exhausted.

He switched on the light and stole a brief glance at her, his eyes dark and unreadable. Then he sat on his chair, pretending to read a book, signaling her with his hand to leave the room. She was reluctant to go. She dragged her feet for a few minutes, but it was clear he was done talking and would prefer to be left alone with his thoughts. She moved toward the door slowly, turning the knob and pushing the door open. He mumbled something incoherent, and she turned around. His boyish face was almost apologetic as he said, "You'll think I'm crazy, but I need to tell you that I..."

He did not finish. The veins on his neck flared with the effort he put into this one sentence. She didn't wait. She went up to him and kneeled on the floor next to his chair. She put her head on his knees and closed her eyes.

The room grew silent. Her heart pounded, first in her throat and then in her ear. The cricket outside the window chirped loudly. A night owl hooted. Michael pushed back the hair from her face and cupped her chin gently. The warmth of his fingers against her skin momentarily mesmerized her. Michael spoke again, but this time his words were almost a whisper, so low that she didn't hear him. She raised her face and brought it close to his. The bottomless depth of his seaweed eyes made her dizzy. That's when he said, "You're my love across the ocean. My only love."

They held each other—their breath rising and falling in unison, drowning them in its perfect synchronicity.

"You will have to talk to my father, you know," she said at last. "That's what we do here in India."

"I know." He sighed. "And I know what'll happen after that. Your father will ask me to disappear. I'm sure he'll drive me to the airport and buy me a plane ticket."

Despite the painful truth hidden in his words, they both laughed.

Chapter 36

After coming back to Mohini's house, Parul tried to set aside all her worries and focus on her everyday housework. She swept the floor—vast areas of marble and mosaic—with her thinning bamboo duster and mopped energetically, sitting on her haunches and dragging along her bucket of dark brown water. She did laundry for the entire house, pulling the dripping clothes from the tin bucket, swinging them over her head, and beating them on the bathroom floor. She stood barefoot in a stream of soapy water, her sari pulled up to her knees as she rubbed the colored material vigorously between her hands. She then wrung out the water, smoothed the creases and dried the clothes on the clothesline on the terrace.

She had not spoken to Rahim at all since she had left Hasina's house, but she'd seen him. Once or twice when pumping water in the courtyard, she had looked up and seen him waiting at the press office window, his face cold and grim. When their eyes met, he had pointed at his watch as if to signal that her mission was incomplete and she was running out of time. His gesture had made her heart twist, as if the last drop of blood was being wrung from it.

It was mid-day when Parul finished mopping Ma's bedroom and headed for Michael's room with her bucket and gray mop. Michael had gone downstairs for his morning exercises. He no longer bothered to lock his door in those days. So Parul pushed aside the curtain and stepped inside. Her eyes widened at the sight of Mohini in the room. Mohini stood in front of Michael's cupboard, shifting and sniffing his clothes.

"What are you doing here, Mohini?" Parul raised her eyebrows at her.

Mohini gasped and gripped a chair for support. "Nothing... I was just..." She flushed.

"And why are you smelling Michael's clothes?" Parul demanded.

Mohini hesitated at first. Then a dreamy shyness came into her eyes. "I need to tell you something," she started. "It is about me and that American boy. We are in love..."

"Love?"

"Yes, we love each other."

Parul looked at her face, gone all intense and shiny, and an alarm bell went off in her head. "How, Mohini?" she asked, trying to hide the distress in her voice.

Mohini picked Michael's shirt up and held it close to her chest. Her face lit up. "I can't explain how," said Mohini. "But I can tell you everything that happened between us, and then maybe you'll understand."

They are in love. The words were so loud in Parul's head that they drowned out all other noise. What had started as simple flirting had turned into love. Everything she had feared was now coming true.

Mohini walked over to Parul and gripped her shoulder. Her eyes sparked like rubies. She told Parul everything that had transpired in the past few weeks, how her own feelings for Michael had grown and how he had confessed his love for her. "But you know Ma and Baba. They would never accept a Christian boy. They would never give their blessings. What should I do? I'm terrified even to talk to them."

Parul opened her mouth to say something, but no words came out. Looking at Mohini, she managed a small nod.

"Maybe I should just forget Michael," said Mohini. "Maybe that is the right thing to do. But how can I make my heart understand that, Parul*di*... you tell me? The heart does not understand any logic. It wants what it wants."

Parul's temples throbbed. Mohini's feelings would get in the way of her mission. How could she harm a boy Mohini loved? Why was fate playing another cruel joke on her?

Parul dipped the mop in the water, got down on her knees and reached below the armoire. Behind her, Mohini clicked her tongue impatiently. She flopped on the floor beside Parul and tugged on the bottom of Parul's sari, forcing her to turn around. "I am not a monk or a *Sadhu* who can keep my feelings on a tight leash. Not being with him feels like a punishment. I don't even want to live in this house anymore. I just wish the two of us could run away somewhere."

This time, Parul could no longer hide her displeasure. "These are all foolish thoughts," she said. "You are being an idiot. The American boy is no good. He is only saying all this to you because he is lonely. He is away from his family, in a new country, and you are his only friend. So he thinks he loves you. The truth is, the moment he goes back, he will forget all about you. Listen to me, Mohini, you need to get him out of your head.... Let him go. Focus on your college work."

Mohini compressed her lips together grimly. "I don't know why you have to speak so cruelly about Michael. You know nothing about him or his life. Do you know how many problems he had growing up? His father had long deployments, and his mother was always very depressed. And when his father got back, the parents had huge fights. They lived a life of constant worry and unending fear where death was always an arm's length away. And last year, all their fear and worry came true. His father was killed in the war in Afghanistan...." Parul tried to listen to the rest of Michael's story but eventually got distracted. She dipped the mop in the bucket and swished it around the floor.

Her lack of interest in Michael's story seemed to infuriate Mohini even more. "Michael is in so much pain, and all you can do is criticize him! Don't judge people so easily, Parul*di*, not before you know their entire story."

Parul stared at Mohini, open-mouthed. She had not expected Mohini to rebel like that. She squatted on the floor next to the bucket, looking down at it wordlessly. Somewhere in Mohini's parents' room, the record player was blaring, and Baba was listening to his English songs. The breeze that came from the open window tugged at her sari.

Parul rose slowly to her feet and caught hold of Mohini's elbow. "Is your head so full of cow dung you trusted that American boy when he told you all these nonsense stories?"

"What are you saying? Michael a liar?"

"I am sure he is one."

"I want you to stop." Mohini tugged her elbow free. She sank into a chair next to Michael's desk and covered her ears. "Don't say another word."

"You just don't want to see or hear the truth."

"Paruldi, I'm warning you. Don't get me any more upset. Anything could come out of my mouth now. You may not be able to bear it."

"You know I only want what is best for you." Parul softened her tone. "Take my advice and leave the American boy before you get hurt."

Mohini's face darkened. She threw the notepads and pens lined up on Michael's desk on the floor and hissed at Parul. "Are you jealous? You're jealous of us—jealous of what Michael and I have."

Parul gave a nervous laugh. "Now listen to this, crazy girl. Why would I be jealous?"

"Are you saying all this because I found true love in my life and you didn't? Is it because your father can't find a groom for you?"

A sharp pain seared through her chest, as if somebody had brought a blade straight through her beating heart. Speechless for a long moment, Parul did nothing but stare at her. Then she shook her head and whimpered, "You would say *this* to me, Mohini? You would say those words to *me*?"

"You are so eager to tell me the truth. I'm only returning the favor."

Parul shook her head. "I can't believe the American boy has made you so selfish that you would fling such hurtful words at your own people."

"You left me no option," Mohini scowled back at her. "I love him. That's the only thing that matters to me now."

"You have known me all my life, and you have known this American boy only a few months, but so easily you could insult me and take his side?"

"Why would I not? You don't understand English. You can't point out America on a map. But that doesn't stop you from judging the American boy, does it?"

"Do you see that? Do you see what you just did?" Parul bit her lips fiercely and pointed at Mohini. "You have always been a chameleon— changing colors on me. I can only approve; I can't criticize any of your decisions. If you don't like what I say, you put me in my place right away."

If Mohini was surprised by Parul's allegations, she didn't show it. She stood and brought her face very close to Parul. "That's because you pretend to be Mother Teresa, always trying to save me. I am tired of hearing, 'I know what is best for you, Mohini.' You have done this all your life and you won't stop. I don't need any saving. Especially not from someone who has only a seventh-grade education. I like Michael, and that's my decision."

Parul picked up her bucket and deliberately slammed it on the marble floor. The bucket rocked from side to side, spilling its dark brown water on the floor and splashing Mohini's bare toes. She jumped back in surprise and erupted in a wail. "How dare you spill this dirty water on me? Wait till I tell Ma what you've done. She will send you back home in no time. You can rot in your stupid village."

For once in her life, Parul did not apologize. She mopped the floor again, collecting the spilled water and wringing it back into the bucket while Mohini continued to scream and hop all around her.

"If my Abbu comes to get me, I'll not say no. I'll go with him," Parul muttered, half to herself. "There is nothing left here for me."

Chapter 37

The *Kalbaishakhi* came. The wind picked up speed, rattling the doors and windows. The sky darkened, and lightning tore across it, followed by the loud clap of thunder. Parul ran around the house, gathering the clothes from the clothesline, closing the window shutters and locking them in place. The widow's cat chased her, tangling in her legs and making her trip.

That night Parul lay on her mat, sleepless. Big drops of water fell on the tin awning outside her window—*tap tap tap*. Nothing and no one stirred inside the house. Parul stared at the ceiling. *How could Mohini hurt her so much?* She adjusted her pillows and turned away from the window. Closing her eyes, she tried to dismiss Mohini's cruel words. *"Are you jealous, Paruldi? Are you jealous of us—jealous of what Michael and I have?"*

How could Mohini let those words come out of her mouth? Why didn't her tongue glue itself to the roof of her mouth to hold back those hurtful sentences? She must have known that Parul would be devastated. Or did she assume Parul was made of stone?

All her life, Parul had listened to Mohini's problems patiently and with appropriate concern. She had sighed and supported and even expressed outrage when the occasion demanded. At times, she had picked fights with other children just to defend Mohini. Yet, her loyalty meant nothing to Mohini. How easily she switched sides, forgot her childhood friend, and defended the American boy. Anger and grief swelled in Parul's chest when she recalled Mohini's hurtful words. *Is it because your father can't find a groom for you?*

Love, Parul thought again, *has made Mohini ruthless. All she can think of is her own desire for that American boy. Nothing and no one else matters to her now.*

It was time to teach Mohini a lesson; she thought to herself, listening to the storm that raged outside. What she was going to do would break Mohini's heart. But didn't she deserve it? After all, to her, Parul was just a maid, nothing more. Mohini paid Parul's wages, and Parul picked up after her. No wonder she thought she could insult Parul whenever she wanted.

Parul pressed her wet eyes against the pillow. Thunder rumbled outside her window, and a sudden flash of lightning lit up the severe edges and sharp angles of her room. Getting up, she wrapped the sari tightly around her waist and opened the terrace door. The rain-washed terrace looked mysterious and unattainable in the moonlight. Staring at the torrential rain, Parul was reminded of their childhood days, when Mohini used to come to the terrace to collect the hail. *Paruldi,* she would say, *I want to make ice cream with this hail. Will you help me catch it?*

They would run out to the terrace with their buckets under the cold, dark sky, lifting it toward the heavens, collecting the blessings in a small virgin pile. Sometimes they splashed in the puddles and ran faster and faster until both of them were out of breath, their clothes soaking wet and water dripping from their noses and eyelashes. They fell back then, dropping their buckets, and rolled with laughter until their stomachs cramped and voices grew hoarse.

Eh Allah, thought Parul now. *All my memories are tangled with this girl. If I harm her, how will I live with such enormous guilt? Even if I atone for a thousand years, will Allah be able to forgive me?*

Beads of sweat gathered on her forehead. She unwrapped her sari and dropped it on the floor. She stepped into the rain, her anklets ringing as her feet splashed water from the puddles. The rain soaked her blouse and petticoat, streamed down her hands and legs. She pulled the pin holding her hair, and it came tumbling down over her heaving breasts. She stuck out her tongue and tasted the rain. Then she lifted her arms and faced the heavy clouds in the night sky. A narrow rivulet dripped into her cleavage and ran down her belly. Her nipples hardened, and the salt from her tears mixed with the sweet rainwater.

The sky was temporarily lit by lightning, and thunder cracked deafeningly. There was a brief flutter inside her belly, as if the new life growing inside her was trying to remind her of its presence. Parul knew then that she simply could not undo the past. She could show regret, ask for forgiveness, and even want to do penance. But she could not go back in time. She was now midstream, and she would either get carried by the current or die trying to fight it. She would have to protect the life inside her. That new life would now triumph over all of Parul's past loyalties, her bonds, and bondage.

Rahim's parting words echoed in her mind, unleashing a fierce burn in her chest. "Succeed in the mission and the child will have my name. Or else..." Parul's nerves stretched like rubber bands, straining her temples and making them throb. If she wanted her baby to have a safe future, what alternative would she have but to carry out his mission? *Even if it meant hurting Mohini.*

Looking up at the angry sky, she fell on her knees and cupped her palms. "Wash away my sins," she pleaded. "Forgive me for what I am about to do."

Breaking out of the trance, Parul moved away from the rain and back to her room. She took off her wet blouse and petticoat and dried them on the clothesline. She thought of her plan now.... The plan had come to her one night, as she lay tossing and turning in Hasina's house, listening to the dogs bark outside her window. She had felt as strongly as if an angel standing beside her had taken a piece of paper and written the perfect solution to her dilemma. What she was about to do would send the American back to his home country and shatter Mohini's family.

Rahim had liked her plan. Before leaving Hasina's house, she had seen him one last time. Hasina had requested him to come for dinner. Parul and Rahim sat on a straw mat with a sari curtain between them. Hasina returned from the kitchen, balancing two plates full of food.

"Move away," she cried to her two children, who got in the way and blocked her. "Don't put *nazar* on the food. It is for your *mama* and our guest."

She set the plates on the mat. "I have some *phirni* and *soan-papdi*. Good food gives good energy."

She dragged her daughters out of the room. Parul waited for Rahim to taste his *phirni* before picking up her own bowl. That was when she whispered to him her plan. Her plan would require some acting skills, she had admitted, but Parul was sure she could pull it off.

"Couldn't be better," praised Rahim, licking the *phirni* dripping off his fingers. He was genuinely pleased. "Give thanks to Him the most merciful, the most kind. Such a perfect plan can only come from Him. This will be a spectacle to watch. We will make big news."

Hasina appeared with cups of milky tea and said she was sending the girls to bed. She was relieved to see Rahim so happy. She made quick eye contact with Parul and gave her an encouraging smile. *So you two made up?* Her eyes seemed to question Parul.

Parul lowered her gaze and stared at the floor. Picking up her cup of tea, she walked to the open window. It was impossible to share her plans with Hasina. Hasina would not approve. "Islam teaches Muslims must treat non-Muslims with respect and forgiveness," Hasina had said. "Muslims should not harm other people."

Outside, two street dogs were eating a dead bird. Wings and feathers lay scattered on the pavement. The scene was repulsive, poisonous. Another cramp came, and she covered her mouth to hold back her vomit.

Rahim got up as soon as Hasina left. He walked over to the window and stood behind her. His closeness made her uncomfortable. A group of men, their faces hardly visible, sat around a clay oven, roasting kebabs and making *Rumali roti*.

"What time is it?" asked Rahim.

"Must be around ten o'clock," said Parul.

"Then the metro rail is closed. I have to take a bus and get off at Garia station. I will meet with the railway slum Maulvi and tell him about your plan. I'm sure he will help us."

Parul turned around. "Maulvi Abdullah?"

"Yes," said Rahim proudly, looking at her. "Maulvi Abdullah will think highly of you. He will know I have chosen well."

Parul tried to imagine what he could mean. Why did he want to include the Maulvi Abdullah in their plan? Did he not want to keep this a secret? All Muslims who lived in that neighborhood highly respected the Maulvi. But why would he take any interest in Parul's plan? It made little sense.

"Is it necessary?" she asked at last.

"What?"

"To tell him?"

Rahim smiled. "He will gather our slum brothers and sisters. He will get them ready. What you'll start, they'll finish."

Rahim's answer bewildered Parul even more. Was there something else that Rahim was planning? This thought rankled. Still, Parul decided not to ask any more questions. *Why should I care? I will only think about what happens to me and my child. What Rahim is planning with the Maulvi is none of my business.*

Now, standing next to the rain-filled terrace, Parul shook the water out of her hair and changed into a dry sari. She switched off the light and slipped under her blanket. Slowly, gradually, calm and equilibrium returned to her. She could reach a firm decision. There were no more conflicting thoughts.

I am ready, she thought. *Tomorrow, the show will start right after Mohini comes back from college.*

Chapter 38

The next afternoon on her way back from college, Mohini found herself in the backseat of a mini-bus idling in the traffic, surrounded by the usual multitude of cars and buses that clogged the city streets. She was still fuming over the way Parul had abandoned her when she needed her the most. All she had wanted was Parul's encouragement, her ever-supportive presence in her life. Instead, what she got was a big lecture. Mohini shook with indignation at Parul's priggish attitude and her hostility toward Michael. She snatched a page from her notebook, scribbled Parul's name on it, crumpled it into a ball and tossed it on the floor.

The bus crept forward an inch and came to a complete halt. Mohini could no longer bear to wait. Her T-shirt clung to her breast in wet, sweat-soaked clusters. It would be easier to walk home than to bake on a sweltering bus. Collecting her college bag, she made her way to the front door, stabbing with her elbows and stepping on toes to push through the crowd.

It was almost four-fifteen in the afternoon when she finally reached her house and clicked open the gate. Black clouds had gathered in the sky, and it looked like it would start raining any moment. Her shoes crunched on the gravel as she hurried past Baba's garage on her way to the house. There was a rustle and an anklet ring, and Mohini caught a flash of color behind the banyan tree. A sound, a little muffled, came from the same direction: it sounded like a low moan and a whimper. *Someone was in pain.*

Mohini rushed to the clearing behind the bushes and discovered Parul bending over the garden tap and vomiting. For a moment,

Mohini forgot to breathe. Her eyes traveled down to Parul's belly. The bulge was barely visible. Mohini stared at her, unable to move, unable to speak.

"Mohini, listen," said Parul. Her voice was filled with urgency. "I have made a mistake. Don't tell your mother."

Mohini's chest knotted, and she tasted bitter bile on the back of her tongue. She covered her ears with her hands, but the phrase drummed rhythmically inside her head.

She is pregnant. She is pregnant. She is pregnant.

Yes, the unthinkable had happened. Parul had crossed the *Lakshman Rekha*, her limits, and brought terrible shame to their family. A storm was brewing, big thick clouds were rolling in and the strong wind swirled around her. Staring at the slight curve of Parul's belly, she realized she could no longer protect Parul. What she had done deserved no forgiveness.

Mohini ran past her father's training camp and up the marble stairs to the second-floor balcony. Her heart hammered inside her chest, her fingers trembled, and thousands of voices whispered in her head. But she suppressed them all. Instead, she clenched her teeth and tightened her fist to prepare herself for what she was about to do. She found Ma in the bedroom.

"Something is wrong with Parul*di*," she cried. "I think she is pregnant."

Ma went completely still. It was as if she had turned into a concrete statue.

"Did you hear what I said? I saw Parul*di* throwing up, and her belly looks larger."

Ma's expression changed slowly as she took in the full impact of Mohini's words. The color left her cheeks, and her whole body trembled. Immediately Mohini regretted blurting out the news; she should have known how traumatic this revelation would be for Ma. She shifted her legs nervously, debating if she should get Baba from the camp.

"Where is she?" demanded Ma, pulling Mohini out of her thoughts.

"Please sit down. You don't look well."

"Just answer me. Where is that girl?"

"In the garden behind the banyan tree," stammered Mohini.

Ma pushed past her and headed down the stairs. "Don't stop me now." She glared at Mohini. "I have to do what I should have done long ago."

Ma ran barefoot to the garden, her cotton sari swishing on the ground and gathering dust. She caught hold of the neck of Parul's blouse with one hand and wrenched her away from the water tap. Then she dragged her all the way to the courtyard. Parul screamed and squirmed, trying to get out of Ma's iron fist. Mohini followed close behind.

Ma pushed Parul down onto the courtyard floor and towered over her. She slapped her face and screamed, "Tell me, you *mukhpuri*, you burned-face woman, whose sin are you carrying in your belly?"

Baba rushed down to see what the commotion was about. The customers and employees from the press room gathered around the courtyard. Hearing the screams, even Baba's students left their training and rushed to the scene. Raising her head and standing on her toes, Mohini looked for Michael in the crowd, but didn't see him anywhere.

Ma slapped Parul's face again and yelled, "I let you in this house, thinking you are a decent girl. You ate our food, slept under our roof, and then turned our house into a brothel. You didn't care for one moment about our reputation. Tell me, *hatatchari*, who are you sleeping with?" Ma banged Parul's head against the brick wall. More men gathered in the shadows behind them. Ma slapped, punched, and twisted Parul's hands, demanding to know who the father was.

Then the rain came. Huge, heavy drops pierced holes in the sky and drenched them all. A flash of lightning lit up Ma's angry face. The surrounding men shifted their feet uneasily. Parul threw herself at Ma's feet. She wept, "Ma, I have made a mistake, and you can punish me any other way you want, but don't hit me anymore, please!"

Mohini's head reeled. Next to her, Baba seemed to have turned into a statue. She caught hold of his elbow and begged, "Do something, Baba. Save Parul*di*."

Baba stepped into the courtyard and tried to separate Ma from Parul, but Ma pushed him back. "Don't stop me today, Mohini's father," she warned. "Things have already gotten out of hand."

She grabbed Parul's braid and gave it a hard tug.

Parul howled in pain. "Let me go... I beg of you."

"Who is the father?"

"Please, don't increase my sin by asking me that question. I can't tell you."

"Yes, you can, and you will. Give me the *name*," screamed Ma.

"The truth is never pretty," said Parul, gasping. "For this family, the truth may be unbearable. I ate your salt, Ma. I cannot bring such devastation on this family."

Parul's gaze flicked to the faces that surrounded her and came to rest on Mohini. For one brief second, a brief glimmer of regret or apology appeared in her eyes before she turned her face away from Mohini.

"The *name*, Parul...." hissed Ma. She gave Parul's hair another hard tug.

"*It's the American boy.* He did this to me."

An eerie silence descended over the spectators. The only sound was that of the raindrops bouncing off the concrete walls and floors.

"American boy? Michael? Are you talking about our Michael?"

"Yes... yes. He is the one. I swear."

Dread filled Mohini's heart. Her legs felt like jelly, and she leaned against a pillar to support herself. Michael was nowhere to be seen.

Parul wept at Ma's feet. "It is him... it is him. The *Saheb* forced me to sleep with him."

"How can you utter such a big lie?" Ma freed her legs from Parul and pushed her back. "I've reared a snake in my house, and I fed it milk and bananas with these hands. How could I have been so blind? Why didn't I see this day coming?"

"I swear on Ma Kali. It's the American boy. May my tongue fall out if I lie."

Ma staggered and lifted her hand to slap her, but Baba and his students descended upon them and separated them. Ma clenched her fists and set her chin. "Parul, go up to your room. I want you and all your belongings gone from our house tomorrow morning. Don't show your face in this neighborhood again."

•   •   •

The storm that raged outside raged inside Mohini. Parul's words rang in her ears and ripped through her heart. She had to find Michael and tell him about this terrible lie. He'd find it hard to believe; he might even lose his temper and go after Parul.

Mohini turned to look at Parul then. *Why, Paruldi?* she wanted to ask. *Why did you do this?* But looking at Parul's burning eyes, she took a step backward. Parul's hair hung in wet ropes over her face; her rain-soaked sari had slipped off her shoulders and lay coiled around her feet like a heavy snake. Her eyes were red and completely focused on Mohini.

The sight of her frightened Mohini.

"Listen to me." Baba grabbed Mohini's shoulder and spun her around to face him. "Your mother needs you. Take her upstairs to the bedroom."

•   •   •

In the bedroom, Mohini passed two aspirin tablets to Ma, along with a glass of water. Ma's fingers were bleeding from striking Parul. Mohini poured some Dettol antiseptic liquid on a cotton ball and cleaned Ma's fingertips. Then she propped up her pillow and gave her a hot-water bag to relax her aching muscles.

Mohini got up to close the door, but Baba pushed past her with great urgency. "We can't keep Michael in this neighborhood. We must get him out of here. Word will spread quickly that he got the maid pregnant, and the whole slum will descend upon us."

Mohini gasped. His words had a chilling effect on her senses. What was Baba saying? Would the slum people attack them? Were they in danger?

"Don't believe a word that comes out of that girl's mouth," snapped Ma. "That girl is a first-class liar."

"Mohini's Ma, this is what I'm trying to understand," said Baba. "Why is Parul putting false blame on Michael? The girl has grown up before our own eyes. She is incapable of such cunning. Who or what is pushing her to do all this?"

Baba turned his head and looked at Mohini with questioning eyes, but she shook her head. This time, she had nothing to offer about Parul. Really, she was just as perplexed as her parents. She didn't know if Parul had a new friend or a group of friends. *Even if she did,* thought Mohini, *why would they want to hurt Michael? Michael was just a foreign student in Baba's camp. Why would anyone take any interest in him?*

Before she could think any further, a wail escaped from Ma's lips. "No one is pushing her to do anything, Mohini's father! That girl is taking revenge on us. Revenge from which life... which incarnation... I don't know. What did we not do for her? Whenever she wanted anything, did we say no? New sari and slippers every *puja* and movie tickets whenever she wanted to see a show." Ma dried her eyes with the end of her sari. "And this is the way she pays us back. The truth is, their class of people can never change. You can keep them in the house like your own daughter, but they will still stab you in the back. It is their nature."

Mohini poured another glass of water and handed it to Ma. Baba asked Ma to calm down and let go of the past. What had happened had happened and could not be undone. But it was important to think about what was about to happen. Parul's allegation could prove very harmful to the family. It could even put them in great danger. The word would spread quickly in the neighborhood. Later that night, everyone would know their American guest made the maid pregnant. The slum people would only believe what Parul had to say, and her accusation would prove devastating for the whole family. Baba blew his nose. "The slum people will come for Michael. My guess is later in the morning... but definitely by mid-day. His life may be threatened," he said.

So many times in her life, Mohini had thought she was afraid. Now she realized that until this moment, she had not known what true dread was. She picked up a shawl and wrapped it around herself. Still, she couldn't stop shivering.

"Don't be so frightened," said Ma, pulling her down onto the bed. "Your father will take care of Michael and our family. He won't let anyone harm us."

Baba sat down next to them and patted Mohini's shoulder. "This is not the time to panic. This is the time to act. You are a brave girl. Won't you help your father get through this crisis?"

Mohini didn't answer him—not because she didn't want to help him, but because she was incapable of thinking rationally. Her world was collapsing like a giant supernova, and she was watching from a distance as a spectator. What Baba said next was even more frightening.

He thought that the slum people might ask Michael to marry Parul. If Michael refused, there would be terrible consequences.

Ma let out a loud sob. "Ma Kali, what have we done to deserve this? Why are you testing us like this? Why is Parul taking revenge on us? In which life, which incarnation did we try to harm her?"

"Stop it, Mohini's Ma," warned Baba. "You are getting your daughter upset. We have to get Michael out of this house. Do you hear me? We have to get him out first thing tomorrow morning. We leave this house before the slum people come looking for him."

Ma dried her eyes quickly. "What should we do?"

"Help Michael pack. Make sure he takes his passport with him. We will take him outside of Kolkata for a few days. Once I arrange a ticket to America, I will send him back home."

Ma motioned for Mohini to follow her down the hall, but Mohini couldn't move or breathe. Her head spun with a nauseous dizziness, and a dark mist blurred her vision.

Chapter 39

Mohini was completely paralyzed with fear. Was Michael really going to leave? Was this their final goodbye? The reality of what was happening hit her. The rain had stopped, and it was a full moon night. The silvery rays washed the balcony outside her parents' bedroom. She paced the balcony restlessly, conjuring up scenarios where she could stop Michael from leaving. The future from here looked dark and desolate... as if someone with cold, cruel fingers wanted to choke out all the joy from her life. She couldn't just give up. She had to find a way to hold Michael back, even if it was by sheer force of will.

Stepping back into the room, she picked up Ma's heavy woolen shawl, wrapped the entire length of it around her body, and tucked in the ends. She ran her fingers through her hair to tame the unruly strands and rolled it up in a bun. Slipping on a pair of rubber slippers, she marched down the hallway toward Michael's room. Every problem, small or big, had a solution, she told herself. *Surely, if we put our heads together, we can find a way out of this present mess.*

A few steps from Michael's door, she lost confidence. She was fooling herself, and she couldn't do anything to hold Michael back. Parul had pushed the family to the bottom of a deep well, and it was impossible to climb back out.

Michael was not alone in his room. Baba and Ma were now with him, talking to him, explaining Parul's allegations and the consequences of them. Baba gave instructions to Michael. Michael argued, but Baba's voice cracked like a whip, silencing him. Ma's shrill voice tried to calm them down. Cupboards opened and closed, and suitcases were dragged across the tiled floor. There was scuffling of feet, things being tossed around, heavy objects being pulled and pushed, and doors opening and closing.

Mohini leaned against the wall and closed her eyes. A bout of intense dizziness gripped her. Soon their love story would end, and the beautiful time they had spent together would be sucked into an invisible vortex, never to be recovered. She sighed, moved away from Michael's door, and went downstairs. The rain had stopped, but the air was cold, sharp with the smell of tuberoses. How ironic that she should smell tuberoses—the flower mostly used for funerals. Maybe she had already started to mourn the death of her relationship with Michael.

The courtyard was now dark and deserted. It was hard to believe what had happened there only a few hours earlier. Other than a few overturned flowerpots, everything looked peaceful. Mohini moved closer to Parul's bathroom at the edge of the courtyard. Next to the narrow drain, where the rainwater spiraled down, lay Parul's silvery anklet. Mohini recognized it instantly. It must have come off during her struggle with Ma. Mohini's skin tingled at the thought of Parul's betrayal. Holding the anklet in her hand, her throat constricted with the kind of breathlessness that preceded hysteria. She dropped the anklet on the ground and stomped on it.

"*Eije Meye.*" The press widow stepped out of the shadows.

Mohini jumped back in surprise. "You here?" she asked. "At this time?"

"How could I stay away?" The widow circled Mohini slowly and intentionally. "I heard there was a circus here this afternoon. Got a call from my employee."

Mohini stepped away from her, but she quickly closed the distance between them. "What is this I hear? The American boy got your maid pregnant?" she asked.

The patch of skin on the back of Mohini's neck burned. "Everything you heard is nonsense. Nothing like that has happened. Our maid is lying."

"Lying? No, no... I don't think she is lying at all. This was inevitable. I knew something like this would happen in this house... sooner or later."

"Believe what you like," Mohini snapped. "I don't have time for this."

"We all know what kind of maid she is. It's her nature to behave shamelessly before all grown men. Your mother encouraged her even more. She thought she could use the slutty maid against me. Now see, her chickens have come home to roost."

Mohini struggled to control her anger. "You are older than me, so I am not saying anything. But, please, don't say things like this about my parents."

"You can stop me all you want. I may listen... after all, I am your relative. But how will you stop the neighbors from talking, *hunh*, after what your precious American boy has done? Things like this cannot be kept a secret."

"Thanks for your concern, but we are leaving first thing tomorrow morning. The American boy will never bother you or anyone in this neighborhood again. So, end of the story. Are you happy now?"

"Leaving?"

"Yes, we are going out of town."

"Tomorrow morning?"

"Yes," Mohini said impatiently. "Our train leaves very early in the morning."

The widow made an owl-like face. "Go wherever you like. Why do I care? It is already hard doing business from this house. I don't know why I still bother to keep my press here."

Mohini was about to turn back when a movement behind the widow caught her attention. She jumped, startled, and looked again. She was sure she had seen a figure lurking in the darkness near the entrance of the printing press. "*Okhane ke dariye*? Who is here?" shouted Mohini.

She was about to go farther into the dark hallway of the printing press when the widow caught her elbow and pulled her back. "Nobody," she said. "It's past office time... All my employees have gone home."

Mohini shook her head. "I saw someone with my own eyes. Someone was listening to our conversation. My eyes don't get fooled so easily." She shook her arm free from the widow and went over to take a closer look. The widow followed close behind, complaining about how Mohini had no business stepping into her printing press.

Mohini located the figure again, this time next to the water tank. "Stop, whoever you are," she screamed. The man didn't turn back. He climbed on top of the water tank and jumped to grab the boundary wall of the alley. He missed the first time and fell back on top of the heavy iron lid covering the tank. He got up, dusted himself and tried again. Mohini fumbled around the wall, trying to locate the light switch. When she flipped it on, a jolt of pain ran through her. The light switch, wet from the recent rain, gave her a slight shock. Suppressing a scream, she turned to look at the intruder. Yellow light that flooded the alley fell on a man in a lace cap and thick black beard, standing on the boundary wall, ready to leap to the other side.

"Rahim?" croaked the widow. "What are you doing at this time of night?"

Mohini had seen the manager in the widow's press, though she didn't know his name. She spun around and glared at the widow. "You said your employees have all gone home. Then why was your manager spying on us?"

Rahim mildly eased himself off the wall and gave them a broad, friendly grin. "I was just locking up the doors, getting ready to leave," he said. "Some fresh supplies just arrived today, and I was making the entries. Didn't realize how much time has passed."

"But wait a minute. Why were you trying to run away from..." began Mohini, but the widow stopped her before she could finish.

"Stop harassing my employees. Is it a sin to work a few extra hours? Every time I make two paisa profits, you are burning with jealousy. You and your whole family, you're all the same. You will be happy if I go out of business."

Mohini gave an exasperated sigh, glared at the insufferable widow, turned around, and went back to the courtyard. She wondered why the widow's manager had eavesdropped on their conversation. What interest could he have in their discussion?

The widow and Rahim walked back from the alley. They talked briefly, and then Rahim picked up a bundle of paper and left the house in a great hurry. His white *kurta* and lace cap melted into the dark night.

Looking at his disappearing form, a terrible sense of foreboding struck Mohini.

Baba said they would drive off right after breakfast. It was still very early. Baba counted the suitcases and beddings and asked the security guard to take them downstairs. They gathered in the bedroom and waited for the driver to bring the car around.

They were leaving for Lucknow, where Baba's cousin lived. They would stay there for a few days until things cooled down. Then they would return to Kolkata and send Michael back to America. After everything that had happened, Baba was reluctant to bring him back to that house, even for a day.

Michael sat with a hot plate of rice and *daal*, putting small morsels in his mouth and washing them down with cold water from the fridge. He looked dazed, but probably knew not to ask too many questions.

Mohini tried to walk past him, but his gaze held her back. "I didn't do it," he whispered to her, a pained intensity lighting up his eyes. His apology made her heart pound. Her golden-haired American was burdened by a sense of guilt, weighed down by the desire to clear his name. He was struggling inwardly, as if getting the message across to her was of great importance to him. "I'm not the father of Parul's child." The words formed on his lips as great anguish clouded his face.

Mohini could no longer see him suffer. "It never crossed my mind... not once." She put her arms around him. "I know you better than I know myself."

A door closed nearby, making her jump. She squeezed his shoulder and moved away quickly.

In the bedroom, Ma took out all the jewelry and cash from her steel armoire and spread them on the bed. She used a needle and thread to stitch secret pockets in her petticoat and hide all her valuables. The crowded Howrah station often saw many pickpockets and purse-snatchers trying to steal from the distracted. Ma was not willing to take any chances.

Mohini could gauge Ma's disappointment from the way her fingers dug into the mattress. All her life, Ma had tried to live within the many restrictions of *bhadralok* middle-class. She never rode the public bus all by herself or stopped to eat puffed rice and chickpeas from street vendors. She knew being seen in public places could smear their family name. She had never tried on a Western outfit or touched a bottle of alcohol. She wore saris every day, all day, and kept her hair long, creeping below her waist. Like all other good Bengali wives, she too applied the vermillion dust in her hair parting, and covered her head in the presence of her in-laws. Being respectable was important to Ma, and she worked hard for it. "There is nothing more fragile than reputation," she reminded Mohini often. "It's like a mirror. Once it shatters, you can put the pieces back together, but the perfection is lost." But Parul had whisked away every bit of that respectability. She had shattered Ma's mirror and brought bad luck to their family. Ma might never recover fully from this blow.

•   •   •

"*Babu*, come quickly," said their security guard, Bahadur. "They are here."

"Who?"

"The slum people. They know about... err... that maid... Parul."

"But how could they come so early? We didn't tell anyone we were leaving." Baba's eyebrows knitted together in a little frown.

Mohini swallowed hard. She wondered if she had made a mistake by telling the widow about their plan. She opened her mouth to confess to Baba, but fear choked her voice.

"I don't know, *Babu*," said the guard.

"Bahadur," Baba ordered him, "run to the neighborhood houses and tell them we are in trouble. Ask them to come and help us."

Bahadur hung his head and looked miserable.

"Didn't you hear what I said?" roared Baba. "Get us help... *now!*"

"They already know we are in trouble, *Babu*. They are watching from their houses. But none of them want to come outside and help us."

"How could they do such a thing?" wailed Ma. "How can they be so heartless when they have known us all their lives?"

They rushed out to the balcony. A big mob had gathered in front of their house. Some men had long bamboo sticks, and the women had bamboo dusters. Mohini studied them with trepidation—the men had thick beards and lace caps; the women had their heads covered with the ends of their saris. Some even wore scarfs and hijabs.

"I don't understand," whispered Ma, standing next to her. "Most of them look Muslim."

Suddenly Mohini had a shock: somewhere among the faces in the crowd, half-hidden behind a guava tree, she spotted a face she knew. She looked again: it was the printing press manager, Rahim. Mohini's head reeled—so it was the printing press manager who had informed the slum people of their early escape plan. There could be no doubt about it. That was why he left their house in such a rush.

Mohini shut her eyes and let the wave of guilt pass over her. Her *dupatta* was drenched, and she could barely move her legs. She opened her eyes with difficulty and looked at the surrounding houses. Friends and neighbors had gathered on the terraces to watch the scene playing out in their front yard. The men stood on the balconies in plain view, while the women peeked from behind the window curtains.

"*Ki kando!*" Ma rushed back inside the room and closed the doors and windows. "Ma Kali, how could you bring such distress on my family? How will we save ourselves from all those angry people out there?"

She picked up the phone and dialed the local police station. "*Daroga babu*, please send us some police protection. We are in a lot of trouble... Yes... yes.... We are locking all the doors and windows... but they may still break in.... The windows have glass panes...."

Baba did not let her finish. He picked up Michael's backpack. "We can't wait for the police. We have to get Michael out of here."

Ma unplugged the phone and flung it against the wall. "What do you want us to do? Don't you see it is already too late to run away?"

"No, it is not," said Baba, grabbing Michael's hand. "C'mon. Everyone just follow me. I checked our back entrance. There is no one there. We can still catch a taxi."

Ma reached for the baggage, but Baba shook his head. "There is no time for that."

As if waking from a bad dream, Mohini followed her parents to the back of the building. Unlocking the door, they darted past the empty children's park and flagged down a taxi. "Howrah Station," said Baba to the taxi driver. "Drive fast and do not stop, no matter what happens."

Ma and Mohini climbed in the back while Baba and Michael squeezed into the front passenger seat of the large Ambassador taxi. The doors slammed shut, and the driver started the engine.

As the taxi turned into the alley connecting to the main road, there was a commotion somewhere behind them—it was a small sound at first, like the buzz of bees. Then the sound grew louder as the voices and footsteps closed in on them.

They all turned and looked through the rear windshield: the slum people rushed toward the taxi.

Someone must have informed them about their back-door escape. The bamboo sticks and dusters rose and fell rhythmically as they ran down the tarry road toward the taxi, yelling obscenities and warning them to stop. "Go, go," Baba pushed the taxi driver. "Don't stop for anyone."

The taxi driver looked terrified. He wrestled with the wheel and turned the taxi around clumsily, almost running over a cobbler and a flower seller. He slammed his foot on the gas pedal, and the car roared loudly, speeding forward. Almost instantly, a rock crashed into the rear windshield, and the glass rained on the backseat like a waterfall.

They stooped forward, slipping between the seats, covering their heads with their arms as more stones clattered against their windows. Baba yelled that the taxi driver was bleeding; a rock had cracked his skull. The car lurched forward in short jerks as Baba told the taxi driver, "Don't stop. We will take you to the hospital." But the driver had lost control of his foot, and the car spun around on the road several times before crashing into something solid. The impact made Mohini's head bang against the front seat.

She sat up. Baba and Michael were bleeding from slight cuts around their foreheads, and the taxi driver appeared to be unconscious at the wheel. Ma had rolled into a small ball. "I am okay," she said.

More voices and footsteps surrounded them. Men and women appeared at the broken windows, looking down at them like predators. Their faces were hard like rocks, revenge blazing in their eyes. The crowd snaked in on them from all sides, trapping them inside the taxi and waiting for the final kill. Slowly, the hubbub died, and the car grew very silent. All Mohini could hear was the collective breathing of the ruthless mob.

Looking back, she could still see her house in a distance: the balconies and terraces, the gravel-covered driveway and the red bougainvillea creeper highlighting the awnings. Beyond the house was a blue sky with scattered white clouds. The guava trees of her childhood lined the street and swayed gently in the wind. This was her house and her neighborhood. This was where her earliest memories were formed. These brick walls, the gray asphalt-covered streets, the little patch of green where the boys played soccer held a bit of her. This was the place where she had felt most safe, most included, and most wanted. Everyone in this neighborhood knew her. She was one of them, and they were an extension of her greater self. Yet looking back at the faces in the windows, blank and still, a dagger of fear struck her heart. The familiar streets of her childhood, her sanctuary in good times and bad, had now become a hostile land—her family was now the hunted.

She leaned forward from the backseat and put her arms around Michael's neck. Michael turned to look at her as if to ask why their fantasy love story was coming to such an abrupt and cruel end. Why was their romance being overshadowed by the story of a maid who was otherwise so inconsequential in their lives? For they knew they were caught up in the dilemmas of Parul's life—which they might never fully understand.

Mohini squeezed his shoulder, not able to answer the questions that formed in his eyes. She would never know what had triggered Parul's hatred. What had prompted this act of revenge? Growing up, Parul had always said, "You are becoming too much of a *memsahib*, a British woman." This had miffed Mohini because she knew Parul meant she was becoming less friendly. She was changing, leaving Parul to find her own world outside the house. Yet she never thought, not for a moment, that the unseen bond of loyalty and affection that stretched between them would one day unravel and Parul would turn on her with such fury.

"Don't worry." Michael turned around to look at Mohini. "I won't let anything happen to you." He threw the car door open and swung his body sideways.

In that instant, Mohini knew what Michael was about to do. "No," she shouted and leaned forward to pull him back. Her nails scratched the back of his neck and ripped the fabric off his shirt.

Michael didn't look back. He jumped out of the car and slammed the door shut. "You are here for me," he told the crowd. "Take me. But, please, spare this family." The men jeered and hissed, measuring up their prey. Then they grabbed his shoulders and dragged him in. Michael's head of gold melted into the ocean of black.

The door opened again, and this time Mohini got out. She ran after Michael. Ma was screaming at them; Mohini couldn't hear what she was saying. She cut through layers and layers of people chasing after Michael.

The police sirens blared in the distance. The road vibrated as if the police vans were coming up from deep underground. The dust rose, and the smell of hot tires pervaded the air.

The police were nearing them.

Mohini hoped they would get to Michael before it was too late.

Epilogue

Panic hit Parul like stepping into a burning pyre. She had followed Mohini's taxi along with the crowd, walking on the sides close to the houses, her elbows and sides scraped by the rough, chipped stone walls and occasional splinters. Inside her, emotions rose, fell, undulated, and filled her with more and more dread. A voice deep within her nagged her to turn around and leave. *Ei Allah, what am I doing? I don't need to see this. I can't bear to see what will happen!* Some men bent forward to pick up bricks from a construction site. *No,* she screamed, even though they didn't hear her. *You mustn't use those.* She tightened the sari around her waist like a thick belt and squeezed through the crowd, fumbling her way forward, almost blindly trying to reach Mohini's car. All around her bamboo sticks and bamboo dusters rose and fell in union—the footsteps grew urgent, and the air crackled from heightening tension. The crowd breathed in sync with each other, as if they were individual pieces of an orchestra. For a moment her mind blanked, unable to decide what her next action should be. For what she had started was now way bigger than she was and impossible for her to control. The mob was hungry and impatient, like a starving tiger let loose from its cage.

Leaning against the lamppost, she tried to shake away the thoughts that clawed against her chest, wanting to rip it apart. That was when she thought of her unborn child. How would she ever tell her child what she had done? Would the answer not scar his young mind, burden his soul forever? Would he not ask her again and again: My life and my name were assured at what cost?

When she was a little girl, Ammi used to say. "Allah sent you to this earth to do great things." She combed Parul's unruly hair with a plastic comb, dividing the strands into equal parts and taming them into thick braids interlaced with red ribbons. She darkened Parul's eyes with *kajol* and placed a black dot on her forehead to protect her from the evil eye.

Ammi's sari smelled of marigold and incense. Parul liked to bury her face into the soft layers. The sari formed a net over her face through which she saw the light scatter and sparkle. In the skylight above their head, a black bird waited patiently for its eggs to hatch. Ammi fed the bird roasted gram seeds. "No point getting attached. It will not stay. As soon as the eggs hatch, it will fly away." Ammi stroked Parul's back and cupped her chin. "You too will leave one day and go to your in-laws' house. All girls have to go. But wherever you go, you will shine like a bright star. You will always make us proud."

· · ·

The sound of breaking glass pierced Parul's heart like a dagger, bringing her back to the present. Mohini's taxi seemed to sway from side to side—the metallic trunk sparkling in the early morning sunshine. Parul's veins tightened, restricting the blood flow to her brain. She grasped her head with both hands to stop it from spinning. *Look at me now,* Ammi, she whispered. *What have I done? For my own happiness, I have burned down someone's house. Are you proud of me now? Am I still a bright star?*

"Don't worry, sister," said a heavy-set woman in a hijab next to her. "The American will pay for what he has done to you." She spit out crimson betel nut juice on the silvery road inches away from Parul's sandals.

More bricks, empty bottles and sticks whizzed past Parul and struck Mohini's car. There's a crash and a loud scream from inside the car. Her legs turned to jelly, and she clasped the lamppost for support. The men surrounded the car one by one, their steps calculated and their intent... *lethal.*

Spare them, she pleaded inwardly. *Don't kill them... I beg of you.*

There was a moment of absolute quiet as Parul watched the American boy climb out of the car and get sucked into the bowels of the crowd. The mob coiled around him like a python, layer by layer, preparing for the last strike. Suddenly, Mohini got out of the car and chased after Michael.

Parul squeezed her eyes shut, for she couldn't believe what was about to happen. "Stop," she yelled. "Have you lost your mind? Get back in the car!" In the next instant, a rock hit Mohini's forehead, and she stumbled and fell face down on the tarry road.

Parul howled. She could no longer hold herself back. With an inhuman amount of effort, she got her legs to move. She pushed forward, stabbing the men with her sandal heels to get to Mohini. Tears streamed from her eyes, and her hair sprang out of its pins and swung on her back like a venomous snake.

In the distance, sirens wailed. The police cars screeched and parked in front of her. The slum people scattered and scrambled in all directions. They dropped their sticks and dusters, hoisted up their dhotis and saris and ran amuck on the streets. Some vanished into the dark alleys while some hid behind the parked cars and delivery trucks. Only a gritty few remained in the center surrounding Michael, unwavered by the police arrival.

Mohini lay face down next to a manhole—mute and motionless. A stream of blood ran down the side of her head. Some boys running away from the police stumbled and piled on top of her. Then they picked themselves up, took a closer look at her unconscious form, and kicked her till she rolled away from them.

"*Haramzada*, sons of pigs." Parul threw her sandals at them. "How dare you kick her? Come here if you have the courage. I'll break your legs and make sure you walk with crutches for the rest of your life."

The boys laughed, pointed at their crotches, and clambered away.

Reaching Mohini, Parul pulled her bleeding head into her lap and wrapped it with her sari. "Wake up," she sobbed. "I beg of you. Please open your eyes."

The police vans were now parked haphazardly on the street. The van doors swung shut and heavy boots approached the crowd. Screams broke out when the uniformed men chased the rest of the crowd with *lathis* and clubs. From the corner of her eye, she detected the crowd in the middle dispersing and leaving the semi-naked body of the American on the street. The mob had peeled off his shirt, trousers, and shoes and left him in his underwear. His face was swollen from the beatings, and blood covered his legs and torso. A stray dog sniffed around him and then bent down to lick his scarred face. The boy neither moved nor opened his eyes.

Parul gasped. *This is not real,* she told herself. *None of this is happening. I will wake up soon and all this will be over.*

The busy street where hundreds of people passed each other peacefully each day now looked like a war zone. Broken glass, rubber sandals, bricks, plastic toys, sticks and bamboo dusters lay scattered and smashed all around her. Farther away was a row of damaged stores, overturned vegetable carts and abandoned *paan* stalls.

Next to the shuttered electrical shop stood the ill-fated yellow taxi with broken windows—Ma and Baba still cowering inside, terrified and helpless, next to a driver who was possibly dying or already dead.

Parul shook her head in amazement. *Eh Allah, what have I done? Am I responsible for all this? I made this happen? Me? An uneducated maid who came from an unknown village? I brought about this destruction?*

She remembered the day her father had brought her to Kolkata. She had looked around in awe at the sky-high multistory buildings, the double-decker buses that belched out black smoke and the endless line of stores on the pavement with rusty discolored signs. Cars honked, peddlers peddled, beggars begged, and customers quibbled. The office-goers pushed past them and speeding cars almost ran them over. Nobody spared a glance.

"It's easy to get lost here," Abbu had said. "One needs to be careful in a big city."

I got lost, thought Parul. *I didn't listen to Abbu. I got lost in the big city and couldn't find my way back.*

Regret, vile and repulsive, nauseated Parul. She slapped her left cheek and then the right. She beat her chest and banged her head against the hardness of her folded knees. She broke her glass bangles and yanked Ammi's locket from her neck.

Eh Allah! Never forgive me for what I have done. I don't deserve your mercy. I am unworthy of your clemency. I deserve to be whipped. I deserve to be stoned. I deserve to burn in the fire of hell for eternity.

An ambulance pulled close to Parul. Men in uniform spilled out of the van and ran towards them holding a stretcher. "Where are you taking her?" protested Parul as they pulled Mohini away from her.

"Get out of our way," they said. "Let us do our work." The ambulance men strapped Mohini onto the main stretcher and carried her down to the ambulance. Parul ran after them frantically, wanting to climb inside the van, but the men pushed her back and closed the door. She felt her throat tighten, constrict, as if the neckline of her blouse was strangling her. She unbuttoned the top buttons and gasped for air. She ran to a roadside tube-well to sprinkle water on her face and neck, but she felt no relief. She walked down the street aimlessly, stumbling on the bricks and sticks, cutting herself on the broken glass. Slowly, the clamor of voices inside her died down, and she felt very still and empty, as if she was gliding along dully in the middle of the surrounding ruckus.

There was movement somewhere in the distance, and then rapid beat of footsteps coming down the street. The heavy footsteps crunched on the gravel and kicked up dust. Turning around, Parul saw the tall dark shapes of men chased by police coming in her direction. For a moment she stilled, wishing them to run her over. Then, with great difficulty, she got her legs to move. She ran behind the tall corporation dumpster and fell on her knees, panting heavily. The footsteps came close and ran past her.

The dumpster was piled high with days-old garbage. There were fish bones and chicken bones and crawling cockroaches everywhere. Blood-soaked sanitary napkins lay scattered near the drain, attended by bloated flies. The air around her was toxic, repulsive. The stench of rotting vegetables and stale rice hit her like a blow. Parul covered her mouth, and vomit trickled out between her fingers onto her neck and breasts and rolled down to her belly.

Looking down at her belly, Parul thought of the baby inside—its small scrunched-up face, velvety-looking hair, tiny fingers and toes all rolled up in a soft ball. She thought of its smooth silky skin and toothless heart-warming smile. She stroked her baby bump lovingly—*sleep beautiful baby... sleep in there.* Then a terrifying thought came to her—what if the filth around her suffocates the baby? The thought made her shudder. As she watched, the trash piles began to grow. They became huge, each pile bigger than the surrounding buildings, rising like small mountains to reach the sky. She pulled her hair and chewed on her nails. The baby was weak and the stench much too strong. How could something so delicate, so fragile, bear such harshness?

Parul covered her baby bump with the end of her sari. She shook her head and made up her mind. She couldn't bring the baby to this vile, unhygienic place. She could not let the dirt stain his satin-like skin, choke his weak lungs. The baby didn't belong here. She would have to send him back to where he came from. He would leave untouched, unspoiled just the way he came. Not a mark of him would remain in this disgusting world.

Parul remembered the day they had brought Ammi back from the hospital. She was wrapped in an immaculately white piece of cloth. Her eyes were closed, and two cotton balls plugged her nose. There were no lines of exhaustion on her face, and her lips held a hint of a celestial smile. How peaceful she looked, as if a lifetime of struggle had finally ended and she could rest. She was even more beautiful in death than in life.

The baby too would look beautiful like her, Parul decided. She would wrap him up in a white cloth and put him in a hole next to Ammi. She would cover him up with marigold, jasmine and tulips. He would smell of flowers when he left this earthly cage. The force of her emotion made her tremble. She dusted off the dirt and food particles gathered in the folds of her sari and stroked her distended belly lovingly. *I brought you to this unworthy world,* she whispered to the baby, *I will take you out.*

Parul did not turn around when Rahim approached behind the dumpster and squatted next to her. A black turban covered his head and forehead, grazing the eyebrows. "I was looking for you everywhere." He squeezed her arm urgently. "You shouldn't be here."

Parul did not respond. Her head hung forward. Grains of rice stuck to the corner of her bottom lip.

"Listen to me," Rahim poked her collarbone. "It's not safe. The police are everywhere. I took a big risk in coming here to look for you."

Parul seemed preoccupied, lost in her own thoughts. She was barely aware of his presence.

"Go back to my sister." Rahim spoke close to her ears to penetrate her dazed mind. "She will take good care of you." He took out a few notes from his pocket pouch and placed them on her palm. "I'll take you up to the corner. You can catch a bus from there."

Parul didn't blink or heed his warning. She bent over and whispered something incoherent to her belly and stroked it gently with her fingers.

"Did you hear a word of what I just said?" demanded Rahim. He slid a finger under her chin, lifting her eyes to his. Her face was colorless and her eyes dull.

"Eh Allah, what has happened to you?" Rahim squeezed her shoulder, trying to bring her back to her senses. "You look like a ghost."

There were voices and footsteps close to them. Rahim cocked his ears and tilted his head to listen. He wrapped the end of his turban around his face, leaving a small slit around his eyes. "We have to get out of here quickly... I can't be seen here with you."

An object whizzed through the air and exploded somewhere down the street with a muffled boom. Women screamed and frightened stray dogs ran past them. Rahim pushed her further behind the bags, almost merging into their creases. "Stay here and keep your head low. Don't make a single sound."

The explosion stirred no fear in Parul. She didn't jump up in surprise or reach out to him for support. Instead, she clutched her tummy and hummed a sad lullaby, rocking herself back and forth. Tiny tears sparkled on her eyelashes like morning dew.

Rahim shook his head and sighed. It was as if she was there in flesh, but her soul had gone missing. He remembered the day she had burst into his printing press office and sat at his desk. Her anklets had rung on the red mosaic and her *bindi* had sparkled like a star in the middle of her forehead. She had tossed her braid from side to side and a half dozen metal bangles rattled on her wrist. Her eyes had twinkled with irrepressible mischief.

Nothing glimmered in her eyes today. Not anger, not complaint, not accusation. She didn't play with her bangles or ring her anklets. She sat lifelessly before him, as if someone had reached into the source of her happiness and extinguished it forever. Rahim longed for Parul to slip back into her old self, to remember him as her teacher and look at him with reverence again. She had trusted him completely, followed him around, and obeyed his every word. *You are my Pir and I am your Murid;* she had avowed repeatedly.

He edged closer to her now till their shoulders touched. Her sari and slippers were soiled and smelly. Her skin was cold. Cupping her chin, he whispered her name. Nothing stirred in the depths of her dark eyes. He gently stroked her hair, his voice soft and coaxing. With his fingertips, he wiped her cheeks dry; then he framed her face between his hands and held it. The commotion in the street moved closer to them and a fire engine went past, whistling loudly. The stench grew stronger and more caustic till it burned his lungs. "For Allah's sake, Mumtaz, think of your condition," he urged, "think of the baby." He lowered his hand and placed it over her belly. Instantly, her body tensed and quivered. She slapped his hand and pushed him back.

It was then Rahim knew his Mumtaz was not *his* anymore. She was with him, but no longer of him.

• • • •

The doctor said Mohini was out of danger. The wound to her head was healing, and they would let her out of the hospital soon. Baba and Ma had spent most of their time waiting outside her hospital room. They were relieved that the internal bleeding, the seizures and other complications had stopped and she had regained consciousness. Baba told her that Michael had gone back to the U.S... His mother, Nancy, had come to Kolkata to take him back. Michael had a broken leg, and an injured spine. He was treated initially in a Kolkata hospital, but he still needed intensive long-term care in the U.S... Michael left in a wheelchair and would probably be in one for a long time. Mohini asked Baba if she could call him, but he told her not to. "His mother blames us," he said. "She has asked us why this happened a thousand times, and we have failed to give her a satisfactory answer. The truth is... we don't understand ourselves. How could such a thing happen? And why didn't we see it coming?" Baba sank into the chair next to her bed, staring into the empty space. "The newspapers are calling it an act of terrorism. They say the radical Muslims from the slum attacked our American boy for making a Muslim maid pregnant."

"But he did nothing..." said Mohini.

"Don't we all know that? The boy was the victim of false accusation. All he wanted to do was to become an excellent athlete." Baba covered his face with both his palms. "Nancy put her trust in me. Thought I'd keep her son safe. And look what happened..."

Ma covered her face with the end of her sari and sobbed.

•

When Baba first told Mohini about Michael's departure, for days she lay on her pillow staring at the walls, an icy lump pressing against her throat. Then, out of the haze of dull pain, the sense of future returned. She told herself that their separation was only temporary and Michael would come back to get her. That was when she played the fantasy of Michael's return for the first time in her mind: A year had gone by and Michael's plane had landed in the Kolkata airport. He walked out of the security enclosure in a crisp cotton shirt and khaki pants. As soon as he saw her, a smile lit up his handsome face. His emerald eyes sparkled and his hair glittered like gold. She ran into his muscular arms, her head leaning against his chest, her fingers teasing the greenish stubble on his chin. He touched her hair, kissed her cheeks, and then held her tightly for what felt like an eternity. After that, she played this fantasy repeatedly. It was so real that sometimes Ma had to pinch her shoulders to bring her out of her trance-like state. Yet it was the fantasy that kept her from getting sucked into the dark hole of despair. She went through all the CAT scans, the drips, the shots and pills by playing out her fantasy repeatedly in her head.

Ma and Baba wanted to take Mohini home from the hospital. They had whitewashed the walls, changed the curtains and bought new sofa covers. The doors had extra locks, and the windows had iron grills. "We'll start over again," said Baba. When she didn't respond, he touched her arm gently. "Let's not look back. Let's try to forget what happened." But even he knew he couldn't turn the clock and start from the beginning. Nothing that had happened in the past few days could be erased from their memory. They had come to dread the ordinary streets, alleys and friends they had grown up with. For they had seen how rapidly the veneer of friendliness slipped away, and the familiar faces turned hostile. Neighborly bonds, made over many years, could ebb away like an insubstantial dream.

Baba always prided himself on being well known in the neighborhood. Small time politicians, athletes, television actors and even neighborhood dons came to him for body-building advice. Local businesses showed respect by adding a little extra to their grocery or moving them to the front of the line. Yet, in the end, none of that mattered—no one batted an eye, no one raised their voice when the mob descended upon them. All it took was a vague accusation and all the goodwill disappeared. Along with the fear came a feeling of desolation—that despite being surrounded by a sea of known faces, they were truly powerless, infinitely vulnerable.

Sometimes Baba sat next to Mohini's hospital bed and asked for her forgiveness. "I committed a tragic mistake by bringing the American boy to this country. The consequences of my actions will haunt us for our entire lives. You almost did not wake up ... and over there in America... I don't know if Michael will ever lift weights. *No, no... forget weights... I don't even know if he will walk again!* Maybe I destroyed his dreams forever. I am a fool, that's all I am... an old fool. Everything I try to do goes wrong." Regret and anguish from his voice chilled her bones and made her teeth clatter. She had a flash of Michael getting out of the car and getting sucked into the crowd, and she shut it out immediately, as if even a glimmer of such an image were offensive.

Beyond the glass doors, Mohini's relatives waited for her. They came to see her every day—uncles, aunts and cousins. They sat quietly on the benches, drinking coffee from the hospital cafeteria and praying for her recovery. Some brought bouquets of flowers and left them quietly by her bedside—roses, gerberas and tulips. The sweet fragrance interrupted her stupor and distracted her with a strange wistfulness. They brought back memories of when Ma had a terrace garden filled with bright flowers, vegetables, and herbs. As children, Mohini and Parul used to sneak away to the terrace and just marvel at the colors.

The thought of Parul made her anxious. "Do you know where Parul*di* is? Is she okay?" Mohini asked Ma as she was arranging the flowers at her bedside.

Ma made loud popping noises with her mouth that sounded like water dripping into a pot of hot oil. "Don't mention her name to me," she said. "I don't care where she is and how she is. To me she is dead."

"But in her condition..." began Mohini.

"Why should I care for her condition after all she has done?" Ma broke a flower stem as if she was ripping someone's head off. She paced the room several times and sank into the chair next to Mohini. "*Hai Isvar*, why didn't I stop her?" She slapped her forehead. "I knew she was up to something. I could just see it in her eyes."

The nurse came into the room to give Mohini her daily injection. Ma got up to leave and then turned around. "Let go of all that. Now is not the time to think of Parul. Get her out of your mind."

Mohini opened her mouth to say something, but Ma covered her lips with her finger. "Don't talk. Try to get some rest."

Mohini lay back on her pillow. She closed her eyes and saw Parul's face, twisted with anger and hatred, wet with tears. Her arm was outstretched as if she were pointing her finger accusingly at Mohini. Guilt sat like a heavy rock on Mohini's chest. For she was alone in knowing she had failed Parul, failed to understand the serious dilemmas of her life, failed to be her ally when she desperately needed one. While Mohini was planning for her future, making new friends and pursuing her dreams—Parul, anchorless and alone, had drifted away in her own miserable ocean beyond Mohini's reach. And now there was nothing left but questions, questions that were as big as mountains with no simple answers. Truly, their family had so little information to go on. They may never understand what drove Parul's actions. A tear rolled down Mohini's cheek and fell onto her pillow.

•   •   •

It had been a month since Mohini regained consciousness, and they had moved her out of the ICU to a private room. She was still too weak and dizzy to get out of bed. She lay under a crumpled white sheet surrounded by oxygen cylinders and hanging glucose bottles. On the other side of the bed was a window open to the main street. She heard the honking of horns, the loud screeching of brakes, the barking street dogs and the whistle of the traffic police. Around mid-day, the primary school bell went off next door, and noisy children spilled onto the outside pavement. And when the day's loud hurry and turbulence died down and darkness fell like a fish net covering the streets and alleys, she stared at the high-rise buildings with well-lighted windows and bright neon signs of the surrounding businesses.

The images and sounds of her old city no longer penetrated the deeper layers of her psyche. It was as if a filter had dropped, tarnishing and obscuring what was once beautiful. Her heart, devoid of joy, labored on. The words *Michael was no longer in the city* were so loud in her head at times that she was afraid that her skull would burst open from the building pressure. She reached for her pillow to drown out the roar.

Then one morning, the nurse stood by Mohini's shoulder and removed the IV from her arm. "You won't need this anymore," she said, smiling. She lifted Mohini up as gently as she could, sat her in the wheelchair and wheeled her to the open window. The early morning sun warmed Mohini's face. The cool breeze played with her hair and whispered in her ears. On the branches of the overgrown trees, birds skipped from top to top. She watched with breathless wonder as they soared up and swept down gracefully, spreading their wings. Through the window came a branch of a blazing pink bougainvillea creeper. Mohini bent forward and touched the smooth petals.

Gradually, the tension left her body, and her shoulders relaxed. The will to live surged through her like a blessing. Baba's thousand regrets and Ma's incessant tears may be their only way of dealing with what had happened to them. But she needed to develop the art of optimism and face life with more vigor. "It's not over yet," a forceful voice in her head insisted. "Like Phoenix, you too have to rise from your ashes."

The next day, while flipping through a copy of National Geographic, she found a U.S. map and looked up Boston. She traced the path between Kolkata and Boston over the blue chilly oceans, and she could see it was far. She tapped her finger on yellow boundary of Massachusetts and felt a strong, impetuous urge to fly. Mohini had never boarded a plane in her life and did not know how to find Michael's home, even if she made it to Boston. She hesitated for a minute, but in the next instant, her eagerness to see him again swept away all her inhibitions.

She swung her legs down and tentatively touched the cool hospital floor. With all the courage she could muster, she pushed herself up. Her legs wobbled, and she felt breathless from the exertion. The dull ache in her head returned, and her eyelids felt heavy. Disregarding the pain, she held on to the metallic bed frame and stepped forward.

A cheer broke out as soon as she opened the darkened glass doors. Her relatives surrounded her—pinching her cheeks and patting her back. Ma wept, holding her hand. Baba pulled her into a bear hug, refusing to let go of her. The nurse ran off to inform the doctor.

And standing there—leaning against the yellowish walls for support, panting and feeling exhausted, she made a promise—*I'll go back to college and finish my degree. Then I'll apply for a scholarship at an American university close to Boston. One day, I'll board the plane that will take me across the seas.*

They all sat down on the wooden benches outside her room. She could tell her relatives were glad and grateful to have her back. Their voices, their laughter, and the squeaking of their shoes rose above the hum of the machines.

"I can't eat the hospital food anymore," Mohini told them.

"We are going to take you back home," said Pishimoni with her usual authority. "You don't have to eat this tasteless food ever again. Your mother will make you all your favorite dishes."

Ma cried again, but this time Pishimoni scolded her using her sternest teacher-like voice. "Mohini's mother, control yourself. How long will you cry? Our bad times have ended and we need to move on. Say your thanks to Ma Kali and take your daughter home with you."

Mohini walked up to the window and inhaled deeply. The windowpanes sparkled like uncut diamonds. The hospital corridor looked golden. Outside the window, the large structures stood silent and remote against the blue sky. She lifted her arms and let the wind course through her hospital gown. Then she leaned forward to look out of the window at the sidewalk below and noticed a young woman in an orange sari, sitting patiently below a tree. Her nose ring glittered in the sunlight and the loose end of her sari flapped in the wind.

Mohini's heart stopped. She knew then that the young woman was none other than her Parul. Parul had come back to see Mohini.

Mohini leaned forward and squeezed her body through the half-closed windowpanes. She called out Parul's name. Parul turned her head to look up at her, looked up at her. That was the moment her eyes lit up with recognition and her face became suffused with a sudden glow of happiness. She raised her bangle covered arms and waved back at Mohini.

"Paruldi, how did you know I am here?" cried out Mohini.

"My heart found you." She pointed to her chest.

Mohini let go of the stale air in her lungs. Parul was not a figment of her imagination anymore. She was more palpable, more fragile, more herself. And she had come back to see Mohini.

Mohini knew she had to talk to Parul urgently. There were so many things to talk about; so many things to explain. She wanted the veil to lift, the hurt to crumble away. She wanted to hold Parul's hand again, put her head in her lap and call her "Didi" again.

The wind ruffled Mohini's hair and whispered in her ears: Like a river, time continues to flow, and we all have to learn to flow with it. We have to learn to bury our wounds, our ghosts and our melancholy and let time sweep us forward.

"This time I won't let you escape," Mohini whispered back to her. "You're my sister, my best-friend."

The End

About the Author

Saborna's debut novel *The Distance* was published by the independent press Istoria Books and received a starred review from *Publishers Weekly*, which commented: "Through Roychowdhury's rich detail and illuminating dialogue emerges a protagonist who is caught in a love triangle and the conflict between rigid traditions and western freedoms." The novel was well-received in other publications in the U.S. and elsewhere, including the *South Asian Review* and *Hyphen Magazine*.

Her short story *Bengal Monsoon* appeared in New York Stories magazine and received a Pushcart Prize nomination. She was born and raised in Kolkata, India, moved to the U.S. for undergraduate work in chemistry. She lives in Houston, Texas, with her husband and twin daughters.

Note from the Author

Word-of-mouth is crucial for any author to succeed. If you enjoyed *Everything Here Belongs To You,* please leave a review online—anywhere you are able. Even if it's just a sentence or two. It would make all the difference and would be very much appreciated.

Thanks!
Saborna Roychowdhury

We hope you enjoyed reading this title from:

BLACK ❀ ROSE
writing™

www.blackrosewriting.com

Subscribe to our mailing list – *The Rosevine* – and receive **FREE** books,
daily deals, and stay current with news about upcoming
releases and our hottest authors.
Scan the QR code below to sign up.

Already a subscriber? Please accept a sincere thank you for being a fan of
Black Rose Writing authors.

View other Black Rose Writing titles at
www.blackrosewriting.com/books and use promo code
PRINT to receive a **20% discount** when purchasing.

CPSIA information can be obtained
at www.ICGtesting.com
Printed in the USA
LVHW091638010623
748639LV00001B/124

9 781684 339594